The Godking's Legacy

by Virlyce

This book is dedicated to Frederick J. and Philip Y..

Prologue

"I was the greatest man in the world.
I killed an elder dragon with a single slash of my sword.
I resolved the eternal war between the three factions.
I tamed the untamable creature—the phoenix.
I created a new branch of magic that heralded an age of magicians.
I concocted pills that brought the dead back to life.
I forged the strongest weapons in the world.
I owned the sword of legends—Durandal.
And then, when I was at my peak,
I died."
-The Godking's Epitaph

***

Some people say my master was the greatest man in the world: The bards sing of his accomplishments in taverns. The parents tell their children stories of his deeds. The youths in training aspire to be as strong as he was. The people made him into a legend, an undefeatable existence that represented the strength of humanity. But I know that's all bullshit. Strongest in the world? More like most shameless.

My master was famous for a lot of things, but his crowning achievement as a swordsman was slaying an elder dragon with a single slash. He slew an elder dragon in a single strike. Are you kidding me? People really believe that? He, a two-meter-tall man, slew an elder dragon, a castle-sized, fire-breathing lizard with impenetrable scales, in a single strike. Read that again and tell me that's not bullshit. I'll tell you the

1

truth—he didn't even try to fight it. He hired the demons to make a potion of great strength with a side effect of sleepiness, which he then fed to the dragon. It hasn't awoken yet, but when it does…, oh boy.

Aside from his (bullshit) achievements in swordsmanship, my master was heralded as a savior of the world because he established peace between the three major factions: the humans, the demons, and the fae. If they knew how he did it, would he still be called a savior? He kidnapped the emperor's son, the demon lord's daughter, and the fae queen's nephew. But wait. Hold on. Isn't that pretty impressive in itself? No. He lured the three of them with a piece of candy, a puppy, and a trail of shiny coins. Then he threatened to feed them to a dragon unless they signed a peace agreement. By they, I mean the children, not the parents.

But, narrator, why would he do something like that? Doesn't that make him a real savior? Maybe. I don't know. I do know he really liked a dessert the fae made called ice cream and wanted to buy it legally. It definitely wasn't for any magnanimous reason like ending the eternal war or solving world hunger. He was too selfish of a bastard to do something like that.

Amongst the beast tamers, my master was heralded as a god for taming a phoenix. Little do they know, he kidnapped a hatchling and tricked it into a contract with fried phoenix eggs. He fed fried phoenix eggs to a baby phoenix. Do you know how immoral that is? Disregarding the fact that he was unusually good at manipulating children, he practically turned a phoenix into a cannibal. Have you ever heard of Stockholm syndrome? That poor phoenix was a captive.

Abuse of animals aside, my master became a genius magician in the public's eye. He was a human—a human becoming a genius magician when demons are the kings of magic. How? Simple. He kidnapped the demons' leading researcher's daughter and exchanged her for the new branch of magic that was under development. The demons tried to protest, but given my master's incredible track record, no one believed them.

Famous alchemist? He should be called famous kidnapper. The prodigal child alchemist at the time magically went missing, and my master became a grandmaster at pill making. I wonder what happened. I can tell you it starts with 'Stockhol' and ends with 'yndrome'.

Godly weaponsmith? He blackmailed the dwarven king and bribed the elvish archbishop to create enchanted weapons which he sold under his name.

Owned a legendary sword with the strongest weapon spirit inside of it? That's the only part that's true. My name is Durandal. I am that sword.

1

As a weapon spirit, I have a corporeal form—all spirits do—which allows me to interact with the world, but only up to a certain distance away from my weapon body. It's a weapon spirit's duty to teach their owners everything they know. We spirits learn from our owners and pass their legacies on to the newer ones. As Durandal, the legendary weapon of the Godking (my previous arrogant asshole of a master), I am doing my best to impart my knowledge to my new master. At least, that's what I would be doing if I had one.

When that asshole was on the cusp of death, he announced to the world, "I'm dying. Only the luckiest of the lucky and the best of the best can accept my legacy," and I was promptly stuffed into a miniature dimension created by spatial magic. Normally, that wouldn't be an issue, but over a few millennia have passed and no one's found me yet.

The miniature dimension is pretty small: there's a warehouse for a bunch of random items, a side room for weapon and armor storage, a library with books on magic, martial arts, and miscellaneous topics such as forging, pill making, enchanting, love making, origami folding, manipulating children, robbing, bartering, fishing. You know, the basics. I've read through all of them multiple times and memorized their contents. There really isn't much to do when you're trapped by yourself when you can't even sleep, eat, or drink. I can't even kill myself. Well, I could, but that would be painful.

So now, I'm waiting. To pass the time, I've been doing body strengthening exercises. Yes, even though I'm a spirit, I can improve my body. But that's only thanks to the abundance of wealth the Godking left behind. There used to be a mountain of spirit stones: the floor used to shine, the walls used to glow, even the sky was always as bright as the sun. I say used to because I absorbed every single stone for my survival and personal growth. Although he was shameless, I have to admit he was very good at making money.

And there's—

"Is this it?"

Holy shit. A voice? Was that a person?

"I think we found it!"

Wait. Wait. I'm not ready. You know how people like walking around naked in their own homes? Yeah. Weapon spirits are like that too. Before I could return to the room with my weapon body, a group of people pushed open the metal gates leading into the dimension.

I stared at them.

They stared at me.

A woman screamed. Despite the fact that I was over thousands of years old, my corporeal body never aged. Even when I absorbed the spirit stones and enchanted my weapon body, my corporeal body has always retained its handsome, rugged looks. I didn't understand why she was screaming instead of swooning. Could the perception of male beauty have changed in the millennia that past me by?

"Who are you?" the leader of the group asked. He was a youth—not old enough to be an adult, but not young enough to fall for the Godking's tricks. Beside him, there was a rotund fellow that could be mistaken for a bear if he had hair. Behind the leader, there was a group of guards wearing sets of white armor. I couldn't recognize the metal they were made out of. In the midst of the guards, there was a female beastkin with a squirrel-like tail and bright, round eyes. On her back, there was a bag that was nearly four times her height and width. A luggage-carrying slave. She was probably the one who screamed.

I pointed at myself and tilted my head. This was my house, and they had the audacity to ask who I was?

"Are you Durandal?" the rotund fellow asked.

I smiled at the group and placed my hands on my hips. "I'm Durandal."

The youth's brow creased. "You're the Godking's legendary weapon?"

My eye twitched. "What? Don't believe me?"

The rotund fellow grabbed the golden axe hanging from his waist. He brandished it into the air and shouted, "Fight me, Durandal! My name is Forseti!"

A sigh escaped from my lips. Looks like he was one of *those* weapon spirits—battle maniacs, the lot of them. I glanced at the youth by his side who had an identical axe in his hand. It looked like he didn't have any intention of stopping his weapon spirit. I guess I should fight. Don't I have some kind of obligation to guard my previous master's … warehouse…?

"What's wrong?" Forseti asked when he saw my head droop.

"Just take it," I said and raised my head. "Take everything. I don't care."

"Huh?"

While laughing, I turned around, ignoring their puzzled expressions, and entered the room where my sword was sheathed. I put on my robes and tied my belt before sitting next to my weapon body, resting my arm over it. I looked at the group. They hadn't moved since I left. The hell were they doing? Hurry up and pick up my body so I can leave this godforsaken place.

When the intruders realized I wasn't going to do anything, the guards spread out and picked up the miscellaneous items lying around. There wasn't much because of me: Bored out of my mind, I had used up all the medicinal ingredients to concoct pills. The bones infused with magic had been drained dry while I practiced enchanting items. The weapons were worthless heaps of scrap because I extracted their raw materials to practice smithing. Only the books had any value, but even those had become unreadable due to the passage of time.

The youth approached me. "I am Bryant Ravenwood, the seventh prince of the Ravenwood Empire," he said. The guards had finished scouring the desolate place and lined up behind Bryant. "I think you understand the hardship I went through to get here."

Nope. I don't. I don't even know where that asshole stuffed the miniature dimension.

I picked my ear with my pinky and noticed the squirrelkin girl glaring at me. What was her problem? Bryant froze for a second before continuing his speech while extending his hand forward. "Will you be my sword?"

"I refuse."

"Pardon?"

I ignored his dark expression and picked up my weapon body. A weapon spirit was unable to hold itself for prolonged periods of time, but it was still possible. I took a step forward, and Forseti made a motion to stop me. I glared at him and placed my hand on the handle of my metal-self. The rotund fellow gulped and took a step to the side. I lowered my hand and patted his shoulder as I walked past him. Out of fear or respect, Bryant stepped aside with beads of sweat dripping from his forehead. His guards parted as well as I walked towards them.

My footsteps echoed through the miniature dimension. When they stopped, I was standing in front of the squirrelkin girl. She shivered and let out a squeak as her shoulders froze up, her hands in front of her chest like a t-rex.

I pushed my weapon body flat against her torso, causing her to stumble backwards. "Accept my sword."

"Eh?" The girl subconsciously grabbed the sword when it was rammed against her body. Her eyes widened as she looked down at the weapon and then back up at me. "Eeeeh!?!?"

***

My name is Lucia. Just Lucia—I lost my last name when I became a slave or, maybe, I never had one at all. I was too young to remember. When I was four, my parents sold me to the traders because they couldn't weather the winter with an extra mouth to feed and I was the weakest of the litter. From there, I was shipped to the human capital where I was bought by a wealthy noble. Due to his status, he was afraid of his daughter going out to play, but she was lonely and needed a friend. That was me.

Even though I was tasked to be her friend, that didn't change my status as a slave. I did the chores around the house: cooking, cleaning, dishes, laundry. When the noble's daughter, Irene, wanted to become a knight, I was told to accompany her. I don't mean to brag, but I was an exceptional knight compared to Irene. That may or may not have been due to my beastkin traits.

As I got older, Irene's family fell into harder and harder times. Eventually, I was sold to the Ravenwood army. I was a strong fighter, but as a beastkin, I could only be relegated to the role of a practice dummy or a luggage bearer. When Prince Bryant announced an expedition to the rumored treasure trove of the Godking, I was one of the first to volunteer. They let me come because every year someone would announce the location of the Godking's treasure, but it was always fake. I never suspected we'd actually find it.

When I was younger, I used to be enchanted by stories of the Godking. He started off as a commoner and, through hard work and perseverance, became the strongest person in the world. The Godking was my idol. During the dark times of my life where I cried myself to sleep every night, I used to think about him and how he overcame all the difficulties he faced. Like everyone else my age, I imagined myself finding Durandal, his legendary sword, and inheriting his legacy.

So when we pushed open the metal gates to the miniature dimension, I knew right away that the handsome sword spirit was Durandal: those washboard abs, those tight pectoral muscles, those toned biceps, those fierce eyes, and that magnificent third le—. Ahem. Anyways. I realized that such a perfect spirit had to be Durandal. There was no way he could be anyone else. I'm ashamed to admit I let out a squeal.

But enough about my embarrassment. I wanted to approach Durandal, to form a contract with him, but I knew my place. Durandal was for the prince, and even the treasures the Godking left behind were for him as well: those … empty … medicine bottles, those … rusty weapons, those moldy books…. What the fuck! Why's everything here crap!? There's not even a single spirit stone! I made my way to the prince and glared at Durandal, who had given up on fighting and sat down like an old person. No! He definitely wasn't Durandal! There was no way this was the Godking's treasure trove, and that spirit was definitely an imposter. 'I'm Durandal' my ass! Who would believe that?

I started looking around the miniature dimension some more, hoping there was something worth scavenging. I was about to check out a rusty sword when all my hairs stood on end and my breath disappeared. Such savage killing intent! My palms became slick with sweat, and I saw Forseti step aside. No way, even that battle freak was scared? The crowd of guards parted, and I followed suit, lowering my head to stare at the ground. When the spirit walked, the whole dimension fell silent. I swear I could hear the heartbeats of the guards beside me. Every one of Durandal's footsteps was like a boulder being dropped on my back.

His foot appeared in my line of sight, and I involuntarily let out a squeak and shiver. Stupid animal instincts! I raised my head and arms, but they froze stupidly in front of my body. Durandal's gaze was colder than ice. He's going to kill me. He's going to kill me. I'm going to die.

Plop.

Something cold touched my chest, and I stumbled backwards. "Eh?"

What? I think he said something. Did he say, "Accept my sword?"

I looked down and saw my hands holding a sword. I raised my head and made eye contact with Durandal.

"Eeeeh!?!?"

"You don't want it?" Durandal asked and raised an eyebrow.

"Want! I, yes!" My head bobbed up and down as I hugged the longsword to my body tighter. All doubts of whether he was Durandal or not were gone. It wasn't possible for anyone else to have such a strong killing intent.

"Drip your blood on the pommel."

Before anyone else could react, I had already bitten my thumb and smeared blood onto the sword. The pommel glowed, and Durandal closed his eyes and inhaled before laughing. He smiled at me. "Good."

"Lucia!"

I froze. That was Bryant's voice. In my euphoria, I had forgotten about him. I bit my lower lip and turned my head. All the guards were staring at me with their hands on their weapons. Bryant's eyes seemed to be spitting out fire. My tail stiffened, and the bag I was carrying on my back felt ten times heavier. "Y-yes?" Even I could hear my voice crack.

"Surrender Durandal or surrender your life!"

Before I could say anything, a hand came down on my head and scratched me behind my ears. I gasped, and a little moan escaped from my mouth. Hey! I snapped my head towards the offender and saw Durandal laughing at me with his hand in my hair. "Calm down," he said and smiled, his pearly white teeth winking at me. His face was perfect. His jawline—. Lucia! Stop. Danger.

I shook my head and straightened my back. "Unsheathe me," Durandal said as he undid the straps of the bag on my back.

I pursed my lips and pulled the sword out of its sheathe. The guards gasped, and Bryant froze in place. My mouth fell open as I stared at the pulsing blade in my hands. Runes danced along its edge, and the light it emitted swallowed the world.

"Close your eyes."

My eyes closed.

"Can you feel it?" Durandal whispered. His warm breath tickled my ear, and a shiver ran down my spine. That's when I sensed it. A thread of mana flowing through my body. I nodded. "Let it guide you."

My body was led by the thread of mana as if it were dancing with me. My arms and legs felt lighter than air, and shivers of pleasure ran down my spine. There was no sight, no sound, no smell. There was only me and Durandal, dancing a dance in a meadow of flowers. I twirled, I leapt, I laughed. When the thread stopped and the blissful feelings faded to nothing, I opened my eyes.

Blood. Limbs. Intestines. The floor around me was a sea of gore. Forseti's axe-body lay broken in twain underneath my feet. Bryant's severed head lay on the floor in front of me, his face twisted in a silent scream. I nearly dropped Durandal out of surprise, but my hand wouldn't let go. We hadn't danced in a meadow of flowers. We danced a waltz of death. Durandal's corporeal body sat on top of Forseti's, his lips smiling at me like the devil with his hand propping up his chin.

Durandal was a demon. I became a murderer. So why did I feel so happy?

***

The squirrelkin girl was impressive. Or maybe it was just my leading that was awesome. Regardless, it seems like my edge hadn't deteriorated with the years. A trivial squad of guards wanted to stop me? Dream on. There weren't even any magicians.

The fat body underneath me began to disperse into thousands of motes of golden light. I had seen the death of a spirit weapon hundreds of times, yet it never ceased to make me feel a sense of loss. Like one more brother devoured by the winds of time. A sigh escaped from my lips as I stood up, Forseti's body fading away into nothing. "Let's introduce ourselves," I said and extended my hand towards the squirrelkin girl. Why did she look so ... lascivious after slaughtering a platoon of soldiers? Was she a psycho? My hand faltered for a second, but thankfully, she didn't notice. It would've hurt my pride to back down from a girl who wasn't even a hundredth of my age. "I'm Durandal."

"L-Lucia!" the squirrelkin girl said as her back stiffened. She saluted me in a style similar to the armies' of my time. Looks like their traditions were long-lasting. The perverted look on her face disappeared, replaced by a serious one with slightly narrowed eyes. Good.

"Just Lucia?"

Her expression dimmed. "Just Lucia," she said, her head lowering.

I smiled at her and placed my hand on her head. I furrowed my brow and closed my eyes. There was no mana flowing within her body. "Like a spirit," I said and scratched her ear.

"Huh?" Lucia asked with red cheeks. Why did her face look so lewd again? Was this going to be a problem? Did I make a contract with a pervert? Wait. Wasn't she the one that screamed? I shook my head. Forget it. She was the only viable candidate amongst the intruders.

"D-Durandal? Can I ask you something?"

Even if I said no, you'd probably ask anyway, right? I stared at her and waited. She gulped.

"You're the sword of the Godking, correct?"

No shit. I nodded.

"Then that means this is his treasure trove?" Her head tilted to the side as her tail curled.

Obviously. Was my new master a bit slow? I nodded again.

"Then ... where's the treasure?"

"Think about it," I said. Her face scrunched up as she seriously listened to my words. "What kind of treasures can last for thousands of years?"

"Eh?"

"Can you name any? Other than me."

"But"—she bit her lower lip—"it's only been eighty years since the Godking died?"

What. I stared at her, and her shoulders stiffened. Her body trembled and a low squeak escaped from her throat. I asked, "Really?"

Her head moved like a stiff doll, nodding once.

What the hell!?!? Did that asshole make the dimension's time pass at a slower rate? Was he trying to kill me? That fucker! Just because you can't use me anymore since you're dead doesn't mean you have to take me with you, asshole. I closed my eyes and groaned. This was totally something that spiteful bastard would've done. If I hadn't used up the spirit stones powering the dimension, who knows how many more millennia I'd have to wait?

"D-Durandal?"

I glared at the girl who was standing in a puddle of her sweat. Wait. That wasn't sweat. The poor squirrelkin girl had tears in her eyes, and her lips were pressed together. She sniffled.

I exhaled. "Stop crying. That's an order."

"Yes!" she said and saluted. A tear ran down her face, but she refused to acknowledge it.

"Clean yourself up."

She nodded and rummaged through the giant bag the army had brought along. At least she was pliable. It felt good to have someone who listened to my commands. No wonder why that bastard was so bossy. But only eighty years have passed since he died, huh? If we had taken out the spirit stones earlier, would I still be the only one left? Couldn't we all have made it?

"I'm done."

I raised my head. Lucia had changed into a set of armor. "The miniature dimension had some special characteristics. Thousands of years have passed in here, so all the treasures rotted away."

"Would the Godking make a mistake like that?" Lucia asked and blinked.

"It wasn't a mistake. That asshole did that on purpose."

"A-asshole?" Lucia asked and took a step back. "The Godking?"

"Yup. He was an asshole."

"No way."

I shrugged. The legends were too prevalent for me to change her mind so quickly. It didn't matter if she believed me or not.

"Then," she said and frowned. "What about the other weapon spirits? Didn't he have a literal army of them? How come you're the only one left? And what about the spirit stones? Those don't rot."

I sighed. I could easily brush off her insensitive question, but why would I want an ignorant master? "A weapon spirit needs a contractor to sustain their life. The Godking died. We lost our contractor. We could've sustained ourselves with spirit stones for an indefinite period of time, but there were too many of us. The weaker spirits taught their techniques to the stronger ones and chose to disperse, leaving the spirit stones untouched. In the end, I was the one who lasted the longest, so I used all the spirit stones to preserve myself for as long as possible."

I was going to continue talking, but Lucia walked up to me and hugged me. Her armor dug into my skin. She whispered into my chest, "I'm so sorry."

"Sorry? For what?" I placed my hand on the girl's head. A drop of water landed on the back of my hand. Was I crying?

"You must've been so lonely."

Was I lonely? Impossible. "I'm just a weapon spirit."

Lucia raised her head and gazed into my eyes. "No. You're not. You are Durandal."

Thousands of thoughts ran through my head at that moment, but only one of them truly stuck out. It was a memory of a time where I was stored on the shelf of a blacksmith's shop. There weren't many customers, and I wasn't what they were looking for. Until he came—the little boy with a head full of brown, mop-like hair. The boy who would be known as the Godking. He bought me with the allowance he saved up over the course of two years.

People laughed at him when he raised me into the air, declaring, "When I grow up, I'm going to be a legend! And this is going to be my legendary sword, Durandal!"

"Durandal?"

I looked down and saw Lucia staring at me with an odd expression on her face—like she wanted to eat me. The expression disappeared so fast, I thought I had imagined it. "Work hard, Lucia," I said and separated her from my body. I placed my hands on her shoulders. "I will make you into a legend."

***

Durandal staring at me while sitting on the corpse of his fallen enemy wasn't uncomfortable like I thought it would be. I was actually at ease. After he guided me, there was a sense of connection—a feeling that I hadn't experienced since I was still a poor farm girl. I wanted to weave that warmth into a blanket and wrap it around myself every time I went to sleep. Thousands of golden motes of light rose up around Durandal's body. He looked like an angel. Ah. Was he talking to me?

"I'm Durandal."

Those words brought me back to reality, and I stiffened before shouting, "L-Lucia!" I saluted him because the aura he was giving off was similar to the captains' in the army.

"Just Lucia?"

He knew. I mean, I guess it was obvious I was a slave. I didn't want to meet his eyes. "Just Lucia," I mumbled. A hand touched my head, causing a shiver to run down my back. He scratched my ear, causing waves of bliss to run through my body. I wanted to tackle him and—. Gah! Stupid, stupid animal instincts! Stop embarrassing me!

"Like a spirit."

"Huh?" What was that supposed to mean? I guess Durandal didn't have a last name either. Was he trying to comfort me? But please stop scratching my ear. "D-Durandal?" His hand stopped, thank the Godking. "Can I ask you a question?"

He didn't say anything. He just stared at me. Was that a yes? A no? I swallowed my spit so I wouldn't sound awkward when I spoke. "You're the sword of the Godking, correct?"

He nodded. Phew. I thought he was going to ignore me.

I asked what was on my mind the whole time. Why's the place filled with crap? Of course, I didn't word it that way. "Then this is his treasure trove?"

He nodded again.

"Then"—where the fuck's the treasure!?—"where's the treasure?"

"Think about it."

Oh. Clearly the outer layer was a disguise. The real treasures must be hidden beneath a contraption or array formation that—

"What kind of treasures can last for thousands of years?"

"Eh?" What? Thousands of years?

"Can you name any? Other than me."

"But … it's only been eighty years since the Godking died?"

Durandal's gaze turned colder than ice, and I involuntarily stiffened. His killing intent was choking me. I'm going to pee. I really am. Please stop. His voice was low like a beast letting out a growl. "Really?"

I'm going to die! I don't know how I managed to, but I think I nodded. The atmosphere got heavier and heavier. I can't breathe. Where'd the air go!? Why's he just staring at me like that? Ah. I peed. Forgive me, panties. "D-Durandal?" My voice was tiny like a mosquito's whine.

The atmosphere loosened, and I regained my clarity. I heard rumors of suffocating killing intent and intimidation, but this was the first time I experienced it for myself. Durandal sighed and said, "Stop crying. That's an order."

"Yes!" I'm not crying. Totally not crying. Ignore that tear that's running down my face.

"Clean yourself up."

Whose fault was it that my legs are like this!? But I held back my thoughts and nodded. There really was no need to provoke the scary fellow's aura. I should listen carefully in the future. At least I carried around a lot of spare clothes and armor in that bag. I hated lugging it around during the trip here, but luckily, Bryant had foresight—because he totally knew he was going to die…. You know what? Forget it. His foresight was shit.

"I'm done," I said to Durandal after changing into a set of armor and turning around. Why did he look so sad?

"The miniature dimension had some special characteristics. Thousands of years have passed in here, so all the treasures rotted away," Durandal told me. Even his voice lost its color. Did he peek at me while I was changing? Was he disappointed in what he saw? Wait, Lucia. Focus on the context. Focus.

"Would the Godking make a mistake like that?" Even a child would keep perishable groceries in mind.

"It wasn't a mistake. That asshole did that on purpose."

"A-asshole? The Godking?" Blasphemy! Blasphemer! That's impossible. The Godking's my idol. He can't be an asshole—he's perfect.

"Yup. He was an asshole."

"No way." I refuse to let anything taint my perfect image of the Godking. If Durandal was telling the truth, then that means I've been worshipping a, a.... Lucia! Stupid squirrely brain. Why couldn't I have been born part crow instead? "Then what about the other weapon spirits? Didn't he have a literal army of them? How come you're the only one left? And what about the spirit stones? Those don't rot." Squirrels are smart sometimes too! See?

Durandal sighed. Did I say something wrong? "A weapon spirit needs a contractor to sustain their life. The Godking died. We..."

Why does he look so sad? Ah. He was lonely. Anyone would be lonely after being trapped for millennia by themselves.

"...was the spirit who lasted the longest..."

But he's not alone anymore. He has me now, doesn't he? We made a contract. I gave him my blood. We danced together. My legs moved on their own until I was right in front of him. He stopped speaking, and I took that chance to hug him. Don't be sad, Durandal. We can be lonely together. Say something consoling, Lucia.

"I'm so sorry."

"Sorry? For what?" He touched my head, but I didn't react this time. This was important.

"You must've been so lonely."

"I'm just a weapon spirit."

"No." I met his gaze. He was crying. Tears rolled down his cheeks, but he didn't even notice them. "You're not." People cry. Weapon spirits cry too. Then weapon spirits are people as well? The transitive property doesn't work here, Lucia. Say something else.

"You are Durandal."

Um. Did I break him? He's not moving. Or breathing. Do weapon spirits even need to breathe? Ah, he looks so cute when he's stunned. I just want to eat him up. "Durandal?"

Oh. He's awake. Serious face now, Lucia.

"Work hard, Lucia," he said and pulled away from me. Was I too clingy? "I will make you into a legend."

"Me? How?" Could I be a legend? With Durandal by my side…, I definitely could!

"You'll s"—my stomach gurgled, drowning out his voice—"ee."

I wanted to bury my face into my hands. So I did. Durandal didn't make fun of me; instead, he laughed and rubbed my head. Ah. That feels nice.

***

Why was Lucia's hair so soothing to touch? Was it because she was a beastkin? She let out soft whimpers, and her tail curled and uncurled. Her stomach gurgled again, louder this time.

"Alright, make yourself some food." Is it just me, or did she look upset that I stopped?

"D-do you want some too?" She lowered her head, but I could still see her bright-red face. While it's true that weapon spirits don't need to eat, it wasn't like we couldn't. Most people wouldn't feed their weapon spirits—why waste food?

"Only if you have enough." I didn't know how much food she brought in that bag of hers, and I didn't know how many days it would be until we acquired more. In fact, I really didn't know anything about the world outside of the miniature dimension. Where was it located anyways?

I watched Lucia walk on the balls of her feet while humming as she retrieved rations from the bag: potatoes, carrots, slabs of salted meat. She took out a pot and filled it with water while whistling a tune that reminded me of my journeys with the Godking in Foresia, the land of the fae. A smile crept onto my face. It really had been a while since I saw someone so happy. Well, it's been a while since I've seen anyone, but still.

Lucia reached into the bag and pulled out … a stack of firewood? Is that something normal people carry around with them at all times? She propped them up and pointed a rusty metal bird at the stack. A small jet of blue flames streamed out of the bird's beak. Ten seconds later, Lucia had a roaring campfire and was setting up a stand for the pot of water to rest on.

"What was that?" I asked. I reached into her pants pocket, causing her to jump and almost drop her pot, and pulled out the metal bird. She snatched it out of my hands and glared at me with a stiff tail. Did I do something wrong?

It didn't seem like she was going to answer my question. Maybe she didn't understand, so I reworded it. "How did you produce fire?"

"This is a magical tool," Lucia said and hugged the bird to her chest after settling the pot. "There's a fire array inside of it that can be used three times a day." Her eyes were downcast. "It took a long time to save up for it."

Magical array? Isn't that what the Godking extorted from that demon researcher? "Are there other magical tools?"

Lucia nodded. "But this one is mine." She stroked the rusty bird's wing and placed it back into her pocket. So these are the results of eighty years of progress—even a layman could cast magic. If thousands of years had truly passed, would I be able to adapt? Soon, the rich smell of stew filled the dimension, masking the smell of blood and carnage. Didn't she have any qualms about killing people? Maybe I really did pick a psycho.

Lucia cheered when the stew finished cooking. Her eyes were sparkling as she ladled the food into two bowls. "Here," she said and handed me one. "Be careful, it's hot."

My mouth watered when the thick aroma entered my nose. That asshole hadn't left any food in the dimension. I hadn't tasted meat in too long. Before I knew it, the stew was gone. I let out a sigh and leaned back. Eh? Why was she staring at me like that?

"D-do you want more?" Lucia asked. She hadn't even drank a sip of her own bowl.

"You need it more," I said. I really did want to take the pot and eat everything in it, but for the sake of my new master, I had to refrain from such actions.

"O-okay."

I stared at her as she ate. She was nothing like the late Godking: There was no imposing aura about her. She was extremely cheerful. And her face was definitely more … lewd. What was she even thinking about while eating? When she finished the stew, including the portion left in the pot, she promptly lay on her back and began snoring before I could say anything. I guess that's one similarity between the two. I sighed and cleaned the dishes as she slept. Then I roamed the field of slaughter and picked up anything that looked valuable. My loot included one small bag of spirit stones and a metal spear. All the other weapons had been broken during the fight. Why were these bastards so poor?

"Mom...."

I picked up my spoils and squatted next to Lucia. Was she dreaming about her parents? Did people who enjoyed slaughtering others even care about their parents?

Lucia groaned as her eyes shuddered before opening. "Durandal?" she asked and blinked while sitting up. "It wasn't a dream?"

"I'm real."

Lucia's mouth fell open. "Why?"

Did my new master suffer short-term memory loss? "Why what? Why am I real? I guess I never really thought about that."

"No," Lucia said and shook her head. Her lips pressed together. "Why me?"

"You're not speaking clearly," I said and sat down, resting the metal spear across my lap. "Why did I choose you as my new master?"

Lucia nodded, causing her hair to bounce up and down. Do I make up a lie and tell her I saw potential in her? Let's tell the truth.

"Because you're a beastkin."

"Eh?" Lucia asked and furrowed her brow. "But the Godking was human?"

Exactly. I nodded. "And male."

"So ... why me and not the prince? You could've become the weapon of a rich master instead of a slave." Lucia's head lowered.

"Humans are devious. I wanted to live under someone more honest and simple." If the Godking had taught me anything, it was to never form a contract with a human again. No way.

"Did you just call me stupid?"

"I called you simple. It's a compliment."

22

Lucia didn't look very happy. Maybe I should pet her—petting seemed to make her happy. I placed my hand on her head and scratched behind her ear. She whimpered and clung onto my wrist. That's when she noticed the spear and bag of spirit stones on my lap.

"W-where did you get those?" she asked with a red face. I noticed she didn't try to move my hand away.

"The spirit stones were from the prince, and the spear was from a guard." Her body stiffened underneath my touch. A constipated look appeared on her face. Did she need to go to the bathroom?

"They're dead," she whispered. I almost didn't hear her.

"They are. You killed them."

Her face paled. "Me?" Tears pooled in her eyes, making them glisten.

"Who else?" I asked. Did she not remember? Maybe I should've gone with the prince instead.... "Did you not notice?"

Lucia bit her lower lip. "I forgot because I was hungry...," she said as she gazed upon the carnage. "What's going to happen now? I killed a prince. They'll hang me with my own intestines when they catch me." Her hands turned white as she clutched my arm. Her eyes betrayed her fear. How cute.

"Then don't let them catch you," I said and laughed. "Calm down."

"You're too calm!"

"It's not the first time I've killed royalty." Honestly, it probably wouldn't be the last either.

"Impossible," Lucia said and shook her head. "The Godking would never kill anyone. He was a saint!"

"Oh, you poor child," I said and sighed before rubbing her ears again. They were so soft to touch. "The Godking's nothing like you think he was. It's best if you just forget everything you know about that bastard."

***

I never knew having my ears rubbed would feel so good. I just want to close my eyes and sink into that feeling of bliss. Shivers ran from the back of my neck down to my toes, causing my tiny digits to curl. Wait. The Godking was a bastard? Is that what Durandal just said? Was he the type of weapon spirit to shit talk his masters? He did call me stupid....

"What do you mean bastard?" I asked, pulling his hand away from my head. Though I was reluctant to part with his fingers, I wouldn't be able to think straight if he kept on rubbing me.

"I mean what I say," Durandal said with a smirk. Did he know what petting did to me? "Forget it. You don't believe me."

It's true. I didn't believe him. The silver spear in his lap bothered me. "Are you sure you should keep that? It's bad karma to loot the dead."

"If that was the case, the Godking wouldn't be so widely praised. He was the one who taught me to plunder the spoils of our enemies." Durandal raised the spear. "Do you have another weapon to give me?"

I'm going to ignore his comment about the Godking. My idol's not a grave robber. Maybe Durandal's impression of the Godking was skewed after spending millennia by himself. That must be it. As for a different weapon...

"No." I wasn't allowed to carry weapons as a luggage-bearing slave. The bag was just filled with necessities for survival.

"Then I'll be keeping this. I don't think you'll be able to keep us out of danger by yourself."

Did he just call me incompetent? I'm very competent! How rude. Actually ... compared to the Godking, I guess anyone would be classified as incompetent. I have to work hard to meet Durandal's expectations! ...Or at least not disappoint him too greatly. I nodded to myself. Work hard, Lucia.

"You agree?" Durandal had a strange expression on his face.

"Eh?" What did I just agree to? Think, Lucia. He called you incompetent. "No! I'm competent!"

He shrugged. "I'm still keeping this spear."

"But you're a sword spirit." I've never heard of a weapon spirit using a weapon that didn't resemble its weapon body.

"And you're part squirrel. Does that mean you fight using squirrels?"

"That's different!" What the hell was he saying!? Was there something wrong in his head? Did thousands of years of solitude ruin his sanity?

"If you can learn how to use a sword, why can't I learn how to use a spear?"

Why did that feel like another jab at my intellect? Forget it. You don't have to argue with the senile, old man who happens to be ridiculously attractive. Gah! He's a weapon spirit, Lucia. When you grow old and wrinkly, he'll still be flaunting his awesome body. You stand no chance in hell.

"Then keep the stupid spear!" Did I just yell? Oops.

"I will."

At least he didn't get angry at me. I don't want to pee myself again—the first time was embarrassing enough. I can't believe I had to clean myself with the prince's towels. Clean? Oh, right. I have to do the dishes. I grabbed the pot. It's sparkling?

"I cleaned the dishes and gathered everything important while you were asleep. We can leave at any time."

He did the dishes? But ... he's Durandal, a legendary sword spirit. What the fuck? That's even worse than making the emperor shine your shoes! "You did the dishes?"

"Is that a problem?"

"Yes!"

"Why?"

"Because you're Durandal!"

"And you're Lucia."

I don't think he understood what I was trying to say. How many people would execute me on the spot for making their idol do the dishes? There'd probably be nothing left of me. I chewed my lower lip. How do I tell that to him in a way that won't make him feel angry at me? While I was thinking, his hand landed on my ears. I raised my head. He was smiling. Not the cold, bloodthirsty kind of smile, but the nice kind. The kind that makes you want to tackle him and snuggle against his chest and lick his neck and take off his clo—. Lucia!

"Don't worry about my status as a godly weapon who's way beyond your league. You're my master now. Do you think the Godking did his own dishes? No, that asshole made me do them."

But it's fine if a legend makes another legend do the chores. I don't have that right. And did he just admit that I was way under his league? Well, I guess that's true, so I'll forgive him. Ah. It makes me tingly when he scratches me there. Don't stop. Sadly, he did.

"Let's leave? We can't stay here forever."

And go where? I can't go back to the empire now that the prince is dead. Oh right, I killed him. Does that make me a bad person now? "Where do we go?"

An evil-looking smile appeared on Durandal's face, and I couldn't help but shiver. What did he have in mind?

"The Valley of Beasts."

Huh?

"It may be a bit dangerous, but danger will help you improve faster."

Was he a sadist? Why did it seem like he was imagining me in perilous situations? But how come I've never heard of the Valley of Beasts? Could he be talking about that place?

"The Valley of Beasts? Is it the canyon that separates the fae from the demons?"

His smile widened. "So you know it."

"Oh." How do I say this? "But it was converted into a trading post before I was even born?"

Durandal's face froze. Did I break him again? I waved my hand in front of his body, but there was no reaction. "D-Durandal?" Ah, he's working again.

"Then the Snow Queen's Forest?"

The Snow Queen's Forest? Did he want to eat ice cream and build snowmen? "The tourist resort?"

Durandal's face cramped. "Tourist resort? I'm talking about the forest that the Snow Queen lives in with the giant, carnivorous rabbits."

"Yeah, me too. The number of adventurers exploring her land dwindled, and it became more profitable for her to turn it into a tourist resort. Now everyone goes there to eat ice cream and play with the rabbits. Can we go?"

"No!"

But I wanted ice cream. A sigh escaped from my lips.

"Are there any dangerous areas with lots of wild beasts?"

Of course. But should I lie to him? If I told him, I think he'd make me go there, and I don't want to die. Maybe I should lie to him. I'm going to lie to him.

"Don't lie to me."

I froze. "Y-you can read minds?" What the heck! That's not fair at all! Has he been reading my thoughts this whole time?

Durandal sighed. "I can't, but I'll know if you're lying."

You better not be able to! There's a giant tentacle monster behind you! Okay, good. He didn't react. But I probably shouldn't lie to him. "There's the southern pass."

"Isn't that where the dwarves live?"

"No? They live in Anvilrock Mountain."

"It looks like all my knowledge of the continent has become worthless," Durandal said and frowned. "Then let's go to the southern pass. I'll teach you there."

"Can't you teach me somewhere more peaceful? Like, um, a meadow of flowers or a small farm in the middle of nowhere?"

"Lucia."

I stiffened. Why's he glaring at me like that!? "Y-yes?"

"Do you know what makes the world go round?"

"Um. Angular momentum?"

"The hell is that? The answer is money!"

"Oh."

"Do you have any money?"

I'm a slave. What money would I have? "No."

"That's why we need to make some. I'm a simple spirit. All I know how to do is kill things. And killing beasts will make me money."

Make you money? Isn't the money for me? What the hell? But I guess he does make sense. I can't survive without money, and killing beasts *is* profitable. And I don't think I'll die under his protection, right? But I should probably get him a sword. What kind of sword spirit uses a spear? "Okay. I'll listen to you."

"Of course." He nodded as if me listening to my own weapon was the most natural thing in the world. But why did he look so sinister? He's definitely a sadist. Goodbye, peaceful days. You were a good friend.

2

The southern pass. It's said to be the most feared area in the continent, teeming with wild beasts, poisonous plants, treacherous terrain, and, of course, bloodthirsty outlaws. When Durandal asked me if there were any dangerous areas nearby, it was the first place that came to mind. We left the miniature dimension two weeks ago and headed straight for the pass, uncovering numerous treasures and legendary artifacts. I trained under Durandal's guidance and became an expert with the sword. Durandal also recovered his peak strength, and we became tyrants of the land. At least, that's what I'd like to say.

"Lucia?"

"Yes, Durandal?"

"Where are we?"

In reality, none of that happened. We're lost, utterly and hopelessly lost.

"Um. A forest?" Please don't stare at me like that. It makes me feel uncomfortable.

"Are you lost?"

"No." I'm competent! I swear! It's just that I get so distracted by..., well, everything. But it only happens sometimes! ...Okay, most of the time. Especially when Durandal looks at me. I still can't believe he's my weapon spirit. It's like a dream.

Durandal sighed. He does that a lot. Maybe he's depressed? Well, it makes sense—he's been all alone for thousands of years. Anyone would feel the blues. Heck, I feel sad if I don't talk to someone every three hours.

"Where are we, and where is the southern pass?" Durandal asked.

"Well," I said and cleared my throat. "We're in a forest. And the southern pass is to the south."

"What did I say to you about lying to me?" Durandal crossed his arms over his chest.

I stared at the ground. "You said I shouldn't lie to you." My eyes watered, but I blinked back the tears. Maybe he won't notice.

"If you didn't know the way to the southern pass, why didn't you say so earlier?"

"I wanted to show you that I was competent." Ah, the tears were falling. Stupid eyes. Stop leaking. My nose started to run, so I sniffled. Durandal sighed again and placed his hand in my hair. He scratched behind my ears, and I closed my eyes.

When I finished crying, Durandal asked, "Do you have a map?"

I nodded. Bryant had packed more than one in the bag. It's amazing how he ended up dying despite how prepared he was. I guess that was my fault. I still feel a little guilty, but the happiness of being with Durandal washes all my guilt away. I think it's because of his head rubs. His finger skills are too perverse.

I took out the map and handed it to Durandal. He stared at it while I stared at his face. I love seeing his serious expression, but only when it's not directed at me. After looking it over for a few minutes, he folded it and put it away into the interior of his robe. Does he have a pocket in there? I wonder what else he stores.

Stupid, leaky nose. I sniffled again before asking, "Do you know which way to go?"

"Of course."

Ah. As expected of Durandal. Sometimes, I wish he wasn't better than me in all aspects. It really does make a girl feel inferior, you know? If he sees someone better than me, would he break the contract and leave? "Which way do we go?"

"South."

I waited for more. Nothing else came. "And … which way is that?"

Durandal stared up at the sky and spoke towards the clouds, "I said I'd teach you swordsmanship, right?"

Oh. Was he finally going to start? I kept bugging him before, but he said I'd have to wait until we arrived at an appropriate area. "Yes!"

"This is how it begins. A swordsman must rely on their intuition," Durandal said and lowered his head until his eyes met mine. "Sometimes, you won't be given a chance to think about your actions, and you'll be forced to make a move. This is an exercise to train your intuition!" My body stiffened as his gaze grew cold. This is why I dislike his serious expression staring at me. It makes me feel so small. "You will trust your instincts to find the way south."

Huh? Why does this training sound like bullshit? Did he think I was a child? Just because I'm easily distracted doesn't mean I'm not intelligent. "You're lost too, aren't you?"

If I were a lake, his gaze would've turned me to ice. "This. Is. Training."

That's not fair! "I, I understand." There's some fights you can't win, Lucia. This is one of them. Just accept the fact that your weapon spirit is a bully. Ah, it's really not fair. I think he'd kill me if I asked him where we were. Anyways, time to use my intuition. I closed my eyes and twirled around and around until I collapsed. The sky spun along with the trees bordering my vision. When the dizziness cleared, I sat up and pointed straight ahead. "That way's south."

Why was Durandal looking at me like that? Was that pity? I've learned to recognize pity. I don't think my actions were pitiful. I crossed my arms over my chest. "If I'm wrong, tell me. I'm sure you know the way."

Durandal cleared his throat and put on a stern expression. "This is a test of your intuition. If I tell you you're wrong, you won't trust your future judgments. And it isn't pretty when an honest and simple person second-guesses herself."

"Stop calling me stupid!"

"I said simple. There really is a difference."

Whatever. I walked in the direction I pointed towards with Durandal at my side. "Can't you teach me anything else other than intuition?"

"I really did want to save it for when we found a suitable training ground," Durandal said and sighed again. Maybe he really was depressed. I have to do my best to be cheerful for him! There are so many things to live for, Durandal. Like the three C's! Candy, cuddles, and ice cream. Okay, maybe ice cream doesn't start with a C, but still.

"Lucia? Hello?"

Ah. He was saying something. "Yes?"

"How much experience have you had with the sword?"

"Well." How do I say this? Maybe if I word it correctly, it won't sound so bad. "If you count that one time I used you in the miniature dimension, then … I've used a sword one time." I've always used a mace. There's just something so satisfying about cracking things open. It must be because of my squirreliness and nuts. It's in my blood. Why wasn't Durandal saying anything? I'm a bit afraid to look at his face, but I'm still going to peek. Eh? He was smiling? It was the nice kind too.

His hand tousled my hair. "Everyone has to start from somewhere. It's great that I get to train you from the very beginning." He held my ear between his fingers and rubbed it. "I look forward to teaching you."

Was it just me, or did those words sound a bit ominous? Ah, I'll worry about it when the time comes. For now, I'll focus on the ear rub.

Everything has a purpose. My purpose is to teach and protect my owner to the best of my abilities. That is all. I have to trust my owner's judgment for everything else. So when Lucia told me she knew where to go, I believed her. I realize now that I made a mistake. For a beastkin, she has absolutely no sense of direction. What happened to her innate animal instincts? I'll admit she does have a sharp nose for food, but that probably contributes to her overall problems.

Somehow, without me knowing, we entered a forest. I didn't even see it on the horizon. One moment, we were walking on a road and I looked at a rock on the ground; then, bam, we were surrounded by trees. After a bit of intimidation, Lucia admitted we were lost. Sometimes, I forget she's not the Godking. I've only ever had one owner—it's a reasonable mistake.

When I traveled with that asshole, he always knew where he was going. He knew the best places to plunder, to hide his spoils, to escape from the law and criminals alike. I've seen him use a map a few times, but he never let me touch it. 'You're a weapon spirit; you won't understand. What do you need a map for anyway? Are you going to roll it up into a paper sword?' What an asshole, right? He wasn't always that way, but puberty happened, and he became unbearable.

I wonder if puberty works differently for different races. Lucia still seems like a child. Now that I think about it, I have no idea how old she is. But the Godking never cried in front of me, not even when he was only up to my waist. I let out a sigh and stroked Lucia's head. It wasn't fair of me to compare her to him. At least Lucia is much easier to deal with than Roland. Ninety percent of the time, she'd forget her problems and feel better if I rub and scratch her ears like this. But why does her face always become so perverted? I should probably stop. "Do you have a map?"

Lucia's eyes brightened, and she dug through her bag before handing me one. Alright, Roland, let me see what's so hard about reading a map. I unfurled the piece of paper and stared at it. ...And stared at it some more. I have no idea what any of these symbols mean. I'm sure if someone explained it to me, I would understand, but there's no way I'll be able to interpret this by myself. Just like those times I practiced alchemy and enchanting.

Although I used up all the medicinal ingredients in the miniature dimension, my success rate in creating pills is a whopping zero percent. The enchantment-weaving was slightly better with one successful low-grade strengthening rune inscribed on a sword. It took about thirty million tries. As for weapon-forging ..., let's not talk about that. For now, I'll put this map away. I'll figure it out eventually. Why was Lucia staring at me like that?

"Do you know which way to go?"

Hell no. But I'm not going to admit that to her. My image would be ruined. "Of course." Maybe she'll figure it out by herself if I stay silent.

Her head slowly tilted towards the side. When her ear reached her shoulder, she asked, "Which way do we go?"

"South." It's called the southern pass for a reason, right?

"And ... which way is that?" She blinked twice.

Alright, distraction time. What would..., oh! "I said I'd teach you swordsmanship, right?"

"Yes!"

Ah, this almost feels like bullying. "This is how it begins. A swordsman must rely on their intuition." I made sure to make eye contact so she knew I was serious. "Sometimes, you won't be given a chance to think about your actions, and you'll be forced to make a move. This is an exercise to train your intuition!" Did I stare too hard? I think I froze her again. "You will trust your instincts to find the way south."

She seemed to be deep in thought. Of course, any random words of mine would be enlightening. Thousands of people would line up to hear me speak about the sword. Well, I bet they would. Roland never let me make any public appearances.

"You're lost too, aren't you?"

She saw through it? Was I looking down on her too much? "This. Is. Training."

Lucia froze like a stunned deer. This killing intent is really handy. "I, I understand." After saying that, she did something inexplicable. Did my aura damage her brain? Was she struck stupid? She spun around and around until she fell on her head. When I was about to say something, she sat up and said, "That way's south."

Maybe I really did damage her…. Isn't she a bit too emotionally frail for a slave?

"If I'm wrong, tell me. I'm sure you know the way."

Never mind. It seems like she's back to normal. "This is a test of your intuition. If I tell you you're wrong, you won't trust your future judgments. And it isn't pretty when an honest and simple person second-guesses herself." I've seen it happen before. His brain literally exploded. Well, that's because a unicorn kicked his face, but still, if he hadn't stopped to think, he might still be alive.

"Stop calling me stupid!"

Yup. She's completely back to normal now. "I said simple. There really is a difference."

She didn't say anything, so I followed after her. "Can't you teach me anything else other than intuition?"

"I really did want to save it for when we found a suitable training ground." A waterfall would be nice. There also had to be plenty of dangerous beasts. A few swinging logs. Maybe some bamboo poles. But I guess we won't be finding a place like that for now. I should start her training soon. I wouldn't be surprised if people discovered I was found. She did kill a prince after all. How much training with a sword did she have anyway? It'd be best if she didn't have any. I asked her, but she didn't reply.

"Lucia? Hello?"

"Yes?"

This girl. How does she get distracted so easily? "How much experience have you had with the sword?"

"Well, if you count that one time I used you in the miniature dimension, then … I've used a sword one time."

Excellent. "Everyone has to start from somewhere. It's great that I get to train you from the very beginning." Maybe if I rub her ears while talking about training, she'll associate training with pleasure. "I look forward to teaching you." I'll definitely make you into the next Godking, Lucia. Even if you want to run away, I won't let you. My owner can't be mediocre. What should I start with? Oh, if I make her do *that*, we can begin right now. It's been a long time since I felt this excited.

***

I'm going to die. I'm really going to die. I'm dying. Ah, the ground feels so cold. It's nice.

"D-Durandal."

"Yes, Lucia?" Was he smiling? He really is a sadist. Why did I agree to this? Wait, no. He didn't even give me a chance to disagree!

"H-help. Please."

"Aren't I helping you get stronger? No need to thank me."

You know that's not what I meant! "I can't feel my legs."

"Just your legs? It seems like you need to work a bit harder."

A whimper escaped from my lips. "No more. I can't do this."

"Really? Then I'll stop," Durandal said and crouched over my fallen body. "But are you sure you want me to? Since you killed a prince, there's bound to be people chasing after you. Not to mention that if any rumors spread about you owning me, then thousands of people will want to rob you."

You're the one who made me kill the prince! I have to admit he does have a point, but I really can't move. My body feels like it's on fire.

Durandal sighed. "How about this?" he asked and stood up. Where was he going? Was he abandoning me after leaving me in this state? "Come over here, and we can stop this training for the day."

Eh? That's too far! He only walked three steps away, but three steps seem like three miles when you have a four-hundred-pound sword on your back. "I really, really can't move my legs."

"Then crawl with your arms. I believe in you, Lucia. You can do it. If you couldn't, I wouldn't have asked."

Please stop looking like you're enjoying this. Shouldn't a weapon spirit listen to his owner? Why does it seem like I'm the subordinate? How can someone so handsome be so cruel? What ever happened to chivalry? Wait. Did he say he believed in me? No one's ever said that to me before. I can't let him down!

Ah, my clothes are getting dirty, but that doesn't matter. This isn't the first time you crawled on the ground, Lucia, but this time, it's so you'll never have to crawl on the ground again. It really is painful though. There's only one step left. He's not going to move away at the last second, is he? No one can be that cruel. My fingers reached his toes.

"Well done, Lucia," Durandal said and squatted down. His hand ran through my hair and rubbed my ears. The numbness in my body was temporarily replaced by pleasure. His voice was soft and soothing. "You really did a good job. I'm proud of you."

I'm sorry for calling you a devil. You're definitely an angel.

His weapon body became as light as a feather, and Durandal turned me over onto my back. "You can rest now," he said and covered me with a blanket. "I'll make sure you're safe."

What about a mattress? At least give me a pillow. "Lap pillow."

Durandal's face blanked. "Huh?"

"Be my pillow!" That's the least you can do for making me suffer!

"Like this?" Durandal asked and raised an eyebrow. He sat on his ankles before lifting my head onto his lap. Perfect.

"Yes." I exhaled and closed my eyes, relishing in the feeling behind my head. Never in my wildest dreams did I imagine myself using the Godking's legendary weapon as a pillow. How many people would want to kill me for this simple action? Too many to count. It'd be best if I got stronger, but I just wish it wasn't so painful. "Head rub."

His fingers ran through my hair and massaged my scalp. Why does this feel so nice? I almost forgot the pain he put me through. Almost. "You were really mean today."

"Was I?" His hand scratched behind my ears. "What do you want to eat for dinner tonight? I'll make it for you."

"Pork chops! Beef stew! Walnuts!" Wait. Stop distracting me! I'm trying to be mad at you.

"If that's what you want, then that's what I'll make." His smile is a cheat. How can I be mad at something so beautiful? Maybe I should just give up. I can't stay angry at him.

Hold on. Isn't he a weapon spirit? "You can cook?"

"I can do anything." Really? You didn't know how to read a map. "Then I want a salad too. And grilled tomatoes with bell peppers, and three scoops of ice cream for dessert."

"I'm not sure we have all those in your bag," Durandal said as he stroked my tail. A shiver ran up my spine to the base of my head, causing me to flinch. Don't do that without warning me! "Does that feel nice?"

My face is definitely on fire. I'm not going to answer him. I wish my arms would work, then I could lift this blanket over my face. Maybe if I close my eyes, he won't be able to see me. What were we talking about? I think it had something to do with food.

Before I could say anything, Durandal asked me, "Why aren't you circulating your qi?"

Huh? I opened my eyes. Why does he look so confused? "My what?"

"Your qi? Internal energy? Lifeforce?"

"I have that?" What is he talking about? Please stop staring at me like that. Your face is turning scary.

"You don't know what I'm referring to?"

I instinctively swallowed my spit. "N-no. Um. Should I?" Tears pooled in my eyes, and his face turned blurry.

"I'm sorry, Lucia," Durandal said. He resumed massaging my head. "I made a mistake."

Mistake? Did he mean choosing me? Was qi or lifeforce really that important? He's going to abandon me? I started to cry.

"L-Lucia? What's wrong? Does your body hurt that much?"

Liquid ran down my nose. I sniffled, but it didn't help. My body screamed at me, but I forced myself to turn around and grab Durandal's leg while burying my face in his thigh. "Don't leave me."

"I'm not leaving. You're my owner, remember? I'll always be by your side."

Does he really mean that? "You called me a mistake."

"Did I? When?"

"Just now!"

"I was referring to the training…. If I knew you couldn't control your qi, I wouldn't have started with something so … physically intensive."

What? "You're … not leaving?"

"No. Where would I even go? I can't go too far away from my weapon body. Silly, Lucia."

Oh. Okay. Did I overreact? Maybe just a little. The tears stopped falling, and I raised my head. "Sorry I yelled. I didn't want to be left behind again." Was that really my voice? It sounds so frail.

His hand stroked my back. "Don't worry, Lucia. I'm not mad or disappointed."

What did I do to deserve a weapon spirit like him? Ah, I'm going to pass out. That training really was too much.

***

I screwed up. Poor, Lucia. She looks so tired. For her training, I decided to increase her strength with the simplest method available—pure weight training. I manipulated the weight of my weapon body to five hundred pounds and had her carry me as we traveled. Of course, I told her I only weighed four hundred pounds to make her feel better. To make sure she didn't cheat, I used her qi to power my transformation, making her rely mostly on her body. Some qi was definitely necessary to prevent injuries from occurring.

What I didn't account for was the fact that she had no idea how to manipulate her qi. Who doesn't know how to do that? Evidently Lucia. I should've asked her, but I thought she knew. Qi exists in every living creature, unlike mana, which is why another name for it is lifeforce. Us weapon spirits can only exist by absorbing our owner's qi which is why all of my friends disappeared in that miniature dimension. I only survived because I used spirit stones as a substitute.

With qi, carrying my five-hundred-pound body would've still been difficult for Lucia, but she would've been in a much better state instead of this half-dead one. Seriously. She can't even move her body without tearing a few muscles. Wouldn't it be super embarrassing for me if my master died due to overexertion? I really did screw up, but the surprising part was how long she lasted. Roland would've collapsed before her when he was her age. I think. I still have no clue how old Lucia is. I tried asking her, but she said something about women and their secrets.

The smell of burning entered my nose. How did these walnuts catch on fire? That doesn't make any sense. And the pot is melting? That's never happened before. Then again, I've only cooked one meal in my life. Roland never let me cook again after that. How was I supposed to learn without some practice? I'm sure a decent meal would've been created after a couple thousand tries.

"Durandal?" Oh. She's awake.

"I'm right here."

"Is something burning?"

Does molten metal count as burning? "No."

Lucia stood up and waddled over to the campfire before collapsing, landing face first in the grass with the blanket still draped around her body. The moon shone down on her head, lighting up her brown hair. "It hurts."

Sorry. "You shouldn't be moving around. It'll take a while for you to recuperate."

"Eh?" Lucia sat up and tilted her head to the side. "But I'm perfectly fine?"

Huh? "What do you mean?"

"I always feel better after sleeping." Lucia stared at me with her big, round eyes. Her stomach growled, drowning out the sounds of the campfire. "Ugh. It hurts.... So … hungry."

The ladle in my hand fell out of my grasp. It passed straight through the bottom of the pot and landed in the fire with some liquid metal sticking to it. Her body recovered already? How is that possible?

"D-Durandal?"

I think I startled her again. Oops. "You shouldn't be able to move. Weren't you dying just a few hours ago?" I squinted at her before placing my hand on her head. Huh? Her qi is overflowing! "Didn't you say you couldn't circulate your lifeforce?" Was she lying to me?

"I don't know how to do that," she said with a pout. "But more importantly, the food's inedible! How did you melt a pot with water in it!?"

Her priorities are definitely skewed. "Forget about the food for a second. Do you know that your qi is already replenished?"

"You haven't even told me what my qi does. How am I supposed to know if it's replenished or not? ...Is this a burnt walnut? You know you don't have to cook these, right...?"

Alright, I can't cook! Sue me. Let's pretend this fiasco never happened.

"Don't destroy everything!" Lucia yelled and stopped me from getting rid of the evidence. She sighed and picked up a slightly burnt tomato that I seasoned. "At least one thing is fine." She bit into it, and her face immediately turned red. "Hot sauce!? Why!?"

"It's good for your circulation."

Lucia threw the tomato into the fire. "I can't believe I trusted you. I never thought a weapon spirit would try to kill its own master."

Hey, hey. My cooking isn't that bad. Forget it. Let's change the topic. "Lucia."

"Mm?" She was rummaging through her bag, taking out new cooking utensils.

"Do you know how to incorporate your qi into your attacks? Have there ever been times where your strike did a lot more damage than you thought it would?"

"Maybe a few times when I was angry."

Hmm. Wasn't there a test that Roland did that related to his qi? There were a few books on it too. "Have you done the water test?"

"Are you asking me if I can swim? Because the answer is no."

"That's not what I meant." I took a cup out of her bag and filled it with water. "Hold out your hand, palm up."

"Why?"

When did she become so suspicious of me? I'm a completely trustworthy person. "I want to see what category of qi manipulation you belong to." Maybe I should release some killing intent. There we go. I placed the cup on her stiff palm. "Now close your eyes. Imagine there's a ball of water below your belly button. Do you see it?"

"Yes."

"Now try to imagine a strand of water rising up to your chest, then to your right shoulder, then down to your palm and into the bottom of the cup."

Lucia's brow furrowed as she bit her lower lip. I peered at the surface of the cup. When qi entered water like this, there were a few things that could happen. The water level could rise or lower. The cup could expand or contract. For Lucia, the cup exploded, splashing water onto both of us.

"Huh?" Lucia asked and opened her eyes. "What was that? How come I never blew something up like this before?" Her eyes stared at me with accusation.

"I didn't break the cup. That was your qi."

Lucia blinked. "I'm special?"

In more ways than one. Ah, I should stop thinking mean things about her. "Not really? Most people can do this, no?"

Lucia shook her head. "I've never heard about this before. Maybe it was more widely accepted eighty years ago?"

That's possible. I guess there are times when she's intelligent. I placed my hand in her hair and scratched her ears.

***

According to Durandal, I am a brute. Even though that's the official name of the qi manipulation category I'm in, I still feel offended. I am a very elegant lady. Maybe I have a teensy bit of a potty mouth, but that doesn't mean I'm a fucking brute. Jeez.

"What are you thinking about now? You're getting distracted again."

Urk. Meditating is hard. How am I supposed to clear my thoughts? I'm part squirrel! Even an acorn on the ground is sufficient enough to distract me in the middle of a fight.

"Isn't there some other way for me to learn to control my qi?" This is way too difficult. I opened my eyes and stared at Durandal. He was practicing with his metal spear. The wind howled and shrieked with every one of his thrusts. Isn't he supposed to be a sword? Why does he feel like a legendary spear spirit instead?

"There is," Durandal said and lowered his spear. He wasn't even sweating after hours of continuous practice. Do weapon spirits sweat? I'm pretty sure they just draw on their owner's.... Wait a minute.... That's my energy he's using! No wonder why I feel so tired! Thief! "It's faster and more effective, but it'll be painful. Are you—"

"No thanks. I'll keep meditating." Pain? I'll pass. I'm not a masochist.

"Lucia..."

I can't hear you. Totally sunken deep into introspective meditation. Mhm. One with the world. Only I exi—gah! Did he just stab me!? He did! "What the hell!?"

"Ahem."

Ah, I shouldn't have yelled at him. His aura's too fierce. "I, I mean, yes, Durandal?"

"We're switching to the other method. You haven't been able to focus once in the past four hours."

"But didn't you say it was painful?" Don't rub my head! You're just trying to trick me. Ah, but that feels nice.

"I believe in you, Lucia. Won't you listen to me?"

Mm. That's a good spot, keep scratching there. What was he saying?

"You can do it, right?"

"Yes!" I think I just agreed to something I didn't want to do…. "What can I do?"

"Mn. Just hold a horse stance," Durandal said and removed his hand.

A horse stance? "Like this?"

"Perfect."

Is that a spike? Where are you going to put that? Don't tell me that's going underneath me…? "Uh…"

"If you fall…. Don't fall, Lucia."

No way. This is inhumane! I'm a girl! What if I lose my chastity to a stick!? Where are you going!? "W-what are those pots for?"

"Nothing really," Durandal said and poured water into two clay jugs. "I'm just going to put these on your thighs." Ah, that's heavy. But I'm not allowed to fall. This is really cruel. "Now, do me a favor and hold these rocks?"

Why are you smiling like that? Aren't the pots enough? "I, I don't want to."

"Hold. The. Rocks."

I'll hold them, I'll hold them. Oh, they aren't too heavy.

"Great," Durandal said and nodded at my suffering. Bastard. "Now instead of meditating, focus on circulating your qi to all the sore parts of your body."

"I don't feel sore though?"

"Give it a few hours," Durandal said. "Unless you want me to add more rocks?"

"N-no. I'll wait for a few … hours…." Hold on just a minute. Did I hear that correctly? "Hours!?"

"Hours."

"But it's midnight! When do I sleep?"

"Martial artists don't need to sleep. They meditate instead."

Can't sleep? "Where's the justice!? Aren't you Durandal, the legendary sword of the Godking? Surely, you're just."

"Just? Me?" Durandal raised an eyebrow. "Did I give you that impression?"

Now that I think about it…, isn't he a cruel, manipulative person? But he's hot, so I guess it balances out.

"You know the Godking started out as a bandit, right?"

"What? No way." How could the Godking be a bandit? He was the epitome of an honorable person!

"Have you heard of Golden Rat?"

"Golden Rat…. Wasn't he the really sneaky thief that the Godking captured? I think the emperor rewarded the Godking for catching him and returning the crown, right?" My legs are starting to feel numb. Let's try circulating some qi there. Oh, that does feel better.

"Golden Rat was the Godking. He was the one who stole from all the nobles and merchants. The Golden Rat that Roland apprehended was a young noble who offended him."

"That can't be true." Stop blaspheming my idol!

"Would the sword of a noble person do this to you?"

I don't think the sword of a thief could be this cruel either. When did these rocks become this heavy? "The Godking really was an outlaw?"

"Yup," Durandal said and nodded as he picked up his spear. Wait! Don't practice! I'll lose my energy even quicker!

"C-can I not do this?" I'm going to die. Didn't he say learning to manipulate qi was the first step of training? I don't want to know what the second step is.

"You have to." The spear pierced the air, blowing Durandal's hair back.

"Why?" What reason could possibly encourage this much suffering on my part?

"Aren't you curious? If the Godking was the strongest person in the world, then how did he die?"

"Wasn't it an illness?"

Durandal snorted. "Illness? He enslaved a pill master that could bring the dead back to life. How could he die of an illness?"

"Then … what happened to him?" Wait. Enslaved a pill master? Ah! That spike is cold! Why is it so close to my butt!? Maybe I can try resting on it…. Nope! Good thing I'm wearing thick pants today.

"He was cursed."

"Cursed?" I should really stop talking. I'm getting too tired. Right, circulate qi. Just keep circulating, just keep circulating.

"Yes. Although Roland was an obnoxious bastard, I can't deny he was my owner. I can't rest peacefully unless I avenge him. And to do that, I need you to be stronger. Do you understand, Lucia?"

I think I do. "But isn't that your problem?"

The world around me froze. Eep! Did I say the wrong thought? "I, I mean, I'll do it! I'll help you by becoming stronger!" …But what's in it for me? Mm. I'll just think of it as the price to pay for owning Durandal. Ah, my body hurts. Tonight's going to be a long night.

***

Is it wrong for a weapon spirit to lie to its master? Maybe. But do I care? Not at all. You can blame my personality on Roland, the most dishonorable kidnapper in the world. Lucia really thought that bastard died of a curse? Sure, probably

99% of the people he's ever met, including me, have cursed him at least once in their lives, but no one's ever succeeded. Mostly because Vera, his amulet spirit, was too strong. I wonder if she's still around. But let's forget about her—we didn't exactly end on the best terms and talking about her irritates me.

Anyways, I actually have no idea how Roland died, but Lucia needed motivation to train because clearly the threat of being pursued by a kingdom isn't enough for her. I had to make her think there's a danger that I can't protect her from in order to stimulate her growth. Is that mean? Well, what Lucia doesn't know won't hurt her. Besides, I'm doing this for her own good. Her growth totally doesn't relate to my freedom in any way whatsoever. I have absolutely nothing to gain from her growing stronger. Except, you know, everything I want.

And that part about avenging Roland's death? What a joke. How many of my brothers have died because he locked us in that miniature dimension? Shouldn't I be avenging them instead? It's a shame that bastard kicked the bucket.

Let's ignore those minor details for now and review Lucia's progress. The first day, she nearly died under the duress of carrying a five-hundred-pound weapon. That very night, she recovered after sleeping for six hours. Then she endured holding a horse stance for eight hours until dawn. And now she's taking a nap after collapsing of exhaustion. She's a lot stronger than I expected her to be, but maybe I shouldn't have been training at the same time as her. I do use up a lot of energy.

Lucia isn't a bad master to have. Compared to when Roland first started, her body is in much better condition. It most likely has to do with her beastkin lineage: her reflexes are sharp, her strength is above average, and her senses are heightened. The only thing Roland beat her in was amount of mana. Lucia has no chance of ever using magic in her life without the assistance of those arrays of hers, but her qi seems to be greater than the average person's. Give and take, I guess. And while I don't like him very much, I have to admit Roland was a lot sharper and more focused.

"I...ce ... cream." Lucia's lips smacked together a few times. Is that what she's dreaming about? Faint snores caused her exposed belly to rise up and down.

Well, a simple master isn't a problem. I do wish she were a little more ambitious. I'm a legendary sword. I can carry her to new heights if only she had the drive. But it's like pulling teeth when I try to improve her strength. Currently, she's at the level of a novice, maybe borderline apprentice. At least, that's what it would be called back in my day. She said she could beat a lot of the knights in the army, so the standards of the current times must have dropped. A novice has to focus on training their bodies and trying multiple weapons until they find a suitable one. Of course, she's going to use a sword. There's no other choice for her. Ignore the fact that I'm using a spear. Most weapon spirits use a weapon identical to their weapon bodies. I ... destroyed mine while attempting to engrave an enchantment on it. I think our first goal is going to be finding a dwarf colony to create a new weapon for my use. Yes. That's a good goal.

Afterwards..., I'm not sure what happens afterwards. Roland always had a goal: live unfettered without scruples. The majority of our time was spent being tyrants while goofing off somewhere. He was the strongest, but he had zero sense of responsibility. Perhaps that's part of the reason why he died. Maybe the people he constantly bullied got sick of him and conspired against him. I wouldn't be surprised if that's what really happened. I don't want Lucia to suffer the same fate. ...Let's pretend I didn't provoke a whole empire, okay? Old habits die hard.

As soon as we escape this godforsaken forest that appeared out of nowhere, we'll be able to plan accordingly. It'd be best if we could leave the Ravenwood Empire and enter the fae or demon territory. Boundaries between nations are respected—the humans should stop their pursuit once we're out of their lands. They shouldn't spread the news of my being found so quickly either. They'd want to keep me for themselves after all. Is that a bad thing that I want to escape from? Yes. No way in hell am I going back to a human owner.

Now that Lucia knows how to circulate qi, traveling with me weighing five hundred pounds shouldn't slow us down as much. As long as we continue walking in a straight line, we'll have to exit this forest eventually. If I'm not wrong, we should be in the Dark Woods. That was the only heavily forested region back in Roland's day, but I'm not sure why there aren't any wild animals or beasts around. It's also possible a new forest sprouted in the time I was sealed. Is eighty years enough time for a forest to grow? I'm not sure. All I know is too many things have changed in the time I was gone. I'll have to keep a low profile until I figure everything out.

Lucia stiffened and sat up. She probably needs to pee. "What's wrong?"

"Something's coming," Lucia said and pursed her lips.

Really? I didn't notice anything. Don't tell me my senses are inferior to a half-asleep squirrelkin lady. "Oh? You noticed?" On the off chance she's right, I have to maintain my image as a master.

Lucia nodded and stood up, quickly putting on her leather armor. She placed my weapon body on her lap and sat next to me, facing the fire. Her ears swiveled back and forth while her tail twitched repeatedly. It makes me want to stroke it.

"Eep! What are you doing at a time like this!?"

Stroking your tail, is that wrong? No need to look so flustered. "Just checking something." I'm curious, okay? Roland didn't have a tail.

The snap of a breaking twig caught my attention. Well, it looks like my senses have dulled. I'm ashamed of myself. Lucia looks so serious—it's really strange. I'm too used to seeing her excited with sparkly eyes, sad with watering eyes, or lewd with her eyes and mouth half-open. I didn't know she had a serious expression. As her weapon, it brings me joy to see her like this. It almost reminds me of the times Roland waited in ambush. If the intruder is a person, I wonder what action she'd take. Somehow, I'm excited to find out more about my new owner. I hope you won't disappoint me, Lucia.

3

Did someone discover that I killed Bryant? That shouldn't be the case, right? If they're able to track me down, then either a miracle or a shitty plot must be guiding them because even I have no clue where I am right now. Mm. It must be a few random strangers passing by: some young village children or a company of merchants. We haven't seen any wild beasts, so this forest shouldn't be a hunting ground for mercenaries. This will be a totally peaceful encounter, right?

I turned to look at Durandal. Why was he staring at me? Shouldn't he focus on the approaching people?

Durandal pointed straight ahead. "Shouldn't you focus on the approaching danger?"

You stole my line! You get to stare at me, but I don't get to stare at you? I see how it is. Hmph. Wait. He said approaching danger? Did he know something that I didn't? My hand tightened around the hilt of Durandal's weapon body. Ah, it's so inconvenient referring to my weapon as Durandal's weapon body. "Hey, Durandal?"

"Lucia…. Did you lose focus already?"

"Erm. No? I just wanted to know, can I call your weapon body mini-DuDu?"

Durandal's expression stiffened. A vein bulged on his forehead. "What am I, a piece of shit!?" The world froze over. Even the approaching people stopped.

Eep! I wasn't expecting that! It sounded a lot better in my head, I swear! "S-sorry! Sorry! I mean, uh, mini-DalDal?" Why does DuDu sound so much like doo-doo? "I-it's just awkward when you say things like grab my hilt firmly, or hold me gently, or thrust me harder, or hide me underneath your clothes…, you know?"

"Is this really the time to be discussing this?"

Ah, I really pissed him off. He looks super angry. I shouldn't have said anything. It's alright mini-DalDal. We're in this together. You won't yell at me, right? Maybe if I get on my knees and beg for forgiveness he'll be in a bett—!? Mini-DalDal! Why have you done this!? You can't turn into a four-hundred-pound slag of metal right now!

"Didn't I say training resumes when you wake up?" Durandal asked and smiled. A shiver ran down my spine. "Oh. I think it's also a good time to increase the weight to five hundred pounds."

"But there's people coming!" Mini-DalDal turned seriously heavy. I can barely prop myself up with my elbows and knees.

"Didn't you learn to circulate your qi yesterday?"

Oh, right. I did. That's much better, but I feel weird. Like mentally exhausted. Maybe I should take a nap?

"Lucia!"

"Y-yes!"

"Danger."

Ah, I almost forgot. This feeling will take a while to get used to. Well, at least this time I don't have to worry about a spike flying up my ass if I lose concentration. That horse stance training was really cruel. I think I'll sit next to Durandal for now until the danger arrives. It's safest here.

"Is that a fighting stance?" Durandal asked, narrowing his eyes at me.

"N-no, but, uh, I'm lowering their guard! Yeah, lowering their guard." Please believe me. I'm not trying to use you as a shield or anything. Not to mention it's a lot easier to sit than to stand with a five-hundred-pound sword hanging off your waist. This kind of weight training won't give me back problems in the future, will it?

Durandal's expression softened. "Acceptable."

Is he evaluating me? I guess he always is, isn't he? The sound of footsteps became clearer. How many people are there? Ten? Twenty? Please be friendly, please be friendly, please be friendly.

"Hello, is there someone here?" A human man appeared from between the trees. He wore a cuirass with a chainmail jacket underneath and plated leggings. There wasn't any visible crest on his armor. A sword hung from his waist. A group of similarly dressed people appeared behind him. "Would it be possible to share your fire?"

They're friendly? What. I usually never get what I ask for. Something's off.

"Of course," Durandal said. Why was he smiling like that? "Have a seat."

The group of armored men walked into the clearing. There were seven of them. The person in the back was holding onto a rope that was attached to a pair of furry hands. Furry hands? That's a beastkin! They're slave traders!

Just like I thought, there was a scrawny, long-haired, beautiful, rabbit-eared beastkin being dragged along by the rope. Pure-white ears pointed directly towards the sky even though the beastkin's gaze was glued to the ground. A white pompom-like tail stuck out of the dirty rags that was a dress. He … He!? That's a terrible candidate for a slave! What the hell!? Rabbits are usually prized for their looks: The males are super handsome and the females are extremely beautiful, but he's clearly a male dressed as a female…. Unless there are some nobles who are into that…? A shiver ran down my spine. I looked at Durandal to gauge his reaction. Why was he staring at me with those judgmental eyes? I feel like I should be offended. Don't categorize me with cross-dressers please.

"Many thanks," the leader of the group said as he took a seat on the ground across from us. "We've been traveling through these woods for many days now, but … I'm ashamed to admit we ran into trouble and our fire array was lost. Do you mind if we cook using your fire?"

"Oh," Durandal said. His smile creeped me out. Was he mad? That's his I'm-going-to-kill-someone-while-smiling smile. "That's fine. Do you know the general area of where we are?"

The leader raised an eyebrow. "This is the border separating the fae from the humans."

Holy crap. That's way off to the east. But I don't recall following the sun? How did we end up here?

"I see," Durandal said and nodded. "Which way is south?"

The leader pointed in the direction opposite of the way we've been going the whole time. "That way," he said. "I assume you're a mercenary? The only thing to the south is the southern pass. It's quite dangerous to travel there by yourself."

Hey. Don't talk as if I don't exist, you filthy slave trader. Ugh. They make me so mad.

"Mm." Durandal nodded. "How far away is the southern pass?"

The leader furrowed his brow but shook his head. "Forget it. I won't try to stop you since you're so determined to go," he said as his subordinates took out their rations. "The southern pass is about twenty days away at a relaxed pace. You know there'll be beasts as you get closer, right?"

"Of course," Durandal said and fell silent. The leader didn't pay him any mind and began cooking alongside his companions. I glanced at the perverted rabbit. Did the slavers dress him up like that? He's even cuter than I am! What the fuck!? How is this even fair? Don't smile at me!

I snorted and turned my head away. What's Durandal planning? Didn't he say there was approaching danger? They don't seem dangerous at all.

"You aren't going to ask who we are?" one of the armored men asked.

"Who—"

"Not interested," Durandal said. Don't cut me off! I'm the owner here! Jeez. Durandal ignored my glare. "We didn't know you before. You didn't know us. There's no reason to change that. Let's go, Lucia."

"Huh? We're leaving just like that?" Don't ignore me and walk away! "Hey, Durandal, why—"

Durandal whirled around and glared at me. My body stiffened. A sigh escaped from Durandal's mouth as he faced the armored men. "I'm sorry, folks," Durandal said and folded his arms over his chest. "Lucia, kill them."

"Eh?" What?

"You just said my name out loud. Do you not know what that means?"

Shit. I forgot. This is why I should've called you DuDu! "I don't want to kill them." I'm not a murderer, at least, not in my heart. Bryant didn't count, okay?

"You're too soft," Durandal said as the armored men rose to their feet. He took the spear off of his back and stepped forward.

"What are you doing!?" the leader asked as he drew his sword.

Durandal answered by planting his spear into the man's face. I didn't even see him move. The rest of the men charged at Durandal, rushing him with their swords. He didn't take a single step. He deflected the swords with no wasted movements and thrust at their vitals. In an instant, the only one left alive was the captured beastkin.

"S-stop!" I couldn't react before, but I'm not going to let him kill a defenseless beastkin!

Durandal's spear halted in front of the beastkin's face, dripping blood onto the rabbitkin's cheek. "You want to spare him?" Durandal asked. "And what are you going to do if he starts a rumor about us?"

"I, I won't."

Durandal laughed. "I don't believe you."

I screamed and ran towards them, but the spear advanced faster than I could and stabbed into the poor … ground? How did he dodge that?

"Not bad," Durandal said and raised an eyebrow at the pale beastkin. The ropes around the rabbitkin's arms and legs fell to the ground. "I knew you were dangerous."

Dangerous? He was talking about the slave? I grabbed mini-DalDal and readied myself for a fight. Ugh. It's really heavy. Oh, right. Qi.

"You're really Durandal? The Godking's legacy has been found?" the beastkin asked and tilted his head to the side. His bunny ears twitched. "You chose someone like her?"

Hey! What's wrong with someone like me!? I'll teach you! Mini-DalDal swung through the air and crashed against the beastkin's head. Crashed? Wasn't he supposed to be sliced? Wait, before that, how did I even hit him? He dodged Durandal's attack.

"Lucia…, you're supposed to use the edge of the blade, not the flat part…."

I knew that. Totally. "But it worked?"

We both turned to stare at the whimpering beastkin. "It hurts!" he shouted as he rolled back and forth on his sides, clutching his head. Wow. His head must be pretty solid. Mini-DalDal weighed five hundred pounds, and the only wound he suffered was a large bump. "What the hell!? How heavy is that sword!?"

Durandal and I stared at each other as the beastkin continued to mutter 'it hurts' over and over again.

"Don't you think you should put him out of his misery?" Durandal asked.

Yes. It wouldn't be right to leave someone suffering like this.

"W-wait! Don't kill me! I can be useful."

"How?" Durandal asked.

The beastkin gritted his teeth and sat up before sticking his flat chest out. "I can seduce nobles!"

POW!

Oops. Mini-DalDal slipped. How careless of me. "Accident." How dare you look prettier than me and say those words with a straight face? Are you saying I wouldn't be able to seduce nobles!? Hmph.

"You used the wrong part of the sword again."

"I said it was an accident!"

The poor rabbitkin looked like he was in a lot of pain. Was that my fault? He gritted his teeth and said, "I'm willing to follow you, so please don't kill me! I swear on my ancestor's grave—I will never do anything to harm you two!"

Follow us? Don't you have a home to go back to? Don't tell me someone as beautiful as you is homeless. I'm totally not bitter. Why would I care if a male was prettier than me?

"Why?" Durandal asked.

"My great-grandfather was the Godking's second-in-command! His name was Cottontail Flopsy. It's been my dream to follow in his footsteps, which is why I adopted the path of the bandit."

"Eh? You're not a slave?" What? Did we just kill a group of righteous people escorting a criminal?

"That's right. My name is Snow Flopsy," the rabbitkin said. "Have you heard of me?"

Hah!? "You're the leader of the Flopsy Gang!" I knew people from different regiments in the army who were assigned to apprehend the Flopsy Gang, but there were never any results.

"*Was* the leader. The gang no longer exists," Snow said and stared at the ground. "Everyone's dead except for me."

Wow. We really did save a criminal. Maybe I'm not destined to be a good person. I should've figured that out when I killed Bryant.

"I have one question," Durandal said and narrowed his eyes. An invisible pressure pressed down on everything. Even the trees began to bend.

"Y-yes?" Snow asked and gulped.

Durandal rubbed his chin. Snow and I waited with bated breaths. "Which way is south?"

Snow blinked three times as his mouth dropped open. "Uh. That way?" He pointed somewhere. I say somewhere because I don't know which direction is south.

"Very good," Durandal said and nodded. Wait. How did he know Snow was pointing the right way? "Welcome aboard, Cottontail Jr."

***

Cottontail Flopsy. That's a name I haven't heard in a long time. When Roland was just beginning his journey, he saved a bunnykin girl from a group of imperial guards. I think that's when he decided to travel the path of an outlaw. If he hadn't met her that fateful afternoon, maybe the name Golden Rat wouldn't have seen the light of day. Like the fool he was, he fell head over heels in love with her. That's right. Roland was a sucker for pretty bunnykin girls. He knew the imperial army was chasing her, yet he forced me, a newly formed spirit, to fight alongside him to save Cottontail. Both of us barely escaped the jaws of death.

After saving the poor bunnykin, we discovered that Cottontail had stolen an armor spirit from one of the princes of the time, which was why she was being pursued. It was at that moment that Roland had his greatest epiphany. If we were in a dark cave, it would've been illuminated by the lightbulb turning on over his head. Roland realized if he became a bandit, he wouldn't have to care about the law, but more importantly, he could join Cottontail in her exploits. And that's how a poor village boy, within twenty minutes of starting his grand adventure to become a hero, became one of the most notorious outlaws the world had ever seen.

But, Durandal, Snow said Cottontail was his great-grandfather, but you're saying she was a woman? Well, to avoid rumors amongst their group of bandits, Cottontail pretended to be a man. Don't ask me why, I'm just a weapon spirit. Did her cross-dressing play an influence on why her great-grandson dressed like a girl? Maybe. And if I'm not wrong, Snow should be one of Roland's direct descendants. Funny how things work out, huh? Roland's great-grandson meets his great-grandfather's legendary weapon, but the legendary weapon's already taken. But it's not like I'm the only legend around here.

"Hey." I kicked Snow's socks. "How long are you going to hide from me?"

Snow's eyes widened as his socks shone with a green light. A second later, a small, white rabbit with a single horn sticking out of its forehead appeared in front of us as the light winked out of existence. Not all spirits are humanoid. The reason I allowed Snow to accompany us was this little critter in front of me. "Hello, Bouncykins."

The rabbit opened its mouth. A deep booming voice replied, "Durandal."

Lucia's tail stuck straight up into the air. "That voice doesn't fit your figure! Wait, no. Rabbits can talk?"

"Bouncykins?" Snow asked and stared at his armor spirit. "T-that…"

"Shut up!" the white rabbit said and thumped its hind leg against the ground. "I am the King of the World, Lucifer, the All-consuming Devourer of Gods and Planets, the Mighty Unstoppable Force of Nature, the Terror of the Eighteen mmph—!!"

"Yeah, yeah." I covered his face with my hand. He always added another title to his name every time he said it. I'm curious as to how many titles have been added in the past eighty years, but I'm not patient enough to find out. "Bouncykins. Let's just stick with that, okay?"

"Dammit, Durandal! Quit destroying my thunder!" Bouncykins thumped his legs against the ground like a kid throwing a tantrum. "How am I supposed to intimidate people with a name like Bouncykins?"

"He's so adorable," Lucia said and scooped Bouncykins into her arms. She pinched his cheeks and twiddled his floppy ears around her finger. Bouncykins and I froze. What? How did she...? "I wonder what he'd taste like...."

"Filthy peasant! Unhand me this instant!" Bouncykins roared as he struggled. His legs waved uselessly in the air as Lucia held him by the scruff of his neck. "Durandal! What kind of monster have you chosen? How can she catch me like this!?"

"I really don't know...." Bouncykins was a spirit of wind and shadow. Even Roland would've had a difficult time catching Bouncykins. So how did Lucia pick him up so easily? Not to mention the fact she hit Snow when I wasn't able to. Was there something special about Lucia? Was her presence so harmless that no one was on guard before her?

"You're thinking mean things about me again," Lucia said and puffed her cheeks out. Her tail twitched a few times, sending ripples from the base to the tip.

"R-release me...," Bouncykins said. Lucia was squeezing his neck, causing his eyes to bulge out of his head. His forelegs pawed at Lucia's hand but to no avail.

"L-Lucia," Snow said and stepped forward. "Y-you're killing my armor spirit."

"Huh?" Lucia glanced at the limp, frothing rabbit in her hand. "Ah! Bouncykins!" She released his neck, causing him to fall towards the ground. Snow dove underneath her and caught him. He glared at me. Why at me? I wasn't the one who almost killed your armor spirit.

"You really are Durandal," Snow said. He placed the rabbit on top of his feet. "Hurry up and recover inside, Lucifer." His socks shone, and the rabbit faded away.

"Durandal?" Lucia asked. "Can you do that too?"

I mean, I could, but it's really boring inside of mini-DalDal. Am I really calling my weapon body mini-DalDal now? "No."

"What?" Snow asked. "But—"

"I. Said. No."

"I, I understand," Snow said and lowered his head.

"Well, I guess you're too big to fit inside this sword, huh?" Lucia asked as she held the six-hundred-pound weapon in front of herself. She thought it weighed five hundred still. Aren't I a genius?

Snow sent a glance at Lucia that said, "It doesn't work that way," but Lucia didn't seem to notice. Like I thought, simple owners were the best.

"Alright. Enough eating." After killing the people who were trying to apprehend Snow, we decided to eat the food they had prepared. It was Lucia's idea. There wasn't much mealtime conversation. Snow and Lucia ate like animals, completely devoted to their meal while ignoring everything else. Would I be the same if I could feel hunger?

"Mn." Lucia patted her belly and wobbled while standing up. It took her a second to balance herself with qi. Compared to yesterday, Lucia's gone leaps and bounds. She was crawling before, but now she can walk.

"Is it ... practical to use a weapon that heavy?" Snow asked and furrowed his brow. He really did look like Cottontail. Was he actually a girl in disguise? I should ask Bouncykins when he wakes up.

"This is training," Lucia said and folded her arms across her chest. Why did she look so smug? Should I increase mini-DalDal's weight again?

"Training?" Snow asked.

"Training," Lucia echoed without elaborating. "Anyways, let's go!" She raised her hand into the air and glanced at Snow. He blinked. Lucia lowered her hand and placed it on Snow's shoulder. "We're counting on you to lead the way."

Snow glanced at me.

I nodded. "That's right."

A deep laugh echoed from Snow's socks. "Still terrible with directions, Durandal? Some things never change."

Shut up. I stabbed at Snow's feet with my spear, but he avoided the strikes. How was Lucia able to hit him so easily?

"You're not going to switch to a sword?" Lucia asked me, ignoring the sweating bunnykin. She gestured at the dead bodies on the ground. I had looted them while the two animals were eating, but I left the swords behind.

"I don't want to use an inferior sword." That's not true, but Lucia doesn't need to know that. It's actually just a lot more fun to use a spear. I've used a sword my whole life, some changes are needed to keep things interesting, you know?

"Bullshit," Bouncykins said.

My spear flashed through the air.

"L-Lucifer, please stop provoking Durandal!" Snow said with tears in his eyes. "They're my feet!"

"What exactly do your socks do?" Lucia asked and crouched down. Snow's socks looked ordinary, except for a ring of carrots circling the ankle.

"Secret," Bouncykins said.

"Lighter footsteps and increased agility." I've worked together with Roland and Cottontail too often to not know all their secrets.

"Oh," Lucia said. "That's pretty neat." Why was she looking at me like that? "Then what do you do, Durandal?"

"Everything." I don't know, okay? Roland was ridiculously good at everything regardless of whether or not I was there. By everything, I mean he was good at kidnapping children and achieving the results he wanted without my help.

Lucia turned to Snow. "Is there some way to check?"

"Not really," Snow said and scratched his head. "Usually people do things without the spirit equipped, then do things again with them equipped and check for differences. It's not very accurate. But most of the time, the spirit should already know?"

Sue me. "Forget about it. You don't want to rely on me too much or you won't get as far."

"That's true," Snow said and nodded. He smiled at Lucia. "It must be nice having such a wise teacher."

For some reason, Lucia hit Snow over the head with the flat of mini-DalDal. "Accident."

Snow fell to the ground, clutching his head with his ears bent down. Poor, Snow. As we traveled south, a thought came to my head. Was Lucia also going to create a bandit group?

***

Snow is really sensible, unlike someone. Durandal's completely useless when it comes to things not involving fighting and training: he can't cook, he can't tell one direction from another, he can't tell what's poisonous and what isn't. I still have stomachaches from that strange mushroom he found and insisted was completely edible. I think Snow didn't stop me from eating it on purpose, that bastard. He definitely knew I was eating poison—he's too smart not to.

So far, we've only been traveling with each other for two days, but it seems like Durandal and I have become completely reliant on him. Even though he looks like a girl, he's manlier than most of the knights I've fought. Maybe it's because of his socks and Bouncykins: he can scavenge for food, he can fight a bear barehanded, and he never gets lost! Why can't Durandal be as practical? All he does is make mini-DalDal weigh five hundred pounds.

"You're thinking bad things about me, Lucia."

No, I'm not. Stop reading my mind.

"I can see it in your eyes."

What am I? A book? "I wasn't. Really."

"She was." Dammit, Bouncykins. Don't side with him! "Make yourself heavier."

Just you wait, Bouncykins. I'm going to eat you one day.

"I'm sure Lucifer is suggesting that for your own good," Snow said. "Maybe he believes you can increase your training?"

Is that it? "Hey, Durandal. When are you going to teach me how to actually use the sword?" All I've done is weight training and a bit of qi manipulation. I've gotten really good at circulating my qi—carrying mini-DalDal for a whole day doesn't even make me tired anymore. Of course, I pretend that I'm exhausted; otherwise, Durandal would definitely increase his weight. That sadist.

"You're not ready yet," Durandal said. He always says that. "When your body has been molded to wield the sword, we can start on techniques. You need a firm foundation to become a legend. A weak body will stray from proper form."

"Uh…. When will I be strong enough to start the basics?" Five hundred pounds isn't enough? Seriously? Is he trying to turn me into a bodybuilder? My already pitiful chest is becoming even flatter. Won't my body become like a man if I continue with Durandal's training session? Well, I guess that would make Snow and me a cross-dressing duo…. No! I refuse to be a weirdo like Snow!

"A ton," Durandal said. "When you can wield me when I weigh a ton, then you'll be strong enough to start practicing."

"No! Don't you have more graceful techniques? Like, um, flowing water style or spring breeze style or even sword of love and grace and girliness, you know, something more feminine?"

"Your qi clearly dictates your path as a brute," Durandal said. "Training in anything else will require ten times the effort to achieve the same effect."

I looked at Snow. Couldn't I become like him? His agility and feminine charm makes me jealous. I don't know why he's unable to dodge my attacks though. Well, that's not important. "Hey, Snow. What are you training in?"

"Don't flutter your eyelashes like that," Bouncykins said and snorted. "You don't have the charm to pull it off."

That settles it. We're having spirit rabbit for dinner tonight.

"Don't listen to him, Lucia. You're beautiful," Snow said and laughed. Why did his laugh sound so hollow? Why are his eyes so empty? Sometimes this duo really makes me mad. It's no wonder why I beat them up daily. Snow flinched and took a step back. "Err, Lucia. Let's put down the sword and discuss this like civilized beastkin, alri—!?"

Thwack!

Mm. The sound mini-DalDal makes when it hits someone is so satisfying. Ah, I almost forgot. "What were you training in? I didn't hear you."

Snow blinked away tears. "I'm an assassin," he said while clutching his head with his hands. "But Durandal is right. You're really suited to be a brute!" His body moved strangely like he was made of smoke, and he vanished before I could smack him again. Darn. How dare he call me a brute? I'm a cute little squirrelkin girl.

"I told you so," Durandal said. Is it just me or did mini-DalDal get a little bit heavier? "Follow my training and you'll become a legend."

The last time I followed you, I almost died of food poisoning. When are we going to arrive at the southern pass anyways? "Snow, stop hiding and come out. I'm not going to hit you. How much longer do we have to walk?"

A pair of eyes and bunny ears appeared in a nearby bush. "Didn't you hear the captain of the guard? He said it was twenty days away at a relaxed pace. We've been going slower than relaxed because of you. Maybe we'll arrive in a month?"

Well, *excuse* me. It's not like you're carrying five hundred pounds of fatness on your back, Mr. My Socks Make Me Run Faster. You think I like traveling this slowly?

"You said you weren't going to hit me!" Snow said. The eyes and bunny ears disappeared again. I guess I wielded mini-DalDal out of habit. Oops.

"You're awfully lively, Lucia," Durandal said. "I think it's time to increase my weight to seven hundred pounds."

Seven hundred!? Isn't it supposed to be a linear increase!? Last time it went from four hundred to five hundred. Now we're jumping straight to seven hundred? Is the next time going to be eleven hundred!? Ah. Mini-DalDal, you're so small, yet you're so fat. I'm going to die even with my qi.

"How is it? Too light?" Durandal asked. Don't give me that gentle smile, you sadist! And don't you dare touch my ears! ...Actually, I wouldn't mind if you did. "By the time we reach the southern pass, I expect your foundation to be passable."

...I'm going to die. Or I'm going to become a manly woman. I don't know which is worse. But if I did manage to fight with a two-thousand-pound sword, wouldn't that make me stronger than most generals in the Ravenwood army? Is that really possible? I remember the first time I joined the army. We were being trained by a lieutenant—well, everyone else was, I was being used as a target dummy because, you know, beastkin—and a general came by. He wanted to check the new batch of recruits and had them all charge him at the same time. He won without even breathing heavily. I wonder what kind of hellish training he went through to become like that.

"Why didn't you give her any magic tools, Durandal?" Bouncykins asked. He was sitting on Snow's head, and Snow was sitting in a tree. Aren't our roles a bit reversed? I'm the squirrel. Wait. Magic tools? Durandal had those? My finger traced the rusted bird in my pocket.

Durandal avoided my gaze and cleared his throat. He took his usual lying pose—head held high, chest out, arms folded in his sleeves, back straight—and said, "Shortcuts ruin foundations. If I let her use magic tools now, she'll become reliant on them."

What a liar. "He didn't know what magic tools were until he saw my fire array!"

"Huh? Huh!?" Bouncykins' mouth fell open. "Really, Durandal? Really?" The rabbit laughed and thumped his feet on Snow's head. "How can you not know what a magic tool is? Your owner practically invented them!"

Hah. How does it feel to be embarrassed, Durandal? Ah. He's going to kill me for this, isn't he? I think mini-DalDal just became a hundred pounds heavier.

"L-Lucifer," Snow said. "I don't think you should make fun of Durandal." He bit his lower lip. "He looks really scary."

"No. Forget it," Durandal said. He wasn't mad? "It's true that I don't know anything about the world that happened in the last eighty years."

"You didn't know anything about the world before that too, you sword maniac!" Bouncykins laughed even harder. He used his ear to wipe away the tears in his eyes and stifled a giggle. "I can't wait to see your reaction when you get your ass kicked by magic. The era of spirits is over. Magic is all the rage nowadays."

"Then what about you?" Durandal asked.

"Snow can use magic," Bouncykins said and smirked. I didn't realize rabbits could even smirk with their mouths the way they are. "And he has an abundance of magic tools. Well, had. We still have to recover them. Even I am a semi-magical tool now. I was inscribed with a fleet foot spell."

"Hey!" Only I can make Durandal feel bad, you stupid bunny. "Durandal is more amazing then you. Look at this!" I swung mini-DalDal against the earth. The ground exploded from the sheer weight of the sword. "See that? That's what seven hundred pounds can do."

"Eight hundred," Durandal said.

What? So it really did increase again? "Then eight hundred pounds. Now imagine if it were a ton!" Wow. I think I realized why Durandal wants me to become a manly squirrelkin girl.

"Yeah, sure. That's impressive," Bouncykins said and rolled his eyes. "Now what do you do if an archer shoots a lightning bolt at you from a mile away with a magical bow?"

"Kick his ass! Durandal's the greatest. I won't ever let him lose. There's no way I can disappoint the Godking's legacy."

***

I chewed on a roasted mushroom while Snow and Lucia slept. Bouncykins was being squeezed by Lucia, her drool drenching his ear. There was a defeated expression on his face. I don't get why Lucia said these mushrooms were poisonous. There's nothing wrong with them at all.

I sighed, leaning against the tree, and stared up at the sky. The stars were still in the same place—Vera had taught me the names of the constellations while we kept guard at night. She was awfully smart for a spirit, but she did exist for way longer than I had. I'm sure I'd be just as intelligent if I lived for as long as her. Ignore the fact I've survived thousands of years in isolation.

"The era of spirits is over."

Bouncykins words echoed through my head. That rabbit spirit might be an asshole, but he's not a liar. If he said the era of spirits was over, then it was probably true, or at least, he thought it was. Had I become useless? No. I guess I always was, wasn't I? It's true that I can't do anything except fight, but what meaning does that have when the world is at peace? Roland united the three warring kingdoms by tricking the younger generation of rulers. I wasn't even necessary back then either. Could I even turn Lucia into a legend? Roland made me into a legend, not the other way around.

"Durandal? What's wrong?" Lucia sat up and tossed Bouncykins aside like a dirty napkin. He cheered and disappeared into Snow's socks. "Is your stomach cramping? Didn't I say those were poisonous?" She stared at the mushrooms roasting in the fire and the ones on my lap.

"Why are you awake? The sun won't rise for another few hours. Aren't you tired from carrying me all day?" Even while she slept, I forced her to keep mini-DalDal on her back.

"I didn't feel right," Lucia said and furrowed her brow. Her nose twitched as she muttered, "Maybe it was the mushroom smell." She raised her head. "But anyway, what's wrong? You look … sad."

I scooted over and made space for her to sit. She grabbed onto my arm and rested her head on my shoulder. I ran my fingers through her hair. "Do you know how a weapon spirit is formed, Lucia?"

"Well, sure," Lucia said. The fire crackled, and I retrieved my roasting mushroom. "When a person loves their weapon very, very much, they plant a spirit seed inside of it; some magic happens between them, maybe some sprinkles and stuff, and then poof! A weapon spirit appears. Right?"

Well. I guess she wasn't wrong. She could've explained it in a less ambiguous way though. "And do you know how a weapon spirit disappears?"

Lucia sat up, her face turning serious for once. "You're not going to die, right?" she asked and grabbed my hand. "I just found you. You can't die."

The mushroom tasted bitter. "A weapon spirit dies when their spirit body is killed or when their core is destroyed. Or depleted." My core was embedded in mini-DalDal's hilt, covered by Lucia's hand when she wielded me. She was right about the spirit seed—it grew into the core. Spirit seeds could be found everywhere. The ones that formed in places with abundant mana grew into stronger spirits. I was a crappy seed that Roland found growing between some weeds. I guess that just attests to Roland's skill. How much more impressive would his legends have been if he had a top-grade seed in a sword made of top-grade materials?

"Durandal…"

"A spirit's core can be refilled by their owner's qi or spirit stones. If we hibernate inside our core, spirits can last for a long time. Do you know the average age of a weapon spirit, Lucia?"

She bit her lower lip. "No. I don't want to know. Stop talking." She leaned against me again and closed her eyes. Her eyelids trembled.

I retrieved the rest of the roasting mushrooms and munched on them. "Five years."

Lucia sat up and her hand flashed. My cheek stung. Did she slap me?

"I said I didn't want to know." Why was she crying? I was the one who just got slapped.

I ignored the feeling in my cheek. "Do you know how long I've lived for, Lucia?"

"Stop!" She knocked the mushrooms off my lap and pushed me down to the ground. I didn't resist. Her tears threatened to fall from her pooling eyes. Her voice lowered to a whisper. "Why are you telling me this?"

"I'm tired, Lucia. Did you know weapon spirits can't sleep? Even when we're hibernating, our minds are conscious."

"I'm really going to be mad at you, Durandal." Her nails dug into my shoulders, drawing blood. Why can weapon spirits even bleed?

"You heard what Bouncykins said. The era of weapon spirits is over. How are you going to kick someone's ass if they're shooting lightning bolts at you from miles away? Even you can use magic with the assistance of a magic tool. Is there even a point of close combat anymore? I've become a relic of the past. Snow can take care of you—he's much more useful than I am."

"Shut up!" Lucia screamed. Snow scrambled to his feet. White lights flashed and two daggers appeared in Snow's hands, his head swiveling. "You said you were going to make me into a legend! You said you believed in me! No one's ever told me that before! Do you understand!?" Lucia's tears fell onto my face and burned my skin. Her hands pounded my chest. "I don't care how useless you think you are! You're everything to me!" She hung her head and sobbed. "I'm just a runaway slave. I can count the number of belongings I have on one hand. I won't have anything left if you leave me, do you understand!?"

She stood up and grabbed mini-DalDal's hilt with a single hand. A vein bulged on her neck as she unsheathed the sword with one arm. I had lied to Lucia earlier—mini-DalDal weighed half a ton, not eight hundred pounds. "One ton. One ton is nothing!" Lucia shouted and swung mini-DalDal into the tree we were leaning against. Wind howled as the tree trunk shattered, the top flying off into the distance. "It doesn't matter! I can do two tons! Ten tons! A thousand tons!" She fell to her knees and dropped mini-DalDal beside her. She wiped her eyes with the backs of her hands. "I don't care how hard I have to work. I won't pretend I'm tired when I'm not. I'll stop slacking off. Just don't leave me, Durandal. I need you."

So she *was* pretending. I knew it. I sat up and leaned over, bringing her into my embrace. "Silly, Lucia. When did I ever say I was going to leave?" I hadn't said anything about leaving at all.

"Promise?" Lucia asked with a sniffle.

"Promise what?"

"Promise me you won't leave, you bastard," Lucia said and grabbed my face, stretching my cheeks.

"I pwomise."

Lucia let go of my face and wiped her eyes with the back of her hand. "Good."

I picked up a mushroom that fell near the fire and ate it. It tasted sweet.

***

Why would Durandal say something like that? Now I can't sleep. He promised he wouldn't abandon me, so everything's good now, right? Ah, I don't want to think about it. It looks like Snow can't sleep either. And Durandal and Bouncykins could never sleep in the first place, so I guess that's fair. Not! "Hey, Snow."

"Huah!? L-Lucia?"

Oops. I guess Snow was asleep. "Why do you dress like a girl?"

"Because I'm beautiful."

…Did he just indirectly call me ugly because I dress in armor like a guy?

"L-Lucia!? You'll strain your back if you hold your sword like that!"

"Just because you're beautiful doesn't mean you have to dress like a girl."

Snow cleared his throat and backed away, sliding his blanket along the grass. "Well, as you can see, I really look like a girl. So why not accentuate my looks? It throws people off guard and makes them easier to manipulate."

Manipulate? Oh, right. I almost forgot Snow was the leader of a gang. He really doesn't act like one. Maybe that was his girly demeanor at work. "You shouldn't manipulate people. It's not nice."

Snow shrugged. "Get some sleep, Lucia. We have a long way to go tomorrow." He rolled over onto his side and faced away from me.

I can't. No matter how much I want to sleep, I made a promise to Durandal. Let's sit in the horse stance together, mini-DalDal. I just wish you were a little less heavy.

"You really should get some rest, Lucia," Durandal said from his seat by the fire. He was still munching on those poisonous mushrooms. I'm a bit jealous of his stomach. Why can't I eat whatever I want?

"I'm not tired." That's a lie, but I can't let him down. I'll just focus on circulating my qi into my arms. How heavy did Durandal say mini-DalDal was? Eight hundred pounds? You're almost halfway there, Lucia. Once you reach a ton, Durandal will definitely be happier if he can teach actual techniques.

"…Should I increase the weight then?"

Why am I regretting my words already? And I'm going to regret this too. "Yes, but just by a little bit, please." The next second, my arms nearly fell off my body as mini-DalDal dipped towards the ground. "That's not a little!"

"Don't yell," Durandal said with a smile. It was definitely a sadistic one. Pervert. Demon. "Snow's trying to sleep."

If I can't sleep well, then neither can Snow. …I'm not a petty person. What makes you say that? Hmm. What if, instead of circulating my qi to the parts of me that become sore, I decide to always fill every part of my body with qi constantly? Oh, it works? Will I run out? "Hey, Durandal. Where does qi come from?"

"From your dantian."

"My what?"

"…"

Don't look at me like that. How the heck am I supposed to know what a dantian is? "I'm serious."

"It's a little ball inside of you that's slightly underneath your belly button."

My womb? That's where that's supposed to be, right? So energy comes from there? Why couldn't he be more straightforward about it and call it what it is instead of a dantian? "Is it possible to run out of qi?"

"If you're dead, yes."

…Maybe I shouldn't be expending it like this. But it feels so relaxing. "How do I get more of it?"

"There's some breathing exercises you can do. But somehow, you seem to absorb large amounts of it when you sleep. Some people meditate with those breathing exercises all night instead of sleeping to get half the amount of qi you do."

Wow. I'm amazing. "That means I should just go to sleep, right?"

"Try sleeping in that horse stance."

That's impossible! Who the heck can sleep while standing? A few birds maybe, but I'm a squirrel! Ah, I really wish I was born part crow. Wait. What are you doing? "D-Durandal?"

"Didn't you say you wouldn't care how hard you had to work?" Durandal asked with a smile. He slid a few spikes underneath me, propping them up on the ground. "Don't tell me that was all talk."

No, no. There's a difference between what I'm capable of doing and impossible. "But how am I supposed to circulate my qi if I fall asleep!? It's impossible."

"It's only impossible because of that attitude. The Godking could do it." Durandal smiled and raised his head, staring at the sky and away from my plight.

I'm not the Godking! But at least I know it's possible. Then I could at least try, yeah? Durandal's right—my attitude is holding me back. Believe in yourself, Lucia. "I'll do it!" …How does this work? "Uh, do I just try to fall asleep now?"

"She's going to turn into a pincushion, you stupid sword spirit," Bouncykins said. When did he get here? Did he want to watch my suffering too?

"Wow, Lucia," Snow said while sitting up. "You're very serious about your training. I was a little jealous of you since you had Durandal, but now I think I'm the lucky one."

Don't snicker at my suffering. I'll smack you. I really will. Wait, what was that bit about being jealous? Wasn't he supposed to be a trusted ally? He wouldn't backstab me in the future, would he? Now that I think about it, Durandal is manipulating Snow a teensy bit. It would make sense for him to be bitter, no? Plus, he's a gang leader with no morals…. This just gets worse and worse! I'll have to keep my eye on him; who knows what he'll do? "G-go back to sleep, Snow."

"She's trembling so hard that she's starting to stutter," Bouncykins said to Durandal as he also snacked on the poisonous mushrooms. "Are you sure she'll be alright?"

I'll be fine! This much is nothing. All I have to do is maintain vigilance and keep up this qi output until the night's over. Who needs sleep? I'd rather have a non-pincushioned body than a good night's rest. Wait. Why did I need to sleep again? To replenish … my … qi. Ah, I feel dizzy. When did my arms become so heavy? Please stay standing, body! My chastity depends on it.

And I fainted.

***

Lucia has surpassed my expectations. It seems like she was serious about not slacking off anymore. She actually forsook sleep to stand in a horse stance. Even though she doesn't know anything about qi or where it came from, that doesn't matter. It's easier to educate someone than to motivate them and keep them disciplined. Hundreds of that bastard's subordinates were like that, riding on the Godking's coattails and doing nothing to improve themselves. Roland's personality was horrible, but I have to admit he was a very determined person.

Well, let's add on to her determination. "D-Durandal?"

"Didn't you say you wouldn't care how hard you had to work?" It's just a few spikes. As long as you don't fall, it'll be fine, Lucia. "Don't tell me that was all talk."

"But how am I supposed to circulate my qi if I fall asleep!? It's impossible." Ah, that frantic expression of hers really is cute. Cute? Maybe a better term would be Lucia-like.

"It's only impossible because of that attitude. The Godking could do it." Actually, Roland couldn't. I've never met anyone capable of circulating their qi while they were asleep. Wouldn't that be too easy? But Lucia was the first person I've ever met who was able to replenish her qi to the fullest just by sleeping. Maybe she'll be able to. Of course, I'm not that cruel. I'll remove the spikes if she shows any signs of falling.

"I'll do it!" That determined face of hers is also very Lucia-like. …Shouldn't every expression she makes be that way? Hmm. Roland's expressions weren't always 'Roland-like'. What's the difference? "Uh, do I just try to fall asleep now?"

Don't ask me. I'm just a leech. I can't generate any of my own qi. "She's going to turn into a pincushion, you stupid sword spirit." When did Bouncykins get here? Did he want to watch Lucia's suffering—err, training too?

Snow said something that was too far away to hear over the crackling of the fire. His voice is really soft like Cottontail's. It'd be nice if Snow could accompany Lucia like Cottontail accompanied Roland. That fluffy beastkin was a good person even if she was a bit … clingy. Maybe she's the reason why I didn't want to form a bond with a human? Beastkin are honest and upright while humans are dirty and manipulative—Cottontail and Roland showed me that.

"She's trembling so hard that she's starting to stutter." Hey, you stupid rabbit, why are you stealing my mushrooms? "Are you sure she'll be alright?"

Lucia looks fine. See? She just closed her eyes to concentrate a bit harder. "Lucia will be fine. I'll remove the spikes from underneath her at the first signs of her falling asleep." Why are you looking at me like that? Do you have a problem? "What?"

"…She's asleep. You didn't notice?"

What? No way. She's … really asleep? How is she still standing? That's amazing. "Do you think her qi is circulating?"

"How would I know anything about your abnormal master?" Bouncykins asked. I think he's still bitter that Lucia can catch him so easily. Now that I think about it, there's many strange things about Lucia. If only Vera were here, she'd know.

"Should I just leave her like this…?" Well, I'll remove the spikes just in case she does fall over. Let's try taking some of her qi. Warmth flowed through my body as I tuned myself towards Lucia's energy. "She's overflowing with qi. Where is it coming from?"

"So … she can hold that monstrously heavy sword while sleeping?" Snow asked. "It still weighs over eight hundred pounds, right? Is there any way for her to decrease its weight?"

"There is, but I'm not letting her use that function right now. I'm in sole control. She'd cheat if she could." Would she still cheat with her newfound determination? Maybe not for a day or two, but motivation is very fickle. I'll withhold the ability to manipulate mini-DalDal's weight until she reaches a ton.

"I see," Snow said. His head and ears lowered. Cottontail used to do that when she was deep in thought. I still can't believe how similar the two are. If Snow wasn't a male, I'd think he really was Cottontail.

"Are you going to teach her the steady sword?" Bouncykins asked. His ears twitched a few times as they swatted a fly away. "I can't think of a better suited technique for her: It's as simple as she is. And she's like an unmoving mountain right now."

Steady sword…. "That really is a good fit." I wanted to teach her the berserk blade though. Her qi is extremely explosive…. Wait. What? How can her qi be explosive and calm at the same time? "Hey, Bouncybounce."

"That's an even worse name!"

"Lucia's qi and water test caused the cup to explode. Doesn't that make her a brute?"

"Huh? Really?" Bouncykins tilted his head. "Are you sure you did it right?"

"Yeah. Put the water in the cup; put the cup in her hand; let her send qi into it."

"And it exploded? Does the current sleeping her look like someone who'd have explosive qi? How peculiar."

"Maybe she's a dual type?" Snow asked. "You didn't test her before you became her spirit?"

Should I have? "I didn't."

"…Really?" Snow's tail inflated. Wasn't that Cottontail's sign of being mad? "I see. Whatever. I'm going to sleep."

I glanced at Bouncykins. He stood up on his hind legs and shrugged before falling back onto all fours. Anyways…, dual type? Maybe I'll teach her both techniques and see which one is the better fit. Yeah, that's what I'll do. With this, it looks like Lucia's future training regimen has been set.

"Why don't you teach Lucia magic?" Bouncykins was staring at my master with a strange look in his eyes. Hey. She's mine; back off. "Well, not you. I already know you're incapable of that. But if you could find someone to teach her lightning or even fire spells, think of how strong she'll be. How the heck can she even lift a sword that heavy anyways? Even with qi, Snow's limit is three hundred pounds." Was that bitterness on Bouncykins' face? It's hard for me to tell with a normal person, but it's way harder to tell on a rabbit's face. "You chose a good master."

Did I? Lucia would be happy to hear that. Too bad she's asleep. And I doubt she'd ever be able to cast spells with her nonexistent amounts of mana. Thankfully, that's what magic tools are for, right? Lucia's right. I promised I'd make her into a legend, and if I have to throw away some of my pride and employ magic tools, then I'll do it. "You said you had a cache of magic tools lying around somewhere that you had to recover, right?"

"Yeah, but it was confiscated by those imperial guards," Bouncykins said. "Those dirty bastards. I, King of the World, Lucifer, the All-consuming Devourer of Gods and Planets, the Mighty Unstoppable Force of Nature, the Terror of the Eigh— mmph!"

"Yeah, yeah. You're going to get revenge on them, right?" Ow. Don't bite me. "If I help you recover them, give me a cut?"

"…Two. I'll give you two tools."

"L-Lucifer!"

"Sorry, Snow. I actually owe Durandal, no matter how much I hate admitting it. Besides, we lost the hoard even with your gang behind us. How are you going to reclaim it without Durandal's help?"

"Two tools, but I get to decide." I wonder what kind of tools they have. Hopefully, they'll be able to help Lucia. …What, you think I'm getting ahead of myself? Do you think a measly group of guards could stop me?

Snow looks upset. "So we're redirecting our course to chase after my cache?"

I nodded.

***

"Lucia…"

"…Durandal? Is that you?" Where am I? The heck? Why's everything so dark?

"Lucia…"

"Quit playing around, Durandal." It's so dark I can't even see my hands. What's going on? What was I doing a few minutes ago? Was—. Ah! That's bright.

A light flashed, illuminating the room I was in. It was white and cubical. That was it: there was no furniture or windows or doors or anything to differentiate the floor from the ceiling. However, there was a figure standing in a horse stance, meditating in the center of the room, floating in space. Was that me? Then what was I? I lowered my head, well, I tried to lower my head, but I didn't have one. My gaze still shifted downwards and landed on the floor. Out of body experience?

"Lucia…"

The walls of the room cracked, little bits of white stone falling away from the cube. The inside was exposed to the outside, and my vision was engulfed in darkness. When I could finally see again, I was standing in the middle of a field, sun shining down on my perspiring body. Mini-DalDal was in my arms which were held in front of me. I was standing in a horse stance?

"Lucia."

My head turned. "Durandal?"

"Finally awake?" Why was his expression so strange? Did I do something wrong? Maybe I drooled on myself while I was sleeping. Wait, sleeping? In a horse stance?

"I did it!" And I promptly fell over due to my excitement. "I fell asleep while holding it!"

"That's right, Lucia, you did," Durandal said and ran his fingers through my hair. Play with my ears, please! Ah, that's the spot. I feel great! All the soreness that accumulated over the past few nights has finally gone away. And Durandal's nice enough to keep mini-DalDal at its base weight. "I'm proud of you."

I could feel my face turning red. "C-can you say that again?"

"I'm proud of you, Lucia."

"Yes!" Ah, if I died now, I'd die happy.

"Perverts."

Shut up, Bouncykins. Don't ruin the moment.

"Perverts."

Don't agree with him, Snow! You're the pervert! At least I don't cross-dress!

"Gah! Lucia!"

An explosion resounded as mini-DalDal whistled past Snow's head and collided against a boulder. The rock shattered and fell apart like a broken cookie. Wait. Wasn't mini-DalDal super light?

"Are you trying to kill me, Lucia!?"

"Uh, no. I just wanted to hurt you a little." Just enough to wipe that annoying expression off your face, I swear. I bit my lower lip and tilted my head. "Sorry?"

"Generally, when you throw a one-ton sword at someone, they die if they get hit," Durandal said while continuing to pat my head. Who cares if Snow's angry as long as Durandal's not? Wait, did he say one-ton? My expression must've betrayed me because Durandal said, "You heard right. While you were sleeping, I planned on increasing the weight until you couldn't handle it anymore, but somehow, you made it to a ton."

I'm that amazing? I should sleep more often! But my stomach really hurts for some reason.

"Also, it's been over a week, and you haven't eaten anything. And you're not at the point where you can supplement meals with qi, which is why I woke you up."

That explains it! How embarrassing would it be if Durandal's newest owner died from starvation? But ... he knows I'm part squirrel, right? "You know, you didn't have to wake me.... Squirrels can hibernate." Eh? Why did his expression freeze?

"Go back to sleep, right now."

No! My food! "S-since you woke me, I have to eat now." Believe me, please. If you don't let me eat, I'll be skinnier than Snow by tomorrow.

Durandal sighed. Hey. I thought he was supposed to sigh less now. Was he still feeling down? Haven't I shown a lot of potential in the week I was sleeping? I did, didn't I? I can wield a one-ton mini-DalDal like it's nothing now.

"Snow! Make me food, please." Why was he glaring at me like that? Oh, right. I threw a sword at him. I should probably pick mini-DalDal up too. Sorry about that, mini-DalDal. Wow, Snow seems grumpier than usual. Well, his food always tastes delicious regardless of his mood. I whispered to Durandal and Bouncykins, "You two didn't bully Snow while I was asleep, did you?"

"No," Durandal said. "Snow's a bit impatient. We decided to change our course to recover his magic tool hoard, and he's upset at giving the people who took it a chance to get further away."

"Oh. Sorry, Snow." The beautiful bunnykin didn't even look up. Rude. "Anyways, I reached one ton, didn't I? You can teach me sword techniques now."

"Yes. Your foundation is passable now."

Just passable? Fine. Maybe compared to the Godking, it really is only just passable. But I'm definitely on the level of a high-ranking general in the Ravenwood army now. Ah, that reminds me. Has no one come after me yet? Did people not realize Bryant was dead?

"…Lucia."

"Yes?" Was he mad?

"Did you hear any of what I said just now?"

"I heard everything. My foundation is passable now." Right?

"So you heard nothing." Durandal sighed. "I'm no longer giving you a choice. I'll be choosing the first technique you learn."

Wait! I like choices! But … I probably won't get any with the way Durandal's looking at me. "Okay…"

"Pay attention." Durandal picked up his spear and raised it over his head. Spear? Why a spear? Then he brought it vertically downwards while shouting, "Break!"

A flood of dizziness assaulted my senses. I wanted to vomit. When I recovered my normalness, I raised my head. The land in front of Durandal was devastated like a typhoon had passed through. "Did you see?"

"I did. I think? But why a spear?"

"Because I don't have a sword. It doesn't matter; it's the same concept." Durandal nodded at his destructive handiwork. "It's a simple technique called Breaking Blade. You simply focus all your qi into your weapon and swing it."

"…That's it?" Seriously? The fuck? I had to wait until I could hold a ton for this? I feel cheated. An icy chill ran down my spine before I could curse Durandal more.

"Are you unsatisfied?" Durandal's eyes were narrowed like a snake's.

"N-no. I'm very satisfied." Yes. Very…. At least something's better than nothing, right?

"That's what I thought. From today onwards, you'll perform the Breaking Blade one hundred times a day."

"One hundred...? I felt dizzy and almost fainted when you borrowed my qi to use it one time! I'll die if I do that a hundred times!"

"The Godking used to have a favorite saying. Do you know what it was?"

...I'm not going to like it, am I? "No."

"On the road to the top, there are only two outcomes: death or glory."

"But the Godking died after achieving glory..."

Durandal held up two fingers. "Then death or glorious death. Those are your only options."

I don't like either! What kind of shitty choices are those!? Where's the option to live peacefully in a meadow of flowers with all you can eat buffets served to you by hot waiters!?

"Now that you know, you should start practicing." Durandal smiled his I'm-going-to-make-you-cry-with-my-next-words smile. "Any Breaking Blades you haven't performed by the end of the day will be converted into an appropriate punishment."

...Maybe I should just pick death.

4

Things have been going well. How long has it been since I last watched someone train? Roland was as diligent as Lucia when he first started, but over time, he dabbled in more and more skillsets, eventually ignoring swordsmanship completely. That's not to say he was bad at swordsmanship, but it definitely wasn't on the stronger end of his skillset. …But that's not to say his swordsmanship was weak—he was still one of the strongest in the world.

"Did the Godking practice the Breaking Blade too?" Lucia asked. She was drenched in sweat, and her hair clung to her skin as if she had just taken a bath. Her hands were on her knees as she panted for breath with mini-DalDal resting on her back. Of course, I increased my weapon body's weight again to 2,200 pounds.

"No." Roland was a much more refined type of fighter, aiming for weak points and openings in his opponents' stances. Would he learn something as crude as the Breaking Blade? In fact, the Breaking Blade was originally called the Breaking Blow from the basic war hammer techniques. When it comes down to it, I might not be very good at reading maps, cooking, making pills, enchanting things, forging weapons, but I'm one of the most knowledgeable beings out there when it comes to weapon techniques. My fallen comrades passed their skills to me before they died after all. If I couldn't remember their skills, then I should just die.

"Then … you're teaching it to me because…?"

"It suits you. Now quit wasting your breath. We still have a long distance to travel, and you still have 86 more strikes to perform."

"Hurry up, you slowpokes," Bouncykins said from atop Snow's head. "We're closing in on them, but very slowly. At this rate, they'll reach their base before we catch them. Can't you save your training for another time?"

"What's the hurry?" Training can't be rushed. Fundamentals and basics are the most important. Lucia is passed her foundational stage, but luckily, her past managed to bring her body to an appropriate level. Being a beastkin probably helped too.

"They can distribute my hoard," Snow said. His tail was expanding and deflating with every one of his breaths. How does he even know how close we are to his magic tools anyway? Maybe there's a connection formed like the one between a spirit and their owner? "Then it'll be impossible to track down my items once their connections are wiped. I already lost a few tools to the guards who're transporting it."

Why does it feel like magic tools are like item spirits? Well, they were designed by people who were unable to contract spirits themselves. I wonder if they'd have a nice sword. Can spirits even use magic tools? It shouldn't be a problem, right? Vera could cast magic despite being an amulet spirit. ...Sometimes, I really wish Vera were here. Why couldn't Roland have stored her in the dimension with me? He probably thought we were going to fight each other. Which was true.

"E-eighty-five left." Was Lucia going to faint? Maybe a hundred was too much to ask for. Exhausting one's qi wasn't a pleasant feeling..., or so I've heard. I don't have my own, so I wouldn't know. Roland used to bitch at me when I used his qi to fight. Maybe that's why he eventually switched to magic.... Was it my fault?

"Can you keep going?" It looked like she couldn't, but she's surprised me before.

"Y-yes! I can..."

Ah. She fainted. I guess I'll carry her then. "So, Bouncykins, how'd you go about transforming into a partial magic tool?"

"Should you be carrying your master like that?"

If I wasn't going to carry her, then who was? "Did you want to?"

"No. I mean, she looks like a sack of potatoes on your shoulder…," Bouncykins said. He shook his head. "Never mind. But why do you want to know? Aren't you practically half a magic tool yourself? You can freely manipulate your weight."

"That's magic?" …Roland gave mini-DalDal that ability one day when I wasn't looking. When I asked him about it, he replied with, "It's magic," in his usually snarky tone. I didn't think he was serious.

"If it's not magic, then what would it be?"

"…Innate ability?"

Bouncykins sighed. "If only your mind was as sharp as your blade. Too bad."

"Gah!" Snow shouted as he ducked underneath my spear thrust. "Quit provoking Durandal, Lucifer! I keep telling you it's *me* who gets hurt in the end!"

"It's good practice for your reflexes." Bouncykins nodded and patted Snow's head. "Besides, can Durandal really hurt you? It's only Lucia that's able to smack you through your evasion."

"It's your evasion too." Snow seems to be getting grumpier and grumpier as time passes on. Maybe he's on his period? Wait. No. He's not Cottontail, but he's acting like her when she was.

"There's someone called an appraiser, right?" Why are you two looking at me like that?

"…Are you intending on announcing your presence to the world?" Snow asked.

"No? I can always silence the appraiser after I'm done." Snow's expression turned into a weird one. Like he was set on fire while eating a lemon. "Is that a problem?"

"You're a very tyrannical sword spirit, you know that?"

"Durandal was raised by the Godking and your ancestor. It's obvious he'd end up as a criminal." Bouncykins snorted. "It's also why he's my sworn brother even if he calls me Bouncykins."

"You two are sworn brothers?" Snow asked. "You don't act like it."

"Is there a specific way sworn brothers are supposed to act?"

Yes. It's true. I decided to become brothers with a rabbit. In fact, I became brothers with all of Roland's and Cottontail's spirits, weapons and armor alike. The only one who wouldn't make the oath with me was Vera.

"N-no," Snow said. "A-anyways, can I increase my pace? You should keep up better now that Lucia's not training, right?"

"Go for it." I look forward to seeing what Cottontail's descendants have hoarded over the past eighty years.

***

Ugh. Why's my bed moving...? Durandal? Why is Durandal carrying me? He's not even carrying me gracefully! Am I a sack of potatoes!?

"Lucia, did you wake up?"

Nope. Still sleeping. Who cares if he's carrying me like a sack of potatoes? Durandal's carrying *me*! Well, probably everyone would hate me if they knew I was making him do physical labor. They'd probably round me up and throw me into a pit before burying me alive. Now that I think about it, nearly all of my actions wouldn't be right in the eyes of Durandal worshippers.

"Lucia?"

Not awake. Not awake at all. Nope, nuh-uh. Hm. Didn't I promise Durandal that I'd stop slacking? Fine, alright. "Yes, Durandal?"

"You can pick two magic tools from the pile. Ask Snow to explain their effects and choose wisely."

Ack! Don't throw me down like a sack of potatoes too! It's bad enough you carried me around like one. "Huh?" I thought we were still super far away from Snow's hoard? "You mean—"

"You slept for three days, Lucia," Snow said. Why was he hiding behind the wall? Did he think I was going to hit him? I'm not that violent! "The people who looted my hoard made it to their base, but Durandal broke inside and conquered it without a hitch. Have I ever told you how jealous I am? I think his prowess in fighting makes up for the hellish training you have to endure."

That's not fair. I didn't get to see Durandal fight. "So this pile of items on the ground is your hoard? Why do you even call it a hoard? There's like seven things." By my feet, there were a few shiny objects laying around.

Snow's ear twitched. "If you sell any of these, you could buy a small house in the city with the funds you'd get."

"Oh." Wow. That's a lot. "...So which ones could I sell for the most?" Gah! Don't all of you stare at me like that at the same time! I'll really freeze to death with how cold your gazes are. Let's cough to break the tension. "That was a joke..., of course."

Snow let out a hollow laugh. "Joke. Right."

Awkward.... Anyways, let's check these out for real. There's a hauberk, a polearm, a bracelet that'd look awfully good on Snow, an eyepatch, an earring that'd look awfully good on Snow, a frilly dress that'd also look awfully good on Snow..., and a fist-sized rock. A rock? "What's the rock...?"

"That's just a rock," Snow said and kicked it away. "There's only six items."

...I was hoping for a magical rock that granted infinite stamina. Oh wells. "I'll pick the bracelet and the dress." It's not because I don't want Snow to be prettier than me. Definitely not.

"Lucia.... You didn't even ask Snow what they did."

Fine. "What do they do, Snow?"

"The dress—"

"That's great! I'll take them both."

"..."

Don't stare at me like that. I slipped my dress on underneath my armor and attached the bracelet to my arm. Eh? How did I wear the dress without taking off these tight restrictions? Don't worry about it.... What you should be worrying about is what they do. "Snow, how do I use these?"

"Are you really fine with her being your master, Durandal?"

Don't look at Durandal with pity! I'm not that bad of an owner. Gosh. With the way Snow was acting, you'd think I was keeping Durandal locked up in a cage while starving him.

"It should be fine. Probably."

Have some more confidence in me! I'm strong, aren't I?

Snow sighed. "Well, the dress is one of my favorites, but you can have it since I did promise Durandal. I might be a bandit, but I'm a man of my words. My grandmother gave it to me when..." Yeah, yeah. Get on with it. I want to know what my new loot does already! "...and now I'll pass it on to you. It has a haste spell array imbued in it. You can cast haste twice a day to increase your speed by threefold for ten seconds."

Oh, that's pretty neat. No wonder why Snow likes it so much. Too bad, it's mine now.

"As for the bracelet. It has a simple barrier spell that can ward off one physical attack. It can be used three times a day."

"I chose well, didn't I, Durandal?"

"You didn't even ask what the other ones did." Durandal might look slightly disappointed, but he's secretly happy for me on the inside since I'm satisfied with what I got. I can feel it. There's no way my happiness doesn't make him happy as well. "But besides that, aren't you forgetting something?"

"Am I?" What did I forget? I don't think there was anything important? If there was, it wouldn't have been forgotten, yeah.

"You missed 285 Breaking Blades."

Shit. Those count even while I'm sleeping? "That's not fair…"

"I said 100 a day, and it's been three days, but you've only accomplished 15 of them. How is that not fair?"

Because I wasn't awake! Demon! Sadist! What was that about my happiness making him happy? He obviously derives more happiness from my suffering!

"Don't worry." Durandal's expression softened. Eh? Was this really Durandal? He's telling me not to worry with a caring expression? I'm definitely more worried now! "The punishment is simple. I've increased mini-DalDal's weight by 285 pounds. One for every missed Breaking Blade."

Eh? Mini-DalDal's still super light though.

"Of course, it might be easy for you now, but as you miss more and more Breaking Blades, what do you think is going to happen?" I knew it. Durandal was a devil. Won't I eventually succumb to the weight of mini-DalDal at this rate? I could only do 15 before, and now it's even heavier?

"Good luck, Lucia," Snow said. He was wearing the hauberk and the polearm was strapped to his back. Darn. I knew he'd look awfully good with the earring. Why couldn't Durandal have taken three instead? The eyepatch looks horrible though. But I suppose it fits. Snow's supposed to be a gang leader after all. I keep on forgetting.

***

The idea behind Lucia's punishment is simple. At the start of the training, she'll fail to complete a large number of Breaking Blades, but as time goes on, she'll be able to do more and more as her body becomes accustomed to the feeling of exploding out with qi. Increasing my weapon body's weight will make it harder for Lucia to accomplish her next set, but the plan is to have her growth outweigh those effects until the weight of her sword is at just the right level. Once she can do 100 in a day, the next phase of her training will begin.

It's been several days since I invaded that base filled with royal guards and took back Snow's hoard. Snow's been considerably less grumpy now that his items are back; though, I don't like the way he looks at Lucia's new dress and bracelet. To be fair, they were his in the first place, but he did give them up in a deal. If it weren't for me, he wouldn't have gotten any of his magic tools back. Speaking of magic tools...

"More please!" Lucia held out her bowl with her cheeks bulging like a chipmunk's. The outline of her body seemed to be shaking, blurring the lines between her and reality.

"Lucia...," Snow said and held his head. "I die a little every time you use haste to eat your food faster. That's not what my dress was made for."

"What's the matter?" Lucia asked and tilted her head. Her hair moved so fast it seemed like it teleported. "The dress was made to cast haste, and I used it to cast haste. And like I said, more please!"

Snow sighed as he ladled her another bowl of stew with a heavy dose of potatoes. In a second, the contents of the bowl disappeared. "More please!"

"Lucia...," Snow said with tears in his eyes. "I haven't eaten anything yet." Poor Snow. Good thing I don't have to eat as a spirit. I think I really would starve with the amount Lucia eats. Where does all that food go? Maybe it's converted to qi. That would make the most sense.

"Sorry, law of the jungle," Lucia said and snatched the ladle out of Snow's hand. "First come, first serve! The weak don't eat. Lucia's the best, yada yada." The simmering pot of stew vanished without a trace as Lucia's stomach bulged outwards. "Don't cry, Snow. I need this more than you do." Lucia picked up my weapon body and raised it into the air with one hand, which was a little ridiculous since it weighed over 3,000 pounds.

...Is today the day Lucia accomplishes 100 Breaking Blades? Yesterday, she reached 75, and the day before that she made it to 56. She might actually do it before we even make it to the southern pass. Well, at least she'll have a technique to fight against beasts with. She can't say I haven't taught her any once I make her fight a spirit beast.

"You just thought of something cruel you could subject me to, didn't you?"

Lucia noticed? Were we that in tune with each other that she could tell what I was thinking? "You're overthinking things. You still have 73 times left."

"I know! Today's the day you're going to stop adding weight!" Lucia cheered as she performed a Breaking Blade, destroying the foliage in its path. A tree in the distance creaked and groaned before falling to the ground with a massive crash. Let's hope no one reports the destruction we've caused in the forest so far. People would think a spirit beast passed through or something.

"72! 71! 70!" Lucia panted as three strikes were performed in succession, tearing apart the earth, revealing the brown beneath. ...Maybe people would even think a divine beast passed through. "Phew. If I do 35 more by dinner time, I can use haste once again to eat faster, and then wrap up the last Breaking Blades before the day's over. I can do this!"

"Then ... I'm not having dinner either?" Snow asked. Hey, don't cry. Aren't you supposed to be a gang leader? "It's been four days since I've eaten!"

"That's okay," Lucia said and patted Snow's back with my weapon body, causing the poor rabbitkin to wince in pain. "You're part rabbit. Rabbits can hibernate, right?"

"Rabbits don't hibernate!" Snow glared at Lucia. "I can't believe I swore to follow you. I thought you would've been at least an impressive person considering Durandal chose you."

"Lucia's impressive in her own ways." Only I can make fun of Lucia. "Don't look down on her."

"Yeah! I'm impressive in my own ways." Lucia smiled at me. It's a good thing her face has become less lewd after all the training she's done. She's almost like a normal person now. ...Not that I'd have many references of normal people. Roland was abnormal and Cottontail was equally strange. And all my spirit brothers were combat freaks—every single one of them. "But can't you just make more food? If you know I'm going to eat a lot, why don't you just make enough for yourself too? I almost felt bad for taking away your meals, but it's not my fault you didn't think of such an obvious solution."

"You think I didn't try that!?" Snow shook his head and stared at his feet while mumbling, "Don't argue with unreasonable people. Don't argue with unreasonable people. Don't argue with unreasonable people." He closed his eyes and exhaled. "I did make more food. Every single time. This lunch you just ate was enough to feed a family of ten."

"What, no way?" Lucia glanced at the fireplace. There were ten empty pots laying around. "Maybe ten really small people..., so it's like a meal for a family of five."

"That's beside the point!"

Poor Snow. He hasn't figured out how to deal with unreasonable people yet. The secret is to be even more unreasonable. That's how I control, err, persuade Lucia to do things. I learnt from the best after all. If Roland claimed to be the number two most unreasonable person in the world, no one would dare claim to be number one.

"Well. Even if it's beside the point. The food energizes me more than it'd energize you, so I need it more. Only 69 more strikes to go!"

It's a good thing Lucia's fired up. I wonder how enthusiastic she'd be about her next exercises.

***

"Uh, Durandal…?"

"Yes, Lucia?"

Don't respond so calmly!

Durandal raised an eyebrow. "Why are you looking at me like that? Is there an issue?"

"Yes." There's a seriously big issue. You could even call it huge. A disaster of epic proportions. "You wanted me to do what? I must not have heard you properly. …Right?"

"Then I'll say it again. Listen carefully this time. Since you've completed 100 Breaking Blades in a day, the level of difficulty obviously has to be stepped up." How's that obvious!? "Pay attention. From today forward, you're going to perform Breaking Blades 100 times a day—underwater."

No. No, no, no. I refuse. "Yeah…. That's what I thought you said the first time. I think I heard it wrong again. Could you repeat that?"

"Get in the water, Lucia."

I stared at the rushing rapids before me. If I took a step in there, I'd be swept off my feet and drowned in no time. If I didn't break my head on the rocks downstream before that, that is. Fierce creatures with sharp scales and massive teeth stared back at me with unblinking eyes, waiting. Waiting for the food known as Lucia to step inside and accept her fate. But I'm not going down that easily!

"I refuse!" Catch me if you can! There's no way in hell I'm approaching those waters! There's no way in hell I'm approaching any water! I already told Durandal I can't swim.

How could he even ask me to do something like that? While I ran through the forest, a white blur appeared in front of me. "Get out of the way, Snow! Breaking Blaaaade!"

"Lucia!?"

I ignored Snow's pained shout and rushed past his corpse—err, unconscious body. He shouldn't have died from that, right? That doesn't matter! If Durandal catches me, I'll die next!

"Lucia, stop! It's just a pond! Why are you running!?"

It's Bouncykins this time? Why does everyone insist on sacrificing me to the river spirits? Were they praying for rain? "Get out of my way, you stupid rabbit! I'm tired of you always making fun of my intelligence. Breaking Blaaaade!" Eh? I missed.

"I'm a hare, not a rabbit! There's a difference!"

"Rabbits and hares taste the same when you cook them! Breaking Blade!" Wow. Now I know why Durandal was surprised when I hit Bouncykins the first time. Why can't I hit him? "Breaking Blade! Breaking Blade! Break! Break! Break! Break, damn you!"

"Lucia! You're destroying the forest!"

"Fuck the forest! My life's more important!" Bah, I ran out of qi. Damn. If I don't get rid of Bouncykins soon, Durandal will catch up. "Take this! Normal strike!"

"Guwah!?"

Whoa. Rabbits fly far when you hit them with a two-ton sword. Good thing I hit him with the flat of my blade, or he'd be dead. I'm so merciful, aren't I? But why did that connect, but the Breaking Blades didn't? Anyways, it doesn't matter, important things, Lucia! Keep running.

I don't know how much time passed, but I ran far enough to no longer hear the sounds of the river. Just when I was taking a quick break, a voice interrupted my peace. "Lucia."

Gack! How did he catch up to me? Wait, he's not here?

"Down here…"

"Mini-DalDal? You can speak?" Why didn't you ever say anything before? You sound exactly like Durandal. I almost got a heart attack because I thought it was him. "Your spirit body is a total jerk! I hate him!"

"...Lucia. It's Durandal." A mist flew out of mini-DalDal's handle and congealed into Durandal's spirit body. "If I'm separated from my weapon body, I'm automatically transferred back inside of it."

"...So I can't run away from you unless I abandon mini-DalDal too?"

"Why are you objecting so much to this training? Didn't you say you'd work hard and not slack off? I don't think I'm asking a lot from you."

"I ... dislike water." Don't look at me with such a baffled expression! What's wrong with hating water? It's not like you need it to survive or anything. Gosh.

"Don't you take the longest amount of time to bathe? Aren't you the one who insisted Snow had to bathe too? Just think of it as bathing while swinging your sword."

"When I bathe, I dip a rag in the water and wipe myself off. I don't actually go inside."

"...You hate water that much?"

Do I tell him? I think I'm going to cry if I do. Maybe I shouldn't.

"Lucia? Are you crying?"

"No!" Stupid tears, quit betraying my resolve!

"Durandal. Lucia?" How did Bouncykins and Snow catch up so quickly? I'm sure I incapacitated both of them! "What did you say to Lucia, Durandal? I know she acted unreasonably, but why did you make her cry?"

Snow, I never knew you were so nice. I think I judged you wrongly.

"I wanted to get revenge and make her cry first."

Never mind. Die in a fire. Stupid harekin or rabbitkin or whateverkin-you-are man.

"You didn't tell her you'd disown her again, did you?" Bouncykins asked.

Again!? Wait, no. There was that one time. I remember now.

"No…" I didn't think Durandal could ever look guilty. Who knew? "Please stop crying, Lucia."

If I could control my tears, you wouldn't have had to have asked. Stupid. Well, since I'm already crying, I might as well tell Durandal and them…. "W-when I was little…" Holy shit, don't all stare at once. I'll get nervous. "My family was very poor. Very, very poor. We can't afford any more kids or we'll all starve to death kind of poor. And, poof, I appeared in that family."

"Oh." Snow's face paled. "Oh. I'm sorry, Lucia." He shook his head and left the area, taking Bouncykins with him. He's a beastkin. It was obvious what was coming next.

"They tried to take care of me and everyone else. I think they did well for a while, but my grandpa really hated me because he got less food. Half a carrot a day, I think? So he took me outside, brought me to the barrel of rain water…, and tried to drown me."

"And that's why you hate water?"

"Right! Good thing my grandpa died of a heart attack the next day and our family finally had less mouths to feed, right? It let me survive for a few years before I was sold off to the slave trader. Happy endings all around! Yay."

***

How can Lucia talk about such sad things with a happy smile on her face? It's unconvincing with the tears running down her cheeks. It'd probably be inappropriate to tell her she looked like a ghoul right now. So instead, I simply stepped forward and hugged her. Isn't that what she did for me?

"D-Durandal?" Lucia sniffled and gazed at me like a frightened animal. "You're not thinking of throwing me in the river still, are you?"

…I was. Water training is crucial to mastering one's body! At least that's what the books say. But she didn't have to do it right now. There were other activities she could do to train her body as I slowly got her to adapt to the water. I didn't think this would be that much of an issue—it's not like she's a cat-type beastkin. "Not right now."

"…Can you amend that to not ever?"

"I'll find a smaller pond than the one before."

"Pond? You call that a pond? That was a fierce river!"

"No…, that was actually a pond. The water was still." I might not be able to read maps, but at least I know the differences in bodies of water.

"But the monsters inside waiting to eat me!"

"Goldfish don't eat people, Lucia."

"I'm sure that's because they haven't met anyone as tasty and helpless in the water as me! I'll be the first person to be eaten by goldfish. Is that the legend you wanted me to leave behind? The girl who was eaten by goldfish?"

"Would you be willing to start with a puddle?"

"A small puddle. A small, small puddle that'll disappear into my socks if I step on it." Lucia's hair bobbed up and down as she nodded at me with puffed out cheeks. Well, at least she wasn't crying anymore. That was a good sign, right? "We can start with that, okay?"

"…I'll sharpen some bamboo spears."

"Eh? What do bamboo spears have to do with water training? Y-you're going to stab me with them, aren't you?"

"No. I'm going to plant them into the ground, and you'll perform some footwork on top of them. Swordsmanship isn't just about swinging your sword. It's also about controlling your whole body to use your sword in the most effective manner. From your toes to the top of your head, every muscle in your body should be in tune with the sword."

"You're going to plant the bamboo spears in the ground spiky end first, right…?"

"Who was the one that said she wouldn't slack off? I think it was you. If you don't want to do the water training, we can start with the footwork training instead."

"Then the spears…. You're going to make me stab myself on the spears! That's even worse than you stabbing me."

"Aren't you a squirrel? This shouldn't be difficult." It's just balancing on bamboo poles. I can do it with my eyes closed. Of course, Lucia will be able to do that by the end of the exercise. I can't wait to get some archery practice in. Hmm? What does archery practice have to do with Lucia's training? Nothing. Nothing at all.

"I'm a ground squirrel! Tree squirrels don't hibernate! And what is that expression on your face? You're definitely thinking of some new way to torture me. Stop it."

"A squirrel is a squirrel is a squirrel. Even a human could do the footwork exercise if they put their mind to it." Roland was the one who insisted on trying it after reading it on a technique manuscript, and it worked out pretty well for him. Not like he used his footwork for anything other than sneaking around though. "But since I don't have anything ready for today, just do 200 Breaking Blades."

"Are we counting the ones I used on Snow and Bouncykins?"

"No. 200 more."

"I'll die."

"Work hard, Lucia." You won't die. If anything, 50 pounds will be added to mini-DalDal tomorrow. Now that I think about it, Lucia can carry a ridiculous amount of weight. She might be on par with the lionkin who always insisted on dueling Roland…. That's just in pure strength though. Why did her family think she was the weakest of the litter when she'd be classified as a high-classed warrior based on her strength alone? It couldn't be that she's weak compared to most beastkin, right? Snow's a wimp, so that's most likely not the case.

"Motivate me." Hmm? How would I do that? "In a positive way! You definitely thought about stabbing me with spears if I failed."

"What exactly do you want for motivation?" It's true Lucia said she'd work hard and not slack off, but she was bound to lose that motivation after a while. It can't hurt to indulge her every now and then.

"Every five Breaking Blades—no, every three Breaking Blades, I want head pats and praise. Every five Breaking Blades, I want ear scratches and praise. Every 10 Breaking Blades, I want a delicious snack made by Snow. When I reach 200 Breaking Blades…" Lucia's face turned red. "I want you to hug me and tell me you'll never leave me."

Before I could speak, a voice came from a nearby tree. Was Snow a tree rabbit instead of a ground rabbit because apparently that was a thing for rodents? "Lucia…. It's not good to fall in love with a weapon spirit, you know that?"

"Shut up, Snow! No one asked you for your opinion!" Lucia threw mini-DalDal at him, destroying the tree he was standing on. I should really teach her a retrieval skill since she insists on throwing my weapon body so much. It'll be possible for her to learn if she can reach 500 Breaking Blades in a day. "Get ready to make me 20 treats!"

I glanced at the rabbit who landed on my shoulder.

"You're going to indulge her in this?" Bouncykins asked, looking at me with a strange expression on his face.

"Why not? It can't hurt."

"You'll get attached," Bouncykins said, watching Lucia chase after Snow. "You both will."

"Isn't that fine? Most weapon spirits die with their owners."

"But you're Durandal."

"So?"

Bouncykins sighed. "Never mind."

5

Before I met Durandal, I was a luggage bearer and sparring dummy for the soldiers in the army. After I met Durandal, I'm a luggage bearer and experimental dummy for Durandal. It feels like my life hasn't changed much. Every day, when the sun rises, I wake up from my horse stance feeling 100% rejuvenated. I do 66 Breaking Blades in the time it takes Snow to wake up and make breakfast—the fact that my training wakes him up is irrelevant. In the afternoon, I perform another 66 Breaking Blades while traveling until it's dinner time. After dinner, I finish up with 68 more Breaking Blades until it's time to fall asleep in my horse stance.

I've been following that routine for a solid two weeks now, eating 20 treats, receiving 40 ear scratches, 67 head pats, and 107 lines of praise from Durandal every day. So this is definitely a lot better than the Ravenwood army—it's satisfying! But today, Durandal finally finished collecting enough wooden spears for a full set of footwork techniques. He said there's a total of 81 positions in the Steady Mountain Footwork's manuscript, and I'm going to have to learn them all. Did I ever mention how he makes me carry those wooden spears while practicing? At least it's not heavy like mini-DalDal whose been upgraded to 5,000 pounds since I, uh, did some … things … to make Durandal mad. It wasn't even that bad!

"Are you ready, Lucia?" Durandal stood atop the field of wooden spears, his image like a dragon perched on its roost. Will I ever look as imposing as him? Snow says I won't, but his opinions don't matter.

"Maybe? I mean, yes!"

"Good. Watch carefully." Durandal stepped from wooden spear to wooden spear, twisting his waist, his legs, even his upper arms on occasion. Even if it's slow, how am I supposed to remember all of this!? After an hour of moving, he stopped and stared at me. "Did you see?"

"Yes." But I don't remember! "Can you show it to me again?"

"Your turn."

"Can you, uh, put numbers on the sticks so I know which one I'm supposed to step towards?" Squirrels aren't good at memorizing things. We store away food but forget where we store it, and it ends up growing into a tree or something. It's very upsetting. Why couldn't I have been a crow instead?

Durandal stared at me like he was staring at a child. He sighed. "Very well. I think that would be the simplest method."

"You're the best, Durandal."

"Isn't that cheating?"

Shut up, Bouncykins. You always pour cold water on my good things.

"Is it?" Durandal's eyebrow rose as he stared at Bouncykins.

"For her to fully comprehend the footwork, shouldn't she not use numbers?" Bouncykins' ears smacked away a few flies buzzing around him.

"There are geniuses who're able to comprehend and memorize actions just upon seeing them," Durandal said and nodded his head. "Clearly, Lucia isn't one of them." Hey. "The only way for her to learn is through repetition. Lots and lots of repetition. Eventually, after the movements become second nature to her, she'll comprehend them fully."

"That's cheating."

"If I have a way to impart a technique on Lucia without going through the standard channels, then I'll do it." Durandal nodded. "Why should she have to create her own path when people before her have already paved the road?"

"I thought you were an old-fashioned stuffy," Bouncykins said and tilted his head.

"What's the old-fashioned way of learning the Steady Mountain Footwork?" I'm curious now. This seems hard enough as is.

"The person who created this wanted to be as strong and as steady as a mountain, hence the name," Durandal said. "He figured the best way to do that would be to walk up mountains during landslides, smashing everything in his way. These are the movements he found most efficient in accomplishing his goal."

"…Wouldn't he have to wait for landslides to occur? How did he do that?" The heck? There's like one landslide every ten years or so in the southern pass. How long did that take?

"I'm just repeating what I read in the manuscript, Lucia. Whether or not it's true doesn't matter. Everyone who learns the Steady Mountain Footwork follows these movements." Durandal was already carving numbers on top of the wooden spears. "Once you memorize the movements, I'll show you how the qi should flow inside of your body to bring the most out of it."

"Can't I just apply qi to every part of my body at once? Then I'll hit all the required spots, right?"

"Theoretically, it's possible," Bouncykins said. "But you'll exhaust yourself. It's like how you're supposed to circulate your qi to only the tired parts of your body during your horse stance. You can only do it because you're sleeping while you hold your stance and your qi regenerates while you sleep, which is beyond abnormal, but you can't do that with the footwork."

You're always pouring water on my good things, Bouncykins. That's the second time in five minutes.

"Don't look so glum, Lucia. I had to do something similar to learn my Wind Shadow Footwork." Snow nodded. "It's why even Durandal has difficulty hitting me."

Bop.

Difficulty my ass. "So why can't you dodge my normal strikes?" I stared at Snow, who was covering the lump on his head with his hands. The culprit, mini-DalDal, was trembling after colliding with Snow's head. Maybe one of Snow's magic tools boosted his defense. Did I tap him too lightly?

"Alright, Lucia. I finished numbering the platforms." Please don't call wooden spear tips platforms. "I'll be following along, correcting your posture as you take each step."

"Before we start. Can we—"

"Establish your motivational goals?" Durandal smiled. "Yes. Yes we can, Lucia."

Wow. How did he know what I was going to say? Maybe he really is a mind reader...

"I don't read minds, Lucia. Anyways, if you manage to memorize 20 steps perfectly by the end of today, I'll tell you a bedtime story."

"I'll do it!"

Snow and Bouncykins had faces that said, "You're being bribed too easily, Lucia," but what do they know? No one's ever read me a bedtime story before. I definitely didn't have to cry myself to sleep while other people had stories told to them and lullabies sang to them. Nope. This is simply for the first-time experience.

***

Lucia is extremely motivated nowadays. Ever since I figured out what drove her to do things, getting her to train was no longer like pulling teeth, but she does complain a lot. Her goals seem to be similar to Roland's. Roland wanted to be the strongest in the world for the sake of Cottontail. He wanted to spoil her by being able to do whatever he wanted without being impeded. Lucia wants to grow strong … for me. Or my praise, at least.

"I memorized them all!" Lucia bounced to my side and stared up at me with big, round eyes. Her ears and tail twitched as she pursed her lips.

"Good job, Lucia." It really was. It only took her a week to memorize the thousands of movements between the 81 positions of the Steady Mountain Footwork. "I'm proud of you."

Lucia closed her eyes and smiled as I ran my fingers through her hair. It was nice that she was such a simple person who could be persuaded by praise. Some people moved only for glory or wealth.

"Perverts," Bouncykins said from the side. He's just jealous Snow's tail isn't as fluffy or soft as Lucia's.

"Hey, Lucia, Durandal, what are your future plans?" Snow asked. He was sitting by the campfire near the field of wooden spears, grilling a chunk of flesh. A large pile of bones lay by his side—Lucia's previous snacks and motivation.

"Become a legend!" Lucia nodded and tackled me, clinging to my torso. She peered up at me with a twitching tail. "Right?"

"Right." Though I already was a legend. "And the most important thing to becoming a legend is?"

"Good looks!" Lucia nodded.

"No. It's your foundation. Now, you'll have to circulate your qi during those movements. And the difficultly will be stepped up." I glanced at Snow while Lucia hung her head. "Did you make it?"

"The bow? Yeah." Snow patted the long-ranged weapon by his side. "Is this for Lucia?"

You could say that. I picked up the bow and retrieved the blunt arrows lying next to it.

Lucia's eye twitched. "Uh, Durandal?" She took a step back and raised her arms in front of her chest. "Are you … going to shoot those at me?"

What. It's not fun if she figures it out before I start. I mean, it's a good thing Lucia's intuition is developing. I'm not doing this for enjoyment or anything. Only a sick person would derive pleasure from someone else's pain. "It's training."

"Don't look at me," Snow said and turned his head away. Lucia was staring at him as if she wanted to cry. "Bouncyki— I mean, Lucifer! Lucifer did a lot worse to me while I was learning my Wind Shadow movements."

"Did you just forget my name?" Bouncykins asked, glaring at Snow, who was beneath his feet. "The Mighty—"

"Yeah, yeah, we get it," Lucia said, cutting Bouncykins off. I'm a bit proud of her for that. "The more important issue is Durandal's trying to shoot me with arrows! This is abuse!"

"You said you wanted to grow stronger and you'd stop complaining."

"How long are you going to hold that over my head!?" Lucia took another step backwards.

"Until it stops working."

"Then…"

"I'll give you a massage tonight."

"I'll do it! Shoot as many as you'd like!" Lucia scrambled up the wooden spears and hopped to the centermost one. "What exactly am I doing?"

"Smash apart the arrows and try not to get hit. The only movements your feet are allowed to take are those of the Steady Mountain's." It sounds simple, but I didn't tell her I was going to imbue the arrows with her qi. "Ready?"

"Yes!" Lucia brandished my weapon body and exhaled while narrowing her eyes. Oh? It's been a while since I've seen her serious face. Maybe a massage was too grand of a reward to bring out just yet? I nocked an arrow and let it fly, letting Lucia adjust to the speed of the projectile. She twisted her lower body and stepped on a nearby spear while swinging my weapon body. How do the spears not sink into the ground despite my weapon body weighing over two tons? …Don't worry about it.

"Good." I fired 81 arrows, guiding Lucia's body through the foundational footsteps of the Steady Mountain Footwork.

"Why couldn't you have been this nice when you were teaching me?" Snow asked the rabbit sitting on top of his head.

Bouncykins shrugged. "I'm not familiar with footwork. I'm a hare, remember? Why would I need humanoid movements?"

"I guess that's fair," Snow said and crinkled his forehead.

I ignored the chatter and focused on guiding Lucia with the arrows. There was one time when she slipped and nearly pierced herself on a spear, but she managed to catch herself with her tail. I didn't realize it was that flexible or strong. It was a shame there weren't any fighting techniques tailored for beastkin in Roland's library. A few of his weapon and armor spirits were beastkin, but none of them were squirrels. "How are you holding up, Lucia?" I've been expending her qi constantly, and she should be struggling right about now.

"I, I can keep going," Lucia said and swallowed the phlegm built up in her throat. "For the reward!" Her eyes gleamed, and I thought I felt her qi reserves replenishing. I should've saved this reward for something more difficult. I didn't think a massage was that valuable.

Well, it was time to pick up the pace. I fired arrow after arrow, aiming for the flaws exposed when Lucia took steps. The easiest way to teach her where her flaws were was to hit them repeatedly until she instinctively guarded against them. Despite the qi-reinforced arrows striking her body, she didn't cry out as she struggled to stay on the spears.

Only after 500 arrows were fired did she finally fall off. By that point, the spears were slick with her sweat and the moon shone overhead. Snow was panting for breath too. He hadn't made 500 arrows; instead, he had to retrieve the ones I fired and return them to me. It's good that he's an obedient lackey, but I'm not quite sure what he wants. He's decided to follow us, but even if he left, I'd have no intentions of killing him. With Bouncykins at Snow's side, the secret of my retrieval wouldn't spread.

"How, how did I do?" Lucia asked. Her arms and legs were splayed as she stared up at the sky.

"You were amazing." She really was. I kneaded her muscles, causing her to groan and relax. When I was done with the massage, she stared at me with a strange expression, her face bright red.

"There's no happy ending?"

…Is that what she was after this whole time? "No…"

"What!? Then what did I work so hard for!?"

"To become a legend." Despite the lack of sun in the sky, my body was unusually warm. "Don't forget your goals."

Lucia grumbled as she sat up. "I feel cheated."

***

I think … I've gotten a bit too freakishly strong.

"Lucia?" Snow stared at the broken bowl by my feet. "Is there something wrong?"

I can't control my strength! I grabbed the bowl and it shattered. My poor stew, stolen by the ground. "Can we buy sturdier bowls?" Ever since completing the Steady Mountain Footwork's qi circulation method and reaching a level that even Durandal found satisfactory, my strength's been out of control. I could wield mini-DalDal earlier even if it weighed over two tons before without breaking anything, but now, everything's so fragile.

Bouncykins tilted his head. "Can you be more gentle?" If I could, I wouldn't have asked for sturdier bowls! Stupid hare. "Do something about your new master, Durandal."

Durandal's gaze traversed my body. "She does seem to be a bit stronger. Her qi is overflowing. Why is this?" He frowned and rubbed his beardless chin. "Perhaps it's a side effect of being a beastkin."

"I don't care why it happened! Just fix it." My food's on the floor, and it breaks to pieces when I try to pick it up. Do you know how frustrating it is to have food in front of you that you can't eat? And the ground cracks when I walk! How ridiculous is this? If I knew this would happen, then I wouldn't have trained so hard. I never even got my happy ending.

"Your body needs an adjustment period." Durandal nodded. "Your strength's grown too fast for your mind to follow. You're still acting like you're the same weak person you were when I first met you."

You could've just said same person. There was no need to emphasize weak. "So if I leave the problem alone, it'll go away by itself?" Will I starve to death before that happens? "How long will that take?"

"How long did it take you to get used to your previous body?" Durandal had a strange expression on his face. I feel like this is a trap...

Ah! "Didn't I tell you not to ask for a woman's age!?" He was trying to trick me. Why did he even want to know? I don't have many secrets, so let me have this one, alright? "But seriously. How long will it take?"

"Maybe a week to a few months or years."

"A week!?" I'll definitely starve to death! "Wait. Years?"

"Don't panic, Lucia. There's a simple way to solve all of this." Durandal had his perverted smile on his face, the one that said, "I'm going to hurt you under the guise of teaching you for your own good."

"I think I'll wait a year." Yup. Waiting's fine too. If anything, I can make Snow feed me. Or I can even have Durandal feed me. Wouldn't that be heaven? Yeah, this is definitely the way to go.

"Pick up your sword, Lucia."

Please, no. "D-do I have to?"

"It's for your own good."

I knew you were going to say that! "Is this going to be painful?"

"Would I ever hurt you, Lucia?"

Yes! You definitely would, you sadistic spirit. "Was that a rhetorical question? Because I really don't want to answer it."

Durandal's eyes narrowed. Thankfully, he didn't unleash the aura that threatened my bladder. "Just pick up your sword."

"What am I doing?" I picked up mini-DalDal and sighed. The ground looked so broken because I stepped on it. Does this qualify as me being fat? The earth shatters when I walk upon it.

"You're going to spar with me." Durandal picked up his spear and pointed it at me.

"Uh. Can you repeat that?" Maybe I heard him incorrectly. The fire's really loud and a fierce breeze is blowing. The insects are awfully loud too.

"You didn't hear wrong the first time, Lucia. Prepare yourself." Durandal lunged at me, thrusting his spear towards my face.

I'm not ready for this! "Breaking Blade!" Somehow, I managed to save myself by knocking away his strike. How can he resist my sword? Don't tell me he's stronger than me even though he's just a spirit...

"I'm using your qi. Don't be too surprised." Durandal readjusted his stance and tightened his grip on his spear. It flew forward like lightning, and I barely managed to deflect it again. And again. And again.

"This is cheating!"

"You never know when an enemy will sap your qi to fight against you." Durandal's blows came faster and faster despite his speech. "There's at least thirteen branches of martial arts that will do this. It's better for you to become accustomed to the feeling now instead of during a real fight."

I'll die before I manage to meet any of them at this rate! Durandal's seriously trying to stab me!

"Hey, Durandal. Those schools that practiced those kinds of arts were destroyed a few decades ago." Bouncykins munched on a biscuit while sitting up on Snow's head. Don't look so relaxed when I'm dying! And stop eating my biscuits, please.

"That's irrelevant," Durandal said, continuing to steal my qi. "What if a weapon spirit lived on and passes the techniques down to someone who finds them?"

"Only a freak like you would be able to survive that long without an owner."

You're also a freak for lasting so long, you damned hare! Don't poke at Durandal's soft spots! He'll become more aggressive towards the person he's fighting—me. "T-time out."

"No timeouts."

"Please?"

"No." Durandal punctuated his word with a spear thrust that caused the wind to swirl and roar. I raised mini-DalDal to block it, and I was sent flying away from the force. Just how strong is Durandal to blow away a two-ton sword? Don't tell me he reduces the weight whenever he strikes me because that really would be cheating. "Take a five minute break. We'll spar until it's time for dinner."

"But it's breakfast time! I still haven't eaten anything."

Durandal sighed and walked over to Snow. He snatched a biscuit out of Bouncykins' stash and sat next to me. "Here. I'll feed you."

...I always thought life was bleak. But now I realize, it's good. It's really, really good. Even better than this biscuit.

***

As long as Lucia continues to perform the Steady Mountain Footwork during our duels, the corresponding movements of her blade will become the Steady Mountain Swordsmanship. Over the course of thirty duels, she's become accustomed to the most comfortable positions for herself to defend and attack from; although she is still vulnerable before my blade. I've dueled Roland a few times in the past, and his skills were on par with mine. I guess that made sense since we grew up and trained alongside each other. But I do think I'm stronger than Roland during his prime, at least for swordsmanship, because I had over a millennia to learn thousands of new techniques.

"Breaking Blade!"

I took a step back and avoided Lucia's strike before blocking the destructive shockwave that followed with a Breaking Blade of my own. Maybe it would've been more appropriate to call it a Breaking Spear. Regardless, Lucia's gotten to the point where it wouldn't be advantageous for me to block her strikes head-on. When we first started, there were dozens of flaws in her footwork, posture, and technique that allowed me to disperse the force with a direct collision, but repeated strikes to her vulnerabilities have taught her well. Pain is the best teacher after all. Followed by head pats.

"Not bad, Lucia." Her hair was damp with sweat and clinging to her face and neck. Even her ears were a bit droopy. With that last attack, she had finally exhausted herself. "Do you know what you did wrong this time?"

"Have less stamina than you?" She looked a bit bitter. If she could steal my vitality instead of the other way around, I imagine I'd have a similar expression on my face.

"Other than that?"

"Have less skill than you?"

"…You're focusing too much on the spearhead instead of following the movements of my body. The body doesn't lie, but the trajectory of a weapon can always change or disappear. It's why you're reacting too slowly in some situations."

Lucia sighed and stared at the floor. She grabbed the hand I moved away and placed it back on her head. I amused her whims as we continued to travel south, following after Snow, who had started walking when our spar ended. How long would it be until—?

"H-help!"

Snow stopped walking as Lucia raised her head and stared towards the direction the shout came from. Now that I think about it, it's been a while since we've seen any other people. "Should we help?" I'll let Lucia decide on how to proceed.

But before Lucia could even react, Snow cupped his hands over his mouth and shouted, "Do you have any money?"

A bloodcurdling scream resounded through the forest before someone shouted, "Y-yes!" It was a different voice this time.

Snow glanced at Lucia. "I guess we can wait until they're dead to loot their corpses." He nodded and sat down on a nearby boulder, propping his chin up with his hands as he hunched forward.

"W-wait." Lucia stuck her hand out. "Really?"

Snow nodded. "We're on the border of the southern pass. Ferocious beasts live beyond this point. Anyone inside should already know the danger they're getting into." Snow picked his ear with his pinky. "It could even be a spirit beast pretending to be a human. There's some who trap prey that way."

"M-mommy! Daddy!" Screams that sounded like they came from a little girl rang throughout the forest. Lucia stiffened as she drew my weapon body.

"I knew you were a gang leader, but I didn't think you'd be so heartless, Snow!" Lucia pointed her sword at the rabbitkin before dashing towards the shouts. Snow shook his head and sighed. He glanced at me and raised an eyebrow.

"I'm going to follow her." Even if I didn't want to, I'd be automatically pulled into my weapon body if she went too far. From up ahead, I could hear Lucia trampling through the forest. It seemed like she lost control of her body since she left behind massive craters and fallen trees in her wake.

"I'll save you!" Her voice wasn't too far ahead. "Wait right there!"

"H-hurry. Please!"

There was a massive crash up ahead, and the sounds of fighting rang out. Lucia had engaged with the enemy. "Die, you stupid fat cat! Breaking Blade!"

A roar echoed through the forest. I made it to a small clearing filled with uprooted trees and broken trunks. A ferocious beast was lying on its side and scrambling back onto its feet as a sword-wielding squirrelkin girl chased after it with a vicious expression on her face. The beast was a large panther with fur as dark as the night. There was no sign of any humans around.

"Where'd they go?" Lucia asked the beast as she repeatedly pounced towards it. Somehow, she managed to appear in front of it every time it tried to run away. Was she reading its body movements? Why couldn't she do that in the spar earlier? Perhaps it was because the panther didn't have a single weapon to focus on.

The panther growled and lunged towards Lucia, but it was batted away by the sheer weight of my weapon body. Watching a panther that was larger than a bear being batted away by Lucia, who was mouse-like in comparison, was interesting to say the least. Perhaps Lucia would be able to kill a dragon with a sword strike if her growth continued at its current rate. She one-sidedly dominated the panther, beheading it after exchanging another seven moves. Five moves too many, but it wasn't bad for her first fight against a ferocious beast even if it was one of the weakest ferocious beasts out there.

"Durandal?" Lucia asked, her expression in a daze. "The family?"

I pointed above her. Snow was right. Three crows were sitting on a branch, staring at Lucia. They seemed to be waiting for her to leave. One of the crows opened its beak and said, "Mommy. Daddy. Help!"

Lucia's mouth fell open.

"Scavenger crows." Snow appeared in the clearing from behind me. "They mimic human voices and beasts' cries to lure creatures into fighting each other. Then they pick up scraps from the aftermath. Their combat strength is on the lowest end of the spectrum, but they're good at fooling simple people."

"Don't call me stupid!"

***

Ever since arriving at the southern pass, I've learned quite a lot: scavenger crows taste like chicken, shadow panthers taste sour and icky, moonlight wolves taste absolutely amazing. I just wish I brought more spices along to eat them properly. Maybe I should get an interspacial ring; then I can stop worrying about space while lugging around a huge bag— though I make Snow carry it. But I heard those rings were super expensive and only available to nobility—I learned that from Snow, by the way. Snow's really too knowledgeable when it comes to survival and money. I suspect he's a quarter crow.

"You're thinking strange things about me, aren't you?" Quit reading my expressions and pay attention to the food,

Snow! What if you burn it? "It's all over your face. …Are you thinking I'm part crow, perhaps?"

"Durandal." Durandal opened his eyes and stared at me. He always meditated while we ate. Maybe he was thinking of cultivation methods and martial arts he could teach me. "Are there any spells that allow you to read minds?"

Durandal shrugged. "That bastard left all the spellbooks with Vera and all the martial arts with me." He scratched his head. "I can't remember anyone reading minds. But who would dare read Roland's mind? Ask Snow."

"I'm asking you because Snow wouldn't tell me the truth if there was." Why would he? I know I'd firmly deny it if I could read minds. Just like Snow denies the fact that he's a girl, but he actually is since I checked underneath his pants at night. …Good. No reaction from Snow. That was a test! I didn't actually take off his clothes at night—I'm not a pervert … mostly. Only when it comes to Durandal, okay!?

"Oh." Snow was staring at the bloody mess in his hands. "There was a beast core in this moonlight wolf. It must have been close to evolving to a spirit beast."

Huh? "A what?"

"…I thought you two wanted to come to the southern pass to make money." Snow's forehead wrinkled as he glanced at Durandal. Hey! I'm the one talking to you; don't look at him. He's mine.

"And training," Durandal said. "Give the beast core to Lucia to absorb."

"Uack!?" A solid object smacked against my forehead. The heck? I picked it up and rolled it around in my palm. It was solid and heavy like a chunk of metal. And Snow threw this at me? I raised my head to glare at him, but he had already disappeared and reappeared in the branches of a tree. "This is a beast core? What do I do with it?"

"Squeeze it and send your qi into it." Durandal walked over and grasped my hand, folding my fingers over the core. It looks like I wasn't being given a choice in the matter. Then again, I didn't mind. Durandal didn't hold my hand very often. His hand was surprisingly smooth considering he was a master of swords. And spears apparently. "…Are you listening, Lucia?"

"Squeeze it and send my qi into it!" Ah. It's hot.

Durandal sighed. "Yes. And then send the energy inside of the core into your dantian."

That weird word again. He totally means my womb, right? What else is beneath my belly but above my squirrely bits? Anyways, focus this heat into my womb, got it. That tingles.

"Make the energy swirl and condense it into a sphere. Locate the boundaries of your dantian and fill it with the beast's energy."

At least Durandal's instructions are always easy to listen to. Is this the boundary? The heck? My womb's not supposed to be spherical, right? Maybe there really is another organ down there. Now what? Were there no more instructions? "And then?"

"And now we spar."

What!? How is that the logical next step? "W-wait. What did that even do?" And where did the beast core go? It disappeared? "The core's gone?"

"You absorbed it and all the energy inside of it. You'll see the changes in your body once you spar with me." Durandal placed mini-DalDal in my hands and picked up his spear. "As you absorb more and more cores, the quality of your qi will increase. With higher quality qi, you'll be able to perform more difficult martial arts. Right now, you're at the lowest level of qi mastery."

"Is that good? I'm as strong as a general in the Ravenwood army."

"You're on the level of cannon fodder. You would've been amongst the first to fight and die during the warring era. If you really are on the level of a general, then the martial abilities of the world have deteriorated."

"Didn't I tell you? The era of weapon spirits and martial arts is over." Bouncykins peered over Snow's head and spoke down on us from the tree. "It's the era of spells and magic. All martial artists are cannon fodder in the eyes of a master mage. No matter how strong or fast you make Lucia, she will never travel faster than lightning. She will never be able to stop an ocean's worth of water. She will never have the destructive power of an exploding volcano."

Hey. Don't look down on me even if all of those are probably true. You'll make Durandal sad again, you stupid bunny.

"You say it as if those are possible for a mage." Durandal's face was expressionless, but I know that's the worst kind of expression he could have.

"They are. Cain Thunderfire. He's currently the strongest mage in existence, surpassing the Godking, but that makes sense, doesn't it? It's been 80 years since Roland's died; new powers will grow." Bouncykins sighed. "With a flick of his wrist, he can call upon thunder. With a point of his finger, he can make lava spew out of the ground. By shouting really loudly, he can cause the oceans to stir and slam tsunamis all the way to the mainland. There's rumors of him inheriting the magical portion of the Godking's legacy."

"I've heard of Cain." He's the hero of the demons. I remember the people in the army thanking the Godking for bringing peace to the three factions because if they had to fight Cain, the humans would lose. "But how come I didn't know he inherited the Godking's legacy?"

"Vera's not as famous as Durandal. And Roland used an alias for his magical deeds."

Really? Then what was the legendary mage of the Godking's generation called? "The Voidwalker?"

"Yeah. That's the one." Bouncykins nodded while Durandal made a sour expression.

"…How many aliases did the Godking have?" I already know about Golden Rat and Voidwalker. Don't tell me there's more.

"Over a hundred." Durandal shook his head. "But the three you know are the most famous. Anyways, don't you think you're forgetting something, Lucia?"

I forget a lot of things, but what specific thing did I forget this time? "What?" A spear flew at my face, and I almost didn't react.

"We're sparring."

***

I've already had that discussion with Lucia. The age of martial arts and weapon spirits is over. But Lucia doesn't care; she believes in me and my ability. I won't disappoint her. That's why I have to strike harder, faster. The spear in my hand blurred, its form becoming more fluid than solid as it struck towards the flaws in Lucia's stance.

Sweat flowed from Lucia like rain from a cloud, and her blade managed to keep up with my spear, deflecting every strike. The beast core she had absorbed was beginning to take its part. All of her physical attributes would rise as the energy of the moonlight wolf was assimilated into her body, including her reaction speed and dynamic vision. Lucia may never move as fast as lightning, but I'll be damned if she doesn't get close.

I drew my spear back, focusing my (Lucia's) qi into the tip. With a short shout, I thrust forward, performing a Breaking Blade with my spear. Lucia's eyes widened as she brought her blade in front of her chest, holding it horizontally and bracing both ends with her hands to block my thrust head on. Like a boulder hitting the surface of a pond, my spear sent ripples into Lucia's body, causing her to fly backwards. She hunched forward and managed to remain standing as her feet left two long lines in the earth. Maybe I should make my weapon body heavier. There's three ways to deal with an oncoming force: redirect it, apply an even larger force towards it, or dodge it. I feel like Lucia would like the second option the most.

"It's over?" Lucia was gasping and her arms were trembling, but I had to applaud her for remaining upright. "D-don't you usually continue until I collapse?"

"Do you want me to?" Right. Didn't she have some masochistic tendencies? "The core has been fully absorbed. If you absorb cores without expending the energy afterwards, impurities will build up and bring more damage to your body than benefits."

"Oh." Lucia nodded before collapsing onto her back. She sprawled out her limbs and exhaled while closing her eyes. She wasn't wearing armor like usual, only having Snow's dress on instead. It was part of an exercise to teach her how to reinforce parts of her body with qi. Armor would remove the sense of desperation, and everyone knows desperation fuels growth the fastest. "I feel smarter."

"Smarter?" That wasn't supposed to be a side effect.

"Like everything is clearer." Lucia opened her eyes. "Sounds are sharper. The ground is rougher. Snow smells funnier."

"Hey!"

"It feels weird," Lucia said and nodded as she sat up. "Like everything was improved by a little bit."

"Do you see why the cores are worth so much money now? Beast cores are used for everything, but the enhancement effect is the undisputed reason why people want cores."

"Not anymore." Bouncykins was here to once again lower my image in front of Lucia. I'm going to stir fry him one day. Or I'll make Lucia do it because I can't cook. "Nowadays, beast cores are used to recharge magic tools to remove the waiting period. You know how you can only caste haste three times a day?" Lucia nodded. "Beast cores can remove that limit."

"Then I should save some beast cores for that?" Lucia's tail twitched as she tilted her head. She glanced at me.

"No. Magic tools are supplements. They aren't your own strength. Wouldn't it be better to use the cores to improve your strength to the limit?" It's not that I don't like magic tools. I'm not bitter or anything. Stupid imposter weapons.

"You're right." Lucia nodded.

"You think anything Durandal says is right." Snow rolled his eyes. He really did look like Cottontail when he did that. I wonder what happened to her after Roland died.

"That's because he is!" Lucia chased after Snow with her sword. "Don't think I forgot how you threw that at my head!"

"It was an accident!"

Snow and Lucia vanished into the forest. Bouncykins and I were left behind by the fire. "It's true that magic tools are supplements, but if everyone is using them, Lucia will be at a disadvantage if she doesn't." Bouncykins stared at me. "There are some magic tools inscribed with ninth-circle magic arrays. Do you know what that means?"

"People have reached the ninth circle?" Back in Roland's time, fifth-circle magicians were considered geniuses and sixth-circle magicians were considered to be at the peak. A lot has advanced in 80 years.

"Cain's reached the tenth. He's the world's first tenth-circle magician." Bouncykins sighed. "Not only that, but the weapons that were called legendary in Roland's time have been demoted to unique. The dwarves achieved a higher level of smithing, and newer, stronger weapons exist. It's possible you and I are only on par with unique equipment these days."

"I see." I'm not sure what I'm feeling, but it's not very pleasant.

"And the elves have gotten better at inscribing enchantments. They're almost on par with magical tool arrays." Bouncykins shook his head. "The only people who haven't made advancements are martial artists. Their standards have dropped instead."

"Is it possible Roland reached the peak of martial arts, so no one could surpass him?"

"There's no such thing as *the* peak. There's only *a* peak. People can only climb higher than their predecessors. They're starting at a higher ground. But no one wants to pursue martial arts. Why go through the suffering when an enchantment can boost your strength? Why torture yourself to learn techniques when magic tools can provide them?" Bouncykins stared at me. It was annoying how dark his eyes were—I could see my reflection in them. "You have to adapt, Durandal. Those who can't adapt can't survive."

"I'll think about it." A weapon spirit … adapt? Not possible. That's what differentiates us from humans. My purpose is to teach and protect Lucia. Even though Lucia doesn't treat me like one, I am still a weapon spirit. I will always be a weapon spirit. But I will still make Lucia into a legend.

6

"When will you let me control mini-DalDal's weight?" It's annoying to pester Durandal every time I feel it's too light. I'm not even sure how heavy mini-DalDal is anymore. Three tons? Four? Whenever I consume a beast core, my strength goes up and mini-DalDal feels off.

Durandal stared at me. Was that not a reasonable question? It's not like I'd slack off on my training just because I could reduce mini-DalDal's weight to nothing. …Maybe. I promise I won't! "Alright. I'll unlock the function for you."

"Wait. Really?" What's the catch? There's always a catch when things go my way. The last time things went my way, I obtained a sadistic spirit who enjoyed torturing poor innocent squirrelkin girls. Does that count as going my way?

"Yes. I think you're—and I somehow don't want to admit it—responsible… enough to control my weapon body freely." Durandal sighed. "You should learn how to control my weight during battles. Increasing it when you need to generate more force, decreasing it when you need to move faster. Why don't we start now?"

There's the catch. Why's the catch always sparring!? "I-I'm not—"

"Send your qi into my weapon body and will the weight you want it to be." Durandal picked up his spear and waited for me. Bouncykins was watching from the sideline, but Snow was dismantling a five-tusked boar I had caught earlier.

"Heavier." Gack! Too heavy! I almost crushed my foot. "L-lighter?" Oh. That's perfect. "I'm ready."

And thus, a brutal sparring session began which once again led to my loss. As usual. But at least I'm more accustomed to the weight changing now. What if I reduce the weight as far as possible, leap into the air, then increase it as much as I can? Wouldn't that be amazing? I—geh! "Why'd you hit me?"

Durandal retrieved the spear he smacked me with. "You're thinking weird things. Stick to the fundamentals: Breaking Blade, weight training, Steady Mountain Footwork."

"…When are you going to teach me something else?" If I had a larger variety of moves, I wouldn't lose so badly!

"When you can beat me in a spar with your current assets. If you haven't noticed, I've only been using the Steady Mountain Footwork and Breaking Blade to fight against you. What's important isn't the number of techniques you learn, it's the proficiency you reach in them."

"It looks like Lucia's going to be stuck with those two techniques forever then."

Say that to my face, Snow! I dare you! Don't look at that boar like it's prettier than me. Oh, is that a beast core? I'll take that. I stuck my tongue out at Snow after stealing away his hard work. Now I see why Durandal's such a bully sometimes. Bullying people soothes my heart. …I'm a good person, okay?

"Lucia's actually progressing very rapidly in the Steady Mountain Footwork. The thousand or so flaws she had when we first started have been reduced to a little over a hundred." Durandal smiled at me. "I'll target them nonstop so you can learn them better. No need to thank me."

Demon. Well, if I'm being honest, Durandal is a really nice teacher. The first time he wants to correct a flaw, he'll lightly tap it. The second time I expose the same flaw, he'll hit it with the side of his spear. And if I reveal it for a third time…, Snow will increase his proficiency in bandaging lacerations. There has never been a fourth time, but I'll probably lose a limb if there were. But anyways, what was I doing? Absorbing a beast … core? Shit.

"I didn't know you were so eager to spar again, Lucia. We can't let those impurities build up." A spear flew towards my face, and I barely managed to block it by reducing mini-DalDal's weight to catch up to the strike and increasing its weight to deflect the spear. This is abuse! Animal cruelty!

After another bout of sparring, new bruises had formed along my arms and legs. Maybe the number of flaws were reduced by a dozen? I hope so. I wonder when absorbing beast cores will lose its effect. I can't keep improving at this rate forever, can I? I swear my vision is almost as sharp as a crow's. Not that I would know how well a crow could see. My sense of smell is probably on par with the moonlight wolves' too. And my constitution is similar to a panther's. "Durandal. When do cores start losing their effect?"

"When you reach the limits of the beast they came from." Durandal poked through the pile of animal corpses and picked up a scavenger crow. "If someone's speed is lower than this crow's and they consumed the beast core, then that person's speed would increase. The same goes for eyesight, hearing, smell. If their abilities are already above the crow's, then nothing will happen. Impurities might build up, in fact."

"Then someone can be as strong as a dragon?" How many dragon beast cores did the Godking consume to kill a dragon in a single strike?

"No."

"Huh?"

"How many scavenger crows have you killed?"

A lot. "Over a hundred? Maybe two hundred?"

"And how many cores did you get from them."

"Like … three?"

"How do you think you compare to the crows' abilities?"

"I'm definitely caught up to them!"

Snow snorted. "You're not even close in the intelligence department."

Shut up, Snow! I'll beat you up.

Durandal patted my head, causing my body to relax. "Snow's right."

Gah! Whose weapon spirit are you anyways!? "Don't agree with him! I'm not stupid!"

"You'll need to consume 30 cores to catch up to the abilities of the crow. How many would you have to kill to get that many cores?"

"Two thousand." See. I can do math. Extrapolating's easy when you put your mind to it. Oh! The wolf I caught earlier is almost ready to eat. Why do they taste so delicious? And why do panthers taste so sour? I don't get it. Could it be their diets?

"So you'll have to kill two thousand dragons to obtain enough cores to be as strong as a dragon. There were maybe 50 dragons living in the wild during Roland's time."

Right. Dragons. "So you're telling me there's a chance? If there's 50 dragons, it's possible for 30 of them to have cores."

Durandal sighed and glanced at Snow while the rabbitkin put the cooked wolf on a plate.

Snow shrugged. "If you ever want to switch masters, I'm always free."

"Durandal's mine!" And that wolf is mine too. Haste!

***

What should Lucia's next step of training be? She's become proficient enough to draw out a battle with me when I'm limited to Breaking Blade and the Steady Mountain Footwork. Her physical attributes have also grown by leaps and bounds—I'm a bit jealous that I can't grow like her, but an increase in her strength is also an increase in mine. Along with those improvements, she's able to freely manipulate my weapon body to the most suitable weight for any situation. I suspect it has to do with her squirrely instincts and balance. Even Roland's growth wasn't as quick as Lucia's, but to be fair, Roland didn't have anyone to guide him.

"Hey, Durandal. I've been thinking. Shouldn't you fight me with other types of footworks?" Lucia tilted her head, causing beads of sweat to drop to the ground. "Won't I become too accustomed to your motions? What if someone who practices a more graceful footwork fought me, like Snow?"

There's a simple way to show Lucia my splendor. Though the basis of the footwork I taught Lucia was the Steady Mountain, I've modified it to include the strongest points of various techniques. "Snow. Spar Lucia."

"…I'll die if she hits me with a full-powered Breaking Blade." Snow shook his head. "When I first saw Lucia, I could beat her with my eyes closed. But now…, after these three months of following you two freaks around, I'm pretty sure I'll die."

"Your growth wasn't slow either, Snow." Bouncykins hopped off of Snow's head. "Lucia's at the peak of low-ranked martial artist. You're a mid-ranked one."

Lucia's tail twitched. That only happened when she was excited or angry. "Wait, how is that decided? I'm stronger than Snow. I can lift more than him."

"It's not outer strength that matters for ranks. It's inner strength," Bouncykins said. "Snow has more qi than you. He'll recover faster, strike harder, move quicker, and be stronger than 99% of low-ranked warriors. But there are some freaks whose constitutions allow them to fight a higher ranked opponent."

"I don't really like being called a freak. Can't you use the term genius instead?"

"Someone as scatterbrained as you doesn't deserve the term genius." Bouncykins sighed. "Also, there's a certain nuance. Geniuses have God-given talents that allow them to excel. Freaks have God-given bodies that provide advantages over other people. If I had to take a guess, you have a unique body that increases your strength."

"I'm amazing?" Lucia asked, her ears perking up. The way they twitch make me want to rub them. Lucia won't mind.

"Perverts..." Bouncykins turned away. "You got a body filled with strength and vitality, but at the same time, you're unable to use mana. Not like that matters due to the existence of magic tools though."

"I-is Snow special too?" Lucia's eyes were closed. I admire her persistence. Normally she would've collapsed by now. Why is teasing her so much fun?

"Snow actually has a special body as well..." Bouncykins glanced at Snow. What was Snow hiding? I didn't sense anything special about him. "He's—"

"Do you have to, Lucifer?" Snow asked and sighed.

"Tell!" Oh, Lucia was reduced to one-syllable words now. Maybe I should stop. No. This is good for her endurance— yes, this is training. "T-tell now!"

"I have a succubus body. I ooze out charm. Usually it only affects people of the opposite sex, but if I change my appearance to a woman's..."

That explains a lot. It also explains why his body didn't affect me—weapon spirits don't feel lust. Was Lucia under his influence? She shouldn't be because he looks like a girl right now, right? ...Maybe Cottontail had a succubus body as well which would explain Roland's sudden infatuation. So he wasn't just a pervert who liked bunnykin girls. Well, I can't exclude that possibility.

"And you call *me* the pervert." Lucia snorted. "So. Are we still sparring?" It seems like she slipped out of my grasp without me knowing. Impressive.

"Didn't I say I'd die? I'm not going to spar you, Lucia."

"You don't get a choice!" Lucia brandished my weapon body and swung it at Snow. The bunnykin's eyes widened as he dodged.

"Lucia! Stop!"

"I can't hear you over the sound of my swings!"

"Then stop swinging!"

"What did you say!? I couldn't hear you."

Bouncykins came over to my side. "You chose a very energetic master. She's nothing like Roland. Will you two even be compatible?"

"She's already mastered my most useful function—weight control. I think we're compatible." She mastered me a lot faster than Roland did as well. But Roland didn't know how to fight when he first started using me. It's really not fair to compare the two. "You and Snow seem to get along well."

"Is that what it seems like?" Bouncykins tilted his head. "You haven't seen it yet, but Snow … can be a handful at times. In fact, I've never seen him so docile before. He's usually the one in charge of everything. He's bloodthirsty, cutthroat, conniving, and overall not a good person. Maybe he's scared of you."

"Bloodthirsty, conniving, and cutthroat…" Those are not words I would associate with Snow. He seems more like a startled rabbit walking on eggshells.

"Lucia, I'm begging you!"

At least they're sparring seriously now. Like I thought, Lucia's winning. I don't think many people her age can defeat her in close combat. Her constitution isn't fair to fight against. Abnormal levels of strength and the ability to recover herself completely by going to sleep is a bit ridiculous. It's like she's blessed by the earth, but hated by the sky. Qi comes from the earth, mana comes from the sky.

I wonder if any of my rivals have survived the years as well. If Bouncykins made it, maybe others have also. Some of them would've made great teachers, but Bouncykins did say that martial arts as a whole has stagnated.

"Hey, Durandal. Why could I beat Snow so easily?" Lucia tilted her head and nudged Snow's body with her toe.

You didn't kill him, right? Let me check for a pulse. …Yeah, he's fine. "The Steady Mountain Footwork I taught you would be more aptly named as Universal Footwork. It heavily emphasizes the Steady Mountain, but it incorporates everything into it. If you can beat me, you can beat every footwork in the world."

"Unless the person is stronger than Durandal." Bouncykins, once again, rains cold water on me in front of Lucia. I should cut off and take one of his legs for luck.

"Durandal's the strongest. Stop being such a downer, stupid hare." Lucia seemed to have similar thoughts. She did mention she wanted to stir fry him once.

***

Ah, it's been half a year since we've arrived at the southern pass. Thankfully, winter doesn't happen this far south or I'd have to hibernate for three months. Okay, winter does happen, but it doesn't snow. I don't think I ever knew the meaning of true happiness until this day. Not even the day I received Durandal can compare to today's bliss. I beat him! I finally wiped that sadistic perverted look off of his face!

But on the other hand, I don't think I've seen Durandal so … upset. Why's he upset? Shouldn't he be happy about his pupil surpassing him?

"…Rematch."

"I refuse!" When you win, take the victory and run away!

"It was a fluke. Rematch."

Even if you spew out ice-cold killing intent like a refrigerator powered by a frost magic array, I refuse! "No fluke! I won."

"Wow, Durandal. You actually lost to Lucia. I didn't think I'd see this day for another few years." Way to go, Bouncykins. Keep rubbing salt into that wound. I'm totally not resentful over the daily beatings I've suffered for half a year.

"Lucia…" Wow, Durandal looks really, really mad. I thought weapon spirits' purpose in life was to help their masters. "I…" He sighed and his face changed back to his normal, handsome one. "To congratulate you on your victory and recent success in breaking through to a mid-ranked warrior, I'll teach you a new technique."

New technique? "This is an excuse to beat me, isn't it…?"

"What kind of person do you think I am?"

"A pervert." …Did I say that out loud?

"Learn this strike with your body." Durandal swung his spear, and something invisible smacked me in the face.

"Geh!?" What hit me? I touched my hopefully not ruined face, but there was nothing there. "What was that?"

"Qi projection. You couldn't learn it before you reached your current rank. It allows you to expel qi from your body to be used in attacks." Durandal put his spear away. I guess this wasn't something that required sparring. "When you become a high-ranked warrior, it'll be possible for you to manipulate your qi outside of your body, but for now, you can only expel it."

"So … it's like magic?" Long-ranged attacks with some invisible force of mine? That totally sounds like magic.

"…To a normal person, this might as well be magic in their eyes. But magic and qi are very different with qi losing to magic in strength and flexibility."

"Does qi beat magic in anything?"

"Anything qi can do, magic can do better," Bouncykins said. "Qi reinforces your body. So does the iron skin spell. Qi reinforces your speed. So does the fleet foot spell. Qi can perform long-ranged attacks and manipulate objects close by, but magic does it better with a simple magic missile or telekinesis."

"…What about recovering injuries?"

"There's magic to fully heal someone even if they're on the brink of death." Snow shook his head. "You're at a huge disadvantage since you can't use magic."

Durandal swung his spear and blew Snow and Bouncykins away with the air pressure. "Don't listen to them, Lucia. If you can transcend the wall, you'll be just as strong as, if not stronger than, a magician."

"The wall?" My head hurts. It feels like I've learned way too much today.

Durandal put on a solemn expression. "The barrier blocking high-ranked spirit warriors from progressing."

"Even Roland couldn't surpass it to become a divine warrior. Don't get your hopes up." Bouncykins had returned after being blown away with a bunch of bananas in his mouth. "Even then, in theory, you'll be on par with a ninth-circle magician. Cain's a tenth-circle magician. You'll have to surpass the divine warrior stage as well. No one knows what's beyond that. Saint? God? Well, if you pass it, you'll get to name it."

"If Roland was stuck as a spirit warrior or whatever, how do you know he could've became a divine warrior?"

Bouncykins nodded. "Extrapolation. You have wild beasts, ferocious beasts, spirit beasts, and divine beasts. There's normal citizens, warriors, and spirit warriors. It only makes sense for there to be divine warriors, no?"

"And magicians are ranked by circles, right?" I know that much. There's lots of complaining in the army about magicians and magic. I think it's mostly jealousy though.

"Yes. Every three circles represents one stage. So—"

I covered Bouncykins mouth. "No. No more exposition. My head will hurt if I absorb too much knowledge."

"...You're not serious."

"Teach me the qi projectile technique, Durandal!"

Durandal sighed. "It's qi projection, not projectile."

"Same thing." A few letters difference, that doesn't mean anything. "How do I use it?"

"Hold your arms straight out in front of you. Good. Now circulate your qi. Close your eyes and pretend your arms are longer than they actually are. Can you visualize your long arms?"

"I'm like an orangutan."

"...Close enough. Now circulate your qi to your new hands, the ones further away from your body."

"Whoa, this feels funny. Like my fingers are breaking and turning into jelly." It tingles.

"She actually did it in one try..." That was Snow's voice. Can I open my eyes now?

"Do you remember that feeling of extending your qi beyond your body?" Durandal's voice is much better than Snow's. Definitely. Maybe if Snow had a deeper voice and looked less girly and more like Durandal and.... Focus, Lucia!

"Yes!"

"That's the foundation of the qi projection technique. Now this step is equally as important. Visualize the normal length of your arms while keeping the projected one alive. Can you see it?"

"There's hands extending from my hands. I feel like a centipede."

"Now imagine a sword swinging down, cutting off the extra hands."

"...Is it going to hurt?"

"No."

Phew. Okay. I can do it then. "Now?"

"Now you've managed to disconnect your qi from your body. You can open your eyes. Try reaching forward and see if you can touch the qi you left in the air before it disperses."

"The air's fuzzy?" This is qi? It almost feels like I'm washing my hands. Ah, it's gone.

"To shoot out qi like I did, you have to extend your qi outside of your body, swing whatever part it's attached to to build up momentum, and cut it off at the right moment. It's like throwing a ball attached to a string."

Like a ball on a string.... "Like this?"

"Gah! Don't shoot your qi at me, Lucia!" Snow wiped at his face.

Hey, it worked. But it doesn't seem very strong?

"To deal damage, you have to change the shape of your qi to that of a sword and pour in the same amount of qi as a Breaking Blade. Like so." Durandal swung his spear, and a nearby tree split into two pieces, bisected vertically. "You have to do two hundred of these a day. There will be punishment for any you miss."

...Back to the grind it is.

***

Two hundred qi blades in a day..., all before dinner. I think I may have underestimated Lucia. ...Or she cheated and reduced the weight of my weapon body. "Lucia."

Lucia stopped staring at the simmering pot and turned to face me. "Hmm?" Drool leaked from the corner of her mouth.

"How heavy was my weapon body?"

Lucia puffed her nonexistent chest out. "Three tons."

Okay. Maybe she didn't cheat.

Snow tilted his head. "Is it always at three tons?"

Lucia nodded. "Usually. Sometimes I bring it to four, but I get tired really fast. Three is a good balance."

"...Even when you eat?"

"Especially when I eat! It helps me digest faster so I can eat more."

Your priorities are a bit skewed, Lucia. Use my weapon body for training, please, not for a digestive aid. Disregarding the incorrect usage of my weapon body, it's impressive how much Lucia can carry despite her thin frame. Even Roland didn't have as much raw strength as her and he was at the peak of high-ranked spirit warrior. He could lift a ton at most. I wanted Lucia to get close to a ton, but I never thought she'd reach it or surpass it. It's amazing how head pats and ear rubs can cause her to reach past her limits. I really chose a good master—it's a shame about the lack of mana though.

"Don't you ever want to relax? Cool down and enjoy your meal? You already finished your daily quota of qi blades, right?" Snow's voice was doing something funny. Slowing down and slurring. Was he trying to hypnotize Lucia? "How long has it been since you last relaxed? Carrying around a three-ton sword all the time must take a toll on your back."

"Shut up! Why are you talking so weirdly?" Lucia threatened to smack Snow with my weapon body. "I'll hit you if you don't focus on cooking. I promised Durandal I wouldn't slack off. So I can't relax. Ever!"

Snow clicked his tongue as he added some spices to the pot of stew. "I was just trying to be helpful. I was afraid you were going to burn out." He shook his head. "Aren't you bored after staying here for half a year? We've collected so many materials but had to throw so many away because we lack space! And there's no alcohol, no dice, no women—"

"Hey!"

Snow snorted. "You don't count, you barbarian. Gah! Don't swing a three-ton sword at me! You'll never get married the way you are!"

…It's great that Snow and Lucia get along well. It's almost like seeing Roland and Cottontail again. But maybe Snow is right. Lucia does need to relax a bit, and we have been a bit wasteful with our spoils. I should teach Lucia how to inscribe enchantments on the bones of ferocious beasts. I could also teach her alchemy with some of the herbs and animal parts. Though I'm terrible at it, I don't believe my teaching will also fail. Yes. Since Lucia has a lot of free time tonight, I'll teach her after dinner.

"The meal's ready! Stop chasing me!" Snow was still terrible at avoiding Lucia. I don't understand why.

"Oh, food." Lucia stopped swinging my weapon body and sat down by the fire. She stared at Snow.

Snow sighed and shook his head. He ladled her a bowl, which vanished in a flash. Before he had even put the ladle back into the pot, an empty bowl was resting in his hand. It seemed like Lucia, once again, used haste to consume her food. At least she was getting practice with it, no matter how mundane the task. Once she finished drinking the pot, she lay on her back and exhaled while closing her eyes, her limbs spreading out like a starfish.

Snow proceeded to create another bowl of stew while I walked over to Lucia.

"Lucia. Get up."

"Tired."

"I'll teach you alchemy and engraving."

"Tired…. Stomach … cramp…."

…Squirrels and their food comas. Well, I did think to let her relax earlier. Why not now?

"Hey, Durandal." Snow had a blank expression on his face.

"Hmm?"

"If Lucia died, what would you do?"

"She won't die." Why? Did Snow sense approaching danger? It was about time for someone to discover Prince Bryant's death, but I don't believe anyone could kill Lucia with me around.

"Hypothetically. Would you search for a new owner?" Snow continued to add ingredients to the stew. He didn't add the spices this time.

"No. I wouldn't." I really won't. "I made a promise to myself. To live and die with Lucia. Don't tell her that though. She won't work as hard if she knows." I stroked Lucia's hair and played with her ears. She squeaked and rolled her head a bit to the side. How cute.

"Why? What's so special about Lucia?" Snow's jealousy was showing again. His tail was puffed up. "Why not me? I can use magic. I'm more capable than her. I have more

139

common sense. I have ambitions, goals. Why did you choose someone as useless as her?"

"You're saying dangerous things about my master, Snow."

"Your master's dying. I poisoned her."

What...?

"What the hell are you saying, Snow?" Bouncykins appeared from Snow's socks and looked around. "Haven't you learned your lesson about making jokes to Durandal?"

"It's not a joke, Lucifer. This is an order: attack Durandal."

"Eh?" Bouncykins' eyes turned red. "Snow. Don't do this."

"I'm your master. You're not allowed to disobey!"

Snow's body disappeared when I stabbed him in the head with my spear. A clone or an illusion technique. Was Lucia really poisoned? Before I could check, thousands of wind blades formed in the sky and flew towards me. It looks like Bouncykins really did get a lot stronger in those 80 years.

"S-sorry, Durandal." Blood leaked from Bouncykins' mouth, eyes, and ears. "I don't want to do this. I knew Snow's personality, told you about it too, but I thought he changed. I really did."

I barely heard Bouncykins' words as I countered his wind blades. I got cut. A lot. I held back on using techniques involving qi, using my spear and body to withstand the onslaught instead. If Lucia really was poisoned, I couldn't afford to use her energy now.

"My, my weakness.... Left hind leg...." Bouncykins' fur stood on end as mana surged from his small body. Before he could cast another spell, I flipped him over onto his back and impaled his left hind leg. He twitched twice and disappeared, presumably reentering Snow's socks. He hadn't lied to me about his weakness.

"Lucia!" Her pulse was weak. There were a few cuts on her body where some stray wind blades had struck. Black-colored blood leaked from the wounds. Her body was turning green, and the tips of her brown hair were turning white. It was my fault. It was all my fault. Snow wasn't Cottontail, yet I treated him like her. I should've killed him when we first saw him like I intended. "Lucia, try to hang on."

What could I do? I've never succeeded in brewing a medicinal pill or elixir in my life. I didn't even know what kind of poison Lucia was inflicted with. Snow had already disappeared long ago while I was distracted by Bouncykins. He wouldn't let me catch him. I'm terrible at tracking people. I can't even read a fucking map. "Lucia…"

But there was one thing I could do. I quickly recorded a message in my weapon body with some qi. There was a lot more I wanted to add, but I was running out of time and there was a limit to the qi I could use. I scrawled out a few arrows in the dirt, pointing at a picture of the hilt of my weapon body. Hopefully, Lucia would understand. I knelt by Lucia's side and stared at her face. It was darkening, with black tendrils crawling up her neck and cheeks. I placed my finger on her chin, knelt forward, and kissed her on the lips.

You have to live, Lucia.

And then the poison surged inside me. It burned my lips, my face, my neck, everything down to my toes. My veins were on fire. At least Lucia wouldn't suffer through this pain. It seems like it'll be a long while before I wake up again, if I ever do. I wonder, how much will you grow by then, Lucia…?

Interlude

Prince. Those who aren't wish they were. Those who are wish they weren't. I am the latter. As the sixth prince of the Ravenwood Empire, I only have one path to survival: I must succeed the throne. If I fail, I die. My brothers understand this concept just as well as, if not better than, I do. I am the second youngest son, and the only one I have an advantage over is my little brother. The crown prince, my eldest brother, has fifteen more years of experience than me. Even the fifth prince has three years on me. I was lacking from the start.

Despite these disadvantages, I do not despair. Though my chances are slim, I still have hope. My mother's side of the family belonged to the household of Cuchulainn, and the weapon spirit, Gae Bulg, has been passed down throughout the ages. Now, he is in my hands. My brothers also have formidable weapon spirits, but I do not believe mine is inferior to theirs. In fact, Gae Bulg has been rumored to fight to a draw against Durandal, the legendary sword of the Godking. I have asked him a few times about it, but he never answered me honestly. But still, all rumors stem from some kind of truth. My weapon is not weak.

A guttural noise entered my ears. "Someone's coming."

I turned towards the speaker, Gae Bulg. His corporal body is that of a beastkin—a werewolf to be exact. He wore deep-blue armor, which covered everything except for a hairy face and clawed hands. I lifted the spear that contained his life and threw it towards the door. I exerted just enough strength for the spearhead to pass through. Someone on the other side screamed and swore. Gae Bulg stood up and retrieved his weapon body before handing it back to me.

The door to the room burst open. "Lan!"

I glared at the red-faced girl who kicked open my door. She wore a purple dress with matching high-heels. She was Evelyn, my half-sister and also the second princess. As my eldest brother's follower, she had no reason to be here. "What?"

"How rude," she said and furrowed her brow. "But I guess that's just how you are." She rolled her eyes before smiling. "His Majesty wants to see you."

The emperor? What did he want from me? I made eye contact with Gae Bulg. He shrugged. I brushed past my sister and stomped into the hallway with Gae Bulg following after me. Evelyn muttered something unintelligible.

"You're not going to change?" she asked.

I looked down. I wasn't wearing a shirt, and my pants were slightly tattered. It didn't matter. The less noble I acted, the less my brothers would see me as competition for the throne. I snorted and continued down the hall, leaving deep footprints in the plush, red carpet. Evelyn sighed as she followed after me.

The emperor's court was a crowded one. My father enjoyed surrounding himself with nobles attempting to ingratiate their family with ours. I suspect he wasn't hugged enough as a child, but that's to be expected. His mother was a lowly servant woman, yet he managed to occupy the throne while his brothers died in happy accidents. Was he afraid I could do the same?

"Lan. Evelyn." My sister kneeled next to me when the emperor spoke. I remained standing with Gae Bulg behind me.

I crossed my arms over my bare chest. "Father." The newer nobles in the court were stunned by my attitude, but the old-timers' expressions didn't change.

The emperor nodded. "Your seventh brother has gone missing."

And he suspected me? It's true I had plans to move against him, but so did everyone else. Everyone had plans prepared. Maybe this was one of my older brothers' plots or even my sisters'. They didn't like me either. I remained silent.

"I want you to find him. He set out on a mission to find the Godking's treasure trove, but we haven't heard from him for quite some time now."

Byrant chased after the rumors? Only an absolute moron would volunteer to throw himself into such an obvious trap. Perhaps inheriting the Godking's legacy was the fastest way to seize the throne, but who amongst us princes doesn't know that? Anyone can set up an ambush, just like anyone can spread a rumor.

"Well?"

Even the emperor is conspiring with the mastermind. Only my eldest brother could do something like this. Just you wait, Algar. If I escape from this trap you've set for me, don't expect to have any more peaceful days. I narrowed my eyes at my father. "I'll go."

"Evelyn will accompany you."

So this really has been planned out quite thoroughly. They're even sending a watchdog to look after me.

"Pardon?" Evelyn looked shocked. Was she acting? If I weren't paranoid, I might've believed her.

The emperor cleared his throat. "You will accompany Lan to discover the whereabouts of Bryant. There is no room for negotiation. You two are dismissed."

I fixed my posture and turned around while Evelyn followed court etiquette and said goodbye to our father. His gaze burrowed into my back, but I ignored the uncomfortable sensation. He already plotted to have me killed. Why should I show him any respect? The nobles didn't dare to meet my eyes as I marched out of the court with Gae Bulg. His wolf-like face was twisted into a sneer, revealing his yellow teeth. The doors to the court closed, leaving me alone in the hall with

Evelyn and Gae Bulg. There were no guards standing watch. My father preferred his bodyguards to hide within his shadows.

"Lan!"

I took the spear off my back and slammed its butt into the ground as I turned around. Evelyn took a step back and gripped her dress. Her knuckles were unusually white.

"What?" I wasn't in a very good mood. After something like that, who would be?

"A-about the mission," Evelyn said while biting her lower lip, doing her best to look scared. But I wasn't going to be fooled. Underneath that soft exterior was a professional alchemist—a toxic alchemist. She was forced to marry an arrogant asshole from an influential family. He died of a heart attack within a week of her moving in. Coincidence? "Should—"

I pointed my spear at her face. "If you get in my way, Bryant won't be the only one missing."

Evelyn's face paled as her mouth snapped shut. Although my mood was bad, it improved after finding someone worse off than I was. Was I smiling? It's been a while since I've done that. Bring it on, Algar. Let's see what exactly you have planned for me.

***

Roland's Authentic Ice Cream. This was where Bryant's lead led him? I took my spear off my back and stared at Evelyn. Who did she think she was fooling? How could this dingy ice cream shop in a backwater village possibly be the location of the Godking's legendary treasure?

"H-hey," Evelyn said and took a step away from me, hiding behind her group of five guards. "I'm starting to question my information as well."

"It's possible." Everyone turned to stare at the speaker. Gae Bulg wasn't perturbed. "The Godking's name was Roland. And he was obsessed with ice cream."

Is that something you find out by fighting someone? You learn their favorite food? Was Gae Bulg also in on this conspiracy to have me killed? Disregarding the coincidental name and favorite dessert, all of us knew before coming here that we weren't going to the treasure trove. We were going to a trap placed by Algar to dispose of Bryant.

"We should at least check it out, right?" Evelyn asked, sending a glance at my weapon spirit. My hand tightened around my spear. Gae Bulg wouldn't betray me. That glance meant nothing.

"You first." I wasn't going to be the first one to walk into a trap. I didn't even have an entourage of guards with me. Act like a savage, be treated like a savage. I think a lack of guards was a fair exchange for my brothers' wariness of me to drop. Besides, guards are one more form of asking to be stabbed in the back. A little bit of gold goes a long way.

Evelyn wrinkled her brow but said, "Fine."

Oh, did I ruin your plans? Sorry. I waited outside of the decrepit shop with Gae Bulg keeping watch behind me. My spear was raised, ready for anything. I was always ready— living while knowing someone can assassinate you at any time does things to a person. Maybe I have become a bit paranoid, but that doesn't mean there aren't people who want to kill me.

"Should we go in?" Gae Bulg asked. Twenty minutes had passed, but we hadn't heard a single sound. Was this part of their plan? I picked up a rock and threw it through the window. Glass didn't shatter because it was already broken.

"Ow!"

Well, at least I know they're still inside.

"Lan! You could've just said something! You didn't have to throw a rock at me." Evelyn sounded a bit miffed.

Other than her aggrieved cries, there were no other sounds. I didn't hear any extraneous footsteps or movements. Either the door was booby-trapped or the ambushers were top-notch experts. I took in a deep breath and kicked the door. It let out an ear-piercing groan as it flew wide open. How old were those hinges? I didn't even kick that hard.

I was greeted by the sounds of chewing. I motioned for Gae Bulg to enter first. He carried a heavy steel spear—not his weapon body—and marched inside. He froze, and a strange expression appeared on his face. What was it?

"It's safe," Gae Bulg said. His voice sounded confused.

I stepped inside the shop and followed my weapon spirit's gaze. Evelyn was sitting in a corner, eating an ice cream cone. Her guards were standing in line behind a counter. In front of them, there was a chubby, bald man wearing an apron. He raised his head and looked at me. One eye was higher than the other, and his nose and mouth were lopsided like someone grabbed his face and twisted it. His smile was crooked.

"Welcome!"

The hairs on the back of Gae Bulg's neck stood erect, and I involuntarily shivered.

"Gae," I whispered and slowly reversed my grip on my spear.

"If you fail, I'm ready."

I inhaled through my nose and let out a shout as I threw my spear as hard as I could. It flashed through the air like a lightning bolt and stabbed into the chubby man's brow. His feet were lifted off the ground, and his body flew backwards until it crashed into the wall. The spear entered his forehead, suspending him on the wall like a painting. Evelyn screamed. The guards drew their weapons and turned to face me.

"Just because you're a prince doesn't mean you can kill disabled people! You really are a mad dog!"

I pointed at the chubby man. "There's no blood."

Evelyn and her guards froze before turning their heads. The dead man's body really had no blood on it. In fact, he was deflating like a balloon. His skin turned grey as he continued to shrivel up like a prune. His legs merged together and revealed a vine while the rest of his body transformed into a leaf-like structure. The vine led towards a door behind the counter.

"What the fuck?" Evelyn asked with a pale face, forgetting her status as a princess. Her hand trembled. Was her acting that good? Or was this really not an attempt on my life?

A guard asked me, "How did you know?"

"How did you not know?" I looked at the ice cream cone that Evelyn had dropped in the corner. "I wonder if that was really ice cream you ate."

Evelyn's face turned even whiter than it already was, and she promptly vomited onto the floor. Maybe this really wasn't an attempt on my life. Gae Bulg kept his eyes on her guards as I climbed over the counter to retrieve my spear. The leaf disintegrated when I pulled the spear out. I pointed at a guard. "You. You're first."

His face paled when I gestured for him to enter the door behind the counter. No way was I going to risk my own life. I didn't feel bad for sending a man to his potential death. They're the ones who wanted to kill me after all. Might as well make it as hard as possible for them to do that. The guard didn't move.

I pointed my spear at him. "Are you disobeying a prince?"

"N-no," the guard said and lowered his head. "I'll go."

I climbed back over the counter and stood behind the guards and Evelyn. It may have been a bit shameless, but there's no point in pride if I die. The guard opened the door, revealing a stairwell heading down. Evelyn turned her head to look at me. Like little ducklings, the guards mimicked her action.

You really think I'm going down there with you behind my back? "Ladies first."

Evelyn's eye twitched. "Go," she said to her guards. They seemed a bit reluctant, but they followed her order. I entered the stairwell after them, but not before stabbing the vine to make sure it was truly dead. It was.

We arrived at a metal door. The vine had snaked through a crack between the floor and the metal. A guard copied my earlier action and jabbed it with his sword, but there was still no reaction.

"Open it," Evelyn said. Her hands gripped her dress as she took a few steps back. I made sure to be behind her at all times. Metal creaked as the door swung open, revealing a room. The smell of carrion assaulted our noses, and one of the guards vomited. Limbs and butchered bodies lay scattered across the floor. The first thing I did was track the vine back to its source. It was connected to a black rose that grew out of a severed head. I recognized the face even though it was rotting and filled with roots. It belonged to Bryant.

Evelyn screamed. I turned around and was about to leave, but I saw an expression of excitement on Gae Bulg's face. I was curious—nothing excited him. "What is it?"

"Durandal," he said in a low growl. "I can smell his scent." His hands opened and closed, his claws scratching the armor covering his thighs. "But it's faded. He's not here anymore, but he was."

"How are you so calm!?" Evelyn glared at me. "Bryant's dead!"

I ignored her. "Do you know what that flower is?"

Gae Bulg shook his head. I kicked one of the guards in the back, pushing him towards the black rose. There was no reaction from the flower. Seems harmless enough. I wandered around the area, keeping my spear at the ready. There was nothing unusual—unless you counted the flower and dead bodies—and there were no treasures. However, there was a library, but the covers of the books were so faded, I couldn't make out any letters.

Evelyn followed me and kept quiet, but I had Gae Bulg watch her in case she tried to kill me.

"Is this really the Godking's treasure trove?" she asked. After getting over the initial shock of Bryant's death, she became curious.

"It should be." I took a book off the shelf and flipped through the pages. A few words were readable, but the majority of the pages had blurred due to mold.

A guard screamed from outside the library, and Evelyn and I dashed outside with Gae Bulg behind us. A flower had bloomed from a severed hand, and a vine had entangled one of the guards. I looked up and saw three motes of purple light descend from the ceiling. When they touched the severed limbs, flowers began to take root.

Gae Bulg and I made eye contact. We both lifted our spears, shouted, and ran away at the same time, shutting the metal door behind us and running up the stairs. Evelyn and her guards had been left behind.

"Should we have done that?"

I shrugged. Not only was Evelyn a professional alchemist, she was also a first-circle magician. She'd live. Probably. I was starting to feel a little guilty. Though I suspected she wanted to kill me, she hadn't made any attempts. "We'll wait for a day." That was the least I could do.

Gae Bulg grunted, and we both sat outside of the ice cream store. The smiling face embedded in the 'O' of Roland seemed to be laughing at us. A few hours later, the doorknob turned. I had my spear ready—Gae Bulg had alerted me of footsteps beforehand. I took a step forward and lunged, thrusting my spear at the opening gap. Evelyn screamed and ducked, dodging my strike. I checked her feet during that time. There weren't any vines.

"Just checking."

I looked past her. None of her guards followed her out. She started to cry.

***

What did I do to deserve a brother like this? Did I assassinate the pope in my past life? Maybe I offended a god during the period of reincarnation. When we found Bryant's last known location, Lan glared at me and threatened to stab me with his spear. If you want to stab someone so badly, stab Bryant! It's not my fault we're at an ice cream shop. Luckily, his weapon spirit spoke up. Thanks, dog-person. I'm sorry you're stuck with Lan for an owner.

Not only did he threaten me with a spear, but when I was eating ice cream, he threw a rock at my head! And then he killed the nice shop owner the instant he saw him. But, then again, the owner turned out to be an evil plant of sorts, but still. He gave me free … ice cream. What if that ice cream was made out of human brains? I vomited.

It was then that Lan pulled the gentleman card. Ladies first? Who would want to be the first one to go down an ominous set of stairs? Don't act like you're doing me a favor. I had my guards go down instead. We arrived at a metal door. When my guards opened it, the first thing I saw was Bryant's severed head. I screamed. I'm not afraid to admit I grew up in a sheltered home while being pampered in my own little bubble. Severed heads were not something I was usually exposed to.

But how was Lan so calm!? He even turned around to leave after accomplishing the mission. Was he used to sights like this? I thought back to the rumors of Lan sneaking out at night to slaughter people. Of course, there was no evidence against him, but I was starting to believe it was true. I glared at him as he talked with his pet wolf-man. Did they say Durandal was here? Regardless, that didn't matter.

"How are you so calm!? Bryant's dead!"

Do you know what he said to me? Nothing. That savage completely ignored me and asked his spirit about flowers. He wasn't sure if the flower was dangerous or not, so he kicked one of my guards towards it. Can you believe that? I don't understand why he was so hostile towards us this whole time. He was like an unchained dog that we had to bring along. This mission would've been so much easier if he wasn't here— except for that shopkeeper bit.

Then he acted as if I didn't exist, but his weapon spirit sure didn't act like it. The wolfkin kept glaring at me with those yellow eyes, and if I stepped too close, he snarled at me. Never in my life have I been treated like this before. I guess if I interacted with Lan in the palace, I would've. How is he nobility? Just what part of him is graceful? He's even worse than my deceased husband!

We entered a library that had more books than our own. I picked up a book and opened it. The words were faded, but I could still make some out. Wasn't this an entry-level alchemy textbook? Well, the Godking did die eighty years ago. There have been a lot of advancements during that time. "Is this really the Godking's treasure trove?" I wasn't asking him. I was asking myself, but he answered anyway. I guessed the silent treatment was over.

"It should be."

And that was when Joey screamed. We dropped the books and rushed out of the library. A scene of carnivorous evil plants greeted us. Joey's hand was being eaten by a flower. Lan and his spirit nodded at each other and drew their weapons. At last, they'd be useful…. Did they just run away!? The metal door shut with a clang, and my heart dropped to my stomach. He really left….

I heard more screaming as another cluster of flowers bloomed on the severed body parts that littered the ground. Joey screamed as a green vine grew out of his nose and blossomed into a flower. Calm down, Evelyn. You're a magician of fire. You can do this.

I sucked in a deep breath and willed my mana into my palms. I raised my hands and pointed them at the flowers. "Conflagrate!" The plants exploded, relieving the pressure on my guards who were fending off vines. They tried to free Joey, but he was already dead, so they hacked off the flower that was binding him.

"What was that?" I asked. None of my guards had an answer. A black vine sprang out of the floor and curled around Jordan, one of my guards. It pierced through his chest, pushing his heart out of his body. It beat a few more times as the vine throbbed in tune like it was drinking something. I ran for the door. I don't want to die!

My guards saw my actions and made it to the door before me. When Josh touched the metal, a vine fell from the ceiling and wrapped around his neck. There was a snapping noise, and Josh stopped moving. I couldn't stop the scream from escaping my body.

"Conflagrate! Conflagrate! Conflagrate!"

All the visible vines in the room exploded. My throat burned, and my legs grew heavy. I felt like I had sprinted for a mile. My remaining guards looked at each other, but neither of them were willing to touch the door first. Before they could decide, the ceiling exploded. Rocks fell to the ground, revealing a massive rafflesia with thousands of vines wriggling around its flower. Three vines shot for the door, blocking off our escape. I was too spent to cast anymore spells.

My guards tried cutting the vines, but they were harder than metal, making their swords ineffective. "The library," I said. They picked me up and ran towards the library. One vine snaked around Julian's leg, causing him to trip. Multiple vines promptly turned his body into a pincushion. Jack continued to run, refusing to let me go to save himself. Before we reached the door, a vine stabbed through his chest, causing him to scream. With the last of his strength, he threw me inside of the library and reached for the door. He smiled at me as it swung shut.

I passed out. When I woke up, my body was sore and my stomach growled. I didn't know how much time had passed. Was I going to die here? Lan wasn't going to come back to save me. I already knew that. Maybe if I surrounded my body with flames, I could make it out alive. My mentor had taught me a human-bonfire spell, but I always thought it was stupid, so I never practiced it. How did it work? I experimented with my mana, attempting to wreathe my body in flames. After a dozen attempts, I managed to get it to work.

I rested and waited inside of the library until my mana was recharged. This is it. I activated the spell and pushed open the door. I was greeted by a sea of black vines. As if sensing the flames around my body, they drew back and parted. I took even steps towards the exit, unimpeded the whole way. A few vines tried to grab me, but they were incinerated before reaching my skin. I pushed open the door, stepped outside, and closed it, maintaining the spell until I reached the top of the stairs. I deactivated it because I didn't want to set the building on fire and closed the door behind the counter. I made it. I was still alive.

I opened the exit, and a spearhead rushed towards my face. I screamed and ducked before shouting curses. I recognized that spearhead from back in the palace.

"Just checking," Lan said as he took a step back.

Just checking? Just checking!? I almost died! My screams reduced to sobs. Why was I stuck with him? Why!?

"Why did you take so long to come out?"

"Because fuck you! That's why!" If my mana weren't exhausted, I would've conflagrated his ass.

Lan shrugged. "Well, at least I know you're still alive." He turned around and walked away. Was he leaving me again? What the hell?

"Where are you going?" I wiped away my tears and blew my nose on my sleeve. Fuck manners.

"Chasing Durandal. You can go back first."

He was walking away from the direction we came from. I watched his back as he left. Good riddance. There was no way I was going to follow him, that was just asking for death. My stomach gurgled, and I stood up. I didn't want to stay in this damned ice cream shop any longer. A bag on the steps caught my eye. I opened it and found a sandwich inside. A note on it read, "It's not poison. – Gae Bulg."

Maybe his weapon spirit wasn't such a bad person. What did Lan do to deserve someone like him? I shook my head and walked away as I ate the sandwich. Our carriage was still where we had left it—no one had the audacity to steal a royal carriage. I boarded it and urged the horses to make haste towards the capital. I think I've had enough adventures for the rest of my life.

7

"Lucia." Durandal's so cute when he blushes! "I love you."

If this is a dream, please, never let it end. "I, I—" Before I could say anything, he rushed up to me and embraced me, covering my lips with his. So forceful! So aggressive! So Durandal-like!

"You have to live, Lucia."

Eh? "You're leaving?" His body began to lose its color. He pulled away and smiled at me before he dissolved into dust. "D-Durandal?"

My eyes shot open. It's nighttime? A dream then. Well, even if I asked for it to never end, it was getting depressing, so it's a good thing it did. "What time is it, Durandal?"

…

"Durandal?" Where'd he go? He always watches over me when I sleep in case I'm about to fall over while sitting in my horse stance. Eh? Why aren't I in my horse stance? "Snow…?"

…

"Bouncykins…? Guys!?"

Did, did they abandon me? What the heck? The fire's out too. "T-this isn't funny."

Rustling sounds came from the nearby bushes. Glowing eyes appeared in the darkness. Moonlight wolves? I don't have the patience to deal with you! "Get lost! Flying Qi Blade!"

Seven whimpers rang out at the same time as my projectile slashed into the darkness, cutting down the bushes and trees. The remaining eyes closed, and their owners ran away. What the heck was going on? At least I still have my fire starter. …Why's there a pot of burnt stew above the campfire? Was Snow in the middle of cooking when he left? First things first, light the fire to prevent anymore beast ambushes.

Okay. I can see. Now, what was I doing last? I drank Snow's stew, then I got super tired and fell asleep. That's it? …What are these pictures of arrows on the ground? Are they pointing at a penis? Wait, no. That's a hilt. Why does it look so ugly? And those squiggles…. Send my qi into mini-DalDal's hilt?

Durandal's voice flooded my head. "Lucia. You were poisoned by Snow. I will try to remove the poison, but if I succeed, I'll fall into a deep sleep. Snow's still alive. Be careful. The fastest way to wake me up is to get stronger. I left some rudimentary knowledge in my weapon body. This is *not* a drill. You have to survive, Lucia. I believe in you."

…Eh? Snow poisoned me? What the fuck? "If this is a joke, it's a really sick one, Durandal." Didn't Durandal say if he was separated far enough from mini-DalDal, he'd automatically enter the weapon? I don't know where he is, but if I go far enough away from here, he'll reappear, right? Or this is a training exercise Snow and Durandal came up with. Some mental fortitude test. Definitely. I'll play along then and pretend it isn't actually a drill. Our massive bag of materials and supplies is still here. I should take it with me. I should also remove the pictures to prevent Snow from discovering them. …Durandal left his metal spear behind. Maybe this really isn't a drill. Fuck. Fuckity fuck, fuck, fucking fuck. Fuck! Fucking whore of a rabbit! I'll kill Snow the next time I see him. Gah!

Calm down, Lucia. Deep breaths. Durandal said he left rudimentary knowledge in mini-DalDal. I should check it with my qi; that's how it works, right? I sent my qi into mini-DalDal's hilt again, and I felt it right away. Durandal's presence. A giant glowing ball of light in the middle of a room filled with darkness. Beside it, there was a speck of blue light that floated towards my qi tendril. Was this it? My qi touched the speck, and I regretted it right away. Nausea. Lots of nausea. My head hurt as something buried itself inside my brain and pulsed. It felt like someone was repeatedly hammering my head while shouting at me.

The art of bone engraving. Engrave runes on bones to draw out their power. Turns bones into consumable items. Rune of strength. Rune of speed. Rune of intelligence. Rune of perception. Rune of…. Dozens and dozens of symbols flashed by my eyes. Rudimentary knowledge my ass! My head's going to explode! …And I passed out again.

When I woke up, the sun was shining overhead. I sat up. The fire was gone, and there were deep grooves in the ground where I had stamped out Durandal's scribbles. Last night hadn't been a dream. Was the art of bone engraving real? I rummaged through our materials bag and pulled out a bone, a small skull from a scavenger crow that Snow had told me was valuable. Let's see…, a rune of focus? I roughly carved out the appropriate rune with 32 strokes of mini-DalDal, inserting my qi in the process. The skull flashed with an orange light. Did it work?

I squeezed the skull with my left hand, and it disintegrated. Work! Lots of stuff to do, Lucia! Carve more runes! Strength! Speed! Focus, focus, focus! Lots of focus runes! Use *all* the bones in the bag! String them up around your body like some macabre decorations for easy use! What are you waiting for, start now! You'll only be focused for another 59 minutes and 32 seconds! 31 seconds now! 30! …Yup. It worked. Busy, busy.

An hour later, I looked like some kind of decorated holiday tree with bones instead of shining crystals. Thank you for the last gift, Durandal. I'll definitely be able to survive with this. But I'm exhausted now. Maybe I should look for something to eat? Or…. I looked at the skull hanging from my wrist. I squeezed it, and it broke. Focus! Hunt! Train! Become stronger! Pick a random direction and flee in case Snow comes back! Kill more animals, consume more cores, create more focus bones! Repeat process until death! Oh, and sleep and eat. Don't forget to do those on occasion.

I can do this! I'll grow stronger, so Durandal will wake up faster! He left me the greatest footwork in the world, the strongest close-ranged burst attack, and … an alright long-ranged attack, I guess. What more do I need? With these focus runes, I don't need head pats or ear rubs for motivation! It's a shame I don't have a guide, but I don't need one. I just have to follow the screams of the scavenger crows!

"S-someone. Help me!"

There! Time to acquire more skulls!

***

Stab the eyes. Deflect the claws. Breaking Blade upwards to bisect the body. Rummage through the brain for a beast core. Store it in my bag. Inscribe a rune of strength on the skull. Consume the bone of strength. Forget all feelings of hunger and exhaustion. Store the corpse. Move on.

Stab more eyes. Deflect more claws. Breaking Blade sideways to cut off all escapes. Chase after the beast core that was sent flying. Inscribe a rune of speed on the tail. Consume the bone of speed. Dismantle all the corpses gathered so far. Inscribe runes of focus. Lie down and contemplate life for three seconds. Back to work.

"Gah! I want to bathe!" Of course, no one heard my shout. Probably. I've gotten extremely good at inscribing runes, and I can do it quickly and efficiently nonstop by consuming bones of strength and speed. A side effect of the bones of strength was decreased exhaustion and decreased hunger and a little recovery of qi. Bones of speed have to be taken with bones of perception or else my mind won't keep up with my body. Bones of focus can be stacked to extend the time limit, so I'll never be distracted like I would be if there was a small window between one effect and the other.

And thus, I haven't eaten, slept, or bathed in half a year. Gross, right? I smell worse than the morning breath of a vulture. I always thought vultures were desert creatures, but apparently they're like upgraded forms of scavenger crows. There's a lot of them in the southern pass, and you can always tell when something's on the verge of death because they gather in the sky like a really loud cloud.

"Help! Save me!"

Speaking of death. It's time to kill some more scavenger crows now that I'm done strapping bones to myself. You can barely see the dress that I took from Snow underneath all my consumable bones. Not like anyone would want to. It used to be white—it's dark red now. Scavenger crow, scavenger crow, here to give me his skull.

"P-please! I have money!"

There it is…? The heck? An actual person? …I wonder how many runes I can inscribe on his bones. How many ribs does a human have? I know there's at least three. Ah, he's being chased by a bear. Bears are great materials for bones of strength. Let's kill it. "Flying Qi Blade!"

The man's eyes widened as the bear stopped moving and split apart in front of him. "S-saved…" He turned around. "Thank—"

Rummage through the brain. Whistle a tune for good luck. Eh? No beast core. What a rip off! Kick its head off, Lucia! Wait, don't. Then you'll have to chase the skull. Haaah. Why are bears so large? They're too bulky to transport around. Dismantle it here then, but first, shoot the vultures out of the sky. Stupid birds. I'm not jealous of your intelligence anymore, not with these focus bones!

"D-demon…"

Oh, right. There was a person, wasn't there?

"Gah! Please don't kill me!"

How rude! I just saved your ass. "Shut up."

"Y-yes!"

What was he? Only mercenaries would go this deep into the southern pass. Why was he dressed like a pansy? "What are you?"

"What am I? A, a human…?"

"Stupid! What do you do for a living!?" Did I mention irritability was a side effect of bones of strength? Maybe it's a side effect of the side effect of not sleeping or eating for half a year.

"I'm, I'm a merchant!"

Gross. Don't pee yourself. …Am I as imposing as Durandal? That's amazing! Fuck. Why was I reminded of Durandal? Stupid, Snow. I'll kill you. Thankfully, these bones of focus let me dismantle a bear, hold a pleasant conversation with a merchant, and think peaceful thoughts about my once-companion all at the same time. I wonder if I'm becoming too reliant on them. …Nah. "Merchant?"

"I … sell things?"

"Idiot! I know what a merchant is! Why are you in the southern pass?" Halfway done with the bear.

"I heard there was a gold mine discovered here…, so I hired a convoy and searched for it. Everyone died except for me."

"…How did the weakest person survive?" That doesn't make any sense.

"We were ambushed by a giant snake. After it ate everyone but me, it laughed at me before curling up and going to sleep…. I still can't believe it."

"It's because you're not worth spending time on digesting." Just a few more runes to carve. Why do bears have so many bones? Have less bones in your next life, please and thank you, bear.

"T-the bear meat. Are you just going to leave it there? Don't you know how expensive their bodies are? You can easily sell a bear penis for ten gold!"

"…The penis?" I'm not going to collect animal penises!

"Nobles eat them for invigoration! Ah, of course, the organs can also be sold. A heart for five gold, liver for three, kidneys for three each, lungs for two." The merchant's eyes sparkled. They were awfully shiny for someone who almost died a few minutes ago. "The bones are worth even more, but I see you can already use them. H-how about this? Escort me back, and I'll help you sell everything! You don't have an interspacial ring, right? That's why you're carrying the bag around?"

There was a plain-looking ring on the merchant's finger. Interspacial ring? "You have one?"

"No! But you can buy a lot if you sell all those bones you're carrying around! What do you say? Help me out of the forest, and I'll help you make gold. I even have connections with the types of people who sell interspacial rings."

"Not interested." I have to get stronger to wake Durandal up! I don't have time to spend on shopping!

"Please! Don't go! I have a wife and child waiting for me to return home!"

Scavenger crow? Oh, no. Just the same merchant. Tsk. Maybe he's a scavenger crow morphed into a human? I should check his brain for a beast core….

"Hiih! I'm sorry, I'm sorry! Please don't kill me!"

Well, if he were a crow, he would've tried to fly away. I totally didn't try to kill him or anything just now. It was only a test. Mhm. Back to hunting! I've already consumed enough scavenger crow, shadow panther, and moonlight wolf beast cores, so they don't increase my attributes anymore, but I can move on to fat bears, hard crocodiles, and ugly vultures! Those aren't their actual names by the way. Snow's not around anymore to be my encyclopedia, so I named them myself.

Ah, the grind really never ends.

***

Despite my best efforts to stay on track killing monsters and consuming beast cores to become stronger, I somehow ended up at a town. No. Why the heck is there a town in the middle of the southern pass!?

"H-hey. Are you a mercenary or a new breed of monster?"

The two people at the gate didn't seem very comfortable with my appearance. How rude. "Do I look like a monster?"

"Yes..."

Oh. Right, I probably do. No one else wears skulls and bones around their body all the time like this. And every inch of me is caked with dried blood except for my eyes. My hair feels all gross too, and my tail can't even be seen underneath all these rib bones. "I'm a mercenary...."

"...Right. The entry fee is ten gold."

"Ten gold!? ...Can I give you this bear penis instead?" Don't ask me why I collected them! I totally didn't! This was on the floor beside the guard. Mhm. It was just lying there; I can't believe they didn't see it earlier.

The two people exchanged glances. Were they going to deny it? "Two bear penises."

Oh, look. There's a second one lying around, what a coincidence. "Here, two of them."

The two people grinned at each other and stored the parts away before opening the gate. "Welcome to Wilderness Town."

Wilderness Town. For a town that's in the middle of the wilderness, it reminds me a lot of the Ravenwood Empire's capital city. The buildings are pretty much designed the same way, but there's some moss and decay showing. The roads are a bit broken but still made of brick and stone. And there's lots of people here too, surprisingly. The only difference is everyone is staring at me instead of ignoring me.

"Monster?"

"No!" I really need a bath. And an interspacial ring to hide all these bones. Maybe I should've accepted that merchant's offer.

"Whoa, those are some finely carved engravings on those bones. Are you selling? I'll pay ten silver per bone." An old man with a bald head slowly walked around me while hunched over. How the heck does an old man survive out in the wilderness? I shouldn't trust him. I'm never going to trust anyone ever again except for Durandal. I won't even trust the people he trusts. Stupid Snow.

"Not selling." Let's find an inn to bathe in. Then I can walk around without all these stares.

The old man's eye twitched. "Do you know whom you just denied?" His body bulged as his back straightened. His muscles grew like water balloons until he was over two heads taller than me. "You should feel honored I even offered to pay for your crappy bones!"

"I don't get it. Are you actually old or just pretending to be old?"

"I'm young!" The hideous, beefy man swung his fist at me. Be skinnier like Durandal, please. Even Snow looked more pleasing.

"Breaking Blade!" It's important to respect your elders. But if they're only pretending to be old, it's okay to beat them up. …Or send them flying. Wow, why was he so weak? I thought he'd be as strong as a bear at least. He looked as big as one. Then again, I did finish consuming bear, crocodile, and vulture beast cores. Don't ask me how much time has passed. It feels like a single day since I haven't slept yet, but the changing of the sun and moon tells me otherwise.

"Strong…"

"He didn't even use any spells."

I'm a she! I need to take a bath to clear up this misunderstanding. "You there, where can I bathe?"

A well-dressed girl stiffened when I pointed mini-DalDal at her. "T-there's an inn down the street. That way."

People tremble in my presence. I feel so much like Durandal—I bet he'd be proud. The inn looked like a standard one from the Ravenwood Empire's capital as well. I can't actually be in the capital, can I? "Innkeeper! I need a bath."

"Yes, you do."

Don't agree with me! "How much?"

"Five gold."

"…If I gave you a bear penis, would you serve me food too?" Wow, there sure are a lot of bear penises lying around, huh? I wonder how much a crocodile's would sell for. Twenty gold? There's two of them from one crocodile after all.

"Yes. I'll have a meal prepared for when you're done."

Thanks, faceless innkeeper who I didn't bother describing. The bath was a simple room with a bucket and a hot-water-generating magic array. …That's not fair. I always had to use cold water arrays in the army. Well, it's a good thing I became a deserter….

Three usages of haste and a bone of speed later, I stepped out of the red bath. It looked like someone had slaughtered an animal in there. Thankfully, there was a drain in the floor of the room that led somewhere. I even managed to wash my dress and bracelet and bones. I feel like a girl again! Now that I think about it, I'm glad I don't menstruate like human women. Perks of being a beastkin!

"Hey, innkeeper, where's the food?" Yes, bones of strength solve my hunger, but I want to taste something! I wonder if my tongue still works. I haven't used it in a long time.

"Here you are."

Wow. Fine. Don't comment on my new appearance. Well, at least the food looks appetizing. …But I shouldn't eat it. Damnit, Snow! All my trust in food is gone now! I'll kill you! Painful death to all bunnykin! It looks like I wasted half a bear penis. Good bye, appetizing meal. You and I weren't meant to be.

"Finished already?"

No need to rub it in! "I eat with my eyes."

"I understand."

Why are you so accommodating!? Question things people tell you! Ah, well, it's not like it's any of my business. I wonder if I can find any stores that sell interspacial rings here. The instant I stepped out of the inn, I sensed a lot of eyes staring at me.

"It's a girl?"

"I wonder where she's from."

"Are beastkin even allowed here? How come I haven't seen any?"

It seems like I don't belong? What kind of place did I step into? Why was I even tempted to enter this town…? Right. Interspacial rings. I need one of those.

"Hey, beastkin. Where's your master?"

So this place is a lot more like the Ravenwood Empire's capital than I thought. "It's her." I pointed at the same trembling girl who I asked for directions to the bath. "Right?"

The girl stiffened. "R-right. She's mine."

Wow. This is fun. No wonder why Durandal likes flaunting his bloodlust. Wait! Does this mean I've finally attained the same level of bloodlust as him!? I've killed over thousands of beasts…. And these bones are pretty intimidating if I may say so myself. Happy days. I looped my arm around the trembling girl's shoulder. "Alright, master! Let's go!"

And I whisked her away.

***

"U-um, can you let me go now?"

I arrived at the edge of the town with my new 'master' held over my shoulder like a sack of potatoes. It seems safe enough to drop her here. "Yup."

"W-why did you claim me as your master?" the girl asked, biting her lower lip.

Why was someone so weak-hearted staying in the middle of the southern pass? "I needed a scapegoat. Anyways, you're going to help me now. I have three goals: sell stuff, visit a magic tool shop, buy an interspacial ring." Obviously I need to sell stuff to make money to buy stuff from a magic tool shop which I can then store into an interspacial ring.

"I-I understand."

She's really obedient too. Why? Was she trying to screw me over like Snow? "And I need you to tell me about this town while we go accomplish my goals, starting now. Lead the way!" I'm a very busy person. Busy, busy, busy. I still have over seven hundred hours of focus bones' effects leftover to spend. All those little bones that I couldn't carry on my body were converted into focus. I think I solved the weakness of all squirrelkin.

"Y-yes! This town is Wilderness Town." The girl walked through the alleyways, heading towards a loud source of noise. "It was founded by the Ravenwood Empire, and its design is similar to the capital as well. Its original purpose was to train the army while harvesting materials from the ferocious beasts nearby, but too many army members died during the training exercises. The empire abandoned the town, and it was slowly taken over by merchants, mercenaries, and, most importantly, promising sect members who're seeking ways to train themselves. Like me."

"Sect members? Like those people who constantly go around preaching in the streets of the capital?" I've seen a lot of them. But they always ignored me. Beastkin aren't allowed to join sects, at least, not in the human capital. I've heard rumors about them, but the army always talked shit about sect members. Apparently, they aren't very good people. Neither are magic clansmen.

"…You could call it preaching, yes." The girl sighed. "Sects need money to run. All members pay monthly fees, and all kinds of training techniques are available. But the sects are hemorrhaging members which is why there's such a huge abundance of ferocious beasts around. Everyone wants to learn magic instead."

"You don't want to learn magic?" Follow the crowd! If people are bailing from sects, why are you staying?

"I took an aptitude test." The girl bit her lower lip. We were getting closer to the source of the noise. "I'll never exceed the second circle if I become a mage. But if I work hard enough in the sect, I might become a high-ranked warrior. There's a better future for me here even if martial techniques are declining. If only the Godking were still around…"

"Why don't magic clansmen have a presence here?"

"…They have their own town. There's a rivalry between the two factions even though the Godking practically created both of them. Silly, isn't it? He united the three races and blended magic with martial techniques, yet 80 years after his death, there's extreme civil unrest between the three races, and magic and martial techniques have gone their own paths."

"A little." Is that all a legend can do? If I become a legend, will all my work be unraveled in 80 years after my death? Well, that doesn't matter to me because I'll be dead, but still. It's sad to think about. I guess that's what legacies are for, huh?

"We're here." The girl stopped in front of the alley's exit. A sprawling field of black tents and stalls lay before us. "You can sell stuff, and lots of magic tools are sold here as well. There isn't really a standard magic tool shop because

Wilderness Town is a bit of a lawless place. There's no one to complain to if your items are stolen. Only really powerful or confident people are willing to open a permanent shop here."

The innkeeper was powerful? I should pay more attention to his face next time. "When you say lawless place, I can also steal stuff from people, right?"

"…Are you that strong? Most people here are mid-ranked warriors."

I have no idea what rank I am. "Compare them to ferocious beasts, please."

"A group of ten mid-ranked warriors can kill a fat bear with a few injuries but no deaths."

No way. The name of the bears I was hunting was actually fat bear? Who's the lazy person who named them!? "What about a high-ranked warrior? Can they kill a fat bear in a single hit?"

"Maybe at the peak of high-ranked. No one here is capable of doing that."

…I think I figured out why bear penises sell for so much. It's amazing how they're just lying around town and totally not in my bag, right? What a coincidence. "Really? No one? Why's everyone so weak?"

"That's simple. This town is where the failures gather. And there's no mages." The girl looked at my bag. "So what are you selling? Do you need help with pricing too? You look like you have the face of someone who's easily tricked."

…She just called me stupid, didn't she? She's lucky she's right. I have no idea how to price these beast cores and bones. If I took my anger out on her now, then I wouldn't have anyone left to help me. "How much do beast cores sell for?"

"What kind? Low-ranked ferocious beasts like scavenger crows have cores that sell for ten gold. Mid-ranked ferocious beasts like moonlight wolves sell for 50 gold. A high-ranked beast core like a fat bear will easily sell for 200 gold."

Holy shit, I'm rich. "How much is an interspacial ring?"

"Market price is 10,000 gold, but you probably won't find anyone selling one here. What failure would spend 10,000 gold on a ring they couldn't defend?" The girl coughed. "Though, promising young masters often come through here for about a week and flaunt their wealth to buy everything." Her voice lowered. "You could buy a ring if they have a spare, or … you can steal it."

…Well, I'm already a murderer. It can't hurt to be a thief as well, yeah? I just have to find a promising young piñata, err, young master.

***

"You, you're really selling this many beast cores?"

It looks like I surprised my unnamed scapegoat of a master with the sheer number of beast cores I've gathered. And this small pile is only made up of the scavenger crows'! Would she faint if I showed her the number of bear cores I have? "But this marketplace really is convenient, huh?"

It really, really is. Everyone's wearing a pyramidal hat with writing on it telling sellers exactly what they want. And the vendors are wearing hats that tell everyone exactly what they're selling. There's even one person selling those hats, which I bought, by the way. But I made the scapegoat wear it.

"How many scavenger crow cores are you selling?" A man dressed in a suit approached me. Maybe he was the servant of someone rich? He doesn't look like a martial artist; he's totally suspicious. "I'm from the Briarwood family."

"T-the Briarwood family?" The scapegoat looked surprised. Were they famous? I mean, I've heard of them too, but I don't know much about the political circles in the upper echelons of human society. "I'm selling fifty cores, easily enough to bring someone's status on par with a scavenger crow's."

"Ten gold each…. Is there a bulk discount?"

"No discounts! Only sell." Money is money! Even if these scavenger crow cores are only equivalent to two and a half bear cores, every single penny counts! I still remember my days of struggling to save even one silver to buy my fire starter. There's no way I can allow discounts. Nuh-uh. Nope.

"...Your servant has an awfully loose mouth."

Your face is loose, you grumpy old man! Look at all those wrinkles and sagging skin.

"Mm." The scapegoat lowered her head a bit. Were the Briarwoods really that powerful? "I'm sorry, but she's right. I don't do discounts."

"Tch. Five hundred gold then." The butler-like man withdrew five bracelets ringed with gold coins from his clothes and placed them into the scapegoat's hands. I took them from her and gave the pouch of scavenger crow cores to the man. Then I changed the writing on the scapegoat's hat to reflect the new sales. Shadow panther cores! 50 gold each! Of course, when I say writing, I mean pictures. Literacy is hard.

The butler-like man stared at me.

I know I'm beautiful, but he doesn't have to stare so intensely. "What? Do you have a problem?"

"No. No problem. How many of those cores do you have?"

"22."

"...1,100 gold then." The man offered me 11 of those gold-coin bracelets and I handed him the pouch of shadow panther cores. He counted them while I once again adjusted the writing on the scapegoat's hat. Moonlight wolf cores! 50 gold each!

The man's expression darkened once he saw the new pictures. "...How many?"

"210." Moonlight wolves travel in packs. It's a lot easier to gather their cores than any other beasts.

The man frowned. "I'll give you an interspacial ring for them."

"Deal!" It looks like I don't have to become a thief. How nice. But I thought people wouldn't want to sell interspacial rings? "Can you trade something as precious as that?"

"…You're not from around here, are you? The Briarwood family has a fourth-circle space magician capable of creating interspacial rings." The man stroked his chin before reaching into his clothes and taking out a simple silver ring. The scapegoat gulped when she saw it.

"Let me inspect it first." I held my hand out. I'm totally not going to steal it and run. I'm not Snow, gosh. The ring was light and no different from any that you'd see from a jeweler. In fact, it probably was made by a jeweler and enchanted later. "How do I use it?"

"Send a stream of consciousness into it."

A whatawhatwhat? A stream of consciousness? Like focus on it? Oh! That's interesting. It's like I'm holding a cube of empty space the size of a room in my palm. How do I put things inside? Go inside, bone! A skull hanging from my shoulder disappeared and reappeared in the space. It worked! Now, come out! It reappeared on my shoulder. "This is amazing!"

The butler-like man cleared his throat. "You can bind it to yourself with a drop of blood. Also…, don't forget why you have it."

Right. I'm a salesman right now. I handed over a bulging pouch and cut my finger with mini-DalDal, smearing the ring with blood. It flashed with a white light, and I had a weird feeling of having an eleventh finger. Right, let's put it someplace safe. Don't look!

Once the ring was safely stowed away in a very private place—I made sure it'd still function properly—I stored all the bones I accumulated on my body inside of it. "Ah, those things were really smothering."

The scapegoat blinked at me. "…You're a lot less scary than before."

I slapped her shoulder, causing her to yelp. Anyways, time to change the writing on her hat again. "Uh, what are those crocodiles called and how much do I sell their cores for?"

"Thick-skinned crocodiles? Their core market price is 250 gold." The scapegoat had a strange expression while clutching her shoulder. "You're selling those?"

"Thick-skinned crocodile cores! 250 gold!" I finished drawing the pictures on her hat.

The butler-like man stared at me. "How many?"

"20." I fell into a river and was swarmed by over a hundred of them. It didn't take too long to harvest their cores and bones because I fed some of their beast cores into my dress to repeatedly use haste. There was no way I was going to spend days on dismantling crocodiles.

"You're a lot more capable than I thought…." The butler frowned and handed me 50 bracelets of gold. It seemed like he was carrying around an interspacial ring as well. In return, I handed him the bag of 20 crocodile cores. "Are you selling more? Death vulture cores perhaps? I'll buy them for the same price as the crocodile cores."

I poked the scapegoat. "Is that a reasonable price?"

"Yes."

The old man's brow was slightly furrowed. Was that concern? He was definitely troubled by something, but he's a big customer! I'll sell it to him. "I have 18 cores."

"4,500 then."

Why was he so good at math? I guess that's why they sent him here, huh? I accepted the 45 bracelets and gave him my pouch.

"…Do you have fat bear cores? I'll buy them for 300 gold each."

Whoa. That's way more than the scapegoat's estimate! "I have twelve."

"3,600 gold." The man gave me 36 bracelets and accepted my last pouch. "I don't suppose you have any spirit beast cores? I'd be willing to buy them for 1,000 gold each."

I don't think I've encountered any spirit beasts yet. "I don't."

"Are you selling anything else?"

"No." I need my engraved bones for personal consumption!

Somewhere along the way of our transactions, the butler-like man's attention had drifted away from the scapegoat completely and focused on me. "You obtained these cores by killing the beasts, right? It was obvious from the bones." I nodded. "Did you hunt the bears by yourself?" I nodded again. The man sucked in his breath. "Then you're at least a low-ranked spirit warrior?"

Am I? I don't know. "Maybe?"

"…That's on par with our magician. Would you … perhaps want to join the Briarwood family as a guest?"

"I'm in the middle of an intense training period right now." It's a shame. Noble families are a lot nicer to work for than the army. If I didn't have to get stronger for Durandal, I'd have totally accepted the offer.

"Can you at least leave me your messenger signature? I'll be willing to buy any future beast cores from you."

"I don't have a messenger." Those are expensive! …But I guess I'm rich now, huh? "…I should buy one." Well, a slave never had a need for one in the first place.

"I have a spare," the man said. He handed me a white tile. "Bind it to yourself."

At least my finger was still bleeding from the earlier cut…? The bleeding stopped? What the heck? And there's no trace of an injury either. But I can still feel the ring down there, so everything that happened definitely wasn't a dream. Well, I'll just cut my finger again and bind this messenger. Gosh, it's like I have a twelfth finger now.

The man tapped a tile against the one in my hand. "I've recorded your signature and stored mine in your messenger. If you need to send me a message, send a stream of consciousness into the artifact, select my signature—I named it Briarwood envoy—and write a message on the surface. Audio messages can be recorded too."

"Okay." I feel like such a fancy person now! An interspacial ring, a shit-ton of money, a messenger. I should go on a spending spree! I'm in a marketplace after all, and money is only useful if it's spent! I poked my scapegoat. "Take me to a magic tool store!"

The scapegoat stiffened. "D-didn't I already say there weren't stores here?"

"Yes, you did, but I wanted to say those lines for a long time." Saying them was almost as good as going to an actual store. Anyways, at least all the sellers have their goods on their hats. ...Even if I can't read them, the scapegoat can. Oh, I should probably take the scapegoat's hat off ... or replace it. Buying combat-oriented magic tools. Will a picture of a sword and shield work? I'll add some squiggly lines. That should do it. Maybe the Briarwood envoy sells tools? "Do you sell magic tools?"

The envoy shook his head. "The Briarwood family only sells interspacial rings for income." He glanced at the sky and frowned. "Well, it was a pleasure meeting you. I didn't catch your name. My name is Poe Briarwood."

My name. Do I lie and tell him something else? What if people connected to Bryant hunt me down? But it's not like I have anything to fear from them! I'm stronger than the generals in the army. "My name is Lucia."

"Just Lucia?"

"...Fluffytail. Lucia Fluffytail." If Snow's ancestor could be named Cottontail, there's nothing wrong with making my last name Fluffytail! And my tail is fluffy. Very, very fluffy. It's a totally fitting name that's not stupid at all.

"Lucia Fluffytail. I'll remember your name." Poe nodded and turned around, disappearing into the crowd of merchants. Was it just me or were there a lot of people looking in my direction? …It seems like they all want to sell me magic tools! Or rob me. Anyways, let's pretend I don't notice them, but if they try anything funny, I'll cut their hands off. I have to hurry up and make my purchases, so I can go back to training faster.

"Come with me, scapegoat."

"Y-yes…"

The scapegoat didn't resist as I dragged her through the market, reading (looking at) the signs on people's heads. "Oh. I almost forgot." I scribbled onto the scapegoat's hat. A picture of a bear's penis.

In an instant, there were a dozen people flocking around us. I had no idea it was such a hot commodity. What other use did bear penises have…? The scapegoat was startled as well. "O-one at a time, please!"

A burly man shoved his way to the front of the crowd. "How much are you selling them for?"

"Ten gold."

The burly man looked at me before turning his attention back to the scapegoat. "Is that right?"

"Y-yes."

"I'll buy twenty!"

…Why would…, you know what, never mind. If people want to buy them, I won't question their life decisions. Right when I was about to take them out, someone shouted, "I'll buy twenty for 12 gold each!"

"15 gold each!"

"20 gold each!"

"I'll trade you my family heirloom which is worth 500 gold for twenty!"

"50 gold each."

The crowd fell silent as a woman dressed in black robes stepped forward, slipping past the crowd like oil through water. No one spoke as the woman flicked her wrist, causing the burly man to be thrown aside. She hadn't even touched him! The woman frowned when she saw the scapegoat. "You're a woman. How could you sell something like this?"

"I-it's not me." The scapegoat pointed at me. "I-it's her."

Wow. I've been sold out by my own scapegoat. But doesn't that mean this person is more intimidating than me? Who is she?

"You, beastkin. This alley may be a black market, but we have some rules. No one's allowed to sell aphrodisiacal materials here."

"…Why not rename this place to slightly gray market then?" Seriously? What kind of black market has rules?

The woman's frown deepened. She flicked her wrist and pointed at me. What the heck? Did she just shove me with magic? How rude.

"…What?" The woman looked at her hand and furrowed her brow. She flicked her finger at me again. I didn't move, but I felt something pushing me. "This…." She turned around and flicked at a random stranger. He was sent flying. "Okay…." She tried to use the magic on me once again without any result. "What's wrong with you?"

"What's wrong with me? What's wrong with you?" Can I justifiably beat her to death in the name of self-defense? "Why are you pushing people with magic?"

"You felt it? I don't understand. The only restrictions on my spell are certain weight limits or…." The woman's eyes widened. "You're a fourth-circle magician?"

…Aren't glorious misunderstandings great? "Yes. That's right."

"Forgive my offenses!" The woman dropped to her knees and knocked her forehead against the ground. Wow. Magicians really hold a lot of sway, huh? "My name is Liana Noctis, third-circle magician. I'm the overseer of this marketplace."

I really understand why Durandal likes bullying people now. It's such a great feeling, ah. ...Does this make me a sadist? I hope not. "Overseer of the marketplace? Help me find some magic tools and I'll forgive you completely. Oh, and buy these penises. You did offer 50 gold for them."

Liana's face cramped. "M-my money's in my office, but I'll take you there right now if you wish, ma'am."

"No, that's okay. I want to buy some tools first."

Liana nodded. "Are there any you have in mind, ma'am?"

"Don't call me ma'am. And I want ten rings with different spells. Another bracelet for my other hand. Two earrings. Goggles! Magical socks and magical shoes. A magical coat and magical gloves. Oh, magical panties and a magical bra as well." Everything I wear must be magical! If I can't learn magic naturally, then I'll use my money to supplement my deficiencies!

"...I understand. But why does a fourth-circle magician need so many magic tools?"

Let's copy Durandal and stare at her until she yields.

"I-I'm sorry I asked. It was out of my bounds. I'm sure you have your reasons, ma'am."

Don't call me ma'am! But anyways, it looks like I can ditch the first scapegoat. I found the boss of the area and made her my lackey. It's smooth sailing from here on out. Maybe she can get me some discounts too. Power is great, isn't it?

8

Magic is an amazing thing. Absolutely, ridiculously, fantastically amazing. I bought a towel that can cast a cleaning spell twice a day, and I have no doubt it'll be the best purchase of my life. All I have to do is wrap myself in it for five seconds, and I and everything on me will be in pristine condition. Yes, it's a simple first-circle magical spell, but it's a life saver for someone like me! Sometimes my grossness would distract me from hunting, especially when my hands would get sticky from all the blood.

"Um, Ms. Fluffytail."

"Hmm?"

The black-robed woman, Liana, lowered her head. "Can we exchange messenger signatures? Since it seems like you like collecting odd magic tools, I'll let you know if I obtain any that might interest you."

…Which one of my tools were odd? Huh!? But, fine. She was immensely useful in finding everything I wanted. "Okay." It feels great to be strong. Everyone wants to be your friend.

After exchanging signatures, Liana saluted me. "I hope we can stay in touch. There aren't many magicians in this area of the pass. We have to stick together."

And she still thinks I'm a fourth-circle magician. Of course, I have no intentions of correcting her misunderstanding. "I'll be busy for a while, but if you need something, leave a message and I'll help if I'm available."

Liana's face brightened. "That's great! I'm glad I met you."

I nodded at her and turned around, facing the exit of the town. As I entered the woods, I could hear Liana muttering, "But what am I going to do with 73 bear penises…?"

I finished hunting the fat bears, crocodiles, and vultures, so it's time to move on to something stronger! And now, I can show off my new equipment! Behold, the legendary second-circle magic fusion combination of Cartography and Eagle Eye, Mini-Map! Just like the name implied, a projection of a miniature map with a blue dot representing my figure appeared in front of me, shooting out of the ring on my thumb. Let's see, Liana marked Wilderness Town with a star, and I have to go southeast to go deeper…. It's that way! Fuck Durandal's intuition training; I know which way is south now!

…Unfortunately, I can only do that once a day. Let's hope I don't lose track until then. But I won't because I'm hyper focused, and even food can't distract me. Why you ask? Because of this new ring I bought which contains the spell, Barbeque! All I have to do is take out a piece of meat, press my ring against it, and shout, "Barbeque!" …Perfection. This is ridiculously delicious. I haven't eaten in who knows how many months. First-circle spells generally consist of spells used to make mundane tasks easier like cooking, cleaning, and waste disposal.

Wait a minute. Didn't I say I wanted combat-oriented spells for my magic tools? Yes, yes I did, but there weren't many because Liana was the only third-circle mage in the area. Most of the tools consisted of first-circle magic, and I was super lucky to obtain Mini-Map which was a combination of two second-circle spells. But Liana did give me a ring that contained an array for her favorite spell, Fling. Apparently, it's custom for weaker mages to give stronger mages spell arrays containing their favorite spell to seek guidance. I think I gave Liana good advice despite not being a mage. I told her to focus on casting the spell in a single area instead of on a whole person. So instead of flinging a person away, she could fling only his leg or his arm to make him lose balance. I'm a genius, aren't I?

But enough self-praise, there's a strange creature in front of me, and I have no clue what it is. It's a dog with two heads and a very pointy tail. Let's smack it. "Breaking Blade!"

Perfect, direct hit! ...Huh? I missed? No, I clearly saw it get hit....

The two-headed dog took a few steps back and growled at me. It pawed at the ground before charging forward and leaping into the air. Alright, it can't dodge if it's off the ground! "Breaking Blade!" Mini-DalDal bisected the dog horizontally, and it died ... is what I'd like to say. But instead, it turned into a puff of smoke and reappeared on the ground away from me where it was standing before. The dog's hackles bristled as both its mouths opened and roared. I prepared myself for its charge. Focus, Lucia! Figure out its technique!

And it ran away.

"...Get back here, you stupid dog! Let me kill you!" No way was I going to let the first prey I encountered escape! Haste! The surroundings blurred as I ran after the dog, gaining on it. If Breaking Blade didn't work, let's try this! "Flying Qi Blade!"

My qi flew straight and true and struck the two-headed dog directly on its butt. It yelped as a cut appeared, leaking blood. It worked! "Flying Qi Blade times 20!" And thus, my first fight against a two-headed dog ended up with an unrecognizable and diced pile of meat. At least there was a beast core—lucky! Let's consume it and spend my qi on engraving the dog's bones. But, first, it's time to use another magic tool! I pressed the ring on my middle finger to the pile of meat. "Dismantle!"

The pile neatly separated itself into shredded skin, piles of bones and teeth, and chunks of meat. How convenient. Thank god magicians are super lazy and invented tools like this for common people like me. The best part about the ring is the blood of beasts can recharge its spell array uses! Now I can spend even less time dismantling corpses, so I can hunt more efficiently! Just you wait, Durandal. I'll become much, much stronger to wake you up as soon as possible. Oh, and I forgot to ask the people in Wilderness Town if they saw Snow. Well, it doesn't matter. If I see him again, I'll kill him, but I'm not going to actively hunt him, not when there's more important things to do. Like getting stronger!

***

I feel stuffy, like my nose is clogged and I can't blow it. But it's for my whole body. Gah! It's driving me insane; what the heck is this feeling!? Did someone curse me? Which bastard was it!? None of these stupid animals could use curses: not the two-headed dogs, not the one-eyed snakes, not the weird eight-legged monkeys with horns, not the stupid, stupid acid-spitting birds in the sky. So why am I feeling this way? Maybe I should ask Liana or that Briarwood envoy. I have no one else to ask after all.

Let's see, where's my messenger?

…cia.

Hmm? That's odd. I thought I heard something.

Lucia….

Okay. That's creepy. Is someone watching me? I don't sense anyone, not even with my web of qi. I recently learned how to do that. If I project my qi outwards like shooting strands out of my body, I can roughly sense everything around me. I guess that's what Durandal meant by high-ranked warriors could control their qi outside of their body. Wait. Durandal?

Yes….

"Durandal!" I grabbed mini-DalDal. Durandal was in here, right? How did I enter it last time? Focus on the hilt and …

whoa. The ball of light I saw last time was shining even brighter than before. There was another orb of light floating around. If I touch it, it's probably going to hurt like last time. "Durandal?"

"Touch the orb, Lucia."

…Dammit. Even when you're asleep, you want me to feel pain, huh? "Are you awake?" I miss you, you stupid sword spirit. You said you'd never leave me. Well, I guess you didn't. But falling asleep for however long it's been is just as bad!

"Fading … consciousness…. Touch the orb…. Get stronger. Lucia, I'll … be waiting."

Just what does Durandal have in store for me now? Please don't be painful, please don't be painful. Deep breaths, Lucia. And … touch it. Gah! Motherfucker! It hurts! It wasn't this painful before! Last time it was like someone hammering open my head. This time, it's like someone's using a chisel to chip away at every single one of my bones at once! I can't feel my limbs. All I can feel is pain. Everything is pain. I am pain. I'm dying. Dying….

It was nighttime when I woke up. A circle of dead animal corpses surrounded me. My body was drenched in blood, and the ground was dark and damp. Did I do this? I sat up and looked around. I'm no stranger to slaughter, but even I thought this scene was a bit gruesome. The animals looked as if they had been torn apart by teeth and claws. Some weren't even recognizable. Mini-DalDal was still strapped to my back, and it didn't seem like it had been used much. My nails on the other hand…, they were pointed, sharp, and curved like a panther's. There was also lots of dried blood and flesh underneath them. Gross.

And there's a metallic taste in my mouth—blood, I guess? It had been an extremely long time since I last slept, and I woke up to something like this. Oh, hey! The stuffiness is gone. I feel great! But first, let's check what kind of nasty surprise Durandal gave me. It better be worth all that pain and suffering I went through. I inspected my body while gathering the corpses. Unfortunately, most of them were so torn apart that the dismantle spell didn't work. But I did find a decent number of beast cores.

My body didn't change much after being tortured by Durandal. Was the orb a prank? I'll review my techniques: Breaking Blade, qi projection, Steady Mountain Footwork, Unrelenting Path of Slaughter, the art of bone engraving. Wait. Hold on a second. What the heck is Unrelenting Path of Slaughter!? When did I pick up something so ominous?

A dull drone rang in my head, followed by an eerie voice. "Listen well, Lucia. You've reached the peak of high-ranked warrior, and without guidance, you'd've been stuck there forever. I forcibly broke you through to low-ranked spirit warrior. Unfortunately, I have no idea what path you'll unlock. Your path will reflect the actions you've done while reaching the peak. Continue following your path until you become a high-ranked spirit warrior."

That was an awfully convenient explanation. I guess this is part of the benefits of inheriting the Godking's legacy—an easy pass to the next rank. And—

"Oh. If I wake up and find out your path is something stupid like the path of sloth or the path of 'hey look, an acorn', then I'm disowning you."

Phew. Good thing I seriously invested my time and energy into improving myself. So what exactly can I do with this Unrelenting Path of Slaughter? This is something spirit warriors unlock, right? Should I know how to use it instinctively?

"To activate your path, send your qi to your forehead and follow the sensation. Your qi will want to flow a certain way. Allow it to."

…You're actually awake, aren't you, Durandal?

"I'm not awake. This is my last message until I wake up. Lucia, there's something I have to tell you. I…, actually, no. When the time comes, I'll tell you in person."

What the heck! You can't do that! What were you going to say!? "Answer me, Durandal! You bastard!!! That was totally a confession flag!" Gah! Forget it. Focus. Send my qi into my forehead and follow the path…? Oh, that feels comfortable. Close my eyes, relax my shoulders, lightly bend my knees, tilt my neck upwards, open my mouth and howl at the sky. …What the heck is this qi path making me do?

When I opened my eyes, my vision was white. There were a few black outlines of trees and leaves and rocks and the dead bodies around me, but the contents were white. Everything was black and white like a child's drawing.

Slaughter….

The space I stood on turned red. Red footprints sprawled outwards from me like a spider web, staining the white landscape.

Blood….

My legs moved without my permission, stepping into one of the red footprints. The rest of the paths disappeared except for the one I took. My other leg advanced forward, stepping into the next footprint, then another. What exactly was this supposed to do? Well, I couldn't do anything except follow the path laid out before me.

Without listening to me, my body continued forward, following the path of red footprints, slowly at first. By the time I figured out the path was leading me to a two-headed dog, the beast was already dead, killed by my body's actions. The beast had a differing appearance than everything else in the world of black and white. Its outline was orange while its insides were gray. Red lines had appeared in its silhouette, and mini-DalDal cut through them like a hot knife through butter, killing it instantly. This was the power of the Unrelenting Path of Slaughter?

Thankfully, my body stored the corpse of the beast inside the interspacial ring. After it did that, another web of red footprints appeared around me, but my body didn't move by itself this time. Was it telling me to copy its actions? I picked a path to the right of me and took a step forward. And I promptly lost all control of my body again. What the heck!? This is *my* body, you stupid path!

My body ran with the footsteps despite my best attempts at stopping it, and I arrived in front of three eight-legged, horned monkeys. The number of red lines on their bodies were less than the dogs, but my body still took action and cut one apart with mini-DalDal. The other two horned monkeys opened their mouths. Stupid body, cover my ears! The monkeys had a stupidly loud howl that stunned me and made me see white the first time I fought against them. …And my body wasn't listening to me at all! Cover your ears, dammit!

The monkeys pounded their hands against their chests and closed their mouths. Huh? There was no howl? Now that I think about it…, I haven't heard any sounds or smelled anything since I activated the path. And if I really think hard about it like a crow instead of a squirrel, was I really seeing? I can only see the bare minimum of everything. While I thought about my vision, my body moved forward and cut along the red lines on one of the monkeys, killing the beast effortlessly. When my head turned towards the final monkey, there were more red lines on it. Did the Unrelenting Path of Slaughter discover new weaknesses?

Whether they were weaknesses or not, it didn't change the fact that the third monkey was killed against my will. My body stored the three monkeys inside of my ring and stood still. Once again, a web of red footsteps appeared around me.

I refuse to pick! Give me back my body!

Choose….

Shut up, creepy voice! I choose independence!

Choose….

No.

Choose....

I refuse.

Choose....

I won't.

Choose....

Aren't you tired of saying the same thing over and over?

Choose....

...Aren't you going to control me anyway? Does it matter which path I pick? Hey, the paths are changing. I guess they reflect where the beasts at the end are? If they're moving around, the path to reach them should change.

Choose....

Why don't you let me control my own body first? Can't we be friends, creepy voice? We're stuck together after all.

Choose....

You're not listening to me at all. A partnership can't work without communication!

Choose....

...

Choose....

I think I figured out why it was called the Unrelenting Path of Slaughter instead of the normal Path of Slaughter.

Choose....

Fine! Dammit! I don't have time to waste on fighting myself when there's a sleeping prince waiting for me to bring him back to life with a kiss! A figurative kiss, that is. Mhm. Totally.

Choose....

Gah! I already said I'll pick! I chose the path leading straight ahead and took a step. Once again, I lost control of my body. This time, I paid careful attention to how my body moved. All of its movements followed the Steady Mountain Footwork, using them more effectively than I could. How's that fair!? ...I'm not jealous of my own body. Even when my body engaged in combat with the massive one-eyed snake, its movements were more efficient. I would've chosen to fight it at a distance, slowly wearing it down with long-ranged qi blades, but the Unrelenting Path of Slaughter dove straight in, disregarding the danger. The spikes on the snake flashed and tried to impale me, but my body avoided them with the distance of a hair's breadth. It even had time to counterattack, striking at the red lines on the snake.

You stupid path! This is my body! What are you going to do if you injure it!? Stop fighting so recklessly!

Never negotiate. Always attack. Evade everything. Don't defend. Simply slaughter.

Fuck you! The best offense is an impenetrable defense! Stop risking my life like—gah! If you mistimed that dodge just now, I'd be sterile! Release me right now! Give me back my body! Of course, the Unrelenting Path of Slaughter didn't listen to me as it continued to practically glue itself to the snake where the danger was the highest. When the snake was dead and its corpse was stored in my interspacial ring, another web of footprints spread out around me.

Your turn....

Really. Is it really my turn, you shitty voice? How about this? I took a step on the white ground outside of any of the red footprints. ...And I lost control of my body again. One dead acid-spitting bird later, I was once again presented with a 'choice' of different paths.

Follow the path....

Will I gain control of my body if I do?

Follow the path....

Answer my questions, dammit!

...Yes.

What. It answered? Fine, I'll follow your stupid path to get back my own body. Since Durandal gave me this path, it can't be something that'll want to hurt me, right? Actually, knowing Durandal..., this path is definitely going to be painful in some way, shape, or form. But what else can I do but believe its words? After thirty footsteps, I messed up one of my movements and fell off the path, losing control of my body once again. It seems like it'll be a long time from now before I'll regain control of my limbs.

***

I'm a murderer. Well, I already was a murderer when I killed Bryant and his guards, but now I'm even more of a murderer. Stupid Path of Slaughter. I'll just pretend those silhouettes were a pack of suspiciously human-looking species of monkey! That's what they were. Totally. They weren't humans. Just monkeys. Maybe spirit beasts. Mhm.

Anyways! On the bright side, I managed to finally gain complete control of my body! It only took 176 tries on my own. Well, I say it only took 176 tries, but that's when I stopped counting. My bones of focus wore off even though I had over 700 hours of them, and I'm not quite sure how many—oh, look, an acorn! …I should consume another focus bone. My body used bones of strength quite naturally during the path, but it didn't use any bones of focus.

That was a horrible experience. I never want to do that again, but I suspect I'll have to. Durandal did say that I had to follow the path to become stronger, and to be fair, I did get stronger after this path ended. I know what steps to take for the most efficient actions, but I still don't like fighting so dangerously. My ass, don't defend. I still firmly believe getting hurt is the worst thing you can do in a fight! Defense and evasion are definitely the most important aspects to winning.

Okay, now that I consumed a focus bone, it's time to dismember the corpses that I obtained during those hundreds of fights. Maybe. My body stopped picking them up and only took out the cores after a while. Someone's going to have a field day when they find dozens of ferocious beasts' corpses lying around. …All those penises I could've sold. The pelts and organs are valuable too! Do you know how many years my family could've lived off of with five gold!? …Neither do I because I was too young to understand, but still. It's a lot.

Somewhere along the way, I ended up out of the two-headed dog, one-eyed snake, eight-legged horned monkey, and acid-spitting bird territory by following the path. Recently, I've been killing massive beasts. Massive, massive beasts. Like I've killed more moonlight wolves, but they were the size of fat bears. Shadow panthers are also here again, but they're all patterned with green stripes and brown splotches. But there's no scavenger crows, or I haven't heard them because I can't hear sounds while I'm on the Path of Slaughter. So, I think it's safe to say I advanced to an area comprised of spirit beasts. Which means their cores are that much more valuable!

I consumed a moonlight wolf core and took out one of the two-headed dog corpses. Haste! It's time to dismantle everything and clear some space in my interspacial ring. I feel like a hoarder. Squirrels are normally hoarders, but that doesn't mean I have to fall into the stereotype! Dismantle! Dismantle! Dismantle! Dismantle! Dis…, huh? It didn't work? I thought it was supposed to recharge from beast blood. …Was I scammed?

Barbeque! Clean! Mini-Map! Barrier! Why isn't anything working!? Stupid fraudulent sellers! I'll destroy that town, just you wait! But first, I'll send a hateful message to Liana for selling me broken goods and then dismantle all of this crap by hand. So much blood and gore and intestines and gross smells. Oh wells. And I can't even have a feast since barbeque isn't working. My life is tragic.

Take out the core, carve some runes, set aside the hides and pelts. Throw the meat in a pile to act as bait for more beasts and pray nothing too dangerous comes out to kill me. I wonder how normal mercenaries do this work. It can't be that all of them have interspacial rings that let them carry things around, right? That thing costs 10,000 gold after all. You could buy a mansion in the capital for that much! Maybe they just don't hunt as many as I do in one go. Yeah, that must be it.

Ding!

Oh, Liana responded? Let's see, how do I, oh, there we go. Her handwriting's super neat! Too bad I can't read! Thankfully, there's an audio playback function.

Dear Lucia Fluffytail,

I've sent out people to apprehend the salesmen of the magic tools, but if they really were scammers, then the possibility of finding them will be low. But, with all due respect, I don't think anyone would sell a fake ring for a single gold. Perhaps it's been a while since you've used magic tools and forgot to tell your apprentice the rules? I've sent you them, so you can easily copy and send them to your apprentice.

1. Every tool can only be used a certain number of times per day.

2. Breaking rule 1 in any way will decrease the durability of the item: this includes sending your own mana into it, replenishing it with beast cores.

3. All magic tools share the same mana around you. If multiple tools are used in the same vicinity, the mana will be used up. This is also why beast cores are necessary for magical warfare.

4. If the array inside of the tool is tampered with, the tool may explode. Be wary.

Sincerely,
Liana Noctis

Hm. Maybe I don't have to destroy Wilderness Town. At least the rules are helpful; why didn't Snow tell me about them? And it seems like Liana still thinks I'm a fourth-circle magician. I'm never going to correct that misunderstanding. Anyways, there's only like four dozen more beasts to dismember....

Three dozen....

Two dozen....

One dozen....

Half a..., oh god. It's the ferocious monkeys that suspiciously look like humans. Do I..., do I dismantle them too? They're a rare breed of spirit beasts, right...? I've dismantled all the beasts so far, it'd be a waste to dispose of these. After all, they aren't human. Yeah. If I don't dismantle them, then that's admitting they were humans and not beasts. I'm not a murderer. They're already half torn apart anyway. You can do this, Lucia! Sing a song—sing a happy song. A nice cheerful tune to distract yourself as you check their brains for beast cores.

"Food is great. Food is tasty.
I like my bread, nice and pasty.
Porridge is bland. Peppers are sweet.
But my favorite ... is a cut of meat!"

All done! And there were no beast cores, but that's perfectly normal! Not all spirit beasts have beast cores! These ferocious monkeys were not humans, not humans at all!

"Oh my god."

Eh!? Who!? Someone snuck up on me? I must've been too distracted by the dismantling process. It's a shirtless human and a wolf-headed man...? The human looks a little familiar....

9

"Oh my god."

Those were the first words out of my mouth when I saw Durandal's new master. After a year of tracking Durandal down with Gae Bulg's sometimes faulty sense of smell, cutting down dozens upon dozens of ferocious beasts, and living a lifestyle more suited to a vagrant than a prince, we finally caught up to the culprit who allegedly caused Bryant's death and claimed Durandal as his, no, her own. A beastkin with docile traits. How did she manage to overpower Bryant and his entourage to claim Durandal? I'd understand if she were a lion or a wolf or even a crow, but a squirrel? And what was she doing? Dismembering a group of mercenaries while singing a song about food?

"...You look familiar. Have I met you before?" The beastkin lowered the skull that was in her hands and placed it on the ground. Half of a rune was engraved on it. A rune of focus, perhaps?

"Lan." Gae Bulg's rough voice drew my attention away from the macabre sight of the squirrelkin girl covered in blood and gore. "The sword in her hand. It's Durandal's weapon body."

The squirrelkin girl's tail stiffened. No, her whole body stiffened. She slowly stood up and brushed aside the dead mercenaries with the sword in her hand. "Who are you?"

"I am Lan Ravenwood. I believe you killed my brother." It seems like a fight is inevitable. I didn't want to clash with Durandal's new owner, but she doesn't seem like the type of person to communicate through words. Her body's drenched in blood, and there are corpses by her feet. I don't have to be

193

paranoid to know she's going to try to kill me as well, especially since Gae Bulg mentioned Durandal's name.

"Lan Ravenwood? Your brother? I have no idea what you're talking about. None at all. Nope." The squirrelkin girl shook her head repeatedly. "I think you have the wrong person. And what was that bit about Durandal? This sword? This is just a cheap iron sword I bought from a street vendor in Wilderness Town. If this were Durandal, the legendary sword of the Godking, would I be using it to dismantle spirit beasts?"

Oi. Spirit beasts? You're not dismantling spirit beasts at all. "Those are humans."

"Huh? These things?" The squirrelkin girl bent over and picked up the skull she was engraving. "This is a spirit beast. Well, it was a spirit beast. It's just a corpse now."

Was she serious? Delusional? Or did she think I was a fool? "What kind of spirit beasts are those? I've never seen any with a skeletal structure like that."

"A super-duper rare species of monkey! They imitate humans, but they're actually beasts in disguise!" The squirrelkin girl nodded her head. "It's very dangerous in the southern pass. There's even crows that pretend to be human to lure you to your death."

That was true. The first time I heard one of those crows speak, I really thought a little girl was dying. "Then … disregarding the spirit beasts." I glanced at Gae Bulg. His eyes were red and saliva dripped from his partially open mouth. "Are you sure that's Durandal?"

"I will never forget his scent," Gae Bulg said and reached into his bag. He opened his mouth wide and roared in a voice I never heard from him before. "Durandal! Come out here and face me like a man! I demand a rematch!"

The squirrelkin girl and Gae Bulg stared at each other. The squirrelkin girl cleared her throat and asked me, "Is your companion right in the head? I know wolfkin men are a bit challenged up there"—she pointed at her skull—"but isn't it obvious that there's no one else here?"

I frowned at her. "Roland's Authentic Ice Cream Shop."

The squirrelkin girl flinched.

"So it really was you." As I thought. Gae Bulg's nose was on point. She was trying to deceive us.

"N-no. I have no idea what you're talking about. I only flinched because you spoke in a really intimidating manner!"

"With the authority bestowed to me by the king, I, Lan Ravenwood, declare you a criminal and put you under arrest!" I can't believe she had me fooled even if it was for a brief moment. I'm embarrassed. How can I proclaim to be paranoid if I almost trust the words of a stranger no matter how persuasive they are? "Gae! Help me subdue her."

"Don't underestimate me! I, Snow Flopsy, will never yield to the likes of you!" the squirrelkin girl shouted out her name before dashing towards us. "Breaking Blaaaaade!"

Weak! A spear will always beat a sword! It's a simple matter of distance and force! "Path of the Spear: Piercing Thrust!" I concentrated my qi into the tip of my spear and followed the blue trajectory painted out in front of my eyes. There was no way I was going to lose to a beastkin as a mid-ranked spirit warrior! I'll pretend to aim for the tip of her sword and dive down to pierce her thigh. Even the most skilled generals can't evade my feints! "Huh?"

Snow Flopsy used her sword tip to follow my spear, positioning her blade in front of her leg. How sharp was her dynamic vision? But that didn't matter. "Pierce through, Gae Bulg!" Even if her blade is blocking my spear from stabbing her leg, she has no leverage to stop my force. My spearhead struck the side of her blade and pierced…, eh, stopped? She blocked my strike?

The muscles on the squirrelkin girl's arm bulged as veins popped up on the surface of her skin. She gritted her teeth. "Ten, ton, swing!"

I held onto my spear and pushed against her blade as she lifted her arms, but it didn't do anything. I was lifted off the ground and blown backwards. Her sword didn't touch me, but the pressure against my spear and the resulting gust of air managed to throw me above the surrounding treetops.

"Lan!" Gae Bulg shouted from down below, but he faded into mist as his spirit body left the allowable range of his weapon body. How far was I going to be launched? Snow Flopsy…, I'll remember this.

***

Run away! I almost lost my leg there! If it weren't for the fact that Durandal fought me with a spear in all our spars, I probably wouldn't have been able to react to that strike. Durandal's foresight is amazing. I wonder how I'd fare against a sword user…. Anyways, it seems like I've finally been tracked down. And by the sixth prince, the man known as the training freak. Why the heck did he leave the palace? I thought he was one of those people who never left their rooms except to eat and use the bathroom. I've only heard rumors about him from the army members. On the days the generals had to spar against him, they always had a bad mood afterwards when commanding the army, which, of course, led to bad moods from everyone all around. It's all his fault I suffered in the army! I should beat him up! …But he has a spirit weapon, and Durandal's out of commission. Fine. Guess I'll just have to keep running. And I forgot to gather those super-rare corpses of the not humans before I left. Oops.

But this is a really big problem, isn't it? If the prince is chasing me, the royal family has to know about Durandal's existence. Gah! Stupid Snow! Why'd you have to betray me at a time like this!? Couldn't you have waited, you bastard? I have to get stronger, a lot stronger if I want to survive. I'm lucky it was the sixth prince that chased after me and not the others. I've heard the first prince is a sixth-circle magician, which would've been a lot harder to deal with than Lan. I guess Lan and I are pretty similar, huh?

"Snow. Flopsy! Get back here!"

Gah! Didn't I launch him really far away!? How did he catch up so quickly? Haste! …Darn. My magic tools still aren't working. How much of the surrounding mana did I use up while dismantling those bodies?

"Gae! Chase her down!"

Large crashing noises came from behind me. Eep! Run faster, legs, run faster! Let's use a bone engraved with speed while I'm at it. I almost forgot I had these. Maybe I should continue wearing them around my body so I never forget. A large boulder flew past my head and crashed into a tree, breaking the trunk and causing it to topple over. What the heck!? If that hit my head, I definitely would've died. I peeked behind myself and saw a rabid wolfkin lunging after me on all fours. "Gah! Breaking Blade!"

The lunging wolfkin collided against my sword with the spear he held in his mouth. How strong are his jaws? Isn't that a bit too excessive? His eyes widen as a shockwave rippled outwards, blowing away the dirt and pebbles by my feet. Then, he flew into the air much like Lan had when I struck his spear.

"Gae! Return!" The wolfkin's body disappeared mid-flight as Lan continued to run after me. Why was a human so fast? He was almost as fast as me! But I suppose princes get all the resources required to raise them. While I only started to use beast cores when I obtained Durandal, the sixth prince was probably eating them right out of the womb. That's not fair. "Gae! Chase her down!"

Doesn't he get tired of repeating the same commands? Jeez. The wolfkin sprung out of his spear and lunged towards me again like a hound chasing a hare. "Breaking Blade!"

Our weapons collided once again and he was launched—
"Gae! Return! Gae! Chase her down!"—and instantly lunged
at me again. What the hell is this infinite respawn cheat!?

Try respawning after I break your face! "Breaking Blade!"
I avoided the wolfkin's spear and struck towards his ugly mug.
He turned his head away and my blade collided with the shaft
of the spear in his mouth. This time, my sword cut deep into
his shoulder after forcing his spear back. Suck it! That should
definitely slow his respawn time.

"Path of the Spear: 1,000 Talons!"

Gah! Lan caught up while I was dealing with his stupid
spirit! My vision was filled with hundreds of spearheads flying
towards me, each one attacking from a different angle.
Durandal's training never prepared me for this! "Barrier!"

…And there was still no mana in the vicinity to use my
magical bracelet. I'm throwing these stupid dismantling and
barbequing rings away! I did my best to block the strikes
while retreating, lowering mini-DalDal's weight to maneuver
it as fast as possible, but dozens of cuts appeared on my skin
and dress. Dammit! I liked this dress too. At least I'm able to
keep my vital spots safe. Durandal drilled protecting my
organs and joints into me through lots of pain and head pats. I
can't disappoint him!

Lan's expression turned fierce like a constipated tiger as
he stopped his attacks. "Path of the Spear: Mirage Thrusts!"
His spear disappeared and reappeared in front of my face.

"Not the face!" I barely managed to avoid it while
shouting. What kind of prince was he!? Doesn't he know a
woman's most important part is her face!? This bastard…. I
didn't even do anything to you except kill your brother!
…Which is pretty bad I guess, but it was totally Durandal's
fault. Speaking of Durandal, can he please deus ex machina
and save my ass sometime soon?

No.

Dammit, Durandal! Don't answer me when you're supposed to be asleep! What other attacks do I have? "Flying Qi Blade!" I fired a blade of qi towards Lan, but his weapon spirit lunged forward and absorbed it with his chest. A bloody line appeared. His shoulder hadn't even recovered, but he didn't seem hurt at all. The wolfkin's eyes were red and staring at me and—gah! Another invisible spear to the face! "W-wait, dammit! What do you want from me!?"

"Stop resisting arrest!" Lan shouted and stabbed another vanishing spear strike at me.

Arrest!? You're trying to kill me! "I'm resisting my death!"

"Then die peacefully!"

Fuck. My shoulder. Why did he aim there when the last three strikes were at my face? A hole in my shoulder dripped blood as my left arm went limp. The wolfkin lunged at me, stabbing his spear towards my chest. I barely managed to block it with mini-DalDal, raising its weight to my limit of 13 tons. The wolfkin bounced off the sword, but he also knocked me off my feet. Damn. This isn't good. This isn't good at all. Consume a bone of strength to recover!

Oddly enough, Lan didn't stop me from using a consumable. Instead, he ran over to his weapon spirit and poured a red liquid onto the spirit's wounds. …Well, I guess I'm not the only one with recovery items. "Can we, uh, talk about this?"

"I don't trust savages!" Lan's voice rose as he thrust forward with his spear. Kuh, why is his range so much longer than mine? It's not fair at all. I can't win if I can't hurt him…. Then I just have to get close?

Dammit. I really didn't want to do this. "Unrelenting Path of Slaughter!"

***

"Unrelenting Path of Slaughter!" Snow Flopsy shouted and raised her sword into the air. She was actually a spirit warrior? It did make sense considering Bryant was a high-ranked warrior. But judging by the usage of her path, she was only a low-ranked spirit warrior at most. She hadn't incorporated any of her techniques with it, but it was a bit unnerving an unknown beastkin had a prefix attached to her path. Even I didn't have one.

"Lan, be careful," Gae Bulg said as he took the spear out of his mouth and stood up on two legs. Though he didn't show it, he must've been sore from the repeated unsummoning and summoning. But it was worth it to catch up to the prey. "She's extremely strong. I think her body may be a divine one." Gea Bulg's hackles were raised, but his eyes were clear. How strong was she? It took a lot to smack Gae Bulg out of his berserk state.

The squirrelkin girl's expression turned from one filled with desperation to a calm one. Her eyes became completely white as she exhaled, lifting her sword. Her posture, which was slouched over before, relaxed even further as her knees and elbows bent while she leaned forward. Why was I giving her time to adjust to her path? Strike while the iron is hot! "Path of the Spear: Lightning Stab!"

Lightning Stab, my fastest long-ranged attack, combined with Gae Bulg's harassment from the side, I don't believe she can defend herself from this—path or not! But she didn't even try to defend. Snow Flopsy charged forwards with no regard to her life, narrowly evading my spear qi. The tip cut off some of her hairs as it brushed by her head, but her expression remained unchanged. Gae Bulg moved in front of her way and thrust his spear downwards, aiming at her abdomen. She didn't flinch as the spear pierced through her stomach, and she exchanged blows with Gae Bulg, swinging her sword diagonally upwards, cutting off Gae's left arm and head.

"Gae!" My weapon spirit dissolved into mist before flowing back into the shaft of my spear. He wouldn't die from something like that, but he'd be out of commission for at least a month—most likely more. How dare she! "I'll kill you!" Since Gae disappeared, his spear embedded in Snow's stomach had disappeared as well, but there was no way she was fine after taking a blow like that. Gae gave up a month of his time for my victory, I won't let him down.

"Path of the Spear: 1,000 Talons!" My most prided technique, 1,000 Talons. It took me four years of harsh training every day to perfect it, and when I did, I broke through the barrier of high-ranked warrior to spirit warrior by unlocking the Path of the Spear. With this strike, I'll avenge Gae's pseudo death!

Dozens of holes instantly appeared on Snow's body as she recklessly charged into the barrage of spear strikes. At this rate, she'd die without a complete corpse. But why was I feeling so uneasy like my older brother was watching me? I ignored the feeling and pushed through with my technique. With Durandal in my grasp, I wouldn't have to worry about Algar even if he was spying on me right now. Wait. Durandal? Why hadn't she called him out? Was she waiting for this moment?

Snow's mouth opened in a silent scream as she lifted her sword despite the numerous holes in her arms. No words came out, but I could tell she was shouting, "Breaking Blade!" as qi surged into her sword's edge. When had she gotten so close to me? How could she move with injuries like those!? My stance shifted from an offensive one to a defensive one, and I held Gae's weapon body horizontally in front of myself to block her strike. It was then that I remembered the words of my first teacher, a famous mercenary with one arm: Never underestimate someone's final struggle for life. Even rabbits will fight back if they're cornered. And never underestimate a dying beast's death throes.

Snow's blade crashed against the shaft of my spear. My arms creaked and felt like they were going to break. My shoulders popped out of their sockets as I was forced to my knees. Her strength really was terrifying! Gae Bulg and her blade continued to shriek and shoot out sparks as she pressed down harder. As if a mountain had descended on me, Gae Bulg's weapon body crashed into my chest, my arms breaking, unable to support my spear any longer. My vision turned yellow as Snow straddled my torso and lifted her sword with a reverse grip, pointing it at my head. The lines of my vision blurred, pulsing with a black light. I barely managed to choke out the word, "T-teleport."

As a scion of the royal family, I was given a ring that doubled as a magic tool. Embedded in it was the seventh-circle magic, teleport. A safety net in case anything ever went awry. I've experimented with it a few times, and I always felt nauseous after every use, but what was worse, death or nausea? But the familiar sensation of needing to vomit didn't come. Snow was still straddled on my torso and her sword was plunging towards my head. Why? Why wasn't it working?

It's funny how time moves so slowly when you're about to die. Dozens of thoughts can flash through your mind that would take you a minute to process under normal circumstances. Almost like a dream. Now that I think about it, Bryant also had a ring of teleportation, didn't he? Yet he still died, most likely to this very person. Why did I think I would escape the same fate? I was too rash. Arrogant. Did I underestimate Snow from the start based on her appearance? How could I declare myself the paranoid prince? …It was Durandal. The thought of obtaining the Godking's legacy, ending the stress of competing for the throne, was too tempting. I gambled, and I lost.

And Snow did say she wanted to talk. If I had accepted her offer, would I still be in this situation? No, I would've made the same decision if I was given another chance. I couldn't trust her. If she had tried to kill me after I lowered my guard, then that would've been even worse. This might be too much to ask for, but I hope she'll take care of Gae Bulg. After all these years of living with the constant threat of death looming overhead, I can finally rest.

***

...There's an awful lot of rare spirit beasts out there, huh? This one could even use a spear, and it summoned another rare spirit beast that was a wolf on the verge of becoming a human. How scary. Surprisingly, I managed to complete the Path of Slaughter in one try and regained control of my body after slaying the beast. I can't believe this rare beast tried chasing me down; it doesn't happen often. I'm scrawny and the meat to bone ratio on my cute adorable figure is not worth the effort of hunting me down.

Lan who? The sixth prince? Why are you bringing up totally unrelated names? Lan's a training freak who never leaves his room. He's in the palace, working hard to become a bodybuilder. This spear contains a weapon spirit? What spear? You mean the one I'm hacking to pieces with mini-DalDal since I'm afraid of more rare spirit beasts being summoned? Oh, look! A spirit seed popped out of the spear! This is the first one I've found by myself; I've seen quite a few on street vendor stalls in the capital.

I can use it on my dress! ...There's a lot of holes in my dress. Is it still viable? You can only see most of my underwear underneath it.... Maybe I won't use it on my dress. I can use it on..., hold on a second; first order of business, remove all the useless magical rings! I'll keep the Mini-Map and Fling rings and put away the rings with Dismantle, Barbeque, Steam, Stir-Fry, Boil..., don't judge my choices! Anyways, that doesn't leave me many options to bury this seed into. Hmm. I'll hold onto it for now then.

Now, let's see what items this rare spirit beast had. If it dressed like a human, it should definitely have some useful stuff! Like that ring. And its clothes. Maybe its underwear too…. I think I'll take everything on it and appraise them later. Yes, that's the best course of action. Let's see…, take this stick and draw on the ground. A picture of a rabbitkin woman with a penis escaping from a net. There we go. Just in case someone mistakes the beast for an actual person, they'll blame Snow instead.

But I really need to buy new clothes. This dress is way too breezy and risqué now. I'll start wearing those bones again. It'll prevent me from being indecent and provide easy access to consumables, win-win! I hope Durandal wakes up soon…. Oh! What if I use the spirit seed to nourish Durandal's spirit? Would that work? …I'll ask Liana; where's my messenger?

While I distanced myself from the crime scene, err, hunting spot, my messenger rang.

Dear Lucia Fluffytail,

I'm sorry, I don't know much about spirit seeds. They weaken the arrays inside of magic tools, so no respectable mage will employ them. You may have better luck asking a martial artist, but I doubt they would know either. Why are you trying to save an injured spirit? Weapons are meant to be thrown away after they're broken.

Sincerely,
Liana Noctis

No! Ms. Encyclopedia has failed me. And who are you calling a broken weapon!? Durandal's just sleeping! I'm going to do it. I believe in Durandal! I grabbed the new spirit seed and pressed it into mini-DalDal's hilt. There was a bright flash of light, and a second later, the spirit seed popped out and fell to the ground. I guess it won't work. Darn. Well, if spirit seeds can only be used on non-magical items, then I'll grow this one in my socks. Magical socks and shoes were the only articles of clothing I couldn't find in the wilderness town. ...Yes, my underwear is magical too. But their functions are for me to know! ...Pervert.

Anyways, how do I bury the seed in my sock? I'll just step on it and see if it works. Oh? It did! A dog's paw print appeared on both of my socks. I guess it counted a pair as a single item. But I thought armor spirits were supposed to take a long time to grow; could I summon it right away? Let's try it. "Come out, Mr. or Mrs. Spirit!"

...

...

...

Now I feel stupid. I guess it really does have to take time to grow. I wonder what it'll become. I obtained the seed off a spear that could summon a rare spirit beast after all. Maybe I'll get a spirit similar to the beast it summoned. Yeah. "It's still a bit sad I couldn't feed it to Durandal...."

"So you're really Durandal's new owner."

"Gah!?" I fell over as a wolfkin appeared underneath my feet. "You're the rare spirit beast!"

"...I'm the weapon spirit, Gae Bulg. Throw away all notions of me being a mere spirit beast." The wolfkin frowned and looked around. "Where is my weapon body?"

"Um. You're a sock spirit now...." I pointed at my socks.

"Huh? Wait. What happened? Where's Lan?" The wolfkin's hackles bristled as he glared at me. His eyes turned red as he reached behind his back and drew a spear...-shaped sock.

"Lan? Who's that?" Deny everything! Lan's in his room in the palace training away like usual! I killed a rare spirit beast that enjoyed impersonating people. Mhm.

"You. Didn't I stab you through the stomach?"

"Nope." Ignore the blood on the dress, please. "Wrong person."

"What happened to Lan!?" The wolfkin dashed forward and grabbed my shoulders. Ah, his hands are soft. He feels like Bouncykins. Are all sock spirits as soft as him?

"Look, Mr. Wolfie, I don't know who Lan is. This is my first time meeting you." Lie with a straight face! Durandal would be proud!

"You called me a rare spirit beast!" His claws pressed against my skin. Oh, that's pretty comfortable. I wonder how nice Durandal's head pats would feel if he turned into a sock spirit too. "Where. Is. Lan!?"

"Return from whence you came!"

The wolfkin's eyes widened before his body distorted and disappeared into my socks like water spiraling down a drain. Wow. I didn't think that'd actually work. "I'll let you out when you learn not to ask totally irrelevant questions."

10

After experimenting with the Unrelenting Path of Slaughter for a while, I realized it's really not that bad. All I have to do is initiate it right when I see a beast to prevent myself from picking fights against rare spirit beasts or creatures that may be too scary to fight against. There've been a lot of those recently. That stupid spear-wielding rare spirit beast chased me really far into the southern pass, and a lot of the beasts I've seen recently have been emitting auras similar to Durandal. I tried going back north using my handy dandy mini-map spell, but... I managed to get lost. First there was an army of bear-sized ants marching in a line that I couldn't go past, so I tried walking around them. Then there was a river with—well, it doesn't matter what the river had because I can't swim. After that, I encountered a mountain with molten rock spewing from its peak. I kind of gave up trying to go north after that. So I've been stuck hunting beasts that can almost kill me, and I've been running away from the beasts that are as scary as Durandal. I've named them Beastrandals.

And thus, that's how I ended up fighting a giant lizard with splotchy green and yellow skin with mucus-like substances dripping out of its mouth. Recently, even when I mess up my steps in the Unrelenting Path of Slaughter, I still have full control of my body which is a bit scary because the path used to always bail me out when I was about to die. But I guess it's a path for a reason and not a cheat that allows me to win every fight. Darn.

"Let me out! I want to fight it!"

"Shut up, you stupid sock spirit! I'm busy!" And I regret planting that spirit seed into my socks. He's very loud, annoying, never shuts up about some person named Lan, and completely not my type. If it weren't for the fact that he made my socks super comfortable, I would've thrown him away a long time ago. "Breaking Blade!"

Whew. It only took thirty Breaking Blades to cut off the lizard's head. How tough is its skin? I bet I could make a house out of it and not worry about it breaking for the foreseeable future. I've also learned through experience that there's a limit to how much I can store inside of my interspacial ring. So I only harvest the most valuable portions of the beasts I've slain.

"Stop cutting off animals' penises!"

"I'll cut off yours too if you don't stop nagging me! Gold doesn't grow on trees!"

"Did you do this to Lan!?"

"I didn't cut his off! I don't even know who Lan is!"

"He's the spearman who owned me previously!"

"Stop shouting at me!" See? Isn't he obnoxiously loud and annoying? Why couldn't he be more considerate like Durandal? "I don't know any spearmen."

"...Are you alright in the head?"

"Don't call me stupid!" Oh, nice. This lizard had a beast core too. I still haven't finished using all the previous ones I obtained from the first time experiencing the Path of Slaughter. Before he had fallen asleep, Durandal had told me to consume them slowly and fully incorporate them into my body or impurities would build up. I can't use this one yet, but I'll be able to soon! I wonder how much it'd sell for....

"You, you're still a low-ranked spirit warrior, yet you're able to kill a mid-ranked spirit beast. It's no wonder why Lan lost." The wolfkin's voice sounded a bit dejected, but that wasn't my problem! I still haven't found a good use for him yet. But how did he know I was a low-ranked spirit warrior? ...Did I discover a new encyclopedia?

"You sound like you know a lot about spirit warriors."

"Of course. My previous owner, Cuchulainn, was an acclaimed spearman at the peak of the spirit warrior realm. One more step and he would've became a divine warrior. But, like the Godking, he couldn't cross that wall." My socks sighed. That tickles!

"How do I become a mid-ranked spirit warrior?" That should definitely count as becoming stronger, right? And if I become stronger, Durandal will wake up faster. Tell me, sock spirit! Lead the way.

"Shouldn't you already know? You're Durandal's owner, aren't you? Why haven't I seen him this whole time? I recognize his weapon body. I'd never forget it."

Well, I guess it couldn't hurt to let my sock spirit know about my weapon spirit, huh? "Durandal fell into a deep sleep before I became a spirit warrior. I have to get stronger to help him wake up."

"Huh? A deep sleep?"

"Right. I was poisoned by a bastard, and Durandal absorbed the poison into his system instead." Why is this lizard's heart green? I wonder if it's poisonous. Well, I'll store it anyway. Now I just have to carve its bones with focus engravings and my next hunt can proceed.

"Durandal absorbed your poison, fell critically ill, and told you you'd have to get stronger to wake him up?"

"That's right." I thought wolfkin were supposed to have a good sense of hearing. Why do I have to repeat myself every single time? It's like that Lan business all over again. Do you see how he's super annoying?

"Out of concern for the stability of my future…, are you a bit stupid?" What. "It'd be better to just tell me now, so I can accept my fate for being bound to such an owner."

"I'm going to set you on fire." I really am. Where's my Barbeque ring?

"W-wait. Don't you know what happens to weapon spirits when their spirit body dies?"

"They die, right?"

"...You killed me earlier, remember? Yet I'm still here. The only way to kill a spirit is to destroy its core. A spirit won't die to something like poison, and they'll recover by themselves naturally. Whether you get stronger or not won't matter.... Durandal will wake up when he wakes up."

"What." I've been deceived! No! I refuse to accept that! What the hell did I work so hard for if that's true!? Do you know how long it's been since I last went to sleep or ate a decent meal!?

"It's true—"

"No. You're lying." It's not true. Durandal wouldn't lie to me. I have to get stronger to wake him up. This stupid wolfy is trying to trick me! He's jealous of Durandal and wants him to never wake up, yes, that must be it! "Just shut up and tell me how to become a mid-ranked spirit warrior."

"..."

"Or I'll set you on fire."

My socks sighed again. "Alright, I'll tell you."

***

"How far along are you on your path? And what exactly is your path?"

"How can I tell how far along a path I am? And my path is the Unrelenting Path of Slaughter."

The wolfkin fell silent for a moment. What was his name again? Gae Bulg? I think I'll just call him Puppers—it's much easier to say. "I thought a squirrelkin would be more in tune with the path of 'hey, look, an acorn', not a Path of Slaughter." Hey. "And you even have a prefix before your path. What is this world coming to?"

"I'm the squirrel here! Stop getting so distracted and tell me how to become a mid-ranked spirit warrior already! Stupid Puppers."

"Did you just call me Puppers?"

That's it. "Where's my Barbeque ring?" Here it is.

"Incorporate your path into your daily life! Live, breathe, eat, and sleep your path. You—"

"Sleep my path? The heck is that supposed to mean. Speak clearly, Puppers!" There should be enough mana in the vicinity to activate this ring, right?

"You know how Lan's skills were preceded with 'Path of the Spear' every time he used one? He incorporated the Path of the Spear into every essence of his life. While he was sleeping, he trained the path in his dreams. As he was eating, well, he exclusively used a spear to eat his food. He bathed with a spear, combed his hair with the spear, wrote on paper with the spear. Everything he did was to further himself on the spear's path."

"Great. But how am I supposed to do that with a Path of Slaughter? How do I eat with slaughter? Slaughter's not even a tangible object!" This advice sucks. I thought he was supposed to make me a mid-ranked spirit warrior.

"That's a good question." Puppers fell silent, so I wiggled my toes to make sure he was still there. "That tickles. Please stop. I'm trying to think of a way. Cuchulainn also followed the path of the spear, but he had a prefix too: it was righteous. He used his spear to help everyone he could, fighting for justice and the weak. The unfairness in the world where the strong bullied the weak, he tried to correct that."

"…Once again, how does this have to do with slaughter? I think I'm just going to keep on killing things." That's right. The easiest way to get stronger is to follow the path, isn't that what Durandal had told me? "I won't sleep or eat, and I'll bathe in the blood of the things I kill. Isn't that the simplest way to follow the Path of Slaughter? I think it is."

"I'm glad my advice has been useful to you."

…I was already doing that before I met him though. But I guess I'll let him feel some satisfaction. It's no good to have unsatisfied socks. What if he decides to tickle me in the middle of a fight? "Yes, it was useful advice." Not really. "Thanks."

"Does that mean you'll let me materialize my spirit form?"

"Who's Lan?"

"Lan Ravenwood is the sixth prince of the Ravenwood Empire. He was my previous owner and—"

"Nope. No materialization for you, Puppers."

"What!? And stop calling me that! My name is Gae Bulg, the spear of Cuchulainn! Hundreds have been defeated beneath my spearhead, and—"

"And you're a sock now. Socks shouldn't be this noisy." Oh, nice. There's another big lizard over there. Unrelenting Path of Slaughter, go! Puppers' protests drowned out into nothing as my senses faded away, leaving me with my vision of white and red. Now that I think about it, the Path of Slaughter no longer stopped me when I strayed off the path. Couldn't I really do everything under these circumstances? Maybe it'll be a little difficult to adjust to if my hearing and smell are gone, but I should be fine, right?

After making quick—read long—work out of the lizard while I was dismantling its body and removing its most valuable part, Puppers' growling voice reached my ears. "Let me spar with you at least. The amount of time it takes to purify the beast core you absorbed will take too long otherwise."

"You just want to materialize, don't you?" I'm not going to keep him in my socks forever. Just until he learns how to behave. "Who's Lan?"

"Lan Ravenwood is the sixth—"

"Stop right there! No materialization, Puppers."

"Why!?"

"Out of curiosity, do you know how to cook?" Is it just Durandal that's terrible at everything save for swordsmanship?

Well, no, Durandal's a good spearman too. I wonder if Puppers would be a good swordsman.

"Cook? A weapon spirit has no need to learn how to cook. There's—"

"I think it may be a long while before you materialize, Puppers." But that bit about sparring was probably true. I remember I could consume three cores a day while fighting against Durandal. It's only a single core when I hunt beasts. "Last chance. Do you know who Lan Ravenwood is?"

A breeze passed through my toes. "Lan Ravenwood? Who's that?"

"Oh, not bad. What's your name?"

"Ms. Fluffytail, please. Don't make me say it."

"What was that? You don't want to materialize today, is that what I heard?"

"Please."

"Okay, I guess that's that then." Well, I don't expect to break him in so soon. It's exactly like raising a dog! I've seen some people in the army raise them. There's lots of punishments for disobeying and plenty of treats for correctly following a command. Too bad for Puppers, I don't have any treats available. Maybe I shouldn't be so mean to him.

"My name...." Another breeze passed through my toes. "My name is Pu, Pu, ...Puppers."

"Nice to meet you, Puppers! My name is Lucia Fluffytail." This lizard's heart is green too. How odd. "What kind of spirit are you, Puppers?"

"I'm ... a sock spirit." My socks felt damp. Was Puppers crying? Oh, no, that was just the blood from the lizard soaking through my shoes.

"Good job, Puppers. Who's a good boy?" And with that, I let the dejected-looking wolfkin materialize in front of me.

***

Sparring with Puppers is nothing like sparring with Durandal. For one, Puppers lives up to his name and fights more like a beast than a human. What kind of human would fight by wielding a spear in their mouth? His claws are super sharp too, and his tail attacks like a whip. It's very annoying because he can strike with the spear or grapple me when I get too close. At least I'm learning a lot! I've started using my own tail to fight. Despite how fluffy it looks, it's actually really solid at its core. Don't judge.

I tried learning how to use a shield—lizard bones and skins crafted into a buckler—but every time I activated the Path of Slaughter, my body would throw it away, so I gave up on it. Who says you can't slaughter someone with a shield? It'd make a perfectly good blunt weapon. Maybe the path knows I want to use it for defense. Why is everything in my life so intent on making me a brute?

Recently, the bones I've been engraving have gotten better effects. The bones of strength heal faster, and the bones of focus last at least three times longer. I'm not sure if it has anything to do with becoming a spirit warrior, or if it's because the quality of the bones are better. Well, it could be both. And—

Puppers froze mid-attack and turned his head. Why did he stop? He pointed, and I turned my head as well while lowering my sword. A cluster of rare monkey-like spirit beasts were gathered at the edge of the clearing Puppers and I had created during our spars. Odd. Usually spirit beasts attack without warning, why were they just standing there? Well, time to get stronger and continue following the Unrelenting Path of Slaughter. I charged at the monkeys and fired off a qi blade. I stopped shouting out my skill attacks since I can't hear them while I'm under the path's influence.

The qi blade flew through the air like a giant pink sheet, and it crashed into the silhouette of one of the monkeys. But instead of falling apart like monkeys usually did, a green film appeared on its orange body and blocked the qi blade. Whoa, what the heck was that? Qi was represented as pink in the Path of Slaughter. Red was the recommended path to take. Orange was living creatures, and black was blood. But I've never seen green before. Magic, maybe?

Well, I don't believe I'd lose! Breaking Blade! I charged forwards and swung mini-DalDal straight down from over my head. The green film appeared again, covering the monkey's body, but it easily cracked and crumbled apart underneath my pink attack. The monkey was bisected and black liquid splashed onto me. I saw the other monkeys panicking and turned my head towards them. Lots of green was flowing into the surroundings, and a green flame flew towards me. I dodged it while Puppers launched his own attack, stabbing towards the monkey who shot the flames. Nice one, Puppers!

The other monkeys turned to flee when the flame-spewing monkey collapsed. I launched qi blades at their heads while pursuing them. Come back, beast cores! Green films covered their heads, but the force from the qi knocked them over, and I made quick work out of them with three Breaking Blades. I looked around to see if there were any more rare monkeys, but there weren't any, so I disabled the Path of Slaughter. Hey, these rare monkeys wore clothes too.

"Ms. Fluffytail." Puppers walked up to me from behind, dragging along the two monkeys we had killed first. Blood covered his muzzle and spear. "I've always been a righteous spear—"

"Sock."

"…Righteous sock. And I don't approve of killing people for no reason. It rubs me the wrong way. If this is how you're going to continue to behave, I think it'd be better for us to part ways."

"Killing people for no reason?" Hmm? "I don't do that."

Puppers stared at me.

What were those judgmental eyes? Only Durandal can look at me like that. Bad Puppers. Bad. "What?"

Puppers pointed at the monkey corpses on the ground. "And?"

"You said you don't kill people for no reason."

"Right. I don't." Do I have to store him back into my socks? He came so far though. Well, a little more reeducation wouldn't hurt.

"Then tell me why you killed these men."

"What men? They're spirit beasts." Those are some really sneaky beasts if they could even fool Puppers. They're like advanced scavenger crows. How scary.

"Is that what you really believe?"

"Of course! I'm not a murderer."

"…"

I'm going to smack him if he keeps staring at me like that. "What do you want?" It looks like I can't activate the Path of Slaughter because Puppers wants to converse. Oh wells. It's not like I need the path to dismantle these beast corpses.

"Delusional."

"You're delusional! These beasts would've eaten us alive if I didn't take care of them, sheesh."

"Beasts can't use magic!" Puppers practically roared at me, and I flinched. Maybe I should've activated my path.

"Then we must've found a very rare variant of monkeys. Do you think the mercenary guild will reward me for bringing them information about a new species?" I heard they do that. Every bit of information helps mercenaries because the unprepared die first! Paying for information is like paying for a higher chance of survival. I wonder how much I'd earn.

"They were magicians! Magicians of the empire! Humans!"

"Puppers. Do you want to go back inside my socks?" Oh, lucky! I finally got a beast core from one of the monkeys! "This beast core's pretty big. Wow."

"Humans don't have beast cores! That's—wait, what?" Puppers snatched the bloody trophy out of my hands and stared at it. "This…, this is actually a beast core…? W-were they not humans?"

"I told you they were beasts! Give that back!" Would I finally gain some mana from absorbing this? Durandal said it was hopeless for me to ever learn any magic, but according to Puppers, beasts couldn't learn magic either. So if I, a manaless person, consumed the beast core of a rare magical spirit beast, maybe I'd gain the ability to cast spells. I have to try it!

That night, I experienced the worst nausea of my life, and I learned a manaless person like me will always stay manaless. The stupid core didn't even raise my strength or speed either. What a waste.

***

Durandal's raised a monster—an absolute monster. If Lucia Fluffytail was around 80 years ago, there's no doubt in my mind she'd be on par with my owner, Cuchulainn, or even the Godking himself. Perhaps she could only reach this far due to finding Durandal, but I can't deny her strength. With the help of qi, Cuchulainn and the Godking could maybe carry 5,000 pounds at the peak of their strength. Lucia can swing a ten-ton sword around as if she were waving paper. How is that even fair? She could disable someone by leaving her sword on top of them, possibly even killing them.

"An opening!"

Durandal's weapon body swung down from above, crashing against my spear which was actually a really stiff sock. As if a mountain had fallen on me, my legs were forced into the ground and my arms creaked as if they would break. Her strength is absolutely unreasonable! Being her spirit is nothing like being Lan's. Sparring with her may actually lead to a temporary death if I'm not careful. It's even more dangerous than living beside a prince who's a target for assassinations.

"Unrelenting Path of Slaughter: Breaking Blade!"

The world froze as Durandal's weapon body emitted a thick, red glow. The light radiating off the blade was heavy, nearly tangible. It engulfed me, and my vision became white. Red lines appeared on my body, revealing all the flaws in my stance. Though I could see them, there was nothing I could do to stop Lucia's blade from descending, carving me apart while following those lines. A sigh escaped from my lips as I fell to pieces before dispersing into a mist that was absorbed by Lucia's socks—my new home.

Damn. I lost again. It's the fourth fight Lucia won in a row, and I'll be out of commission for at least a week now. What kind of person would kill their armor spirit in the name of training? But I suppose that's what Lucia's path does. When she activates her path, there are only two outcomes: her opponent dies, or she becomes disabled. The path can only be disabled when she kills something. At first, I didn't understand how someone could obtain a path like that, but after seeing her train for the past few months, I understand: she doesn't eat, she doesn't sleep, all she does is kill. She used to dismantle the corpses of the beasts she killed, but I've been given that duty instead. Surprisingly, my capabilities to do things other than fighting have increased after turning into a sock spirit.

And once I hand over the bones, she uses her qi to carve some engravings to convert them into consumables that she uses right away. I think she's become dependent on them, but I can't deny their effects. Though it costs her qi to convert a bone, once the bone is consumed, she gets back an even greater amount of qi than what she had spent. Her strength, speed, and concentration are increased which allows her to function as a machine purely built for killing.

Speaking of killing. I still can't believe those people who I thought were magicians were actually spirit beasts. I don't believe they're a variant of monkey, but it's possible for them to be a slime of sorts that absorb the characteristics of the things they eat. However, even if some of them are really spirit beasts, there's no doubt in my mind that some of the people Lucia have killed were actually human. But that's the frightening part—with every person she kills, her Unrelenting Path of Slaughter advances by leaps and bounds. She's become a mid-ranked spirit warrior in a few months. It took Lan a year and a half to advance to mid-ranked from low-ranked.

Despite Lucia Fluffytail's prowess, she does have quite a few shortcomings. For one, she's pretty stupid; maybe it'd be nicer of me to say she has a single-track mind. It's sad, really. Once she thinks something is true, her mind doesn't change about it despite evidence to the contrary. Or it isn't stupidity, and she's just delusional. Either way, she's not exactly your normal person. But I can't look down on her for it. She's been alone, hunting spirit beasts in a jungle without sleeping or eating for over a year. Before that, I'm pretty sure she was living as a slave. Only a slave beastkin would've been allowed to accompany Bryant to the Godking's tomb.

"Puppers!"

Has a week passed already? When a weapon or armor spirit dies, our sense of time is distorted. A few brief moments for us can be weeks or months to our owners. Also, I really dislike having to respond to the name Puppers. I was a renowned spear, Gae Bulg. Criminals would tremble when they heard my name. Now—

"I know you're awake, Puppers! Dismantle these things!"

Is that a tree-devouring centipede? She killed something like that? ...Does it even have bones?

"This too! And this! Also do these things! Why did you have to die again? Do you know how much slower my hunting became without my little helper!?"

Little helper…. I'm not sure if Puppers is better or worse. But I'll begin because materializing outside is infinitely better than living inside of her socks. I still can't believe I've fallen from a mighty spear spirit to a sock spirit. But I guess I'm lucky to be alive. Lucia completely diced apart my weapon body, but she just missed my core. If her blade had struck even a millimeter closer when she was breaking apart the spear…, I probably wouldn't be here right now. It's a shame about Lan. Though Lucia won't admit it, I know she killed him. After all, that's what her Path of Slaughter does—it kills. If Lan weren't so paranoid, maybe he'd have been willing to talk with Lucia rather than fighting, but that was his one shortcoming. Perhaps I'm doomed to have mentally unstable owners. Even Cuchulainn had something wrong with him that compelled him to exterminate evil.

11

Aren't I strong enough for Durandal to wake up yet? I remember him telling me the Godking was at the peak of high-ranked spirit warrior, and according to Puppers, I've just passed the boundary from mid-ranked spirit warrior to high-ranked. Aren't I almost as strong as the Godking? In terms of qi at least. The Godking could use magic too, which automatically makes him stronger than me, but that was quick! It's only been … two days since Durandal was poisoned. Totally. A day only passes when I fall asleep.

It's so lonely when Puppers dies and reenters my socks. Ever since the day I became a high-ranked spirit warrior, Puppers hadn't won a single fight against me. He used the excuse that he couldn't show his full potential as a mere sock spirit, but I think he's just a sore loser. After reaching high-ranked spirit warrior, I've gained the ability to…, I'm not sure actually. Puppers said I can shrug off normal wounds, and fatal wounds become non-fatal. I'll only die if my head is cut off, but I'm not willing to test that! If someone told you you'd be fine if he cut your heart out, would you believe him and cut your heart out to test it? Hell no!

Other than that, my qi has become visible. It's red and viscous and kind of sticky like blood. Puppers says I'll be able to figure out what it can do if I play around with it, but I don't have time for that! If I have spare time, it'll be spent on sparring Puppers, carving bones, or hunting beasts. I also feel like I control the Path of Slaughter more than it controls me now. I can turn it on and off at will, but it's a bit painful. Maybe when I reach the peak, I'll be able to control it completely, but for now, I'll just make do. Hey, what's this strange green pattern on the ground?

Green means mana, right...? Maybe I should throw Puppers on top of it to check.

"Puppers?"

...Darn. I forgot he was dead at the moment. Let's turn off the Path of Slaughter and poke around. Wow. There's a massive chunk of meat sitting in the center of a glade. This isn't suspicious at all. ...But it does smell really tempting. How long has it been since I've last eaten? I'm not sure if I even have a stomach anymore. Why couldn't bones of strength be tasty? Then I wouldn't be so tempted. Maybe I should poke it..., no! Back to hunting!

Leaving the obvious trap behind, I reactivated my Path of Slaughter. I've finally absorbed enough cores of all the beasts around that none of them give me any more improvements. I have dozens of really high-ranked beast cores sitting around my interspacial ring. I should find a shop and sell them. Disregarding them, I'm pretty sure I reached the deepest point of the southern pass. Running north leads to weaker beasts as expected, but when I head south, the beasts become weaker again. Heading east and west bring about the same result. Clearly, I'm in the most dangerous spot, which isn't really dangerous for me anymore. The deadliest creature I killed was a black and red lion with three heads. I almost died 73 times during that fight, but through perseverance and hard work, I managed to kill it.

...

Just kidding. I ran away, poisoned Puppers, and fed him to the beast. Then I killed it in a fair one-on-three fight—because each of its heads counted as one person. It dropped a suspiciously evil-looking beast core that I still haven't absorbed yet because Puppers told me to save it. I'm not sure if he told me to save it because he was giving me bad advice out of bitterness for feeding him to the lion, or if he was actually serious. I'm planning on waiting for Durandal to wake up before I do anything with it.

Anyways, there really isn't anything left for me in the southern pass. I won't grow anymore by staying here. I could go to the desolate mountains in the north, but they're really far away and I'd have to travel through civilization to do that. I'll be interacting with actual people—how scary. I mean, I'm still a wanted criminal, I'm sure! I killed Bryant after all. I'm surprised no one's been sent after me yet though. Then again, only two days have passed. And—, hey, look! It's the green circle again.

After turning off the Path of Slaughter, I realized it was actually a different area. And sitting in the center of the circle—

"Miss. Can you hear me, miss? Please, help."

—there was a spirit beast waiting to be slaughtered. Ignore the fact that it looks like a helpless child. After being fooled by those scavenger crows at the very start of my journey, I refuse to be fooled by anything else ever again! And Snow. I still hate that bastard.

"Miss, please. I lost my mommy."

"Hey. Look here, spirit beast. There's no way a child would be able to navigate to the center of the southern pass completely unharmed."

The child shut his mouth and blinked. Large droplets formed in the corners of his eyes. His mouth opened and wails rang out of his mouth. He blubbered and sobbed as snot and tears ran down his face. What an ugly-looking child. Didn't he know crying would make it worse? Anyways, there was no way I was going to approach a suspicious magic circle with such obvious bait.

"Bye."

The child stopped crying and put on a neutral expression. "Bye."

I nodded at him before leaving. Hmm. Should I head towards the north? If I can't grow anymore in the south, then Durandal will never wake up. Yeah, I'll head to the north. I'll have to cross through the northern part of the southern pass, a few human towns, the border between the humans and the demons, and then the demons' territory. …Should I slaughter my way across? That'd definitely improve my path, but I'm not an evil person. I wouldn't kill people for no reason! That's what crazy people do and I'm not crazy. Nope—

Hey, look, an acorn! Whoa, it's a really big one too, I don't think I've ever seen one this … large…. Damn. I just stepped into one of those magic circles, didn't I? The ground is glowing, so yes. Yes I did. Shit.

***

Where am I? What is this? A cage? I really hate cages. "Breaking Blade!" Alright, the cage is no more. But what the heck is this place? It looks like a noble's basement, and those are definitely spirit beasts trapped in cages. Was that magical circle a teleportation array? Someone was capturing beasts that way, huh? How despicable. At least fight them honorably with poison.

A beast growled at me, its eyes glowing red in the dimly lit area. "What? I wasn't the one who trapped you here, stupid mutt." It clawed at the cage, but its paw bounced off the bars. Whoa, those bars are awfully sturdy. They could take a bear-sized shadow panther's attack without breaking. I guess that makes me amazing, right? Too bad Durandal isn't around to praise me.

Will this work? "Mini-Map!" Sweet, it does. It looks like there's an exit that way. This place is circular and the only way out is through that suspicious-looking spiral staircase. It's also covered by a trapdoor. This is definitely some perverted noble's basement. I wish I didn't kill Puppers though. He could've acted as a scout for me. Oh wells, with any luck, I'll have been teleported somewhere closer to the desolate mountains. I hope I don't run into anyone on the way out. It's been too long since I've talked to actual people. I'm nervous.

"Who's there!?"

Welp, there goes that wish. Why did the trapdoor have to be so loud? I guess it had to be since I broke through it with a Breaking Blade. "Just a talking squirrel. Don't mind me."

The gruff voice from before called from another room, "Oh. That's fine then. Carry on."

It worked?

"Teacher! Squirrels can't talk!" It was a younger voice this time. "That sound came from our fishing room. I think you accidentally caught a person again." No! Stupid voice of reason, don't convince the scary sounding man to take action! "Please, put the bottle down, Teacher! You're drunk."

"Drunk? I'm not drunk! I'm fishing for ideas! My best work comes after I blackout!" the gruff voice shouted back as I tiptoed towards the sound because it was the only way out of the room I was in. An old man and young lady came into view. They were both tugging on a half-filled bottle of alcohol, and the old man was winning. The strange part about them was their skin color: purple. Were they demons?

"Ah! Teacher, I told you it was a person!" The young lady's eyes widened when she saw me, and she scrambled behind the old man. Was I that scary?

"Person? That's a squirrel, you blithering idiot," the old man said and took a swig from his bottle. "Look, round furry ears, large fluffy tail, and a cute pair of socks. It's evident she's a squirrel."

"My socks are cute too, but I'm not a squirrel!" the young lady said. She grabbed a nearby stick and pointed it at me. "She's a beastkin. Your stupid bait caught a beastkin."

"Is the bait stupid if it worked?" the old man asked and rolled his eyes. "Hey, talking squirrel, which trap did you fall for? It was the acorn, wasn't it?"

…Should I kill them? Demons aren't people, right? Actually, they probably fall under the demi-human category like beastkin. Well, I'm not going to admit I fell for the stupid acorn; that'd be confirming his stereotype! "It was the helpless child."

The old man stared at me. Then he burst out into laughter and slapped his cushioned armrest. "What an idiot! You thought a child could make it to the center of the southern pass by himself?" His laughter shook my ears as he nudged his student with his bottle. "Get a load of that. I told you the helpless child could catch something! I never thought a person would be stupid enough to fall for it though! Ha ha!"

I'm going to kill them.

"Don't make fun of someone who broke out of your cage!" the young lady said and used the opportunity to snatch the bottle away from the old man.

"Huh." The old man's expression changed in an instant as he looked at me with narrowed eyes. "How *did* you break out of my cage? Did my mana-dampening runes run out of juice?"

"She's a warrior, Teacher," the young lady said. "Look at her sword. And there's no way a mage would have muscles like those."

That was a compliment, right?

"But that doesn't explain how she escaped the cage. I'm sure—with the materials it was made out of—the cage could've kept even the Godking inside of it. You know it can store a divine beast without problems." The old man scratched his chin. "That sword. Durandal?"

What? He's the first person to identify Durandal on sight! Just who is this guy? I should really kill him. I have a feeling I'll seriously regret it if I don't. But I'm not a bad person…. "Who are you?"

"I am Rogath Winemark, an eighth-circle magician." The old man leaned back and crossed his arms over his chest. "This is my pupil, Ilya…, uh, Ilya something."

"Pentorn! Ilya Pentorn! Teacher, please, you're not old enough to be this forgetful." The young lady glanced at me. "Is that really Durandal? So you're the wanted criminal. You're, uh, fluffier than I thought you'd be."

"Wait. I'm a wanted criminal? And how did you know this sword was Durandal?" So word really has spread about me killing Bryant. Darn.

"The Godking kidnapped me when I was younger," Rogath said and snorted. "I burned everything about him into my memory to enact vengeance one day. But he died before that."

"Wow. You're ancient." He must be really old—at least 80. "So, uh, now that we've become acquainted, I'll be taking my leave…? Is that okay?"

"No. That's not okay," Rogath said. Great. He wants to fight. I don't know how well I'd do against an eighth-circle mage. They're supposed to be on par with divine warriors, right? "Take Ilya with you before you go. Thanks."

"You asked for it! Breaking Bla—wait, what?" I lowered my sword. I imagine the look on my face was similar to the one on Ilya's.

"Right. Take her off my hands." Rogath nodded. "Unless you want to fight."

"No, no fights. I'll take her." Of course, the first thing I'll do is abandon her once I get out of here. No way am I going to accompany another person.

"Teacher! Don't throw me away like this!" There were tears in Ilya's eyes. Poor girl. "She's clearly going to throw me away once she gets out of here!"

Don't read my mind!

"Hmm, maybe you're right," the old man said. "Also, Ms. Squirrel, I don't like the way you've been eyeing me. I'm not a beast you can cut down." Before I could respond, he pointed at me and said, "Topsy-Turvy."

Urk. I feel sick. Like I was flipped over onto my head but not really.

"You're still standing?" The old man's voice sounded surprised. "Then what about this? Upsy-Daisy."

Gah! What the heck!? When I want to move my hand, my foot moves instead! How am I supposed to beat him up like this!

"Amazing. As expected of a warrior who managed to escape my cage somehow. Then…. Twisty-Turny."

I'm going to throw up. What did he do now? Oh great, now moving my right arm moves my left leg. Just what I needed. Then I'll use my qi to activate the Unrelenting—

"And for good measure, Wishy-Washy."

I can't control my qi!? So this is the power of an eighth-circle magician. No wonder why Bouncykins said the era of warriors was over. What can a warrior do without control of his qi?

"Teacher, I'm glad that you did something, but I'm the one who has to clean up her puke if she vomits, you know?" Ilya was concerned for all the wrong reasons! I'm dying here! Besides, I haven't eaten in a very long time. There's nothing for me to vomit out.

"That's fine, silly girl. What did I teach you the clean spell for?" Rogath asked and snorted. His drunken demeanor was completely gone, replaced by the dignity one would expect from a top tier magician. He pointed at me again and said, "Wishy-Washy."

Stop doing that!

"You should still be able to speak just fine. Why don't you say something?" Rogath asked.

"What am I supposed to say? You're a bastard. There."

Rogath burst out into laughter. "Excellent. The inheritor of the Godking's legacy should have this much spunk at least.

You don't have to make a face like that; I'm not going to hurt you, I swear." He scratched his chin. "Well, any more than I have already. Now, the reason I'm keeping you alive even though you wandered into my laboratory is simple. Did you know that the Godking's legacy is split into two parts? The first part is the martial path with Durandal. The second part is the magical path with Vera. Since you've found the martial path, I suspect finding the magical path will be easier for you. Call it a hunch."

"You mean, you want me to inherit Vera?" Ilya asked, her eyes widening. "You were serious about that!?"

Why does she look so startled? ...And devastated?

"Of course I was serious," Rogath said with a nod. "Speaking of the Godking's legacy, why hasn't Durandal shown himself? I want to give that weapon spirit a good smack for ignoring me when I begged for his help as a child."

Never reveal your weaknesses! "He doesn't want to come out because he recognizes you."

"Oh, really?" Rogath's eyes narrowed. "Then what if I tortured you until you summoned him?"

"You said you wouldn't hurt me! I'll definitely bully your pupil if you do!"

"Bully her all you want. She's a very meek girl. A little roughhousing will shape her right up."

"Teacher! Are you really looking out for what's best for me!?"

Wow. They sure have a nice relationship with each other. It's like the relationship between Durandal and me. I'm a bit jealous. Why can't Durandal wake up already? "Durandal's a lot like you. He'll let you torture me to build character." I think he really would if he was awake.

"Huh. I see." Rogath leaned over and took the bottle out of Ilya's hand. He pointed at me again and said, "Wishy-Washy."

Apparently, it was only a temporary spell. And it's not like I can't control my qi; it just doesn't move in the manner I'd like it to.

"So what do you say?" Rogath asked. "Take my pupil with you on your journey. If anything happens to her, I'll know and teleport over there to deliver punishment. She can also be very useful; it's not like I'm throwing a completely useless burden on you."

"Does that mean I'm partially useless then!? Teacher, why are you so mean!?"

"Can I refuse?"

"Ilya, take Durandal away from her."

"So I'm not useless enough to do that?" Ilya grumbled and came over to me. I tried to get away, but ended up falling over instead. Stupid arm-leg nonsense spell. Don't touch Durandal, you whore! "Eh? I can't pick it up?"

"What do you mean?" Rogath asked and stood up. "Durandal should be bound to her, but anyone should be able to use him like a normal sword if they get their hands on him."

"I'm serious; I can't pick her sword up."

"Let me try," Rogath said and nudged his pupil aside. His hand was enveloped in a layer of green as he bent down to grab Durandal. He couldn't lift Durandal's weapon body enough to fully wrap his hand around the hilt. "What is this?" He shrugged and grabbed me instead. "Well, if we can't move the horse away from the water, we'll move the water away from the horse."

And thus, I was dragged away and thrown into another cage. It took all of three minutes before I was begging them to let me out. Pride? Dignity? Forget that! Durandal is way more important! I get panic attacks when Durandal's not somewhere on my body!

"That was a lot quicker than I thought." Rogath had a strange expression on his face. Don't judge me! "But you agree to bring my pupil along with you?"

"If she does anything suspicious, I'm going to kill her."
I'm not letting another Snow incident happen ever again!

"Did you hear that, Ilya? Don't do anything suspicious."

"Teacher!" Tears threatened to fall down Ilya's face.
"Please don't do this to me! You're entrusting my life to a
complete stranger! I came here to learn magic from *you*, so
why—"

"Magic stems from experience. Not just experience with
the spell you are casting, but life experiences. Without
traveling the world, you'll never break through to the seventh-
circle. Haven't you been stuck in the sixth-circle for thirty
years now?"

Thirty years!? What the heck! She looks like she's
thirteen! How old is she?

"Teacher…, you're thinking about Elaine again. I'm Ilya,
the third-circle magician."

"Ilya, Elaine, what's the difference? They both have two
syllables. Now get out of my sight."

And that's how I met my new traveling companion, Ilya
Pentorn.

12

My name is Ilya Pentorn. I'm the only child from a prestigious noble family, the Pentorns. I'm supposed to have a bright future based on the test results gathered from me after my birth. My father is a duke. My mother is deceased. My teacher is a drunkard. And my current companion is a bamboozling squirrelkin lady. Where is my promised future?

As the oldest scion of a noble family, I'm expected to inherit my father's title after he dies. But since my father is a duke, I'm expected to be strong enough to fulfill his role by the time he dies. I have to be at least a seventh-circle magician, but eight or nine is preferable. So my father sent me off to Rogath Winemark, an eighth-circle magician, to learn from him when I was twelve. Before that, I had reached the third-circle. My father had taught me himself, but due to some recent tensions between the three factions, he wasn't as free as he used to be. Six months after arriving at Teacher's laboratory, I finally convinced him to accept me as a pupil. And three months after slaving under Teacher without learning anything, my current companion, Lucia Fluffytail, was caught in one of his traps. And three months after that…, I crossed the first wall and became a fourth-circle magician. I also nearly lost my life seventeen times.

"Keep up or be left behind!"

Those were the only words Lucia said to me during the whole time I've known her. I'm actually a little thankful for that. I see how her words mentally destroy her ex-weapon spirit, which she stuck into a sock, and I don't know how long I'd last if those vitriolic words were directed at me instead. I'd probably have a nervous breakdown and cry. Can you believe she named someone older than her Puppers? A sentient being! Puppers! You name a newly born fox Puppers, not an experienced weapon spirit who can swallow your face without chewing.

Anyways, I'm doing my best to adhere to her words. What I didn't know at the beginning of our journey was that being left behind meant I would die. Seriously. I will die if I let this eccentric squirrelkin lady out of my sight. As much as I loathe to say it, my livelihood depends completely on Lucia. And the reason for my dilemma is that beast chasing after me—the four-meter-tall creature with two heads, six legs, and a snake for a tail. Well, it's not only that, but that's just an example of the average beast I run into at least eight times a day.

"Unrelenting Path of Slaughter: Breaking Blade!"

And the creature that could kill me if it even looked at me the wrong way was promptly killed in a single strike. I don't know if Lucia is at the peak of martial arts or not, but if she isn't, then I'm willing to bet my left pinky toe that she's extremely close. Her fighting style is very simple: approach, dodge, slash, repeat. She never blocks, never disengages, and doesn't care about getting minor injuries. She's a completely self-destructive fighter who reminds me of a blood magician. Her personality probably has something to do with it too.

"Oh, nice! There were two cores! Like I thought, two-headed beasts are the best."

When she talks to herself like this, I've learned not to say anything or else she'll glare at me with a bloody aura. Why did you leave me with such a crazy person, Teacher? No, why did my father even choose you to teach me if you were going to abandon me like this? Experiences? Worldliness? I'll die before I learn anything. And keeping up with her is extremely difficult. That's actually how I broke through from the third circle to the fourth circle. Everywhere Lucia goes, she engages in a battle which attracts the attention of many beasts because of the bloody smell in the air. We have to leave the area quickly before a swarm of beasts arrive.

To keep up with Lucia, I had to use all the wind magic I knew. But even that wasn't enough, and the motivation of not wanting to die spurred some kind of breakthrough in my magic. I transcended the wall and learned how to control my wind magic in a more efficient manner that allowed me to barely keep track of my crazy companion. Not only that, but Lucia doesn't sleep. It's odd, yes. She doesn't eat either which I had trouble adapting to. She occasionally gives me bones to consume—which are extremely addictive by the way—to rid me of my weariness and hunger. I don't think she realizes what consuming the bones are doing to her body. I don't think she realizes anything at all.

A faulty machine. If I had to use three words to describe Lucia, those are what they'd be. How does someone become like her? What kind of life has she lived so far? What about her—dear lord, that's not a normal tree. Why do even the trees want to kill me in this place? "Lucia! Help!"

"Unrelenting Path of Slaughter: Flying Blade!"

I dove down as the massive red surge of qi flew towards my head. I felt it shave off years of my life as it passed by and bisected the giant tree that had a mouth and face. It screamed so loud that I thought I'd be hearing ringing noises in my ears for the rest of my life. When I finally managed to pick myself off the ground, Lucia was staring at me with completely white eyes—no traces of irises or pupils. She opened her mouth but closed it again before turning away while muttering something about a fluffy cross-dressing bastard.

And with the narrow escape from the tree, I've nearly died eighteen times now. That's an average of six times a month. Six times too many if you ask me. I wonder how long I'll have to live like this. I don't think I can take much more.

***

Ilya's sturdy! I hate to admit it, but she's a lot more competent than I was when I was her age. Which wasn't too long ago! I'm not old. Gosh. She also eats a lot. I really, really want her to cook for me, but the last time someone did that, I was poisoned and Durandal nearly died. Maybe if I watch her as she casts the barbeque spell on the meat, it'll be fine. But there's no way for me to know if it's barbequed or barbequed and poisoned. The safest bet is to not play, so I'll continue being bitter—err, not jealous of her food at all! How come magicians don't have to worry about running out of mana in the vicinity? It's not fair.

And she also has the clean spell which I am also completely not jealous of. I'd ask her to use it on me, but I haven't talked to her in a long while and it'd be awkward to start now. Besides, I have it too! But if I overuse it, I might not have enough mana to cast barrier and haste when my life is in danger, so that's a no-go. Especially since we're in the desolate mountains in the north. Wasn't it super convenient that Rogath's laboratory was situated right outside the mountain range? I didn't have to cross the human kingdom or the demons' territory. It's almost like there's someone out there plotting out my life and helping me avoid all human interaction. It's great! And with that super-long-ranged teleportation, anyone tracking me will be bamboozled by the lack of my traces!

I still can't believe Rogath let me go like that though. Does he really think I'll uncover the Godking's legacy part two? The legacy's a once in a lifetime lucky chance; I already spent mine on finding Durandal. There's no way I'll find what's her face's necklace too. But I'm not complaining! Rogath was even kind enough to give me his four favorite spells—the ones he used on me. He told me I'll probably only be able to use them once every two weeks though, and no other magic tool will work for a week after their use. It's in the form of the totally cute red ribbon tied to the base of my tail by the way. It used to be white, but, eh, beast blood does that, you know?

Speaking of beasts, the ones in the outskirts of the mountain range aren't much different from the fat bears I used to kill in the southern pass. They're definitely a step up though. I bet I'll find ones stronger than the three-headed lion in the center of the range. I wonder if Ilya will survive. She's been having a really tough time keeping up with me. She almost died like … two times? I guess that isn't too bad, but for someone as young as her, it can be awfully scary.

Well, I'm sure she's been left some life-saving items from her teacher. Maybe an instant teleportation button, or a three-week shield, or an instant-kill needle. …Now I'm scaring myself. What if she does have an instant-kill needle? Do those things even exist? Hmm. Somehow, it feels like my focus bones are becoming less effective over time. Obviously, I need to consume more. There we go. Why's Ilya looking at me like that? Does she want one? I guess I can give her a spare.

"Thanks."

It wasn't out of kindness! Don't thank me. It's because your teacher would definitely punish me greatly if anything happened to you. But I'll let her think it was kindness. I've been giving her a lot of my bones; she probably has a positive image of me in her mind. Did you know I could sell these bones for at least 50 gold each? More for the bigger ones too. But it doesn't matter since I won't be going to civilization for an awfully long time.

I say a long time, but I plan on going as soon as Durandal wakes up. With all the beast cores, bones, and penises I've gathered, I'll definitely be able to buy a mansion! I'll have dozens of servants to cook for me and clean for me and do everything I don't want to do. Then I'll hire some financial advisors, invest in the right things, and maybe start a dojo where I can put Puppers to work. I'll be set for life and Durandal and I can live happily ever after! I'll pay for surgery to alter my appearance, or if the emperor is willing, I could pay him off and free myself of my bounty forever. Anything can be solved with money; Durandal was right. Screw angular momentum—money makes the world go round!

I feel like I'm forgetting something though that would ruin that dream. But I'll deal with it when the time comes. Mhm. For now, I have to focus on getting stronger. I'm definitely approaching the peak of high-ranked spirit warrior. I can even hear things and make out details during the Path of Slaughter. Durandal should wake up when I reach the peak, right? I'll be as strong as the Godking was, so...

Holy shit. I'll be as strong as the Godking was! Aren't I qualified enough to be a legend!? Wait. Lucia, you're forgetting the existence of mages. Any seventh-circle magician is stronger than a high-ranked spirit warrior— remember Rogath? The guy you were just talking about that rendered you helpless with eight words? Darn. It seems like I'll have to transcend the peak to become a divine warrior. But how do I do that if no one's ever done that in the past? ...I'll worry about it after I get stuck at the peak.

"Lucia! Help!"

Again? Didn't I already kill a tree like ten minutes ago? What's trying to kill her this time? "Unrelenting Path of Slaughter: Flying Blade!" I renamed Flying Qi Blade into Flying Blade because Flying Qi Blade was too unwieldy to shout every time. Now, what was trying to kill her...? Oh, would you look at that: Purple rare spirit monkeys.

"M-murder."

Aww. Ilya doesn't know about the specialty of the beasts. She looks absolutely terrified with large, rabbit-like eyes. How cute. "Don't worry. They were spirit beasts." See? I'll prove it to you. ...Hmm, no beast cores. Welp, can't get lucky all the time. I'll prove it to her during the next batch we run into.

***

"Don't worry. They were spirit beasts."

Those were the words Lucia said to me before she proceeded to bash open the demons' heads and dig around through their brains. Teacher, why have you left me with such a person? I'm not sure what's worse: if she truly believes they were spirit beasts or if she was making up an excuse for murder. Granted, I did call out to her for help. I sensed someone trying to disable me with magic, and I couldn't do anything about it on my own. I hadn't considered how much of a target I was as a young demon traveling through the wilderness. People didn't only hunt beasts. Sometimes it was easier to hunt the people hunting beasts. It may be a bit barbaric, but the imperial family allows it—if only in the wilderness. Perhaps because it'd be too hard to regulate; I don't know.

But to be hunting in an area like this; they must've been fifth-circle magicians at the very least. One out of 500 people have the potential to reach that level. Magic isn't like martial arts where anyone can improve so long as they try hard enough. Besides, there's—wait. Wait, wait, wait! What is Lucia doing!? Lucia was humming while, while…! She cut it off! She cut all of them off!

"Most expensive parts, get! They're kind of small though. Would anyone still buy them?" Lucia shrugged and the, the things disappeared into her interspacial ring. "Whew. My space is getting full. I wonder if there'll be a town conveniently placed nearby like Wilderness Town was."

Don't be stupid! There's no way anyone would establish a town inside of the desolate mountains. How would the town defend against beasts? You'd have to have seventh-circle demons guarding the walls day and night in case a divine beast attacks. Only one out of ten thousand people will ever reach the seventh-circle; it's much more difficult than becoming a sixth-circle magician. That's why people call the boundary between six circles and seven circles the second wall. Elaine, Rogath's first pupil, is still stuck as a sixth-circle magician after thirty years. I wonder if her travels bore any fruit.

But now that I think about it, Lucia really … is leaving me behind! "Wind, encircle my feet! Earth, lighten my body! Fire, give me stamina! Water, maintain my temperature!" Wait for me, dammit! Let me monologue inside my head some more! Thankfully, those bones of strength that Lucia give me restore my mana; otherwise, I really won't be able to keep up with her. And we already saw what happened when I lagged behind. Maybe it was my fault those demons died. If I hadn't been targeted, Lucia wouldn't have struck to kill them. Actually, she might have done that regardless if she sincerely believed they were spirit beasts.

"Oh sweet! It's a person-faced lion with wings! And a pointy tail!"

A divine beast! I never thought I'd see a manticore before I was even an adult! We're so dead. O lord, if you exist, please, let me die a quick and unmiserable death.

"Take this! Unrelenting Path of Slaughter: Breaking Blade!"

Lucia's sword was tiny in comparison to the beast. In fact, she was only as large as its face, but she didn't look scared at all. The manticore roared and blocked the strike with the tip of its tail. "Pitiful warrior." It could speak!? "Trying to fight *me* without *magic*? Realize your folly and die."

Wow, it sounds awfully snobby. Then again, it is a divine beast. I don't imagine many things can even hurt it. If I tried to escape right now, could I make it? Why didn't Teacher give me something life-saving like an instant teleportation button, or an instant-kill needle, or at least a three-week shield? I'm sure dying does *not* build character. Maybe negative character.

"Go! Puppers, use poison attack!"

Right! Lucia had a sock spirit that looked pretty fierce. He can definitely—he was eaten!? What the hell!?

"Success!"

What the hell was successful about that!?

"Y-you! Warrior! What did you do!?" The manticore looked like it was in a lot of pain. Don't tell me Puppers was actually poisonous to eat. Was he meant to be used this way...? I wonder how he feels about it. I imagine not very good.

"Let's try it again! Haste! Unrelenting Path of Slaughter: Repeated Breaking Blades!"

A red aura surrounded Lucia. The aura was so dense around her sword that it looked black. She turned into a red blur that repeatedly crashed against the manticore's body. The manticore swiped at Lucia with its claws and tail, but Lucia didn't stop. Blood flew into the air. I wasn't sure if it was Lucia's or the manticore's, but there was a lot of it. A droplet landed near my feet and burned a hole in the grass. ...Probably the manticore's then. Will Lucia be alright if she's covered in that stuff?

"Gah! Warrior! Cease your struggles!" The manticore spread its wings. It was about to leap into the air, but it let out a scream that caused my eardrums to burst. It hurt a lot, and I couldn't hear anything, but the manticore was definitely hurting more. One of its wings had been severed and fallen to the ground.

My lord, Lucia was an absolute monster. "Light, please heal my injuries." I wasn't sure if I said it correctly because I couldn't hear myself, but I think I did because there was a buzzing feeling in my ear afterwards.

The manticore's massive body seemed like a detriment as Lucia darted around like a fly. The beast couldn't hit Lucia at all. It even tried stopping, dropping, and rolling in the hopes of crushing her, but it didn't work and the manticore lost an eye because of that action. Wasn't it a divine beast? How could a manticore be so weak? Or was it that Lucia was just too strong? Literally too strong because she had picked the manticore up and thrown it after it tried rolling on her. It must've weighed at least 10 tons, but she..., she only used one hand....

"Wah! That was a tough fight."

It was over!?

"Sweet! A beast core!"

You didn't even hesitate to smash open a human-like face!

"No! Dammit, why!?"

What was she cursing about now? I still can't believe she killed a divine beast so easily. The manticore's corrosive blood didn't even have any effects on her.

Lucia kicked the manticore, causing its corpse to fly off the ground and fall a few meters away. "This stupid thing was a woman! My money!"

***

Cheated. Swindled. Why can't I make any money off of this man-faced lion thing? Well, at least, I obtained a beast core from it. It looks red and black and omninous like the one I got from the three-headed lion back in the southern pass. And Puppers isn't around this time to tell me whether I should save or consume it. He'll probably be bitter again since I fed him to the beast. Maybe Ilya will know?

"U-um, this body, are you leaving it here?" Ilya flinched under my gaze. Why was she approaching the divine beast? "C-can I have it?"

"If you want?" Where would she even store it? Unless she has an interspacial ring. That'd make sense considering how powerful her teacher was. "I'll take the bones later though."

"Thank you!" Ilya bowed at me before touching the beast. It vanished and disappeared, presumably, into her space.

"Hey."

"Y-yes!?" Ilya stiffened. Was that guilt on her face? What was she feeling guilty for? Hmm. Hmmm. Hmmmmm. Oh wells.

"Do you know what'll happen if I consume this core?" If she knows, she'll probably become my new encyclopedia. I've tried messaging Liana and the Briarwood envoy a few times, but I don't think the range of the messenger extends that far.

"Um. You might explode?" Ilya asked and bit her lower lip. "Please don't explode. I'll die if you die."

Explode, huh? "What happens if I don't explode?"

"...Increase in strength?" Ilya lowered her head. "I'm really not someone you should be asking about this. Most people don't consume cores. It takes too long to remove their impurities."

"Eh? But a day of sparring is all it takes." Right? And it takes around 30 cores of an animal to develop their attributes. That's only a month of training. And it goes by even quicker the more you take. Some cores won't even give you any strength if you're already beyond their abilities. Wouldn't it take a year at most to develop a body equivalent to that of a spirit beast? Of course, it only took me a day. Mhm.

"A day?" Ilya asked. "Maybe for a beastkin. Demons have a lot of mana, and mana interferes with beast cores a lot. Even ingesting a beast core brings about a lot of nausea for a first-circle magician."

That probably explains those magical monkey beast cores then.... Their cores had magic in them, and that was an absolute nightmare to absorb. Mm. No absorbing beast cores with mana. Wait. Aren't I super lucky that I can't use magic at all then? Well, it depends on what you call lucky: the ability to use magic, or the ability to absorb beast cores easily. In that case, since I'm specialized to absorb beast cores....

"Um, Ms. Fluffytail. What are you doing?"

"Absorbing the beast core." Ah, her stupefied expression is so satisfying to see.

"Didn't you hear what I just said?"

"Loud and clear, young encyclopedia."

"Young encyclopedia? Wait! What if you explode? Lucia!"

"Then I guess we'll both die then." Mhm. How unfortunate. Wow, this feels amazing. Like I'm being massaged everywhere at once!

"Y-you're really absorbing a divine beast's core…. You could've bought a small town if you sold it…."

…Say that sooner! But I do have enough money regardless. I think. But with this, I'm really getting a lot stronger. I can probably lift 14 tons after I'm done absorbing this! Durandal will definitely, definitely, definitely wake up soon! Peak of high-ranked spirit warrior, here I come!

"It was around here, right? The manticore's aura suddenly disappeared. What the hell?"

"What do you mean its aura disappeared? We hired you to track it down, and you dragged us through this forest for three weeks. You're trying to tell us it disappeared?"

Wow. Someone sounded grumpy. A nearby tree was knocked to the side as a group of six people appeared in the clearing that was created during my fight with the divine beast. Well, since they could talk, it didn't seem like they were rare spirit monkeys. Probably.

"A young girl and her slave?" The demon at the head of the group stared at me and Ilya.

Oi. Don't call Ilya a slave. She's an encyclopedia. I don't mind you calling me young though.

"A fight clearly happened here. Hey, girlie, did you see a manticore?"

"Nope. No manticore." I answered since I was obviously the person in charge. "Right?"

"R-right," Ilya said. "No manticore. We'd be dead if there were."

"Hmm. What's a young girl like you doing out here in the desolate mountains?" one of the demons with a blue staff asked.

"Hey," another one said. "Leave her alone. She's probably the heir to a noble family."

"So what? Everyone is equal in the desolate mountains," the blue-staffed demon said.

"Are you members of the Arcane Arts Academy?" Ilya asked. She was inching behind me. Was she scared? They're probably going to attack us, aren't they? I should horribly maim them, but I won't kill them because I'm not a murderer. Mhm.

"Oh? You know about us? That's right, we're students of the Arcane Arts Academy," the blue-staffed demon said. "Are you—"

"Unrelenting Path of Slaughter: Flying Blade!" Oh, wow. They weren't expecting that at all. I almost feel bad. Now, grab Ilya and run!

"L-Lucia!" Ilya screamed louder than the demons did when they had lost their legs. "Don't grab me so suddenly! I'm going to be sick!" Her purple face turned green, and my dress was covered in vomit. It was already bad enough with the blood as it was. I'm definitely making her clean this off of me.

Wait a minute…. Why am I running? I killed a divine beast; I have no reason to fear a bunch of legless demons! They weren't legless before by the way.

"Wait, Lucia! Why are you going back?" Ilya asked. At least she didn't struggle in my grip. What a nice little encyclopedia. Much, much more compliant than Snow.

"To gather loot! Everyone knows mages are rich."

13

"Save us…. Please…."

Lucia ignored the demons' cries and continued to flip them over and rummage through their belongings. "Why don't these people have interspacial rings?" She glanced at their lower bodies. "Unless their hiding them down there…."

No one would hide their interspacial ring down there! "Um, Lucia. The earrings you took from them earlier. Those are interspacial ones."

"Oh. Thanks, Ilya," Lucia said and patted my head. Great, now there were bloodstains I had to clean out of my hair. "I guess we're all done with them then."

Is she just going to leave them there? They were students of the Arcane Arts Academy, one of the most prestigious magic schools around. Of course, as the daughter of a duke, my stature was above attending it, but many of the lesser nobles had their children attend. The graduation rate was only around 25%, but all the students who graduated became magicians of at least seven circles. It was a very vigorous course that took twenty-five years to complete, and there were rumors that students could hunt beasts in the desolate mountains to earn better grades. Dangers were accepted as normal, but if the academy found out Lucia did this…, they'd retaliate.

"Um, Lucia. Are you going to leave them like that?"

"They'll be fine," Lucia said with a nod. "Their limbs will regrow in time and they'll make it out of the forest a-ok." She stuck her thumb up before turning around to leave.

Limbs … regrow? Demons aren't salamander people! "Lucia! Lucia, wait, Lucia!" But it was too late, Lucia had already ran off into the forest and resumed her hunting spree. I could stay behind and help these people and most likely die, or I could follow after Lucia and most likely die. …Why do both options feel the same? I glanced at the pale demon lying in a puddle of blood and quickly made up my mind. Follow Lucia!

"Um, Lucia," I asked after catching up to her. She was running pretty slowly because she was looking over her loot. "If you were going to do that to them, shouldn't you have just killed them?" I wasn't sure which was worse: cutting off someone's arms and legs and leaving them to die in a forest or killing them outright without leaving a strand of hope. I wouldn't want to select either option.

"What? Kill them? I'm not a murderer." Lucia frowned at me. "Sheesh. Just what do you think of me as? Oh, and clean my dress since you barfed all over it."

"…Clean." With a word and a flick of my wrist, Lucia's dress turned back to its original red…, white? Her dress was white before? Then what was the red? Oh. "So, um, why'd you cut off their arms and legs?"

"Well, I cut off their legs so they wouldn't chase us," Lucia said with a nod as she inspected her dress. "But then I realized I wasn't weak and they were rich, so I went back. And everyone knows magicians can't cast spells without their hands, so I cut those off too."

Huh? Where did she hear that from? The only thing required to cast a spell was mana. "And you don't think that counts as killing them?" Did she really not? Sometimes, I can't tell if she's an idiot or if she's actually really sinister on the inside.

"Of course not," Lucia said. "If they're out hunting divine beasts, then a mere flesh wound like that won't kill them. I can regrow my limbs easily if you cut them off." She turned her head away. "At least that's what Puppers told me. I haven't actually lost a limb to test it out. Anyways, I only did enough damage to them to make sure they wouldn't have any ideas to chase and kill us after they recovered. I'm a totally nice person. If Durandal were around, he'd have killed them."

"I see." I don't, but if I abandon some of my common sense, I can see where Lucia's coming from. Maybe. "And you know magicians don't need hands to cast magic?"

"Huh!?" Lucia's eyes widened. "Really!? They're always doing hand flicks or weird motions when they do magic though."

"Those are just tics. You don't even need to chant a spell to cast it either. As long as you circulate mana the right way, a spell can be cast. It's like how you don't have to shout out the spell name when you use a magic tool."

"...You don't?" Lucia looked ... crestfallen. I think I broke one of the strange rules of her world. She shook her head and continued to run at a slow pace. Was she doing that out of consideration for me? "Anyways, what's the Arts Arcanium School?"

"The Arcane Arts Academy?" Please. The name alliterates.

"Yeah, that thing. You seemed really scared by those people which is why I attacked first."

So she attacked out of consideration for me? ...I don't believe her. I have a feeling she'd have attacked even if I wasn't present. "The Arcane Arts Academy is a place for elite magicians. They're the largest academy in the empire, and the strength they hold is no joke. The principal is a ninth-circle magician, and most of the teachers are at eight circles."

"That sounds scary. Dozens of demons as strong as Rogath gathering around in one place? Yeah, I'm never going there." Lucia nodded.

"You may have attracted their attention by assaulting their students though. On missions, there's usually a teacher to chaperone. And if he finds out his students didn't come back and personally went out to investigate..."

"Why didn't you tell me this earlier!?" Lucia whirled around and ran back towards the direction we just came from, going at a speed I could barely keep up with. "Remove all evidence!"

"I thought you weren't a murderer." How does she run so fast without the assistance of magic? Imagine if she could use spells to augment her physical abilities. She'd be unstoppable.

"I'm not a murderer! I'm an angel of mercy! Didn't you hear that demon pleading to be saved? I'll definitely put him out of his misery."

Why didn't she hear him the first time around? How did someone like her inherit the Godking's legacy?

***

When we got back to the spot where I killed the manticore, there was already a ferocious beast in the process of eating the six demons. Well, there were only two of them now, but they weren't conscious. That was a pretty fast spirit beast; in fact, once it caught sight of me, it picked up the two demons with the spikes growing out of its back, turned tail, and ran away.

"That was a corpse stalker," Ilya said from behind me. Way to go, encyclopedia! Right on time. "It specializes in stealth. It follows after a creature stronger than itself and picks up the remains left behind. They're like vultures."

"Why do you know so much?" I didn't know anything about beasts. Like, at all. Then again, I didn't have much of an education concerning … anything. I should become more learned. At least I know how to draw! Don't judge me.

"Studying dangerous beasts was a part of the curriculum my father had me take," Ilya said. "In the case of a beast invasion, nobles are expected to step up and defend their territories. Learning about future threats is mandatory."

That makes sense. I didn't know nobles had to fight to defend their territories. I thought they just conscripted an army of villagers. Maybe demons and humans are different. I wonder what it's like in fae territory. Do beastkin have nobles and peasants? They should, right?

The hairs on my tail stiffened. "Run!" I turned around, grabbed Ilya, and ran as fast as I could. What the heck!? Squirrely instincts, at least tell me why you want me to run away before doing it! Surprisingly, Ilya didn't panic, scream, or vomit on me like last time. She was actually pretty stiff as well.

"Six? No, seven," Ilya muttered. There was a massive boom that echoed through the mountain range before I could ask Ilya what she was talking about. But I knew from the scary green lights floating behind me after I activated the Unrelenting Path of Slaughter. A seventh-circle magician had appeared.

Ilya chanted, "Wind, heed my call, bless this crazy squirrel with your gift of speed."

Nice! I'm a little faster than when I'm hasted. I should make Ilya inscribe this array on my dress.

"Earth, hear my pleas, lighten the burden on this crazy squirrel's body."

Quit calling me a crazy squirrel, please.

"Water, if you will, clear this crazy squirrel's sight and maintain her temperature."

The sight spell didn't do anything since I already had the Unrelenting Path of Slaughter. At least it feels like I won't sweat even if I run through a desert. Wind, earth, water..., then the next one was fire, right? I know this! She's going to give me a stamina boost.

"Fire, do as I say! Set this crazy squirrel's tail ablaze!"

...What? Gah! It's hot! "What the fuck, Ilya!? Put it out! Put it out!!!"

"There's a pool of water ahead, Lucia! Run with all your might!"

I tossed Ilya aside, but somehow she had tethered herself to my body with a rope made of mana. She spread her arms and a thin film of mana appeared between her arms and her sides, and she flew up into the air like a kite. I'm going to set her ass ablaze and see how she likes it! But first, where's that pool of water!? "Haste!"

"Run faster, Lucia! He's gaining on us!" Ilya shouted down from above while I focused on running as fast as I could. My beautiful tail! Now it's going to be all burnt and crispy, and Ilya is definitely going to heal me or I'll skin her and feed her to her teacher. "Lightning, hear my call, stun my enemy!"

I flinched as thunder crackled overhead. If I didn't have my Path of Slaughter active, I'd probably have went blind for a moment there as well. "I hit him!" Ilya said. "Lightning—"

Ilya yelped as a massive purple lightning bolt struck a nearby tree. "But all it did was make him mad!" The mana rope between us shrank, and Ilya was soon clutching onto my back. The flames on my tail went out when she made contact with my body. "He's going to catch up to us, Lucia. Can you fight a seventh-circle magician?"

"You're the encyclopedia; why are you asking me!?" I'm not bitter about her setting my tail on fire. Not at all. But a seventh-circle magician.... Why is he chasing us? Probably because his students were eaten, huh?

"Well, you shouldn't have been able to kill the manticore since it was a divine beast," Ilya said. "But that's because your physical abilities are absurd. The magician should be on the same level, but he'll be using magic. Will you be fine?"

"I can't use my poison attack." Puppers is still out of commission.

"Poison attack? You mean.... That wouldn't have worked on a demon!"

"Why are you two running? Cease all movements or face the consequences!" an angry voice shouted from behind.

Like hell I'm going to stop!

"I just want to ask you some questions about my students!" the voice shouted again. It was closer this time.

"No! Yes! C! Thirty-three! Manticore! I'm taken!" I took a quick glance behind myself, but the person was still chasing after us. Wasn't one of those the answer? Jeez. The demon was wearing a suit and tie, and he was holding a briefcase in his right hand.

"Earth, rise up!"

The ground rumbled and a massive wall of dirt rose up in front of me—"Breaking Blade!"—and I went through it with ease.

"I won't forget your face, you bushy-tailed creature!"

What? One spell and he was exhausted? "He stopped?" Of course, I kept running just in case.

Ilya looked behind us. "Yeah," she said. "He stopped. Maybe we were getting too far away from…"

"What's wrong?" Why'd she stop speaking all of a sudden?

"Lucia," Ilya whispered. "Turn around, right now."

"Huh? But he's back—"

"Turn around! Turn around! Turn around!" Ilya tugged on my ears and twisted my head.

"Don't yell at me!"

"We're in the predator's territory! It's a beast that's even killed ninth-circle magicians!"

"Huh? Oh. Turning around it is!" How'd she even know it was this predator's territory? "What marking gave it away?" Usually there's dung droppings. Or skeletons hanging from trees. Or weird scent markings.

"You can't feel it? The aura that disrupts your mana?"

"Nope. But that aura sounds super useful." Can't I have that? Could magicians even fight me if I did? What if I absorbed this predator's beast core…? Maybe…. A loud roar caused my tail to stiffen. Nope! Nope, nope, nope! Anything that makes my tail stiff is too dangerous to fight! Flee!

***

In the situation of being stuck between a rock and a hard place, I believed the seventh-circle magician was the less hard one compared to the predator. The predator's a well-known beast amongst these parts. Physically, I have no idea how strong it is, but demons have concluded it to be a top tier divine beast based on the fact it wiped out a small group of three ninth-circle magicians during one of their explorations. Because of that, the deeper parts of the desolate mountains remain unexplored. The empire couldn't risk another loss like that. With three of their powerhouses gone, the fae and the humans pressured the demons greatly, but thankfully, Cain Thunderfire, the world's first tenth-circle magician appeared. There are even rumors of him inheriting the second part of the Godking's legacy, but no one can prove it. Personally, I believe it hasn't been found and the rumors are a scam to prevent humans and fae from flocking to our territories. If it was found, Cain should've announced it to the world; he's already the strongest magician. No one would try to take Vera from him.

Wait, why am I giving a history lesson? Well, it did serve to calm me down. Maybe I should become a teacher in the future instead of a duchess. I think I'd be much happier that way, but sadly, neither Teacher nor my father would agree to that just because I'm the world's youngest third ..., fourth-circle magician. Fourth circle...? Doesn't that mean I surpassed the first prince? He became the world's youngest fourth-circle magician at eighteen after he had a lucky encounter with a dryad and ate her heart.

...I think Lucia's rubbing off on me. My thoughts aren't coordinating like they're supposed to. Focus on the task at hand. Deep breaths. The seventh-circle magician waiting for us most likely set some traps while he retreated in case we came back or provoked the predator. "Light, with your gift, please, show me the path." There, a simple spell to illuminate unseen dangers based on abnormal amounts of mana present. "Lucia, avoid those red patches."

"Red patches? You mean the green ones? I was already doing that."

Was she colorblind? I took a quick glance behind myself. There were dozens of red patches on the ground that Lucia had already avoided. How did she…? I think setting her tail on fire was probably not the best idea I've had. And it's already fully furred again without my help. Maybe she won't be too angry at me? I did put it out for her once I clung onto her back. Oh, is this what you'd call a squirrelback ride? …Bad pun, sorry.

"Darkness, take heed, show me the path to my enemy." If helping her see the traps didn't work, at least I can show her the direction to avoid. And she's running on it. Great. "Lucia, avoid the black path."

"You mean the green one? Turn it off; it's interfering with my footprints."

I have no idea what Lucia is talking about. Why would her footprints be affected by my path? But I'll listen to her since I have to put on a good impression. Sure, Teacher said he'll appear if Lucia killed me, but how does that help me? I'd be dead. It's better not to agitate Lucia further.

"So you finally realized?" a gruff voice asked. It was the teacher with the suit, tie, and briefcase. He was floating in the air with hundreds of fireballs, wind blades, and icicles revolving around his body, a display that would make even a manticore hesitate. "I just wanted to ask you a few simple questions; why did you have to run off and attract the attention of the predator? I see it hasn't chosen to chase you."

Lucia stopped running and stared up at the demon in the sky. She took in a deep breath and opened her mouth to shout.

Was it going to be a declaration of battle? Lucia cupped her hands around her mouth. "I will give you a hundred and two penises if you let us go!"

The spells revolving around the demon's body stopped. They started again after two seconds. "I, I think I misheard you there."

"If you let us go," Lucia shouted again, slower this time, "I will give you a hundred and two penises."

The demon opened his mouth before shutting it. He opened it, raised an eyebrow, then stopped and closed it again. He scratched his head while Lucia glared at him with her hands on her hips. "Why don't you just answer my questions?" he asked. "If they're what I want to hear, I won't need any … compensation at all."

Lucia tilted her head. "I can keep my penises?"

"Yes, yes, all the penises shall be kept by you," the demon said. "Do you know what happened to my students? There were five of them, and they chose a mission to hunt down a manticore in the nearby area. I haven't heard from them in a while, so I decided to track them down, and what do you know? At the end of the trail was a squirrel and a little girl."

"Oh…," Lucia said with a nod. "Yeah, they're dead. Sorry. Can't help you. There was a … what was it called, Ilya? A corpse lover?"

"Corpse stalker."

"Right. There was a corpse stalker eating them when we found them. But it saw me and ran away."

"Is that so?" the demon asked and rubbed his chin. "And the manticore? I saw signs of a struggle."

"It was already gone when we got there." Lucia nodded twice. "Any more questions?"

"Why did you run when you sensed my presence?"

"Because my tail stiffened."

"…Pardon?"

"Because my tail stiffened," Lucia said again, louder this time.

"Last question. What's the name of the demon sticking to your back?"

I spoke up this time. "My name is Ilya Pentorn. Daughter of Duke Pentorn."

The spells floating around the demon's body stopped and disappeared. "Very well," the demon said. "Thank you for your time. If you go to the base the academy has set up in the mountains, you can use my name, Bartholomew Shinx, to gain access to our systems. Pass a good word to your father for me, will you?"

"Thank you, Sir Shinx," I said, keeping my head level like my father taught me to in his etiquette lessons. "Which way is the base?"

"It's east of here, about three mountains away." Bartholomew smiled at me and adjusted his tie. "Do you need to be escorted?"

"Nope. We're good," Lucia said. "Thanks."

"Ms. Pentorn?" Bartholomew asked, ignoring Lucia's glare.

"As my companion has said, we won't be needing your assistance. I appreciate the offer."

Bartholomew nodded. "Then this is farewell."

***

I'd be lying if I said I wasn't a bit jealous of Ilya. She can drop her father's name and even a seventh-circle magician will respect her. How is that even fair? It's not like she's her father, sheesh. Duke Pentorn...., that sounds like a really high position of nobility. I'm pretty sure it is. The first noble I was sold to was a baron. I wonder how different their statures are.

Anyways, I've decided to head east towards the base that the demon was talking about. The main reason being my interspacial ring ran out of space to hold anymore valuables. Like penises. Also, it's taking me a lot longer to absorb this beast core than expected, and I feel like I've reached a wall in my Unrelenting Path of Slaughter. Usually, when I kill things with the path on, I'd get a rush of excitement. But after always having the path on, the excitement's faded and following the path does nothing. I'm not sure how I'm supposed to breakthrough from a spirit warrior to a divine warrior. I'll just ask Durandal when he wakes up, which should be really, really, really soon. Please.

On the way to the base—I've already crossed two mountains and halfway through a third—I've killed a total of thirty-three divine beasts, twenty-four of which dropped cores. That's a lot more than the usual core rate! But during that whole time, the manticore beast core still hadn't finished absorbing. Even sparring daily with Ilya doesn't speed up the rate—probably because Ilya doesn't present any challenge at all. The sparring's mostly payback for setting my tail on fire, but she doesn't know that.

Speaking of beasts…, that one looks awfully familiar. "Oh, look, it's a corpse lover!"

"Corpse stalker," Ilya said. I'm not sure when it happened, but Ilya's been riding on my back more often than not. It's because she refuses to consume any more bones to restore her mana to maintain her spells to keep up with me. Well, that just means more for me!

"These corpse stalkers follow strong beasts, right? I wonder what this one's following." Ah, it's running away. How did it notice me? I think their sense of smell is stronger than mine. I have a few of their cores, but I can't absorb them until this manticore's is done digesting. Stupid divine beasts.

"Are you going to hunt another divine beast?" Ilya asked. Why does she sound so tired—no, that's not the right word. Helpless?

"Of course. I need to get stronger." Maybe if I kill whatever the corpse stalker was following, I'll breakthrough. I doubt it though. I shouldn't have fed Puppers to the manticore; he still hasn't reappeared yet. He'd probably have an idea or two on how to become a divine warrior.

I circulated my qi to activate the Unrelenting Path of Slaughter. The red footprints showed me the way to the beast ahead. I wonder how that works. Can it be subconscious scents, sounds, or markings on the ground? Wait a minute…. Wait one gosh darn minute.

"Lucia? Why'd—"

"Shut up. I'm thinking." I've had the Unrelenting Path of Slaughter active more often than not due to Puppers' advice of live, breathe, and sleep the path. It's always consuming a little bit of my qi every second it's active, but the bones of strength refill it without an issue. Wasn't the first time I used the path like a guide? It told me what to do and how to follow it. Well, it didn't tell me, more like forcibly took control of my body until I listened. Then it slowly gave me freedom until it became like a navigation tool, which I've been using a lot. Maybe, the next step is to follow the Unrelenting Path of Slaughter without actually having it activated? Wouldn't having it be active passively be the real meaning of living, breathing, and sleeping the path? Then my next step is to figure out how the path figures out where creatures are, where their weaknesses are, what mana lo—

"Lucia."

Didn't I tell her to stop bothering me? I have to figure out—

"Lucia!"

I'm going to throw her away if this isn't important! "What!?"

"Beast!"

Oh. I was so lost in thought I didn't even notice. "Unrelenting Path of Slaughter: Breaking Blade!" Ah, I forgot to turn off the Unrelenting Path of Slaughter to try to figure out the giant snake's weakness on my own.

"You killed an imugi in a single hit...," Ilya said and climbed off my back.

Why does she sound so surprised? "Wasn't it just too weak?"

"Oh, no, it was already weakened," Ilya said and pointed at the gashes all along the beast's body. "See?"

"Hey! Step away from our prey! It's dangerous.... You killed it?" A group of demons wearing robes emblazoned with three A's, the Arcane Arts Academy's symbol, appeared from behind the imugi.

Oh, sweet, the imugi had a beast core. I'll pretend it didn't have one if anyone asks. Ilya's good at talking, I'm sure she's distracting them.

"Sorry about that," Ilya said. "My companion wasn't paying attention and killed it on accident. We would've left it alone if we knew you were chasing after it."

The leader of the students stared at Ilya. "No, it was our fault for letting it get away. But do you mind if we keep the body? We need it as proof."

"That's not an issue," Ilya said with a nod before looking at me. "Right?"

"That depends; is it male?"

"Male?" the leader asked. "No, it's a female. Why?"

"Never mind, you can have it." Ilya and I have left over a dozen divine beast corpses lying around mainly because we ran out of space in our interspacial rings. And Ilya has seven of them! Seven! For the record, I have three. The ring I got from the Briarwood envoy and the two earrings I conveniently found on a dying student. Of course, I hid them with the ring just in case the well-dressed demon teacher appears again and notices me wearing his deceased student's jewelry.

"Thank you," the leader said. He glanced at Ilya. "Are you a student of the academy?"

258

"No," Ilya said, "but I'm an acquaintance of Bartholomew Shinx."

"Teacher Shinx?" the leader asked. His eyes widened—from fear, I think. I have to admit that teacher was pretty scary. He even made my tail stiff. "I see. Were you heading to the base? We can escort you if you'd like."

Everyone gives Ilya face. How come I don't get any? It's not fair.

***

I'm impressed. Bartholomew Shinx, his name can get me anywhere. How does a seventh-circle magician hold so much sway over this community? Unless he's an eighth-circle magician, that would explain it, but I don't think he is. No one's even questioned my relationship with Mr. Shinx: they didn't ask for proof, they didn't ask how I knew him, they didn't even harass Lucia when I said she was with me. Demons don't take too kindly to beastkin.

The Arcane Arts Academy's base is well-guarded. I know, earlier, I thought it'd be impossible to set up a town inside of the desolate mountains, but I've been proven wrong. There's hundreds of spell arrays outside of the walls, and I think the dense mana hanging over the area dissuades beasts from coming. But there are still guards on the walls even with the many formations laying around. Most of them are at the sixth circle though; I only saw one seventh.

The walls are simple, made of earth and camouflaged with vines and trees. There are also corpses of dead beasts laying around in specific ways. There's a dead elephant-like creature hanging from a tree, mimicking the prey of a divine shadow leopard. As long as beasts think stronger beasts live here, then they wouldn't advance. Lucia was a bit nervous about entering this place as well, saying the territorial markings were unsettling.

The interior of the base is set up like a small section of the capital. There are buildings surrounding a plaza that has a teleportation array set up in the center. Stalls line the array where leaving students can sell their unused consumables and arriving students can buy useful items. Lucia said she wanted to hold off on selling our stuff until right before we left. She didn't want to be surrounded by hundreds of demons who knew she had a fortune on her. I say our stuff, but really, it should all be Lucia's. She just didn't have enough space to carry all the corpses of the beasts she's killed. I thought seven interspacial rings would be enough, but who knew it'd be too little?

After the group of students we were traveling with brought us here, they went to their commission area, and we tagged along. The academy has a nice system set up. They exchange spell books as rewards for handing in beast corpses. The beast corpses are used as materials to train alchemists, engravers, chefs, and necromancers who give their products to the school. These products, potions, bones, and meals, are also put up as rewards for killing beasts or accomplishing commissions. It's a very self-sufficient economy that Lucia and I will be able to take part in because of Mr. Shinx. But I don't know how useful Lucia will find this area; the academy is centered on creating magicians after all. A martial artist like her won't get as much use out of it compared to someone like me.

"I want to take a hot bath," Lucia said. She was staring fixedly at a sign that said lodgings. It was for the students who hadn't booked their rooms in advance or visiting teachers. "I want a fluffy bed to sleep in too. I want to eat barbeque and drink beer." Her tail twitched from side to side and she turned her gaze on me. Her face was akin to that of a divine beast's. She pointed at the building.

"Okay. Let's go." Lucia made all the decisions, but I had to help her. All the demons we've encountered so far completely ignored her and focused their attentions on me instead. I've managed to deescalate the situation in every instance, but it's only a matter of time before Lucia's temper explodes and an incident occurs.

"Hello," a feminine voice greeted us when we entered the building. "New student? You look awfully young. May I see your I.D.?"

"I'm not a student," I said, "but I'm an acquaintance of Bartholomew Shinx."

"Oh," the woman at the counter said, bringing her hand to her mouth. "Teacher Shinx, is it? I understand. Will he be staying with you two as well?"

"He won't," I said. At least, I don't think he will. He seemed like a very busy person with his briefcase and all.

The woman nodded. "Usually you'd have to pay with your contribution points, but considering you don't have any, I'll put the tab on Teacher Shinx's account," she said. "Would a regular room for two be sufficient?"

"VIP!" Lucia shouted.

The teacher glanced at Lucia, then turned her gaze back onto me.

I resisted the urge to scratch the itch that appeared on my neck, and I nodded. "We'll take a VIP room."

"Not *a* VIP room," Lucia said and placed her hands on the counter while leaning forward. "*The* VIP room. The best one you have." She glared at the unsettled woman with her tail twitching like it was smacking away flies. "It better have a hot bath."

The woman smiled at Lucia while taking a step back. "The luxury suite does have a bath. It also has access to the private roof with a swimming pool and grill. The—"

"We'll take it!" Lucia said. She turned her gaze onto me, and I involuntarily gulped.

"I'd like to book the luxury suite then," I said to the woman. "Does Mr. Shinx have enough contribution points to afford it?"

"That depends on how many nights you're staying," the woman said. "Teacher Shinx has enough contribution points to book the room for a week."

"Then we'll stay for a week!" Lucia said.

It seemed like I had to tell my father about Mr. Shinx. If I used up all his contribution points and didn't do anything in return for him..., terrible rumors would start about the Pentorn family. Who would want to help me out in the future if that were to occur? "Yes, we'll book the room, but it's possible we might leave in less than a week."

"Impossible!" Lucia said, shaking her head.

Sorry, Mr. Shinx. Your sacrifice is appreciated.

***

Hot water! Fluffy towels! Clean clothes! The most gosh darn comfortable mattress I've ever rested on! Well, it's like the second mattress I've ever tried before, but I'm sure it's incomparable to others. It's like I'm lying down on a cloud—ah, if only Durandal were here, then I could light those scented candles, kick Ilya out of the room, put on some nice music, and have my way with him. ...Of course, that means beating him in a fair fight. I didn't get to win enough before he fell asleep!

"Lucia, um, are we really going to stay here for a week?"

Of course! I need to rest! It's been way, way too long since I've had any time to destress. "Mhm." Ah, I can splay all my limbs and not leave the boundaries of the bed. This is great.

"Don't you feel a little bad for Mr. Shinx? His students' deaths were directly related to you, and now you're abusing his trust in me."

"That's your problem, not mine." One day, everyone will have to give me face. People will be able to say, I know Lucia Fluffytail, and they'll be treated as well as Ilya is when she calls upon Bartholomew's name. Mm, that's a good goal.

"But, Lucia, what if he gets mad?"

"Then you kowtow to him and apologize. Throw in some dukes and other noble sounding titles too." Sheesh, Ilya has so much power because of her father, but she doesn't abuse it at all. What's wrong with her? If my dad could make people tremble in their boots just by hearing his name, you can bet that I'd wear a sign, blatantly saying I was his daughter, on my forehead.

I heard Ilya sigh. She muttered, "We could've gotten a normal room. Could've lived modestly. Stayed in good favor with everyone."

I lifted my head and looked towards the side. Ilya was drawing circles on her mattress with her finger while sitting with her knees against her chest. She looked so sad. Was I a little too excessive? May—

"The grill is ready. Would you like me to man it?"

A student interrupted my thoughts. Apparently, you could even earn contribution points by doing mundane chores like cleaning and cooking. The student who asked the question was standing by a sliding glass door inside of our room that led to the roof outside. A sparkling pool and grill could be seen just beyond the puffy red curtains. I really want to make him man it, but I can't guarantee he won't poison me. "I'll do it. You can leave."

The student ignored me and looked at Ilya. I'm really going to smack the backs of these demons' heads one day. They're always ignoring me. I wonder if they'll ignore a sword to the face.

"Thank you," Ilya said. "You can leave."

The student nodded and made his way out of the room. The door clicked and locked itself as it closed. Meat! I can finally eat after not eating for so long; I can't wait. What do I have to cook? ...Not penises, those are for sale. Hm. Ilya has all the corpses, I'll take hers. What was I thinking about earlier before I was interrupted? I can't remember. "Ilya! Meat!"

"You ... want to eat a divine beast?" Why was Ilya backing away from me? I killed those things! Their bodies belong to me. "D-do you know how valuable their meat is?"

"Beasts are born to be eaten! Don't tell me their price or you'll make my heart hurt." I held my hand out. "Ring, please."

Ilya gulped. Why did she look so scared? "We can order uncooked meat from—"

"No." She's hiding something, or she's just very reluctant to give up the corpses. It can't be that she already ate them all, right!? If she did..., I might have demon for dinner. "Take out that manticore. I'm going to eat it, and you're not going to stop me."

Ilya pursed her lips. "What if I said it was poisonous?"

"I'll let you try it first." Obviously. I'd test it on Puppers, but he's not alive yet.

Ilya tilted her head. "You ... were going to share with me?"

What am I, a savage? "Of course, what the heck? Unless you're not hungry?" I went through a life-and-death ordeal with Ilya. I won't trust her to make me food, but I won't be so cruel as to starve her. Plus, I really don't know if manticore is poisonous or not, so it's always good to have a trial dummy.

"N-no," Ilya said. "Here." She gave me one of her rings. Great! Let's start! "But what if Mr. Shinx comes here and realizes you're eating a manticore?"

Did she say something? I couldn't hear her over the sound of the grill starting. This is a really fancy cooking implement, much better than a campfire. There's some buttons you can press to increase or decrease the level of flames. And there's even this handle that you can rotate to make the meat cook more evenly. Magic's amazing. This probably counts as a magic tool, doesn't it? Well, I doubt I'd need to use my mini-map, and Ilya can cast a better version of haste than my dress can.

I rifled through Ilya's ring and pulled out the manticore. I better cut off a part of it and store the rest just in case Bartholomew comes in here and realizes we're eating a manticore. Why am I so smart? I think I'll eat the hind leg first; I think that's the best cut of meat? I wouldn't know. All I know is that I was never fed that part of an animal before. I was always fed with vegetables or the gross parts of animals like intestines. Until I met Snow that is, but I like pretending that part of my life never happened. Which part?

Anyways, I should ask Ilya why divine beast meat is valuable. I'm curious because she gathered enough courage to try to keep it for herself. "Hey, Ilya. What does eating divine beast meat do?"

"...Makes you feel full?" Ilya asked. She put on some slippers and stepped outside of the room, standing next to me by the grill and pool. She looked around. "I feel like I'm in a mansion. But we're still in the desolate mountains; it's a bit unsettling."

"Stop trying to change the subject! Why'd you want to keep the meat for yourself?"

Ilya looked down. "Divine beast meat is very rich in nutrients. Of course, it's nothing like absorbing a beast core, but for magicians, it's a godsend," she said. "We're not good at absorbing beast cores, but we can, at the very least, eat the beast's meat for a minor boost in our abilities."

"But aren't you rich enough to buy it since your dad is special and all?" A duke's supposed to be pretty high up there in nobility, right?

"It's very hard to kill a divine beast without damaging its meat," Ilya said, "since, you know, explosions are what magicians are best at. My family only eats divine beast meat on special occasions, and only direct descendants of the emperor can afford to eat it every day. Like I said, it's very valuable." She smiled at me. "I really didn't think you'd share any with me, but you're a nicer person than I thought."

...Maybe I shouldn't eat this.

***

I feel guilty. I'm shamelessly using up Mr. Shinx's contribution points, living my life in debauchery in the first-class suite of an inn with the finest service, feasting on the meat of divine beasts with an expert cook, and freely studying all kinds of spells through the scrying orb in the corner of the room. But it feels. So. Good. I want to live this way forever, but I know it's temporary, and at the end of it, I'll have to confront Mr. Shinx's anger. Is this what it means to live your life to the fullest knowing you'll die the next day? Abandoning every restraint and forgetting all the consequences because your time is limited? It's only been three days, but I have a feeling I can sink much, much further into depravity if I don't stop myself now.

"Before we leave, I'm going to steal this bed. And grill. And pool. And peeping-Tom orb." Lucia rolled around on her bed and sighed, her tail twitching occasionally. At least she knows it's stealing. "Ilya. More meat!" She sat up and stared at me. "Quit peeping and give me the ring."

But a teacher was lecturing on the intricacies behind fifth-circle magic.... Ah, if I don't give her the ring, she might break the orb. I didn't want to, but I released the scrying orb and tossed Lucia one of my interspacial rings. I think that one had a dead beast inside of it. I put my hands back on the scrying orb, and the image of the teacher and blackboard reappeared. Good, I didn't miss anything important.

"Do you want some?" Lucia asked, her voice coming from outside the room.

"Yes, please!" I called back. Lucia is an amazing cook. She's infinitely more times better than Rogath, who only had bread stocked up in his pantry. Maybe it's the materials Lucia's working with, but she's also better than the chef working at my dad's mansion. Now that I think about it, the prince had a lucky encounter with a dryad to become a fourth-circle magician. I guess, Lucia counts as my lucky encounter. …Even though she's using my father's influence. I should use it more often.

"There's no divine beast in this one!" Lucia shouted. A ring flew into the room and bounced off the wall. It looks like this lecture will have to wait. At least there's a recording feature built into the scrying orb. How convenient is that? After turning on the feature, I picked up the ring and checked inside. It really was empty except for a few engraved bones. Then was it this ring? No, this one's filled with bones too. Then, this one…?

"Um, Lucia. There's no more meat." Even I couldn't believe my own words.

"What!?" Lucia stomped into the room with wide eyes. "Did you check all your rings!?"

"Yes. You didn't take any when I wasn't looking, right?" I always left the rings on the counter for Lucia to rifle through whenever she wanted to. She enjoyed engraving the bones of the beasts.

"No way," Lucia said and shook her head. "Besides, do you really think I can eat seven house-sized spaces filled with divine beasts in three days? I could eat one a day at most."

"Then there's only one explanation." Well, there were probably more, but this was the only one I could think of. "The cleaner stole them."

"That little greasy bastard!" Lucia said, her eyes widening. "I knew he looked sketchy! I should've cut his head off when he ignored me." Her eyes narrowed into slits, and her tail violently twitched. She lifted her head into the air and sniffed twice before her eyes glazed over and turned white. "Found him."

Oh dear. White-eyed Lucia was the scary Lucia I knew from my time traversing the mountains with her. When her irises and pupils reappeared, she became a lot nicer. I think it has something to do with the Unrelenting Path of Slaughter that she's always shouting about. It'd also explain her colorblindness. I should probably follow after her in case she gets targeted by a teacher or a patrol.

The door to the room flew open as Lucia dashed outside, her sword in hand. I had to cast my standard spells to keep up with her, and I didn't forget to lock the door before I left. The receptionist smiled at me as I ran past her. A few demons in the streets pointed at us, and I could feel my face turning red, but I didn't stop chasing after Lucia. My gut told me if I lost sight of her, something extremely bad would happen.

Lucia continued to run until she arrived at the street vendors surrounding the portal into the base. I saw the student who cleaned our room talking with one of the merchants. He turned his head, and his eyes widened when he saw us. A yelp escaped from his lips as he whirled around and ran. But he didn't get very far because Lucia shouted, "Unrelenting Path of Slaughter: Flying Blade!" And his legs fell off. The demon screamed and planted face first into the ground. He rolled over onto his back with the help of his arms, constant shrieks coming out of his mouth.

"Bastard!" Lucia growled and leapt forward. Her sword plunged into his shoulder and came out the other side, shattering the ground beneath the demon. "Where'd you put them?"

"I, I don't know what you're talking about," the demon yelled. It was hard to make out his words through his sobs. I'm not sure why I followed after Lucia. I don't think anything I could do can change the current situation.

Another shriek pierced the air as Lucia twisted the hilt of her sword. The demon's shoulder cracked, and his arm was severed as Lucia pulled her sword out of the ground. "Where'd you put them?" Lucia asked again as she plunged the sword into the demon's remaining hand, pinning it to the earth. "Your neck is next if you lie."

"That, that merchant," the demon said through whimpers. "I sold them to him!"

Lucia whirled her head around, and the merchant at the street stall stiffened. Lucia snorted and pulled her sword out of the demon's hand. She stomped over to the merchant and held out her palm. "Hand them over."

"T-this is robbery," the merchant said. He glanced behind me, and I turned my head to follow his gaze. The patrols were approaching. "Help! Over here! Help!"

Well, the three days of debauchery were good while they lasted. I just hope Mr. Shinx's name is good enough to get us out of this mess. I don't see Lucia taking down a group of sixth-circle magicians led by a seventh-circle leader.

***

"Hold it right there!" a voice shouted at me. "Release your sword!"

They want me to let go of Durandal? There's no way in hell that's happening. I pointed mini-DalDal at the merchant. "This man has my items. What is the punishment for trafficking stolen goods?"

"That's not true!" the merchant yelled. "I pay for every one of my transactions. Is it my responsibility to check the source of my items? The beastkin is insane! Look at what she did to that man."

Wow, there aren't many people who become more talkative when there's a sword pointing at their face. Maybe I should move it closer.

"Stop!" the patrol leader said. One of the patrol members ran to the fallen demon's side, picking up his legs and arm along the way. "Let's discuss this calmly like civilized folk."

He looked around. "Who's the one responsible for this beastkin?"

"I am," Ilya said, raising her hand. She bit her lower lip and ran to my side. "Lucia, put down the sword, please. The merchant isn't going anywhere. I'll get your stuff back, I promise. I want to eat it too, remember?"

Well, if Ilya can get those corpses back without an issue, then I won't have to use force. My tail isn't stiffening, so I can probably fight these people if Ilya fails. Yeah, I'll let Ilya handle this. I lowered mini-DalDal, making sure to cut the merchant's stall on the way down.

"Can I see your I.D.?" the patrol leader asked Ilya.

Ilya shook her head. "I don't have one," she said. "I'm a close friend of Bartholomew Shinx; my name is Ilya Pentorn."

"A friend of Teacher Shinx?" the patrol leader asked and furrowed his brow. His eyes widened. "Did you say Ilya Pentorn? B-by any chance, is your father…"

"Duke Pentorn," Ilya said and narrowed her eyes. Wow, there it is again with the name dropping.

The patrol leader paled and looked behind himself. The patrol members looked away and lowered their gazes to the ground. The leader pursed his lips before facing Ilya. "I see, Lady Pentorn," he said. "May I ask what the situation is?"

Ilya pointed at the demon I dismembered. "That man worked as a cleaner for the VIP room of the lodgings I was staying at," she said and snorted. "He stole the contents of four of my interspacial rings and had the audacity to sell it off to this merchant over here. If it weren't for my bodyguard, he would've gotten away with it. Can the Arcane Arts Academy shoulder the responsibility of having my goods stolen?"

I became a bodyguard? To be fair, it *is* in my best interest to keep Ilya alive. I guess I *am* her bodyguard. …I demand a wage!

The patrol leader cleared his throat. "No, ma'am," he said. He glanced at the merchant. "What are you waiting for? Give her back her goods."

The merchant bit his lower lip and glanced between Ilya and the patrol leader. "I, I paid for these," he said. "You can't do this."

The patrol leader's face turned red. "Who's your backer?" he asked in a low voice.

"I'm an independent merchant," the merchant said. "The merchants' union is my backer."

"Let me see your I.D.," the patrol leader said, holding out his palm.

"I have to show you my I.D., but she doesn't?" the merchant asked, pointing at Ilya. "How can you believe she is who she says she is?"

The patrol leader's brow furrowed, and his gaze shifted onto Ilya. She placed her hands on her hips in return and snorted before asking, "Can you afford to offend the duke?"

How domineering! I want to be able to do that too! Life isn't fair. But I already knew that, didn't I? Power is everything, which is why I have to get stronger! Wait, I thought I was getting stronger for Durandal to wake up faster. And to become a legend. ...Welp, three birds with one stone; becoming stronger will solve every single one of my problems.

The patrol leader turned his head back towards the merchant. "I.D." he said, his voice practically a growl. The amulet around his neck glowed bright orange, and I saw tendrils of green in the air flowing towards the man. How am I supposed to see mana without the Path of Slaughter if my theory is right and I have to incorporate the path without actually using it? I turned the path off, but I couldn't see anything out of the ordinary.

Wait, I can project my qi outwards. I could do that for a while now, but I forgot about it because of the path. How did it work again? I willed my qi out of my body, letting it expand outwards like a hemisphere. When it touched the man's amulet, I felt a faint sensation like a single hair brushing along my arm. I tried to focus on it, but the amulet stopped glowing when I was getting close. The merchant had handed over his I.D. to the patrol leader.

The merchant's eyes widened as a tearing sound rang through the air. The patrol leader threw the two halves of the I.D. over his shoulders without even looking at it. "You're no longer welcome here," the patrol leader said. "Return Lady Pentorn's items or drastic measures will be taken."

"T-this is illegal," the merchant said and fell to his knees.

"In these parts of the mountains, the Arcane Arts Academy is the law," the patrol leader said and took a step forward. "Your union didn't tell you about this when you came here?" The leader looked around at the merchants and students who were watching the spectacle. His voice echoed over the area. "Are all the merchants this uninformed?"

One merchant called out, "No. We all know the rules."

The merchant on the ground laughed. "You want your goods back?" he asked and stared at Ilya with wide eyes. "Then take them!"

A mountain of beast corpses appeared in the center of the market. The pile was easily five times my height even though there were only nine beasts. Divine beasts are big, okay? Ilya's face paled as she pulled out her rings and stored the corpses as fast as she could, but everyone was staring at her when she was done.

The patrol leader opened and closed his mouth a few times. "W-were those all divine beast corpses?" he asked in a low voice.

Ilya took in a deep breath and placed her trembling hands on her hips. She cocked her head to the side. "Birds risk their lives for food. Do you know what people risk their lives for?"

Sex?

"Treasure," the patrol leader said, his face returning to a neutral expression. He bowed. "I asked something I shouldn't have. I apologize."

Ilya nodded and came to my side. She whispered to me, "We should take the teleportation array to the academy grounds back in the capital. If we return to the wilderness, we'll be attacked."

"Can I sell my penises first?"

"There'll be a better market for them in the capital," Ilya said and tugged on my sleeve. "Please, Lucia."

Well, I guess that's fine. I still have 24 divine beast cores in reserve for when I finally finish absorbing this manticore's. A break from killing divine beasts would be nice. And if we go to Ilya's mansion, I'll definitely get better treatment than I was in the VIP room, right? A warrior needs a calm and relaxed mind to breakthrough! Slacking will make me stronger! This is training.

14

Thankfully, I managed to convince Lucia to leave the desolate mountains via the academy's teleportation array. It wouldn't have been very smart to stay in those lawless lands after everyone found out about our wealth. I've told it to Lucia before, but divine beasts are *valuable*. It wouldn't have been a problem if only the students came after us, but I'm willing to bet patrol leaders and teachers would've been tempted by nine divine beast corpses.

When we arrived in the capital, we were asked for our I.D. once again, but Mr. Shinx's name was enough for them to stop hassling us. I wanted to find Mr. Shinx and apologize for spending so many of his contribution points, but he was visiting family in the countryside; thus, we had to leave. I hope he won't be too angry with me when he finds out. His contribution points were only enough to rent a room for a week, so either he had an abysmally low number of points or that room was insanely expensive. I think it's the latter.

It's been a while since I've been to the capital. It's an ugly, crowded place. There's people everywhere. It's loud and noisy. Tourists stand in the middle of the streets or walk side by side along the narrow paths. The roads are littered with horse dung from all the carriages and taxis. The smell is unbearable at times, especially when it rains. It's nothing like the countryside. I've only been here three times: when I begged my father to take me on one of his business trips, when my father was recognized for his deeds, and most recently, when the crown prince came of age. I was ten at the time, which means the prince should be in his twenties now.

Speaking of ages, I wonder how old Lucia is. "Lucia? How old are you?"

Lucia blinked and glanced at me before raising her head again. It seemed like she didn't like crowds—crowds of demons at least. I'd probably be just as uncomfortable as her if I was thrown into the beastkin's capital. "Age has no meaning to a warrior." Lucia nodded twice.

Well, whatever. It's not like it matters once she's above the age of marriage, which I'm sure she is. "You wanted to sell your ... stuff, right?"

"Right," Lucia said and pushed me in front of her. "Lead the way!"

Under normal circumstances, I'd avoid the marketplace and have my father buy everything Lucia was selling, but I'm positive my father has no use for beast penises! He hasn't remarried after my mother died after all. Though I haven't been here often, I memorized maps of the major demon cities and the human and beast capitals as part of my education to becoming a duchess. I'm pretty sure the mercantile section of the capital is towards the south.

And I was right. It was to the south, but now the problem is choosing which store to sell to. Apothecaries have been known to create tonics with the goods Lucia's trying to sell. But chefs have also been known to buy the goods Lucia's trying to sell from butchers. They're a delicacy sold in high-class restaurants. And I also have to take into consideration which shops are aligned with which political faction. It wouldn't reflect well on my father if I sold a tremendous amount of materials to someone unaffiliated with my father. Then I have to take into consideration the beast cores Lucia wants to sell. Those can go to alchemists, magical blacksmiths, or the apothecary again. Price also plays a major role; I can't let anyone scam Lucia. ...I think I figured out why my father hired a butler who used to be a merchant.

"Are we here?" Lucia asked. "Why'd you stop?"

"I'm trying to figure out the best person to sell your goods to," I said. "There's a lot of things to take into consideration."

"Eh?" Lucia tilted her head. "I'll take over since we're here." She sucked in her breath and tilted her head towards the sky. "Beast penises! Beast penises! Come get your beast penises! They come in all shapes and sizes: one head, two heads, three heads; you name it, I have it! Special limited time offer! Buy a package deal and receive two complimentary beast cores!"

…I think I should hide.

"But wait!" Lucia shouted. "There's more! How many of you have seen a divine beast's penis!? Not only can you look, but you can buy your very own today!"

Lucia's voice echoed through the whole mercantile district, and a few curious shop owners stuck their heads out of their stores. A few mothers had covered their childrens' ears with their hands, and men were laughing at Lucia's advertisement. One shop owner walked up to us. "Can I see your wares?"

Lucia nodded and grabbed my hand. She put an earring in my palm and patted my back. "This is the seller. I just work for her." She leaned closer and whispered to me, "They'll scam me if I try to sell them goods. You can do this for me, right? Thanks, Ilya, you're the best."

I looked up at the expectant merchant before sending my senses into the interspacial earring. A sea of dicks awaited me. When Teacher told me to gather experience by exploring the world, I don't think he ever expected me to have this kind of experience.

What happened next has been forever scrubbed from my memory.

A few hours later, Lucia was smiling with an interspacial earring filled to the brim with gold, silver, and copper coins. If I had to take a guess at Lucia's fortune, then I'd say she had as much money as an established marchioness would—more than a common person would ever make in fifty lifetimes. I never realized there were so many depraved people in the capital. I feel tainted after ... after that event that never happened.

"Ah, it feels good to be rich," Lucia said and stored her earring somewhere beneath her dress. "So, what's next? Why don't you take me to your home? There's so many new things to explore! Ah, the world's so bright."

I think I'm going to cry.

***

Just as I expected! It feels good to be rich. I don't get why Ilya looks so glum despite mooching off my money by riding the super-expensive carriage I hired to take us back to her home. She didn't lose anything, and she's getting benefits! This carriage comes with a portable refrigerator powered by magic; there's even free drinks! Of course, I offered them to Ilya first to test for poison. I should just hire someone to test all my food for me before I eat it; I think it'd make my life a lot less stressful. That's right, in the future, I'll hire a poison tester when I have my own place.

I took a bone of focus out of my storage and absorbed it. I was starting to get low on its effects, and they didn't give me as much focus as they used to, but they still work fine. I just have to consume more. And even though I'm eating and sleeping properly now, I still use my bones of strength. I've gotten a few tingly feelings and headaches when I don't use them. One time, I even vomited.

"Hey, Lucia," Ilya said. She was hesitating. Was she going to say something that would offend me? "You, um, probably shouldn't use your bones...."

What? Nonsense! I have so many; I'd feel bad if I didn't use them. Waste not, want not; that's what one of my fellow beastkin army members told me once after licking moldy sauce off of his plate. I avoided him after that.

I must have given Ilya a strange look because she continued and said, while biting her lip, "They're addictive. Like really, really addictive." She withered under my gaze, her shoulders hunching. "And, um, they're not healthy for you. I didn't say anything earlier because it looked like you really needed them to sustain your unsustainable lifestyle, but now…" Ilya stiffened. She barely managed to whisper, "I'm going to pee if you keep staring at me like that."

Oh, I was activating my Unrelenting Path of Slaughter. I hadn't even noticed, how odd. But does that mean my aura is as intimidating as Durandal's was? No, I actually peed under Durandal's bloodthirst. But then again, Ilya does seem more levelheaded than I was when I first met Durandal, so maybe, my aura's the same as Durandal's, but Ilya's just better at holding it together. …I feel like Ilya was saying something important before? What was it? Darn, this bone of focus is already running out; I should use another.

"Lucia…," Ilya said when I took out another bone and consumed it. "Are you doing that just to annoy me?"

"Doing what?" Oh, right! She was saying bones were addictive. That can't be true. "Don't worry, I can stop whenever I want."

Ilya furrowed her brow, her face looking like a concerned puppy's. "You do know that's what all addicts say, right?" she asked and pursed her lips.

"Well, I'm willing to bet that's what all non-addicts also say." After all, a person who's perfectly sober wouldn't claim to be addicted. That's me; why admit a problem when there is none?

"No they, I mean, well, that's true," Ilya said. "But the thing is, they actually can stop whenever they want. I don't think you can."

"Hey, it's my life, and if I'm ruining it by absorbing bones, how's that your problem? Besides, they're really helpful." These bones really help me, okay? They're all I have to remind me of Durandal—other than mini-DalDal. The ability to engrave symbols onto bones was Durandal's parting gift to me—other than the Unrelenting Path of Slaughter. I definitely couldn't have made it to the peak of spirit warrior without them.

Ilya lowered her head and looked up at me through her lashes. "But are they helping you now?" She sighed. "You're eating and sleeping. You don't need to constantly maintain vigilance. So why are you using them?"

"Because it makes me feel better. And why are you asking so many questions? Are you upset that I'm not sharing any with you? What's so bad about using them anyways?" I don't see a problem. Sure, I can sell them for money, but I'm rich! I don't need money. I could buy a mansion full of bones if I wanted to.

"I'm not upset," Ilya said. "And they're bad for your health. Everyone who's used them has died an early death."

"Correlation does not imply causation! Most people who would use these bones are mercenaries. And mercenaries have a high rate of death. It's not the bones' fault."

"But major schools ban bones of focus even though students live a life filled with a need to stay focused." Ilya's lips were trembling, and she bit her lower one to make them stop.

"Clearly, they don't want rich people to win out over the poor." What a considerate school. "Everyone deserves a fair chance."

"If that were the case, the administrations wouldn't put the wealthier students into the classes with the better teachers," Ilya said. "It's the bones that are the problem. If you want me to, I can list out their major problems."

"You should've done that from the start." She can't just say bones are bad without explaining why. It doesn't make for a very convincing argument.

"Well," Ilya said and hung her head. "I don't know them off the top of my head, but I'll show you the books in my father's study! There's lots of them about addictive substances and their corresponding health hazards. But I do know nearly all addictive substances tears families apart because of communication and financial issues."

"Hah! I'm an orphan. There's no way my family can be torn apart."

Ilya scratched her head. "They're … they're just bad, you know?"

"No, I don't. And you haven't said anything to convince me that they are." Sheesh, why's she so persistent about this topic? It's not like my bones are interfering with me becoming a divine warrior, right? …Right? "Ilya! Do you think these bones interfere with becoming a divine warrior!?"

"Oh! That was one of the side effects!" Ilya said, her eyes widening. "Consuming bones hampers mana circulation in the long run because of the beastly properties!"

"But I have like literally no mana circulation. Do you think it hampers qi too?" That would be a serious problem! A serious, serious problem! But wait, Durandal wouldn't give me something that prevents me from advancing. But then again, the Godking probably consumed bones too, and he never crossed the wall to become a divine warrior.

"Maybe? I'll check my father's books when we arrive." Ilya nodded.

I guess, for now, I'll have to … stop. …After this last one.

***

I may have created a monster. Lucia had handed over all her bones to me and told me to hold onto them to prevent her from consuming any for no reason. I didn't think my persuasion would work, and I have no idea if consuming bones affects her qi circulation, but my words worked. The first few minutes weren't too bad. That's right, just minutes. Maybe she got anxious from not having them on her, but she threatened to tear my lungs out if I didn't return them to her, so I did.

After that happened, she consumed a bone and gave the whole thing back to me again, and told me to not give them to her no matter how much she asked. But as anyone who's had a sharp object pointed at their face would know, if the wielder of said object asks you for something, you hand it over without objection. When Lucia realized handing the bones over to me wouldn't work, she decisively dumped them out the window of the carriage. Five minutes later, the carriage driver was forced to turn back under the threat of never having kids in the future.

So Lucia did the most logical thing to do when she realized as long as the bones existed, she'd seek them out. She consumed all of them at once—a whole interspacial ring's worth of them. I thought she'd explode or at least turn into an idiot from the backlash, but I guess someone who would consume that many bones at once had no fear of turning into an imbecile because they already were one. Did I just call Lucia stupid? Well, as long as the person in question doesn't know, it's fine.

After consuming all the bones, Lucia sat around in a daze for a while, letting out the occasional burp or hiccough. The peace and quiet lasted for nearly a day, but after that is when the nightmare started. Lucia trembled and muttered to herself like a homeless person in the streets, staring at her hands while licking her lips. Her sock spirit, the wolfman named Puppers, finally came back to life around the time Lucia started chewing on her tail, and she, uh, dismembered him to acquire a new set of bones to engrave. I don't know what the poor spirit had done in his past life to deserve an owner like Lucia, but it couldn't have been good. But disregarding his unfortunate fate, Lucia's newest supply of bones has dwindled severely over the past few days, and I'm afraid I'm going to be next if she runs out before we make it to my home. Now I know why addicts are scary; they'll do anything to get their next fix.

The carriage driver is also frightened, and in turn, the horses are frightened too. They've been running nonstop through the nights to reach our destination faster. Of course, I've been renewing their stamina and increasing their speed with magic, but there's only so much I can do. I've thought about giving Lucia the corpses of the divine beasts I currently have stored away, but I'd like to save that as a last resort lest anyone discovers them. It's unlikely anyone would have designs on me or my father to steal away some corpses, but it never hurts to be careful. …Unless a slightly crazy beastkin wants to rip the bones out of your body to draw pictures on them.

I have never been as relieved as I was when I saw the statue of my father on the horizon, signaling we were getting close. Lucia hasn't spoken a word since she tore apart her spirit, mostly keeping her eyes closed with a pile of bloody bones in her lap. The past few days in the carriage with Lucia have been like sitting in a cage with a sleeping manticore. The stress has caused my mana levels to soar, and looking inwards, I could tell my fifth circle was starting to form. Meeting Lucia, I'm still not sure if it's a blessing or a curse.

Just a few more hours and I'll be back home. I hope my father's doing well. He had chosen to pass me off to Teacher because he was busy with work, and anything that could keep a high-ranking magician occupied for extended periods of time was most likely troublesome to handle. I wonder what Father would think when he meets Lucia. Speaking of Lucia, she's still muttering to herself with her eyes closed. Eh? They opened? But why are they so … strange? They're not as white as they are when she turns cruel and savage, but her irises and pupils are definitely dimmer.

"Someone's looking to die," Lucia said, her eyes narrowing. She glanced at me, and I stiffened. It was almost like she could see past my eyes, right into my head. "Sixteen? No, seventeen."

What? "Are you sober?"

"Shh." Lucia put her finger to her lips. Her ears twitched a few times. "So that's how the path knows where to find prey: sounds and smell." She grinned at me, her smile brightening up her face. It was almost like the deranged companion I had for the last few days had never existed. "There's seventeen people hiding behind that particularly large mound of dirt. Is that normal? They're talking like bandits, saying things like, 'hush, they're coming', 'do you see their crest', and 'how many are there?'"

"Bandits? This close to my father's lands?" That's definitely not normal. My father would never allow bandits to exist along his roads. No one would be stupid enough to anger a duke either; what are they thinking? "What do they look like?"

Lucia rolled her eyes. "Do you think I can hear appearances?"

I guess that's impossible even for someone like her. But I bet if she could, and I didn't ask, she'd respond with something like, 'But you didn't ask me if I could do that.' Anyways, as my father's daughter, there's no way I can let bandits roam free like this. Sadly, I can't take care of seventeen people by myself if they're all magicians. "Will you help me subdue them?"

Lucia's tail twitched. "Will I get paid?"

A typical Lucia response. "Yes."

"Then I'll gladly help!" Lucia beamed and drew her sword. She muttered to herself, "I wonder if I can use bloody qi without activating the path."

***

Lucia signaled for the driver to stop and hopped out of the carriage. "I know you're out there," she shouted and pointed her sword at the hill. A moment of silence passed with Lucia standing as still as a statue, the wind causing the hairs on her tail to rustle. "Come out!"

Were there really bandits? Now that I think about it, how trustworthy are Lucia's words? I'd believe her if she told me this two weeks ago when we were still in the desolate mountains, but now...? She's crazy and suffering from withdrawals. I wouldn't be too surprised if she heard everything in her head. Her eyes did look a bit glazed over when she 'noticed' the ambushers.

"If I have to walk over there, I'm not going to spare any of your lives," Lucia said and snorted. She took a step forward, causing the earth to fracture and tremble. It seems like she's making her sword extremely heavy; I'm a bit proud of myself for figuring out that mechanic. I had always wondered why I couldn't lift her sword back in Teacher's laboratory. I only figured it out when Lucia forgot to lighten her sword while climbing a tree, causing it to fall over.

There was another heavy thumping sound as Lucia took another step. A group of heads appeared as the bandits started climbing up the hill from the other side. They were dressed in rags and filthy clothes, but their demeanors didn't fit those of bandits at all: their backs were straight and their posture was immaculate—like they were soldiers. The bandit leader—I could tell because he was wearing an eyepatch and stood at the front of the group—stared at Lucia before asking, "A beastkin?" Then his gaze turned onto me. "Three people. Do you want to surrender yourselves or struggle futilely?"

The bandits standing furthest in the back raised their hands into the air. Massive fireballs sprang into existence above their fingertips. All of them were at least fifth-circle magicians. There was no way these bandits were actually bandits. A fifth-circle magician was a respected figure in society; bandits wouldn't even make a quarter of what a fifth-circle magician would make as a guest teacher. There's something really fishy about this. I might as well be straightforward and see how they react. "Are you soldiers?"

"Soldiers? We're bandits; can't you see?" the leader asked and gestured towards his eyepatch. He raised his hand and hooked his index finger in front of his face. "Arr."

"Those are pirates," Lucia said.

"Shut up!" the leader said, pointing at Lucia. Black lightning, symbolizing a seventh-circle magician or higher, crackled around his hand. "Surrender yourselves peacefully. You have no other choice if you wish to live."

"Alright," Lucia said and nodded. Wait, what? She was surrendering just like that? What happened to our deal!? Her tail's not even stiff! Lucia glanced at the sword in her hand before making eye contact with the leader. "You'd feel better if I wasn't holding a sword, right?" She grabbed her sword by the blade and gently lobbed it to the leader, hilt first. "Catch."

"Good"—the leader caught the hilt—"choice!?" The sword dragged his arm towards the ground, and his face followed. Lucia dashed over and grabbed the leader's legs while he was stunned. The leader screamed as he was lifted into the air and swung around like a ragdoll.

"Captain!" the bandits shouted. A few of them charged forwards while the magicians with the fireballs hesitated.

"Breaking Substitute Blade!" Lucia shouted, infusing the bandit leader with her qi. She swung him with one hand, using him as a makeshift sword. His body collided against his subordinates, and soon, they were all scattered along the hilltop. One of them tried shooting a fireball at Lucia, but after she blocked it with the leader's body, the rest of them stopped. Without their spells, there was nothing they could do to her. Only when all the demons were groaning on the ground did Lucia stop beating them with their leader's body. She looked at me. "All done. Or did you want me to kill them? I'm not a murderer though, so you can do it if you want."

I climbed out of the carriage—I should've done that earlier, but I was too surprised by Lucia's actions—and walked over to the fallen bandits. The leader was such a bloody mess that I wasn't even sure if he was alive or not. I walked over to a groaning bandit while Lucia picked up her sword and polished it with her dress. "Who sent you?" I asked the man on the ground. "You're obviously not bandits."

"I'm a bandit," the man said and stared at me. "My comrades and I have always been bandits."

It didn't seem like they were willing to talk. Someone probably ordered them to silence. I could always resort to torture…, but that was a job for my father. We're almost at my home anyways; I can take them with us. There's only one problem though. "Lucia, do you have any way to prevent these people from attacking us while we transport them?" It'd be bad if they started casting spells in the carriage; tying them up wouldn't work.

"Aren't you the encyclopedia? Shouldn't you have methods?" Lucia asked and tilted her head. "Just bonk them over the head with a stick to knock them out." She nodded. "Why am I so smart?"

"What if they wake up?" I asked. It would be possible to transport them if they were all unconscious. But if one of them woke up, pretended to still be asleep, and cast a fifth-circle spell, it'd be a disaster.

"I'll just hit them every five minutes or so regardless of whether they're awake or not," Lucia said. "Easy."

And that's what we did. I thought it was a bit wasteful for Lucia to spend several gold on such a large and luxurious carriage, but I'm glad she had; otherwise, there wouldn't have been enough space for all the prisoners. And capturing the so-called bandits was a good thing for Lucia. Hitting them every so often distracted her from her withdrawal symptoms.

Ah, just like I thought, hitting people is super relaxing. By projecting my qi out of my body and sending it into the bandits we captured, I can sense when they're about to wake up. And when I do, I hit them over the head with a bone. Like this!

Ilya flinched and glanced at me. She pursed her lips, but she didn't say anything before turning her gaze back onto the road. Maybe I hit him a bit too hard.

I actually didn't know I could send my qi into people until recently when I used the bandit leader as a substitute sword. There's a little bit of resistance, but if I apply some more qi, it goes away. It's a lot like life; if something's blocking your way, hit it until it isn't. That's how most problems are solved, right?

"We're here," the driver said as the carriage slowed to a halt.

I poked my head out the window and looked around. What a picturesque scene! The carriage was positioned in front of a massive gate with brick fences on either side that extended far beyond what I could see. Trees with pink leaves were lined up along the road inside the fence, leading to a fountain. Beyond the fountain, there was a white mansion with gargoyles positioned on its roof. Around the carriage, patches of colorful flowers decorated the bright-green grass. A few decorations—cute animal statues—were littered about. And there were even sun-bleached skeletons impaled on bloody stakes all around us.

"There's no guards to receive us?" Ilya asked and stood up to peer over the driver's shoulder. Her face paled as she took in the beautiful scenery. She muttered, "What's going on?" before departing from the carriage.

Okay, maybe, the skeletons weren't normal. I tossed the unconscious bandits out of the carriage before storing the portable refrigerator inside of my interspacial ring without the driver noticing. After I paid the driver, the carriage whirled around and departed without a word. Ilya didn't seem too ecstatic after returning home. Maybe her family tried to drown her too? "So…."

Ilya glanced at me before touching the gate. A circle of mana appeared in front of her fingers. It pulsed a few times, and a ringing noise sounded through the air. A few seconds later, there was a click, and a voice asked, "Hello?"

"It's Ilya," Ilya said to the circle. "Open the gate."

"Young Miss? You've returned?" the voice asked. "I'll open the gates right away." There was another click, and the circle in front of Ilya disappeared. The gate rumbled, and the chains holding the gate shut loosened before falling to the ground. As Ilya pushed open the gate, the doors to the mansion opened, and a procession of well-dressed demons, humans, and beastkin stepped outside, forming two lines on either side of the road underneath the pink-leaved trees.

A demon, who was wearing a monocle, approached us and bowed until his chest was parallel with the ground. Seeing how well Ilya was being treated made me feel a bit uneasy because, well, I treated her like crap in the desolate mountains. She wouldn't hold that against me…, right?

"Young Miss, I apologize for not noticing your arrival earlier," the monocle-wearing demon said. "Forgive me."

That's something he needs to be forgiven for? We just got here.

"It's alright, Matthew," Ilya said and gestured behind herself. "Bring these bandits inside for Father to interrogate." Then she turned her head towards me. "And this is my…"— her brow furrowed—"punishment for the sins I've committed in my past life. Treat her like an esteemed guest."

Hey. I'm not that bad of a person, right? …Right?

"Understood," Matthew said and nodded at me. "Welcome, esteemed guest." He glanced to the side at the beastkin with tiger-like features. "Take the bandits to the dungeon."

Ilya's mansion has a dungeon? Isn't that a bit excessive? Why would anyone have such a depressing place inside their own home?

"Let's go, Lucia," Ilya said and pursed her lips. She stared at my face. Did I have food stuck between my teeth? Wait, no, my mouth was closed. "How are you feeling?"

Feeling? "Uh, normal? Like always."

"You don't want to consume any bones...?" Ilya asked. "I can—"

"Ilya!" a voice interrupted. My tail stiffened as the air in front of us fractured and split apart like a broken mirror. A demon wearing black robes appeared from within and tackled Ilya before she or I could react. "You're back. Where's Rogath?"

Ilya struggled to remove her face from the demon's chest. "Father," she said and tried to wriggle out of her dad's hug. "You're squishing me."

"Sorry, sorry," Ilya's dad said before releasing her. He smiled at her before glaring at me. "You dare point a sword at me?"

Out of reflex, I had readied mini-DalDal for combat when my tail stiffened. Good thing I didn't attack him right away because I'd probably have lost. With my qi, I could sense the air around him vibrating from the sheer amount of mana guarding his body. If I activated my Path of Slaughter, I don't think I would even be able to see him beyond a wall of green.

"Father," Ilya said and tugged on her dad's sleeve. "This is Lucia. She's ... special. Don't hurt her, please."

Damn right I'm special. That was a compliment, right? "Hello, Mister..."—what was Ilya's last name again?—"Ilya the First." Well, close enough; I can't think under pressure, okay? "Nice to meet you."

Ilya's dad stared at me for a few seconds before looking at Ilya. "She's certainly special," he said with a nod. "But what happened? Why are you here? Where's Rogath?"

I feel like I've been completely ignored. As usual.

"Teacher…," Ilya said and furrowed her brow. "Teacher captured Lucia with a trap and convinced her to take me on a journey. And now I'm here."

"I feel like you've skipped a lot of things," Ilya's dad said. He glanced at me. "But you're saying I can trust her?"

"No," Ilya said and shook her head. Hey! I'm very trustworthy! "Her perception of the world is skewed. If you ask her what color a red wall is, she'll tell you it's green, firmly believe it's green, and believe she told you the truth. She won't try to lie to you, but her words will be lies simply because she's wrong."

I'm going to smack her. …As soon as her dad leaves us alone that is. How strong is he? Eighth circle? Ninth?

"It sounds like you've had it rough," Ilya's dad said and put his hand on her shoulder. His eyes widened to a comical size. "You're almost at the fifth-circle?"

"Yes," Ilya said, her face darkening. "Thanks to Lucia."

Why did her words sound so spiteful? "You're welcome."

"Excellent!" Ilya's dad said and lifted her into the air. She yelped as he spun her around in a circle.

"Dad!"

"Sorry, sorry." Ilya's dad grinned and placed her back onto the ground. "A fifth-circle magician at the age of thirteen! Oh, you're almost fourteen now, aren't you? We'll have to hold a banquet." He glanced at Matthew. "Prepare a birthday banquet for Ilya. Invite everyone important."

I'm being ignored.

"I'm extremely proud of you," Ilya's dad said. "Which element did you attune to?"

Ilya pursed her lips. "All of them," she said before glaring at me.

Did I do something to make her mad recently? What's with all the glaring?

"All of them?" Ilya's dad's eyes widened. "How!?"

"It was because of Lucia," Ilya said. "If I didn't use all the elements, I'd have never kept up with her and died instead."

Ilya's dad beamed at me, and my tail finally relaxed. Was he no longer hostile? "Thank you," he said and nodded at me. "Thank you for taking such good care of my daughter. You've been really helpful. Please, allow her to accompany you longer."

"Of course! I'll do my best!" It's been a while since I've been praised! Puppers is always such a bitter person and never compliments me. Ilya's praise feels like I'm being insulted. And Durandal still hasn't woken up yet. I don't understand why though. Puppers has died and woken up dozens of times, but Durandal's still recovering. He couldn't have abandoned me and given up on life, right?

"Father...," Ilya said with hints of tears in her eyes. "You're supposed to support me, not throw me to the lions."

Her dad ruffled her hair. "How can you compare Lucia's guidance to throwing you to the lions?" he asked. "Look at how well she's treated you. You'll be the youngest fifth-circle magician in existence!" He smiled at me. "Welcome to my residence. Feel free to treat this place like your own home."

***

A few hours had passed since we arrived at my home. I was in my father's study, reading up on the side effects of consuming engraved bones when I heard a commotion coming from outside. Of course, it had to be Lucia. I left her to her own devices, and it wouldn't make sense if her withdrawal symptoms didn't act up. I opened the door and poked my head out. Our chef, Mr. Ei, was storming down the halls, looking like he had run into a mama bear with her cubs.

"Ilya, what's going on?" my father asked from his seat. He was reading over the information the bandits had provided after a session of interrogation involving water and towels. He didn't expect the truth to come out of their mouths, so he interrogated them one at a time and was currently looking for differences between their stories.

"I'm not sure," I said. "But it looks like our head chef's been mauled by a bear."

"Duke Pentorn!" a booming voice echoed through the halls as Mr. Ei approached me. He was a demon, but his face wasn't purple like it should've been. It was bright red with anger instead. "Is this how you treat the members of your household? I'll have you know, my skills are respected amongst even the imperial family—I could've chosen to work anywhere I liked, but I was persuaded by your butler to join the Pentorn's. Never did I imagine that you'd treat me so rudely. I quit!" The chef threw his hat and apron onto the floor before my father could say a word.

"What was that about?" my father finally asked once the chef's footsteps could no longer be heard echoing through the halls. "Isn't it almost dinner time?"

"It's probably Lucia," I said and hung my head. Good chefs were hard to acquire. A commoner wouldn't be experienced with handling expensive meat and vegetables while a noble wouldn't aspire to be a chef unless they were really passionate about food or had no other paths in life. The only exception is Lucia, and I'm not sure if that's because I hadn't eaten properly cooked food in a long time or if it was just because Lucia was working with divine beast meat. It's not like she has divine beast meat to work with right now. I have the corpses in my rings. ...My rings? Where'd they go!? Only Lucia knows where I hide them!

"You look like you're panicking," my father said. "What's wrong? Lucia could train you to become a fifth-circle magician; I don't think she'd do anything without a good reason. I won't punish her even if she did scare away the chef; you don't have to worry."

No! Punish her, please! Before I could say anything, a servant with whiskers and a curved tail appeared at the door to the study. There was a noticeable bump on her head that didn't look natural. She bowed at me and my father while saying, "Master, the esteemed guest is causing trouble in the kitchen."

"How so?" my father asked and crossed his arms over his chest. Good! The sterner he looks, the higher the chance of Lucia getting her just deserts.

"She forcibly expelled everyone from the kitchen, claiming she couldn't trust us to handle her food. When Mr. Ei confronted her, she beat him with a whisk before threatening to cut off his manhood and force it down his throat," the servant said. "She's in the kitchen right now. I tried pleading with her, saying we had to make meals for you two as well, but she said she would handle it and threw a pot at my head."

I glanced at my father. What would he think?

"As expected of a genius," my father said, causing my mind to blank. "How domineering; I wouldn't expect anything less from that girl. Allow her to do as she pleases."

You can't be serious! How good of an impression did Lucia make on my father!? Who's the daughter here!?

"I understand. I'll inform you when the meal is ready," the servant said before exiting.

"Didn't you say to never offend Mr. Ei?" I asked my father. "Shouldn't you throw Lucia into the dungeon for what she's done?"

"It was my fault for not requesting your teacher to not offend Mr. Ei," my father said and smiled at me. Lucia's not my teacher! "Besides, I want to make a good impression on her. If you keep accompanying her on her journeys, just imagine how far you'll go in your magical studies. You don't want her to be reluctant in bringing you along."

"Am I your daughter?" I asked, hanging my head.

"Of course, Ilya." My father looked at me with an odd expression. "Do you think you're not?"

"Is Lucia your daughter?" I asked in return.

"No," my father said, looking even more confused.

"Then if I'm your daughter and Lucia isn't, shouldn't my opinions and feelings matter more than hers?" I asked.

"When did I ever neglect your feelings or opinions?" my father asked, tilting his head. Realization dawned on his face. "You really liked Mr. Ei's cooking, huh?"

That's not it! I don't want to journey with Lucia anymore! Wait, I didn't actually tell my father that though, so he didn't ignore my feelings or opinions. "No," I said and shook my head. "That's not it. I don't really like traveling with Lucia. In the future, can I, um, not?"

My father's eyes narrowed, and the air around him fell by a few degrees. "Absolutely not," he said. "You're following her until you become a ninth-circle magician."

What happened to not neglecting my feelings!? "But, father," I said. "There's—"

"No buts," my father said, cutting me off. I could feel tears welling in my eyes. "In life, there are some things you have to do whether you like it or not. Traveling with Lucia is one of them. Eating your vegetables is another."

So this is what it feels like to have your hopes absolutely crushed. The last time I felt such despair was when I was nearly eaten by a divine beast with three mouths while running after Lucia. At least I can take comfort in the fact that I ate the beast in the end, but it's not like I can eat Lucia.

"Master," a voice said from behind me. "The meal is ready."

My father nodded and stood up. "Let's go, Ilya."

I sighed. I can only hope Lucia makes a terrible impression on my father during dinner. Please, lord, let it be so.

***

I thought the inn Ilya and I had stayed in was fancy, but that place was nothing compared to Ilya's home. She has so much food! There's a refrigerator similar to the one that was inside the carriage, but it's huge. It's almost like a separate house that I could walk into. I actually got lost and had to use my mini-map ring to show me the exit. There was even a section of the refrigerator that was so cold it froze things, mostly meats, but I saw a few bodies inside there. I'm not sure if I was supposed to see them, but whatever.

And the kitchen is ten times as large as my previous owner's. Even though I was still a child when I was enslaved and had to use a stepstool to reach the stove, Ilya's kitchen makes the current me feel even smaller than I did back then. There are super-sharp swords on the walls to cut things with. The cutting board is as large as a table made for a banquet. Okay, maybe that was actually a table saved up for a banquet, but I'll pretend those cut marks weren't made by me. And most importantly, they have a grill! Barbeque is the only way to go when you're cooking divine meats! It's crude and meant for commoners, but everyone can enjoy a good ol' barbeque.

The best part is I have free access to all the food since I was told to make myself at home. I did have to shoo away an annoying person with a white hat, but that was pretty easy. There's so many different kinds of dead animals stored away, and a few of them look as imposing as divine beasts. Obviously, I chose those first. And don't even get me started on the spices! I didn't know what some of them were or if they were poisonous or not, so I grabbed a few servants and sprinkled them on their tongues first. I had to grab a few servants because some of them died, but luckily, there was already a pile of bodies in the refrigerator anyways. No one would notice a few more, right? In the end, only the salt wasn't poisonous, so I threw away everything else.

I had another few servants check the finished products for poison, but there wasn't any, so I told them to invite Ilya and her dad over since I said I was going to make their meals too. I hope I wasn't supposed to make the servants theirs. I don't think I was.

Ilya's dining room is even more amazing than her kitchen. First off, the size is absurd: the doorway is three times my height, a normal person would probably break their legs if they fell from the ceiling to the ground, and it's about two times the size of the training field of the Ravenwood army. I wonder if there are giant demons; the scale of things would make sense if there were. But at the same time, despite the open space, it feels so lonely. The table's big and proportional to the room, but you can't touch the walls if you lean back in your chair. You have to practically walk the length of a field if you want to leave the room. It's too big; there's no sense of coziness at all.

"Esteemed guest," a servant said to me. "Are you sure you don't want us to help?"

"Nope. I got this."

The maid stared at the towering plates of food stacked upon my head. "If you say so," she said and lowered her head before backing away.

Obviously, I'm carrying all the food to the table by myself. All the poison tests would go to waste if the servants poisoned the meals in transit! But I wouldn't mind some help from Ilya if she were here. She wouldn't poison good food, but I wouldn't trust her to make me any. Her cooking's worse than Durandal's if she doesn't use magic. Footsteps echoed behind me. Think of the devil, and the devil appears! "Ilya! Grab these for me and bring them to the table."

Ilya's face darkened as she trudged over to my side and helped me carry some plates. The maid who I just rejected glared at me with wide eyes, looking a little like a ghost. She could contend for first place with Durandal in a scary-face contest. Ilya glanced at her dad, but he just smiled at her and said, "Excellent. Developing a hardworking foundation that refuses a life of luxury, no wonder why you could advance so far in such a short time."

I think Ilya felt a little aggrieved, but I wasn't too sure. Well, she'll feel better when she eats.

After the plates were set up, Ilya's dad took the seat at the head of the table while Ilya sat to his right. I sat beside her, causing her face to make a strange expression. Was that happiness mixed with confusion? "Lucia," she said. "You're supposed to sit across from me."

"Don't tell me where to sit." I flicked her forehead. How am I supposed to steal her food if I'm sitting all the way over there? Despite her inability to cook, Ilya's very good at picking out the most delicious portions. I always force her to trade, but recently, she's been taking the suckier parts and trading those to me for the better ones. She's too sneaky, have to keep a close eye on her.

"You shouldn't offend your master over a minor matter like seating positions," her dad said and smiled at me. He glanced at the table, and his smile faltered. His head turned towards a sweating servant. "What are you doing? Bring out all the dishes."

The servant's expression when he smiled was uglier than a crying person's. "All the dishes have been brought out, sir."

"But there's only meat," the duke said.

"The esteemed guest prepared the meal," the servant said.

Ilya's dad stared at me. I'm not a rabbit! Vegetables aren't made for me. But Ilya's dad does look a bit upset even though he's trying to hide it.

"Yeah, Lucia," Ilya said and nodded so hard her hair was bobbing up and down. "Balanced meals are important. I can't believe you've served us this."

Wow. I've been betrayed. Mm, what's the best way out of this? I'll copy Durandal, talk nonsense while stating it as fact! I slammed my hand on the table, causing the plates to rattle. Ilya flinched while her dad jumped. "If you want to be as strong as a divine beast, you have to eat like a divine beast! If you want to live your life as a tiny rabbit, I'll make you a meal of lettuce and grains! What do you want to be?" I glared at Ilya while unleashing my Unrelenting Path of Slaughter. "A rabbit or a divine beast?"

"A, a divine beast," Ilya said with a whimper. I continued to glare at her because that's what Durandal did to me a lot. I'm not sure why, but it's intimidating! Ilya slipped out of her chair and lowered her head to the ground. "I'm sorry! I was wrong!"

Wow, that's usually how I react. This feels great! No wonder why Durandal's such a bully.

"If you want to be as strong as a divine beast," Ilya's dad muttered and rubbed his chin, "then you have to eat like a divine beast." He nodded. "Well said. Why should we aspire to be lower than what we can be? If you behave like a rabbit in everyday life, when the time comes for you to behave like a divine beast, you won't be able to. Amazing." His eyes closed as he crossed his arms and legs.

Ilya's eyes widened at her dad's posture. "H-he's breaking through," she said. "He's breaking through the eighth circle to the ninth." Her eyes widened even further when she stared at me. "Your nonsensical words enlightened him!"

Damn. I'm amazing. …Wait a minute. Wait just one minute. Isn't that it!? The way to break through to the realm of divine warriors? I understand! I've been doing it wrong this whole time!

"Lucia!?" Ilya shouted as two dozen divine beast cores appeared next to me. "What are you doing?"

"A divine warrior should be able to easily absorb all of these at once! If I want to be a divine warrior, I have to act like one." And thus, I proceeded to absorb all the cores at once.

"Don't listen to your own nonsense! You'll explode!"

Those were the last words I heard before my vision went black.

15

"I understand how you've reached the border of the fifth circle so soon now," my father said once his eyes opened. But I wasn't paying attention to him because Lucia was lying on the ground, froth coming out the corners of her mouth with her eyes rolled all the way up so only their whites showed. Her tail occasionally twitched as the cores around her body shrank and melded into her like ice melting in the sun. "What's wrong with Lucia?"

"She's an idiot! That's what's wrong with her!" Lucia's body spasmed once all the cores disappeared. I tried taking one away, but it still shrank and melted away into nothingness. "She absorbed two dozen divine beast cores all at the same time."

My father's eyes widened. "She's going to explode," he said. "Wait. Did you say divine beast cores? Where did she get that many?"

"From the desolate mountains." Should I just leave Lucia here? I'm not sure anything I could do would be able to help her. But it'd be bad if she ruined the dining room by exploding. "She can kill divine beasts easily even though she's only a high-ranked spirit warrior."

"She's a warrior?" my father asked. He was as oblivious as Teacher Rogath! How could he have not noticed the sword and her muscles? No wonder why he sent me to study under that drunkard. "What do we do?"

"You're the adult! You should be the one with the answers, Father." Why does everyone depend on me!? I'm not even fourteen yet! Gah, Lucia's thrashing around now! "Don't try to lift—"

I tried to warn my father, but it was too late. He bent down by Lucia and attempted to pick her up, but a thrashing limb smacked into his side. I thought I heard a rib break as he was sent flying. He tumbled a few times on the ground before crashing into the wall. Lucia could throw a manticore with one hand. It made sense for a single one of her smacks to send people flying. "Are you okay, Father?" Great, now I have two injured people to attempt to take care of.

"Amazing!" my father said and coughed out a mouthful of blood. He clutched his ribs as he chanted a simple healing spell. Though my father was more attuned to destructive magic, namely earth and water, he could still use healing spells from the lower circles. "You chose a good person to follow."

That's what you're thinking of in a time like this? Care more about your safety! It'd be terrible for the empire if a duke died. "Do you need me to call a healer over?"

My father grunted in reply. "It was just four ribs. I'll be fine after ten minutes or so," he said and sat up, resting his back against the cracked wall. "You should do something about Lucia though. Can she survive with all those cores inside of her? Imagine how she must feel; even absorbing a low-ranked beast core can cause me to feel nausea. But dozens of divine beast cores?" He shook his head. "I can't fathom how much pain she must be in."

Great, now I can't help but feel bad for Lucia. It's not her fault she was born an idiot. I'll drop a few healing spells on her and hope they alleviate her suffering. "O water, heed my prayer, cleanse—"

"Wait! No! That was just a dream!?" Lucia sat up and looked around. Devastation painted her face.

"...This poor squirrel beastkin and alleviate her mental illness." I can't stop a chant midway! But I could change the contents, which I did. A fountain of water gushed out of the ground and sprayed onto Lucia. Her eyes widened as she spluttered and shook herself off.

"Ilya! What the hell was that for!?" Lucia glared at me.

"S-sorry," I said and lowered my head. Why was her gaze so fierce? I was just trying to help. "I was trying to heal you."

"Do I look like I need healing?" Lucia asked and snorted. She sighed. "That was such a nice dream too. All the divine beasts I killed were trying to eat me, but I beat them all up and cut off their penises. But it was just a dream! Do you know how much money I could've made if it were real!?" She grabbed me by the shoulders and shook me until I felt dizzy.

I have a feeling she just underwent a tribulation. I couldn't help but feel bad for the divine beasts she encountered in her dream. No doubt, parts of their soul still existed in their beast cores and were trying to take her body over after she absorbed them. It's just such a Lucia thing to do, surviving through ignorance. I guess simple people do have resolute and pure souls.

"Hey, what are you all sitting on the ground for?" Lucia asked as she climbed onto her seat. "The food's going to go cold, and you better not blame the lack of flavor on me if it does." She reached over, grabbed onto a drumstick, and munched on it while looking at me and my father.

"Are you okay, Lucia?" I asked. Were there seriously no side effects? Did she break through? Wasn't she curious, or was food that much more important to her?

"I'm okayer than okay," Lucia said. She engraved a symbol onto the drumstick's bone before absorbing it. Then she picked up another chunk of meat and bit into it, showing no regard for the utensils the servants had pulled out. She probably thought they were poisoned. I wonder what happened to her to make her so paranoid. No doubt, she had been poisoned while eating before, but why? Who did it? "There won't be any left for you two if you just keep standing there."

Well, I can always figure that out in the future as I adventure more with Lucia. ...Did I just think that? I actually want to adventure with Lucia? Or, maybe, I just resigned myself to my fate. Ah, whatever. I should eat before the food gets cold.

***

Phew. That was a good meal, but I feel like I ate a lot more than I usually do. Well, I did warn Ilya's dad to eat soon otherwise it'd all be gone. I think he got a piece or two. Now, let's see how much my strength improved. Why isn't there a convenient way to check? Like a stone that measures qi when I place my palm on it, or a magical orb that shifts colors depending on my strength. I guess I'll have to do this the old-fashioned way.

"Lucia," Ilya said as she wiped her hands on her napkin. "What are you doing?"

I raised mini-DalDal over my head, keeping my arm straight while pointing it at the ceiling. "Testing my strength."

"Don't test it here!" Ilya shouted. "Are you trying to destroy the dining room!?"

Wow, when did she become brave enough to start shouting at me? And it's not like I was going to swing mini-DalDal or anything, I was just increasing the weight, jeez. Ten tons ... eleven ... thirteen ... eighteen ... twenty-two ... twenty-seven ... thirty...!? Oops. I dropped it.

Ilya screamed as massive fractures spread along the floor. Well, I'm rich enough to pay for it, so that shouldn't be a problem. Anyways, thirty tons! That's more than twice what I could lift before. Those beast cores were super useful. Does this make me a divine warrior? "Unrelenting Path of Slaughter!"

Ilya screamed again before stiffening. Her eyes rolled up to the top of her head, revealing their whites. She fell over backwards like a log, and froth appeared in the corners of her mouth. What brought that about? I didn't even attack her. But there's this super-ominous aura surrounding my body. It looks like strands of blood are floating around me. And according to the mirror that's conveniently placed in the dining room, I can tell that my aura's taking the shape of a cute goat's head, horns and all.

"Devil," Ilya's dad said. He was looking at me with wide eyes.

"Devil?" Aren't I supposed to be a divine warrior? Shouldn't I look more like an angel than a devil, the heck? I've been swindled! It's definitely Durandal's fault for giving me a defective path to follow. What else changed? Ilya's not awake, so I can swing my sword a few times! I'll blame it on her dad if anything bad happens. "Unrelenting Path of Slaughter: Breaking Blade!"

I lifted my sword into the air, focused my qi into it, and swung downwards. When my qi entered the blade, blood-red wisps of mist leaked out of it. When my sword cut the air, a howl filled the room as a massive, red vertical line slashed outwards, cutting through the ceiling and wall of the dining room. Holy shit. Silence filled the air until a few clattering sounds broke it. Bits and pieces of the ceiling were falling onto the floor. Then, without warning, the whole room collapsed inwards, burying me under chandeliers and stone rubble. Of course, I saved Ilya, but I have no idea if her dad was okay or not. Eh, he's a ninth-circle magician, he'll be fine!

A head popped out of the rubble. "What was that?" Ilya's dad asked me as he shook his head. His expression froze when he looked off to the side. I followed his gaze. Holy crap! Did I do that? I'm amazing! Look at that beautiful fissure in the ground! I even split a cloud in half, a fucking cloud! As far as the eye could see, there was a straight blue line leading into the horizon. Everything in its path was split: the ground, the trees, the clouds, a few houses, a field of grain. I know I said this before, but damn, I'm amazing. I think it's safe to say I became a divine warrior.

"Was that magic?" Ilya's dad asked. "I know some magicians who specialize in wind magic that can do something similar."

"She's a warrior, Father!" Ilya said as she wriggled out of my grasp. When did she wake up? Maybe it was the loud noises. Her eyes widened as she looked around before staring at me. "Did you do this?"

"Uh, nope." Deny everything! "Your dad did it, right?" Maybe winking at him will make him catch the hint.

"It was all Lucia," Ilya's dad said.

Ouch, that was cold.

"Duke!" someone shouted. "What happened? Are you alright!?"

"It's nothing," Ilya's dad said to the approaching servant. "There were some minor complications. For now, just clear the rubble. Have Matthew hire an architect to draft up a design to rebuild the dining room. Ilya's birthday is in a month, I want this fixed by then."

"Duke!" another voice shouted. "What happened? Are you alright!?"

They care about Ilya's dad a lot, huh? How many more times am I going to hear those two lines? Maybe four or five more.

"Everything's alright," Ilya's dad said.

"Duke!" a third voice shouted. "The prisoners escaped! What happened? Are you alright!?"

"The prisoners escaped?" Ilya's dad asked. "Didn't I cut their legs off?"

"The array holding back their mana was destroyed by something!" the servant said. "All I saw was a flash of red and the wall was gone. I couldn't do anything; the prisoners all worked together to cast a large-scale teleportation spell."

Hmm, flash of red. That was me, right? Oops.

"Did you uncover any more information before they left?" Ilya's dad asked. He dusted himself off while standing.

"All their words have been recorded," the servant said with a nod.

"Bring me the report," Ilya's dad said. He turned around to face me. "Thank you for the meal, Lucia. It tasted delicious. But next time, please refrain from destroying my dining room."

No punishment? Sweet! These must be the perks of becoming a divine warrior!

"Wait, Father," Ilya said and grabbed her dad's sleeve. "Are those imposter bandits a serious problem?"

"Serious?" Ilya's dad rubbed his chin. "I'm not sure. But there's been a lot of unrest in the capital recently, and I think I uncovered the culprit behind it. The Flopsy Gang."

Flopsy Gang? Why does that sound so familiar…? Snow! That bastard! I'll rip him to shreds!

***

Lucia became a monster. Whenever she projects her qi outwards, chills run down my spine and I want to curl up into a little ball and cry. Her aura takes the form of a goat's head with red eyes which many people associate with the devil. In fact, blood magicians have many spells that have a similar hazy red tinge to them, and their symbol is a devil's head. I've seen pictures of them drawn in books, but there's only been one blood magician who's ever broken past the wall of the sixth circle. The empire has forbidden magicians from practicing blood magic because they require tons of sacrifice to advance.

I never realized the similarities between martial arts and magic until I met Lucia. She explained to me—after I bribed her with food—her attacks unnatural strength are powered by qi, and it circulates in nearly the exact same way as mana does. When she told me that, I went to my father's library and did some reading on the subject. Qi is the energy of the world produced from the earth. Mana is the energy of the world produced from the sky. Researchers aren't sure how either of the energies are produced or why the earth and sky would produce two different but functionally similar types of energy, but that's just how it works. They did note something interesting though: a seventh-circle magician who has also practiced with qi has never been recorded. Even the Godking, also known as the Voidwalker, was stuck as a high-ranked spirit warrior and sixth-circle magician, but that brought him to the peak of the world at the time.

Maybe Lucia broke through to the level of divine warrior because she never used mana. It would make sense, seeing as every warrior learns at least simple spells like clean or barbeque. If qi and mana inhibit each other, it's no wonder why warriors never breakthrough. ...No wonder why this was a book exclusive to demons and forbidden from circulating to the human and fae kingdoms. Demons figured it out long ago, but only our nobility have profited from the information. That explains why my father never let me know about the existence of qi. I always thought warriors did basic strength training to fight beasts.

But anyways, back to Lucia. She's been practicing her techniques in the training field of my father's personal army, and she's been challenging all the seventh-circle magicians to duels. They've been losing, miserably. But to be fair, they all train large, wide-area spells because that's how armies work. And they're not used to dueling at the seventh-circle level since my father prohibited it ever since that incident with a neighboring noble's house. But really, I'm just making excuses for them; I didn't realize how weak they were until now. The majority of them can't react to Lucia's speed, so once she closes in on them, it's her guaranteed victory. One person tried to fly, but Lucia split the sky in half with a single swing of her sword and no one tried it again.

My father's army doesn't have any eighth-circle magicians employed; after all, an eighth-circle magician might as well be a noble. Why would they work under someone else? Instead, my father decided to duel against Lucia himself, which is why I'm sitting out here, under the hot sun, instead of relaxing in my room with a cold drink and exciting book. When will my father arrive for their duel? Lucia's been moving across the field with strange footwork for over an hour now. I'll admit, it's a bit entrancing to watch—like some sort of devilish ritual.

"Sorry for the delay." My father flew down from the sky and landed in the field while Lucia stopped her motions and drew her sword. "I caught a clue in one of the reports and had to dig deeper. Were you waiting long?"

"Nah," Lucia said and shook her head. She smiled at him, showing her teeth. "What are the rules?"

"Don't destroy my mansion, please," my father said. "That's it. Everything else is allowed. I don't think you'll be able to kill me, so give me your best shot." He grinned. "I'll take it easy on you."

I knew my father was arrogant—it comes with being a duke—but I didn't think he'd underestimate Lucia after all her victories. The first seventh-circle magician she dueled with said almost the same exact words. It's been engrained in our culture, I guess. A warrior will never beat a magician of the same rank. And now that my father's reached the ninth circle, he must be feeling invincible.

"Then I won't be polite," Lucia said as her eyes turned clear. The bloody aura rose up around her body, and I couldn't help but shiver. Lucia took two steps forward and leapt towards my father as fast as a divine leopard could pounce.

"Earth: Wall of Diamonds!" my father shouted and raised one hand. A massive transparent dome rose up and engulfed him, protecting him from all directions.

Lucia's blade clashed against the diamond wall. There was a booming sound followed by a yelp as Lucia bounced off and tumbled along the ground. "What the heck!?" Lucia shouted as she sat up.

"It doesn't protect him from underneath!" I shouted. "Dig your hands into the ground and lift it up." My father couldn't hear me inside his dome, so he wouldn't know I was helping Lucia. ...Why was I helping Lucia? I shouted out of reflex. The soldiers nearby stared at me with strange expressions on their faces. Please stop.

"Water: Storm of Icicles!" Though my father couldn't hear the outside world, his voice was still projected out of his dome. In a serious fight, a real magician wouldn't let his enemies know what they were casting, but it seemed like my father was treating Lucia as someone to be tutored.

From the clear sky, hundreds of icicles rained down. The smallest were the size of my foot while the largest were easily taller than me. Lucia tapped on her socks and shouted, "Puppers, use human shield!"

I pity her sock spirit. I pity him a lot. After Puppers' brave sacrifice, Lucia charged forwards, acting like she was going to cut the dome once again, but she dived towards the ground and slipped her hand under the protective layer. With a grunt, she lifted it with one hand and swung it downwards at my father like a club. This may be the first time in history that a magician's earthen shield was wielded as a blunt weapon against himself. Apparently, my father wasn't expecting it either because he stood there with a blank expression as it crashed down on him.

"Ah! He's dead?" Lucia asked with wide eyes.

Some mist leaked out from underneath the dome. "It was an illusion, Lucia! Watch out!" I shouted. ...Why am I doing that? Do I secretly resent my father for forcing me to suffer under Lucia and want him to suffer the same? That's probably it. "Most magicians strike from above once they fool their opponent!"

"Am I your father or is Lucia your father?" my father's voice shouted. As expected, he was in the air above Lucia.

"Sorry, Father. You're just too strong; Lucia needs a handicap." Yes, this is all for the sake of fairness. I'm a good person who forgets her grudges.

"Unrelenting Path of Slaughter: Breaking Blade!" A massive red line extended from Lucia towards the sky. She had stopped using her flying blade technique ever since her breaking blade technique got the long-ranged aspect added to it.

My father dodged to the side, narrowly avoiding the surge of qi. "Earth: Grasping—" His words cut short as he dodged again and again and again. …And again.

"Unrelenting Path of Slaughter: Storm of One Thousand Breaking Blades!" Lucia shouted out an absurdly long technique name as her arms turned into a blur. The sky turned red as blade strikes soared into the air. I bet my father wished he was a space magician to teleport out of that mess.

"Stop! Stop! I surrender!" my father shouted from above. It was a terrible idea for him to fly in the sky. He should've positioned himself in front of the mansion, so Lucia would feel guilty about launching a single Breaking Blade. And my father does have skills to counter Lucia's storm of qi, but the spectators, me included, would've been implicated if he used them. It seemed like he was handicapped enough even without me aiding Lucia.

My father landed on the ground and gave Lucia a bitter smile. "Don't you know how to do anything else?"

"Nope!" Lucia said. "If one slash doesn't work, then I'll do two. And if two don't work, then three!" Now that I think about it, that's always how Lucia fought divine beasts. Is it possible her skillset only involves Breaking Blade and Flying Blade? If only she had a teacher to guide her….

***

So I won a duel against Ilya's dad. I wonder what Bouncykins would think if I told him I trounced a ninth-circle magician. He probably wouldn't believe me, huh? That rabbit was always praising magicians for their power and undermining warriors. It's a good thing I stopped traveling with him; otherwise, his negativity may have dragged me down. I'm a divine warrior! I'm stronger than the Godking was! Now I just have to figure out a way to become famous.

"Are you listening, Lucia?" Ilya asked and poked me.

Gah! Don't poke me while I'm eating! I stole the food off her plate before asking, "What?"

Ilya's expression fell. "That was the best piece...," she muttered before shaking her head. "My father asked you if you'd be willing to represent him in the upcoming tournament."

"Tournament? What tournament?" How convenient; when I want to become famous, a stage appears where I can display my power. The god of this world must love me. "This is my first time hearing about a tournament."

"My dad asked you about it yesterday and the day before that, but you didn't respond," Ilya said with a blank expression. "You said you'd think about it a week ago."

Hm. Hmm. Hmmmmm. Nope, I don't recall any of this. Did it really happen? I've been doing as Ilya asked and started weening myself off of these bones, but I've been getting really bad headaches and, apparently, memory loss at times. The past week's been a blur of luxury and relaxation. Ah, that reminds me, I need to obtain some more beast cores since I consumed all the ones I had while breaking through. I wonder if they sell any at the capital or if I'd have to travel back to the desolate mountains again.

"Lucia...?" Ilya asked and poked me again.

Stop poking me! "What?"

"About the tournament," Ilya said, her voice slowing down. I don't know whether I should feel offended or not. "Will you represent my father?"

What tournament? "What do I get out of it?"

"My dad just wants the prestige," Ilya said. "You can have the reward for first place—if you manage to get it." Her eyes lit up. Was the prize a precious treasure? "The first-place prize is a legendary beast's core. It's an elder dragon's. Cain Thunderfire personally killed it; not only that, but you'll get a chance to meet Cain himself!"

Legendary beast's core?

"Legendary is the tier above divine," Ilya answered.

Don't read my mind! Gosh, am I that easy to read?

"I'm not a mind reader, Lucia," Ilya said. "Your face is just very ... filled with expressions."

That's not very fair.

"Don't worry," Ilya said. "I heard nearly all beastkins wear their hearts on their sleeves. Except for the rabbits; you have to watch out for those."

...How come I haven't heard about that?

"Anyways," Ilya said. "You'll do it, right? Don't you need the legendary beast core to get stronger?"

"I'll do it. When does it start?" She's right. If Durandal finds out I had any downtime where I wasn't absorbing cores, he'd beat me. ...Could he? Aren't I stronger than him now?

"Lucia...., you're making a very perverted face right now," Ilya said and bit her lower lip. "Are you sure you're going to remember this conversation in the morning?"

"Just tell me about the tournament." I'll remember! Even if I don't, Ilya will remind me and manage to convince my forgetful future self that this conversation happened.

"Okay," Ilya said. "It's called the Godking's Brawl. It's a really famous tournament that happens once per decade."

"If it's really famous, how come I've never heard about it?"

Ilya stared at me. "Lucia, you've never heard of blue cheese before. I'm not surprised you've never heard about the Godking's Brawl."

That's fair. Even though I do feel a bit insulted.

"Anyways, it's scheduled to happen within two months. The three factions are going to send twenty representatives each," Ilya said. "It's a massive tournament to uncover the top talents of the decade. Cain is pushing really hard for it; in fact, he's the one who insisted on continuing the tradition even when the three factions were in tense times."

"Cain's not competing?"

"No, he's the host," Ilya said. "Everyone knows he's the strongest person in the world; why would he have to compete?"

"And I'm allowed to compete for your dad?" I don't get it. Wouldn't I be representing the beastkin for the fae? What kind of demon would choose a beastkin as their representative? Right, Ilya's dad would.

"As a duke, my father automatically gets one of the representative positions," Ilya said. "But he's old, and Cain insists for the participants to be younger than thirty." She made a strange expression. "You're younger than thirty, right, Ms. A Warrior Doesn't Age?"

"Of course I'm younger than thirty!" Seriously, I am. How old did she think I was? Jeez.

"Then there's no issue," Ilya said. "Though we're demons, it's not unusual for humans or beastkin to compete for us, just like it's not unusual for beastkin or demons to compete for the humans. Ultimately, the representative slots go to the schools and rich nobles, and sometimes those nobles think they'd have a higher chance of winning if they chose someone that's not their race. The participants and the person they're representing both get a prize; the participant for winning, and the other for unearthing the talent."

So Ilya's dad gets to leech off of my hard work? Well, that's fine as long as I get the beast core. First place will be a cinch with my newfound strength! Ah, that's a difficulty and hardship flag, isn't it? I think I just jinxed myself. Well, it's not like I'll have to deal with poison or betrayal or anything of that sort, right?

"Oh, and it turns out the Flopsy Gang that's been messing with my father's territory has designs on this tournament, so there might be some unexpected danger," Ilya said. "At least that's what my father told me, but that shouldn't really concern you, right? ...Um, Lucia? Are you okay? You're making a really ugly face right now."

16

Lucia's been acting strange ever since I invited her to partake in the Godking's Brawl under my father's position. She's been muttering to herself in her room and drawing strange pictures on the wall. I'm not sure where she obtained the paint from, but the drawings are a little creepy. They're almost like her engravings that she carves on bones to give them power. Perhaps it also has to do with the fact she's been abstaining from her addiction; I've considered having my father throw her in a dungeon to prevent her from hurting herself, but I don't think it's possible to keep Lucia caged up. If Teacher Rogath was here, he could disable her, but my father isn't specialized in controlling magic like Teacher is.

"Ilya, what are you thinking about?" my father asked from his chair in the study.

I was reading up on properties of divine beasts to see how many similarities I could find between them and Lucia. Since the majority of Lucia's power came from her absorbing beast cores and not her qi, it'd make sense for her to adopt some animalistic characteristics. It's a shame I don't have any divine beasts locked up to compare their statuses with Lucia, but I suspect her base stats are similar to divine beasts' albeit weaker. For example, divine leopards specialize in speed, but while their strength may be low compared to divine gorillas, it should still be stronger than a spirit gorilla's. So while Lucia might not have absorbed enough divine leopard cores to be as fast as one, she should be as strong as one since she absorbed 25 different divine beast cores. Likewise, her speed should be on par with a divine gorilla's even if her strength isn't.

"Ilya?"

Oops. I got lost in thought. "Yes, Father?"

"Mm, never mind," my father said. "Are you ready for your party? Once the emperor heard about you almost breaking through to the fifth circle, he ordered the princes and princesses to attend." My father gave me an odd smile. "I heard that the first prince has taken an interest in you; what do you think?"

"I'm only going to be fourteen, Dad." Marrying young isn't unheard of amongst the upper nobility; however, I have no intentions of doing so. I'm almost a fifth-circle magician; in the future, I might even be as strong as Cain. Why would I bog myself down with the inevitable fight for the throne if I marry into royalty? It scares me a bit to say this, but I'd rather go on an adventure with Lucia than deal with the first prince.

"Isn't fourteen when most people start noticing the opposite sex?" my father asked. I glared at him. "Alright, alright. I won't place any unreasonable expectations on you, but I do want to see grandchildren within my lifetime. Anyways, did you invite Lucia to attend?"

"I was going to, but she was … preoccupied." Alongside drawing creepy pictures on the wall, I saw her creating dolls made of straw and driving nails through their heads. I think it's a form of black magic created by the humans called voodoo, but Lucia has no mana, so it shouldn't work…? I hope she's not possessed by anything; it's very difficult to destroy a lingering soul.

"I'll invite her," my father said. "Can you bring her here? There's also something I want to talk to her about, namely, the bodies in the refrigerator."

"The what?" Bodies in the refrigerator? Did Lucia kill people? Wouldn't that place the responsibility of those lives on me since I brought her here?

"Just bring her here, please," my father said and sighed as he leaned back into his chair.

316

What the heck did Lucia do!? I made my way out of my father's study and approached Lucia's room. I knocked on her door, but there was no response. "Lucia?"

A really loud yawn came from the other side of the door. There were some clomping sounds, and the door swung open. Lucia was sloppily dressed with her hair in a complete mess. Her eyes were half closed, and dried saliva was stuck to her cheek. "Ilya?" Lucia's head flopped to one side while her tail flicked back and forth on the floor. "What's up?"

"My dad said he wanted to talk to you about the … bodies in the refrigerator." Will she know what I'm talking about? I hope not.

"Oh, those," Lucia said with a nod. "Okay." She placed her hands on my shoulders and stared down at me. "Clean, please."

So she knew. I hope no serious issues arise from this. I sighed before casting a simple clean spell on Lucia. Then she fell over on top of me, knocking me to the ground. "Lucia!?"

"Carry me," Lucia said and yawned again. She closed her eyes and turned into dead weight.

"You're not serious." I managed to crawl out from under her, but her hands were grabbing my ankles. "Why are you like this, Lucia?"

"I stayed up all night making voodoo dolls," Lucia said. "And I stopped abusing bones of strength to remove tiredness."

"Even still! With qi, you should be able to stay up for months at a time without sleeping." I read about it in one of the books on warriors. As long as they circulate their qi, they can remove fatigue and hunger. A peak spirit warrior wouldn't need to sleep or eat at all. What went wrong with Lucia?

"I'm tired," Lucia whined and shook her head.

Why was she more childish than me? "I'll give you something good to eat if you cooperate."

Lucia's tail perked up into the air, but she remained motionless.

"Matthew just came back from the capital, and he bought a ton of sweets. You know what chocolate is, right? But have you tried hot chocolate? It's a melted form that you can drink." For some reason, sweets and desserts were her weakness. I suspect it's because she never had any while growing up.

Lucia raised her head. There was a gleam in her eyes as she sat up, resting her butt on her ankles. "You're not lying?" she asked and stared at me with narrowed eyes.

"I'm not. He bought it all for my birthday banquet that's going to happen in a week. I can let you have some earlier than everyone else."

"What are you waiting for?" Lucia asked and stood up. She grabbed my waist with one arm and slung me over her shoulder like a sack of potatoes. "Let's go!"

…If only she would've carried me like this while she was hunting divine beasts, then my life would've been a lot less stressful during that period. I'll have to bring lots of dessert for our next adventure.

***

This hot chocolate is delicious! Whoever created it must've been a genius on par with the Godking. But I wonder how Ilya's dad found out about the bodies in the refrigerator; there was already a stack there, so obviously someone else had put them there first. How'd he know the other ones were me? Maybe, Ilya's dad is the one who stores them there and noticed some extras! That would explain it. Nobles *do* have creepy hobbies.

After finishing my hot chocolate, Ilya insisted on heading to her dad's study right away even though I wanted more. I decided to listen since she said she was saving it for her banquet that I'm inviting myself to whether she likes it or not. Her dad's study is like a library, filled with books and couches everywhere. There's this massive desk that faces the door, so the first thing people get to see is her dad's face staring without blinking, watching every step they take. ...Why is he watching me so intently? He couldn't have fallen for me, right?

"Have a seat, Lucia," Ilya's dad said and gestured across from him.

This smells suspiciously like an interrogation. Do I have to take part? Well, I'll sit because I don't want to stand.

"Did Ilya say anything about why I called you here?" Ilya's dad asked, folding his hands on top of his desk.

"Nope." Deny everything!

"I did!" Ilya said. "The bodies, remember? You even said, 'Oh, those. Okay.'"

"Mm. Nope, doesn't ring a bell."

"Lucia, a magician has ways to tell if you're lying," Ilya's dad said.

"Oh, really?" Let's test it then. "I have nine toes. True or false."

"False," Ilya's father said.

"Hah! You're wrong. It's true." It isn't actually true, but there was a time in the past when I was cooking and dropped the knife I was holding and tried to catch it with my foot. Yeah, I lost my pinky toe then. But it grew back when I became a spirit warrior!

"Wait, really?" Ilya asked, her eyes widening. "Now that I think about it, I've never seen your feet before. You're always wearing those socks."

Of course. Puppers is too comfortable to not wear. I think my world would collapse if I took Puppers off. I can never go back to wearing normal socks or walking around barefooted again. "Mhm. It's really true."

"Forget it," Ilya's dad said and shook his head. "Do you happen to know anything about the bodies inside the refrigerator?"

"They were there when I got there." That's the truth, technically. Bodies were there—just not all the ones that currently are there.

"I see," Ilya's dad said and rubbed his chin. Was that it? Was the interrogation over? "I was just wondering; the servants noticed the spice rack is empty of everything except salt. Do you know what happened to the rest? I mean, you've been cooking a lot, so I thought you'd know."

"Yeah, they were poisoned, so I threw them away." Why would you even keep poisoned spices in your kitchen anyways? It's almost like someone wanted to assassinate the duke.

Ilya's dad tapped his chin slowly before smiling at me. "You know, something that the bodies had in common were the fact that they were all poisoned with spice residue inside of their mouths," he said. "How did you know the spices were poisoned, Lucia?"

I've been bamboozled! Why are magicians so sneaky with their words? "Uh, I saw the servants eat the spices. Mhm. Are you suspecting me? I'm not a murderer, okay?"

"Huh," Ilya's dad said and blinked. "The lie-detection spell didn't go off when you said you weren't a murderer."

"That's impossible!" Ilya shouted and stood up. "She's killed so many people in front of me! How's she not a murderer!?"

"No, no, those were beasts, Ilya." Jeez, how many times do I have to correct this misunderstanding? Super-rare spirit beasts that can talk and cast spells are not people. It's not murder to kill them—it's population control. And moneymaking.

"That's what the spell says," Ilya's dad said and shrugged. "Then it wasn't you who killed those people. Did you put poison in the spices by any chance?"

"Nope." The only thing I put poison in is Puppers. Other than being eaten, he's completely useless while fighting divine beasts, so why not make him injure the divine beasts while he's being eaten?

"Then it was the chef," Ilya's dad said. "Ilya, who did we hire to cook for your banquet? Was it Mr. Ei?"

"Yes," Ilya said. She blinked and pursed her lips. "Do you think he's an assassin?"

"It's possible," Ilya's dad said. "Or it could be one of our servants." He sighed. "This is troublesome."

"Why?" How is it troublesome? Just interrogate everyone. "Don't you have a lie-detection spell? Why not just use it on all your servants?"

Ilya's dad cleared his throat and turned his head away. "The lie-detection spell..., the lie-detection spell only works on those who aren't burdened with great mental capabilities."

Those who aren't burdened with great mental capabilities.... I'm being called stupid again, aren't I? I'm going to smack him.

"Ow!"

"Lucia, assaulting a duke is a serious crime," Ilya said. I smacked her too. "Ow!"

That's right; fear me. "No, seriously, why don't you use the lie-detection spell on all your servants?"

Ilya's dad held his swollen cheek. There were tears in his eyes when he said, "I wasn't lying when I said what I said before."

Well, if assaulting a duke is a serious crime, then it looks like I'm going to be a criminal. A few minutes later, Ilya was casting a healing spell on her dad's face. Her dad cleared his throat and stared at his hands while asking, "So ... would you like to attend Ilya's banquet? The upper echelons of demon society will all be attending. It's understandable if you're uncomfortable and choose not to."

It seems like I don't have to invite myself! That's great. Is it just me, or is Ilya's dad a lot friendlier now? I'll keep this trick in mind for the banquet. If any demons aren't friendly, I'll smack them around a few times until they are. Maybe just one more smack.

"Ow! What was that one for?" Ilya's dad asked with a frown.

"I'm still upset you called me stupid." The requirement for the lie-detection spell can't really be based on intelligence, right...? I'm not a dumb person!

***

Ah, I'm so nervous. The day of the banquet has finally come, yet Lucia still looks totally relaxed despite the fact that dozens of demon nobility will be here in a few minutes. I tugged on her sleeve. "Aren't you nervous?"

"Nervous? About what?" Lucia asked and tilted her head. She had changed out of the white dress that she always wore and had on a red backless dress that plunged down far enough for her tail to be freed. A black leather belt was strapped around her waist with a scabbard attached that held her sword. Despite the fact she was wearing high-heels, she insisted on wearing her socks with the cute wolf and paw print patterns on them. I honestly didn't know Lucia could look so ladylike. In my head, she's like a blood-covered demon. It's a bit unsettling to see the stark contrast.

"About meeting nobility," I said. "The emperor is coming, you know?"

"So?" Lucia asked again. She yawned and fiddled with her hair that had been tied into a bun by our maids. A pin fell loose, and her hair cascaded down to her back. "Ah! That wasn't supposed to happen. Oh wells." She shrugged and poked me with the pin in her hand. "Are you nervous?"

"Yes." I'd be lying if I said I wasn't. With a ticking time bomb like Lucia attending my party, it'd be a miracle if nothing disastrous happens. And other than that, the emperor holds the life of all his subjects in his hands. Though it's unlikely, he can strip my father of his title and lands. How can someone not be nervous around someone who controls their life? Wait a minute....

Lucia, the one who controlled my life for over three months, slapped my back. "Chin up! Pretend they're divine beasts and all your feelings of nervousness will turn into hunger." She nodded and stared off into the distance with a glint in her eyes. Her stomach growled.

"I don't think seeing a divine beast provokes hunger in normal people," I said. But I have to admit divine beasts are delicious. Eating their meat has almost spoiled all other kinds of food for me. Lucia's right; what do I have to be nervous about? I've seen over thirty divine beasts die in front of my eyes. Someone like the emperor can't strike fear into my heart.

Lucia yawned and shifted her weight from foot to foot. "When are they coming?" she asked. "And why do I have to stand here with you? I'm not the birthday girl; I should be allowed to slack off and eat all your food without repercussions."

"You already do that." I grabbed her hand. "Can't you stand here with me? I don't want to stand up here by myself." My father had me and Lucia wait inside the dining room, which had been repaired with the help of magic after Lucia destroyed it. A stage had also been set up by one of the walls in the center of the room. We were waiting on the stage with the curtains down because my father wanted to do something like a grand reveal with music and flashy effects. But it's scary standing up here alone! Under the guise of protecting me from assassins, I managed to convince my father to let Lucia stay up here with me.

"The food's not going to be poisoned, right?" Lucia asked. Her tail swept against the floor as she closed her eyes, most likely imagining the delicacies prepared for the banquet.

"Just wondering, but why are you so paranoid about poison in your food?"

"Because I was poisoned once," Lucia said as her eyes snapped open. For a second, they turned white like she had activated her Path of Slaughter, but her irises and pupils returned when she blinked. "Sneaky little bastard. Once I get my hands on him, I'll chop his ears off and make a stew out of them."

"That sounds a bit like cannibalism." She's talking about a person, right? Unless a rare spirit beast that specialized in poisons poisoned her.

Lucia looked at me as if I were an idiot. "I never said I was going to drink the stew. I was just going to make it." She raised her head. "Oh, they're finally here."

Moments later, I heard faint chattering and the sound of the dining room doors opening. My father's voice rang through the air followed by the shuffling of footsteps and scraping of chairs against tile. Earlier, my father had his servants place nametags at every round table for the guests. Once everyone was seated, he'd direct their attentions towards the stage and the curtains would rise.

I glanced at Lucia. She was fiddling with her sword while humming. Wait. Why was her sword out!? "Put your sword away," I said in the sharpest but lowest voice I could muster. Seriously, what was she thinking?

Thankfully, Lucia listened and rolled her eyes before sheathing her sword. "It's just a habit," she said and patted my head. "Besides, if you're angry at me, you won't be nervous." She frowned. "But I don't get why you're always angry or bitter at me."

Am I? Have I been treating Lucia unfairly? I don't think so. I think anger and bitterness are completely normal emotions to feel when dealing with Lucia. And it's not so much anger as it is frustration. She doesn't understand social norms or etiquette when dealing with people. But is that her fault...? Right now, she might be dressed like a noble, but I'm not sure what her background is actually like. I always assumed she was nobility because commoners aren't powerful: their starting points are lower and they won't have the same amount of resources. Now that I think about it, how much do I actually know about Lucia other than she's a divine warrior who can kill divine beasts and has an obsession with gold and good food?

"Hey, Lucia."

"Hmm?"

"When the banquet's over, can you tell me about your past?"

"Huh?" Lucia stared at me. "It's not that exciting, but okay."

My father's voice rang out before I could speak. "And now, if you'd so kindly turn your attention towards the stage. I'd like to introduce you to the youngest fifth-circle magician in history, my daughter, Ilya!"

I took in a deep breath and held my head high while Lucia took a few steps back and whispered, "Relax, if anyone makes fun of you today, I'll beat them up for you." With those reassuring words behind me, the curtains rose.

***

Wow. That's a lot more people than what I was expecting. The whole dining room is filled and I already elaborated on huge it was before, so I won't do it again. Most likely all the servants are working right now because there's no way the usual number can service this many people. It's almost like being in the streets of the capital again. Oh, and they're all staring at me. Why me!? It's Ilya's birthday; stare at her!

"Good evening, everyone," Ilya said and curtsied. Wasn't she supposed to be nervous? She's really good at hiding it. "I'd like to thank you all for attending my birthday banquet."

Why am I up here again? Ilya said it was to prevent assassins from targeting her or something along those lines. Then, I guess, that makes me a bodyguard. An underpaid one, that is. Why do I feel like I'm a slave to nobles again? Hmm. Well, Ilya doesn't treat me like a slave at all, so it doesn't matter. What are we anyways? Traveling companions? Friends? Is this what friends do? I've never had any before, so I wouldn't know. I thought Snow was a friend, but that bastard poisoned me. Ah, like I thought, the path of a genius is a lonely one.

"Aren't you going to introduce the esteemed guest behind you?" Ilya's dad asked. He was holding something in front of his mouth that caused his voice to echo through the whole room without shouting. I wonder how it works. Magic? It would've been so much easier to sell those penises if I had one of those things.

Ilya glanced at me, her brow crinkling for a second. Her expression returned back to normal as she faced the crowd. "This is Lucia Fluffytail. For the Godking's Brawl, she will be representing the Pentorn family. She is also my good friend, so please treat her as you would treat me."

"My lord, she's a masochist," a voice whispered from my socks.

"Shut up, Puppers. No one cares about your opinion." I made sure to whisper so no one in the crowd could hear me. I wonder if Ilya thinks of me as her friend or if she's just saying that. Then again, I did save her life, so she should have a positive impression of me. And I feed her! I tried to give her lots of head pats and teach her tricks too, but she gets offended when I do that, so I stopped.

"Lucia," Ilya whispered. "Say something to the crowd."

Great, everyone's staring at me again. What do I say? I was never taught any noble etiquette. Ilya, help!

"Say it's my honor to be here tonight," Ilya whispered.

Thanks for the help, but don't read my mind! "It's my honor to be here tonight."

"And lower your head," Ilya whispered.

I lowered my head. Ilya's dad clapped, and a round of applause soon followed. "Let the banquet begin," Ilya's dad said and walked towards an empty table. He gestured for Ilya and me to follow after him. The center of the dining room was left empty with the tables close to the walls. Servants strode through the doors on either side of the dining room, bringing in trays with glasses and bowls.

I took the seat next to Ilya, who sat beside her father. It was a round table with twelve chairs, and the other nine chairs were occupied by demons wearing purple clothes. ...Their fashion sense sucks. Their skin is purple, but they're wearing the same exact shade of purple for their clothes? I almost thought they were nude.

"Welcome, Your Majesty," Ilya's father said to the man sitting beside him. So the naked-but-not-really man with wisps of white hair was the emperor. Interesting. Huh? You're wondering why I'm not scared of him? Obviously, it's because I'm not a demon. I don't have to abide by his laws. ...That's how diplomacy works, right? Yeah, I'm positive that's how it works; if I'm not his subject, I don't have to respect him.

"Duke Pentorn," the emperor nodded at Ilya's dad. His attention turned towards Ilya, and he smiled at her. "So this is your daughter." His eyes narrowed before widening. "She really is a fifth-circle magician."

"Greetings, Your Majesty," Ilya said and lowered her head, staring at the empty space on the table where her plate should've been. Why aren't there any plates? Wasn't this supposed to be a place with a lot of food?

"Mm," the emperor nodded and Ilya raised her head. The emperor put his hand on the shoulder of the demon sitting next to him. "I presume you already know who this is? Daniel, I think you'll get along well with Ilya, don't you think?"

This person? He looks older than me! Then again, everyone looks older than me because I'm super-duper young. Mhm. Ilya nodded at Daniel. "Greetings, First Prince."

"Miss Pentorn," Daniel said and nodded back. His red eyes shifted and stared at me. What kind of look is that? You want to fight, old man? I'll take you on any day!

Someone tugged on my sleeve. "Please don't growl at him," Ilya whispered to me. Was I growling? I didn't even notice.

"I'm unable to sense any magical fluctuations from you, Miss Fluffytail," Daniel said. "Could it be your attainments in magic are higher than mine? No wonder why the duke has chosen you to represent his family."

Mm. Misunderstandings are the best understandings especially when it comes to people overestimating me. "That's right. I bet I could teach you a thing or two."

Daniel smiled while Ilya's expression paled. "Please," Daniel said and stood up while cupping his hands. "It's always an honor to receive the guidance of an elder."

Huh? Ow! Why did Ilya pinch me?

"You just offered to have a magical duel with him. He's a seventh-circle magician," Ilya whispered and bit her lower lip.

…Why did I act so arrogantly a few seconds ago?

"Oh, Lucia, please demonstrate your skills," Ilya's dad said, his eyes twinkling. "In magic."

Damn it, old man! You're just upset I beat you in a duel!

"Go on, what are you waiting for?" Ilya's dad said and gestured towards the center of the dining room. "Usually the demonstrations are reserved for after the meal, but I'm sure no one would mind one match before."

"Father…," Ilya said. "I think—"

Wait! I still have Rogath's ribbon with his four skills inside of it. I'll just use that and make it quick. "It's fine, Ilya." I patted her head to stop her from speaking and gave her a thumbs up. "I got this."

"Ladies and gentlemen!" Ilya's dad said through his magical talking device. I followed after Daniel to the center of the dining room. "It's a bit early, but these two couldn't wait to begin the demonstrations! The meal will proceed after the conclusion of this duel."

I stood opposite of the first prince. "What are the rules?"

"The loser surrenders," Daniel said. "Please, take it easy on me."

"The two contenders are the first prince and Lucia! Please don't destroy my dining room again, Lucia. Ready, set, begin!"

I raised my hand and pointed at Daniel and shouted before he could react, "Topsy-Turvy, Upsy-Daisy, Twisty-Turny, Wishy-Washy!" The ribbon attached to my tail nearly scorched my butt from the heat that came off of it, but thankfully, nothing caught fire.

Daniel's eyes widened and rolled up to the top of his head. Then he fell backwards like a log and started frothing from his mouth. …Was that supposed to happen? That didn't happen to me when Rogath did it…. Maybe if I tiptoe away, no one will notice. …And everyone's staring at me. Well, this is awkward. "So, uh, did I win?"

No one answered.

***

In complete silence, Lucia squatted next to the first prince, heaved him over her shoulder, and walked back to us. She pulled out the seat beside the emperor and placed Daniel onto the chair before dusting off his suit. The prince's head lolled to the side with froth still leaking out of his mouth and dripping onto the floor. Lucia nodded and dusted her hands off before sitting beside me and smiling sweetly at the emperor. Then she turned her gaze towards me. "Can we start eating yet?"

I turned towards my father, who turned towards the emperor, who turned towards his son. I hope the first prince doesn't turn into an imbecile. I forgot Lucia had my teacher's spells stored inside her ribbon, and I didn't expect her to use all four of them at once. Topsy-Turvy scrambles the target's senses. Upsy-Daisy randomly changes the force of gravity on different parts of the target's body. Twisty-Turny temporarily rewires the target's nerves, ruining their motor functions. And Wishy-Washy reverses the flow of qi and mana in the target's body. A combination of all four is enough to fry someone's brain, turning them into a vegetable with no hope of recovery. That's actually why Teacher Rogath can own such a massive property without having a noble title; no one wants to provoke him lest they live a life worse than death.

"Will he be alright?" the emperor asked Lucia.

Lucia nodded. "Definitely! They were four harmless spells anyways. They're just minor inconveniences."

Right, Lucia almost had the same exact thing done to her. Maybe she wasn't as badly affected by the spells because there isn't anything in her head to target.

"Minor inconveniences...," the emperor muttered and looked at his son again. He closed his eyes and shook his head before sighing. He met my father's gaze. "The banquet may begin."

My father cleared his throat, breaking the unnatural silence pervading the room. "Wasn't that quite unexpected? Sorry for the delay; the banquet will now proceed." As soon as my father finished speaking, the servants bustled and passed out plates along with glasses and bottles.

The old butler, Matthew, was servicing our table. "Is there anything you'd like to drink, Your Majesty," he said and bowed at the emperor while keeping the tray in his left hand perfectly steady. "A cocktail or a glass of wine, perhaps?"

"The wine," the emperor said. The rest of the royal family echoed his choice, and their drinks were served.

"I'll also have a glass of wine," my father said. He rarely drank, but it would've been rude of him to not accompany the emperor's choice. Oh, I should tell Lucia to get the wine too; she has no idea how etiquette works.

"Lucia—"

"Hot chocolate!" Lucia said, her eyes round and bright and practically shining at Matthew. The butler gave her a wry smile before taking out a steaming mug of hot chocolate from an interspacial ring. Evidently, Lucia had gotten along really well with him in the kitchen over the past few weeks. "Thanks!" She looked at me, her tail twitching back and forth. "Were you saying something?"

"No, it's nothing." Well, too late to salvage that. "I'll have a glass of wine as well."

"*Half* a glass," my father said to Matthew.

So I'm old enough to be considered for marriage, but not old enough to drink a glass of alcohol? How does that even make sense? Even the youngest princess has a glass of wine.

"I'm curious, Lucia," the emperor said from across the table. Lucia's tail perked up, her face still attached to her mug of chocolate. "Where did you learn those spells? And to be able to cast them all instantaneously with a simple incantation, your attainment in magic must be high indeed."

"I got them from Rogath, the old drunkard," Lucia said. Is that how she thinks of Teacher? Well, it is accurate, I must say. He's drunk more often than not.

"As I suspected," the emperor said with a nod. "Is he here today?"

Lucia looked at me, clearly indicating she wanted me to answer. So I did. "Teacher is in the middle of a crucial experiment right now, and he wasn't able to attend." That's a lie. Teacher was actually just too lazy to come, and he doesn't get along well with nobles. He calls them prudish twits with paper livers.

"How unfortunate," the emperor said without any sincerity. He smiled at Lucia. Was he hoping to rope her into his faction? "How come I've never heard of you before? If you don't mind me asking, how many circles have you established?"

I sipped on my glass and waited for Lucia's answer. But it didn't come. Lucia? ...And she wasn't paying attention. Her head was facing away from me, staring at the steaming tray of food a servant was carrying over. I pinched her tail, causing her to flinch. "Huh!?"

The emperor's gaze seemed to pierce through Lucia as her head whipped from side to side. He cleared his throat, attracting Lucia's attention. "How come I've never"—Lucia tilted her head up and sniffed the air before turning back towards the approaching tray—"of you before...?"

"My apologies," I said. If I didn't say anything, I think the emperor would have her executed for not showing proper manners. "Lucia tends to get easily distracted. It's a side effect of being her."

"I see...," the emperor said and turned his gaze back onto Lucia. She wasn't paying attention to us at all. What was even being served for dinner? Is that ... divine beast meat? There's no way my father could've afforded enough for all the guests. If anything, it should just be limited to this table. As for the divine beast corpses Lucia and I had gathered during our time in the desolate mountains..., we already ate them all.

"This is the meat of a divine three-headed snake," my father said as the tray was placed in the center of the table. It filled up the majority of the space, not leaving any room for anything else.

"Where did you get it?" the emperor asked. His eyes flashed as Lucia's utensils struck the meat like lightning, taking a massive chunk for herself.

"Lucia brought it," my father said.

"Huh?" Lucia asked through a mouth full of meat. "Me?"

"Right," my father said with a nod. "I replaced the one in your interspacial ring. Just think of it as rental fees." He beamed at Lucia, who started making strange clicking noises.

"Scoot over, Ilya," Lucia said. "I'm going to smack him."

I firmly approve of Lucia's decision. This snake was ours—yes, I'm taking credit even though Lucia was the one that killed it. I knew that snake we ate a week ago wasn't as tasty as a divine beast should've been. I moved my seat back, making space for Lucia to lean over and reach my father.

"Ow! Not in front of all these people, please!"

***

Ilya's dad is a thief! He stole my divine beast corpse and replaced it with, with…, I'm not sure what he replaced it with. How did he even find my interspacial ring? That's the biggest issue! I hide my rings in a very personal place. That pervert. How did he raise someone like Ilya? She's so much easier to get along with, jeez.

"Is that true, Lucia?" the emperor asked. "You killed this divine beast?"

"That's right. It's mine." Back off! This whole thing belongs to me. I risked my life for this; well, not really because it was kind of weak. But still!

"Please, feel free to dig in," Ilya's dad said through swollen cheeks. "A dish made out of a divine beast is the only meal appropriate to serve at my daughter's birthday banquet."

The emperor and the rest of the royal family, except Daniel, turned to stare at me. …Were they asking for permission? Gah! Don't poke me, Ilya. And stop looking at me like that. Fine, okay? "Yeah, sure. Dig in."

After I said that, they pounced on the dead snake like hungry demons. …No one said I was good at similes, okay? I'm a warrior, not a bard. Ilya did say divine beasts weren't that easy to obtain because they were expensive, but I didn't think even the royal family would turn into savages when given the chance to eat some. Couldn't I become a legend by hunting divine beasts and selling their corpses to the nobles? I'd become super rich too…. Yeah, Durandal wanted me to be a legend, but he never said how. This is a totally legitimate path I can take.

"Delicious," the emperor said and wiped his mouth with a cloth napkin. "Simply amazing." He smiled at me. "Was it difficult to kill this beast? I've never seen one as intact as this. It's almost as if magic hadn't been used at all."

Right, Ilya did say most divine beast corpses were charred beyond recognition by magic. "It was pretty easy." Should I make the offer to sell divine beasts right now? Obviously! I'm in front of the emperor, I don't think there's any chance better than this. "If you want, I can go hunting and bring some back for you—for a price, of course."

"Oh?" The emperor raised an eyebrow. "How many could you hunt in a month?"

I'm not sure. "Hey, Ilya." I poked her side because she always did that to me. She choked for a while before finally glaring at me. "How long did it take to get to that academy base after meeting … that teacher guy whose name I can't remember?"

"Teacher Shinx? About a week," Ilya said. She glanced at her food before looking back at me.

"Mm, okay." I wasn't going to poke her again. I'm not as mean as her. The emperor was still staring at me with that strange smile on his face. Kind of like a pervert, but isn't he, like, really old? Maybe it's in a grandfatherly way. Not like my grandfather who tried to drown me in a barrel, but an actual nice one. "So I killed 33 divine beasts in a week. And there's four weeks in a month. So ... around 130 beasts a month?"

The emperor's eyes widened as dozens of utensils hit the table at the same time. The whole royal family—and Ilya's dad—had dropped their forks and knives. One of them, I think the empress, even spilled wine all over herself. "One, one hundred beasts a month?" the emperor asked. Wow, now he's looking at me like those people did back in the southern pass when I still wore my bones like armor. "You're serious?"

That's right; be amazed! "Yup. But I'd need a few more interspacial rings to hold that many."

"Lord," the emperor said and picked up his utensils with trembling hands, "over a hundred divine beasts a month." He raised his head to look at me. "And they'll all be in the same condition as this one?"

"Mhm."

The emperor gritted his teeth and furrowed his brow. "By any chance," he said slowly, staring at me with a strange expression, "are you married? Daniel here might not be as strong as you, but he's set to inherit the throne. The whole empire will be under his control. He's also single and looking for prospective marriage partners. I guarantee you'll have the position as the main wife even if you're a beastkin."

What. "Eh, I'll pass." I mean, Daniel hasn't even woken up yet. He's still frothing from both corners of his mouth. And I have Durandal! As soon as he wakes up, that is. Why the hell is he still asleep!? It's been literal years. Years!

"You're making a really scary face right now," Ilya whispered to me. "Is everything okay?"

"No, everything is not okay." Damn it, why am I so angry and frustrated? There's an itch in my chest that I can't scratch, but instead of an itch, it's pain. The last time I felt like this was … was when my parents sold me to the slavers. Fuck. Why is it so hot in here? Who's cutting onions?

"…Lucia?" Ilya asked and placed her hand on my shoulder. Her touch felt like fire, and I shoved her away. Aren't I strong enough now, Durandal?

"Whoa," Ilya's dad said. "Let's not pull out swords at the dinner table, please." He stood up, and an overwhelming chill ran down my spine. Tendrils of mana swirled around my body, forming a giant hand that closed its fingers around me. I wasn't even using the Path of Slaughter, but I could see the outline of the mana hand easily. It even distorted the view of Ilya behind it. "I'm sorry about stealing your imugi corpse; I'll make it up to you, promise." Ilya's dad floated into the air, bringing me with him. I didn't resist. What was the point? "Stay here, Ilya. I'll bring Lucia to her room and be right back." He paused. "Sorry about this, Your Highness. She must not be feeling very well."

"I understand," the emperor said with a nod. Then he muttered, "Is Daniel so ugly that he made her cry? It can't be. What does that say about me if it were true?"

17

I'm not quite sure what's wrong with Lucia. After that outburst at my banquet, she holed herself up in her room. She doesn't respond to food, sweets, hot chocolate, or even acorns. If it weren't for the fact that I saw her mumbling to herself while staring at her ceiling while lying down, I would've thought she was dead. I did walk in on her one night, and she was crying in her sleep. I stopped checking on her after that; I hope she's okay.

It's been about two weeks, and the Godking's Brawl is set for two months from now. The emperor said he was looking forward to seeing Lucia compete. Thankfully, the first prince had woken up during the banquet, but the imugi was completely consumed by then. He was regretful he missed out on it, and he was a bit devastated to hear about Lucia and how his father had proposed a marriage offer for him.

Puppers has been wandering around a lot outside of Lucia's room. I tried asking him what was wrong with her, but the only response I got was, "Everything. Everything is wrong with her. There is literally nothing right about her." Given how badly Lucia treated him, it's not a surprise for Puppers to sound so bitter. But I think he cares about her deep down on the inside. If he didn't, he wouldn't be scouring our library for information about squirrelkin.

The guards and servants are concerned about Lucia's health too. I hadn't realized how much of an impression she left on them during her short stay here. The guards miss training with her, and the servants smile less ever since she locked herself away. Lucia promised to tell me about her life after the banquet, but she's not in the right state of mind to do that; though, I highly suspect the answer to why she's being like this is hidden away in the details of her past. Could it be Durandal's fault? The only other time I had seen her breakdown like this was when Teacher took away her sword and locked her in a cage. She had become a blubbering mess in less than five minutes and begged to take me on a journey.

According to Puppers, he's never seen Durandal after meeting Lucia either. And Puppers actually turned out to be Gae Bulg, a pretty famous weapon spirit. The losers aren't really glorified by the winning side, but even I've heard of Gae Bulg when studying the history between demons and humans. His owner played a great contribution to the human side, winning battle after battle. Of course, he was overshadowed by the Godking who officially ended the war by coercing the leaders of the three factions. The commoners are told a different story involving the Godking's overwhelming might, but every noble knows how the Godking really did it—that kidnapper. And alongside the stories about the Godking, Durandal's always there. It's hard to imagine a legendary weapon like him being under Lucia's control due to the differences between Lucia and the Godking. But to be fair, Lucia is a serious powerhouse that can influence the politics between the three empires directly with her words. A divine warrior? Simply unheard of. Thousands of mercenaries and soldiers will flock to her side if she announces her status. It's a bit scary to think about. Not to mention she has a ton of money, and the strength to fight off a ninth-circle magician. No doubt, the fae will do their best to rope her in once they see her at the Godking's Brawl.

But even scarier than Lucia is Teacher Rogath. He managed to tie her fate together with mine, linking her to the demons. There's no doubt in my mind that Lucia is the scion of some rich and powerful family of beastkin, tempering herself by traveling through the world. She jokes about being an orphan or a slave sometimes, and she even tried to say she didn't know how to read, but I simply don't believe her. Anyone as skilled and talented as Lucia has to have been raised by nobility. The ignorance and lack of common sense she displays also points to her living a sheltered life amongst her family. Who doesn't know the value of a divine beast corpse? She was fully intent on leaving a manticore's body behind. Only someone raised by wealth can think like that. And the fact that she showed no respect to magicians in the desolate mountains—no commoner would ever be that arrogant.

At first, I thought Lucia was an idiot because she was a bumpkin. But after seeing her behavior at the banquet, completely natural and relaxed in the presence of the emperor, I can't help but suspect her position. How high up there is she in the upper echelons of beastkin society? Illegitimate daughter of the beast king? Direct descendent? She has a family name, so she can't be low. I've never heard of the Fluffytails before though, so she's most likely an illegitimate child of the emperor. She'll probably deny it if I say it outright, so I'll have to lure it out of her. It shouldn't be difficult since she's an airhead.

There's supposed to be a new moon tonight. I've heard beastkin are most agreeable when the moon isn't out, so I'll try to figure out what's wrong with Lucia today. That's actually why I'm standing in front of her room with a cup of steaming hot chocolate right now. I took in a deep breath, worked up my courage, and pushed open the door. Knocking on the door only results in Lucia throwing a sword at the offender, which is why I went in acting like I owned the place—which is close enough to the truth.

I froze. Lucia was lying in bed, with tearstains running down the side of her face. A stuffed animal was covering her eyes, and soft snores escaped from her lips. But that wasn't why I froze. There was an average-looking human male standing over her by the window. There was a puzzled expression on his face as he stared at Lucia. Then, he raised his head and met my eyes.

"Who are you?" His gaze was like a spirit beast's, encasing my body in a layer of imaginary ice. If I hadn't encountered all those divine beasts on my journey with Lucia, I may have been intimidated. Instead, I channeled my mana, readying one of my stronger spells.

"Me?" the strange man asked and raised an eyebrow. "I'm Durandal."

***

I wasn't sure what I'd see after waking up again. I thought waking up to a new owner had a very high probability, but luckily, that didn't happen. I noticed Lucia absorbed the path seed I left behind for her; I wonder what path she unlocked when she became a spirit warrior. I was serious about disowning her if she unlocked the path of 'hey, look, an acorn'. What I certainly didn't expect was to see her in the living quarters of a noble demon. The demons' furniture and designs are easy to differentiate from the fae and humans. Was she kidnapped and turned into a servant? I wouldn't be surprised. Is it sad to say that I wasn't expecting too much from Lucia? It's a miracle she even survived.

Footsteps caught my attention. I waited for the knock on the door, but it didn't happen. A young demon girl had kicked the door open, not caring about Lucia's privacy. So they're treating her this poorly, huh? Perhaps I should teach them a lesson.

"Who are you?" the girl asked. A servant girl? No, she seems more dangerous than that.

"Me? I'm Durandal." Why did I freely give out my name? I wanted to see how she'd react. Her reaction would tell me a lot about the place I was in. Besides, if the demons become greedy and start lusting after me, then it'll be a perfect training ground for Lucia. Strength increases with proportion to danger. I've let Lucia slack off for far too long. It's been over three months at most, but that's enough of a grace period. No doubt, the human royalty are sending someone to chase her down by now. She has to grow stronger to repel them by herself. If I'm knocked unconscious again, she has to be strong enough to take care of herself. There's no guarantee she'll get as lucky as this time.

"Oh, you're finally awake?" the demon girl asked. "Thank the lord. Take care of your mentally damaged master, please." She walked over and placed the tray she was carrying onto the nightstand by Lucia's bed. She could move so freely after experiencing my aura? Let's do it again. The demon girl stiffened for a second before frowning. "Stop doing that, please."

...Did I become weaker during my time of slumber? I can't even intimidate a child? "Uh—"

"You have no idea what she put me through," the demon girl said before I could speak. "It was terrible, an absolute nightmare. But it was helpful, kind of. Were you the one who taught her to train that way?"

"I guess you could say that?" I'm not sure what way she's talking about. But it has to have been me, right?

"It's all your fault!" The demon girl stamped her foot. "What the hell is wrong with you? Light, heed my call, smite this sinner to the ground!"

Huh? A beam of light rained down from the ceiling and smacked my forehead. My body grew heavier, and I was forced to my knees. I didn't even have a weapon to defend myself with! I'm also not sure of Lucia's condition; otherwise, I'd use her qi to resist. "W-wait. Can't we talk this out?"

"Let me vent my frustration first," the demon said. "I can't beat up Lucia, but evidently, there's no issue with dealing with you."

She can't deal with Lucia with this level of power? "Are you saying I'm weaker than Lucia?"

"Don't try to act like a tough guy! I know the Godking's great at manipulating young children, but I'm old enough to not fall for any tricks," the demon said. So she knew about Roland's kidnapping deeds. Well, a lot of demons do since Roland wouldn't be the main contributor of a new school of magic if he hadn't kidnapped that child back then. What was his name? Rogath? Urgh, this light is getting unbearably heavy. But I'm not weaker than Lucia!

"Darkness, listen up, sap his strength!"

What are these tendrils? They're taking away my senses! Is this what Bouncykins meant by the era of warriors is over? A young magician holds this much power. What if she were older? How would any warrior hope to deal with her?

The demon crossed her arms over her chest. "Water, be gentle, spray his face with a fine mist every five seconds."

What..., what is this!? Am I really this helpless? Did I really lose my strength after sleeping for so long? Or was I always this weak...? And Lucia's supposed to be stronger than me? Can I even help her anymore?

"Had enough?" the demon asked. "Kowtow to me ten times and apologize for your master's misdeeds, then I'll let you go."

"Do you know who I am?" The only thing I can do is appeal to reputation. It's very sad to admit, but as I am right now, weaponless and unable to draw on Lucia's qi, I'm weaker than this young demon. And for some reason, I can't even retreat into mini-DalDal.

"Do you know who my father is? He's a ninth-circle magician," the demon said. "And do you know what Lucia did?"

Why do I dread the answer? "No...."

"She slapped him until his face turned puffy in front of the upper echelon of demon society while the emperor was beside him. So I don't care if you're Durandal or the Godking himself. Right now, I'm bullying you into apologizing." The demon snapped her fingers. "Earth, be sharp, form a spike and pierce the center of this unrepentant soul's hindquarters if he doesn't kowtow within ten seconds."

A chill ran down my spine as an earthen spike appeared where I'd rather it not appear. Now I know why Lucia had such an objection to holding a horse stance above a spike.

"Nine."

Do I do it? Do I give up my pride as the Godking's weapon? Or do I draw on Lucia's qi and fight back? But I might harm Lucia if I do that.

"Five seconds left."

That wasn't four seconds!

"Two seconds."

I'll do it! To preserve my last shred of dignity, I'll repent for sins I'm not aware I committed. "I'm sorry for the trouble Lucia has caused you! It's all my fault as her teacher and mentor!"

"Now do it nine more times," the demon said. There was a bright smile on her face. What a sadist. Are these the kinds of people Lucia has been associating with? As I kowtowed nine more times, I could hear the demon mutter, "Ah, it's like all the stress I've built up over the past four months has all been released at once. I can feel my sixth circle beginning to form."

***

Ah, Mr. Fluffy Toy Bear sitting on my face, I miss Durandal. "Durandal...."

"Yes?"

Huh? "Durandal?"

"Yes, Lucia?"

That sounds like..., is it really...? "Durandal!"

"That's me."

Wait. That's not Durandal. What the heck? Why's there a stranger sitting in the corner of my room pretending to be Durandal? Why does he sound like Durandal? "Who are you?"

"Did you really forget who I am?" the strange man asked. He tried to do Durandal's intimidating gaze, but failed miserably. I didn't even feel it. Durandal's tall! Buff! Handsome! This man is ... well, he's a bit pudgy, short, and it looks like his face had an unfortunate encounter with a grindstone. "You don't remember me?"

"Eh...? You're really Durandal?" I thought I would flying tackle Durandal after he woke up, but ... I don't really want to now. "What happened to your face?"

"Before anything else, can you please put some qi into mini-DalDal," the false Durandal said. "For some reason, I can't draw on yours. I'm withering."

Hmm. Well, he knows mini-DalDal's name, so I guess it can't hurt. Let's put some qi inside. Oh? The false Durandal's growing! His abs are forming! His jaw is re-sharpening! Durandal's really back! "Unrelenting Path of Slaughter: Flying Tackle!"

"Lucia!?"

"You're back! You're really finally back! Do you know how long I waited for you?"

"How long?" the real Durandal asked and patted my head. Oh, I missed these. Do my tail too. "About three months?"

"Over two years!" Ah, did I smack him too hard? That was supposed to be a playful, flirty smack to the chest, but he flew into and cracked a wall. Oops. "I'm a divine warrior now!"

"Huh?" Durandal asked. His eyes widened. Stupefied Durandal's the best! I bet that brought about a bigger reaction than if I told him the Godking came back to life. ...Hey, isn't that insulting myself?

Oh! And there's Ilya; I should introduce the two. "Hey, Ilya, this is Dur—"

"Wait," Durandal said and blocked my mouth. "Do you have a weapon? A spear perhaps?"

"Um, I have this pointy divine beast's spinal cord. Will that work?" I took the bone I was saving for consumption out of my interspacial ring.

"Don't give it to him!" Ilya shrieked. She turned around and ran, spells blazing around her feet.

"Wait here, I'll be right back, Lucia," Durandal said as he snatched the bone out of my hand and chased after Ilya. What was that about? Moments later, I heard Ilya's shrieking and Durandal roaring, "Trying to bully me because I had no qi or weapons!? I'll learn you! I'll learn you real good!" followed by more of Ilya's shrieks.

"Save me, Lucia!" Ilya shouted. Her voice made it seem like she was crying, but Durandal's a nice person! He wouldn't make a little girl cry. ...That asshole, he totally would. Did something happen between them? Mm, well, Durandal told me to wait right here. Ah! I should introduce Durandal to Puppers too. I patted my socks, and they glowed with a white light. A few seconds later, a blur rushed into my socks from outside the room.

"Did you call?" Puppers asked with a sigh.

I'm your master; you should be happier to see me, gosh. "Yeah, c'mon out. Durandal's awake!"

"Finally!" Puppers said as he sprang into existence. "I can finally be free from this torture! ...Right? You don't need me anymore because Durandal's back, right? Please say yes." His tail wagged back and forth while his eyes gleamed.

"Nope. Down, Puppers. Be a good boy and sit patiently."

Puppers whimpered and sat on the ground beside me, looking like he lost all purpose in life. Ooh, Ilya brought me hot chocolate while I was sleeping too. She's the best; maybe I should've helped her. Oh wells, I'm sure she'll be fine. But Durandal's really back! Everything is right in the world.

"Pervert...," Puppers said under his breath, but I could still hear him anyways. I'm in a good mood though, so I won't do anything bad to him. I'll just pretend I didn't hear that because I'm such a magnanimous person.

Right when I finished my hot chocolate, Durandal strode back into the room, holding Ilya by one of her legs. She was face down on the ground, looking like a dead deer. A streak of blood and tears marked the path the two had taken back into the room. Durandal unceremoniously tossed Ilya onto the bed. She bounced off and fell to the ground, but she didn't make a sound. She wasn't dead, right? That would be pretty bad, especially since Rogath is still out there.

"Durandal!" Ah, I missed saying his name so much. "Durandal, look. Durandal! It's Puppers."

"Puppers?" Durandal looked at Puppers, who lowered his head and looked to the side. "Gae Bulg...? Is that you?"

"No. I don't know who you're talking about," Puppers said. "Must be someone similar."

"It really is you, Gae," Durandal said and blinked. "What happened to the old spearman? Why's Lucia calling you Puppers?" Durandal looked at me with a strange expression on his face. Did I do well? Head pats? Please?

Puppers sighed. "The old man died of old age. I was passed down to Lan, one of the princes of the Ravenwood Empire. Lan decided to hunt Lucia and died in the process. So now I'm here."

"...I see," Durandal said. He patted my head and rubbed my ears. "She beat you, huh? Just like in the past, my master's greater than yours." Durandal smiled at me before looking around. "Where's your weapon body?"

Puppers sighed, rolled over, and crawled under the bed.

"I made him into my socks!" I pointed at the cute little paw prints on my socks. "See?"

"You … turned Gae Bulg into a sock spirit?" Durandal asked. His face paled. "Then what that demon girl was saying—"

"Ilya?"

"Yes, Ilya. She said you disrespected the duke in front of the emperor of the demons. Was that true?"

"He deserved it! Bastard stole my divine beast corpse."

"Divine beast corpse?" Durandal asked. His brow furrowed as he sat down, shoving Ilya's unmoving body out of the way. "You sound like you have quite the story to tell."

"Mm! I beat things up, drained their cores, cut off their penises, and met Ilya. Then I beat divine things up, cut off their penises, and sold them to perverts in the capital. I decided to visit Ilya's home, then consumed all the divine beast cores and became a divine warrior. Then there was a party, and now you're back! Praise me!"

"Wait!" Ilya shouted. So she wasn't dead. "How come 'met Ilya' comes right after 'cut off their penises'!? That doesn't make any sense!"

"It makes sense chronologically." Right? I didn't miss anything at all in that story. Wow, maybe I should've been a bard.

***

Lucia…, Lucia's surpassed me. She went above and beyond my expectations: unlocking a path with a prefix, becoming a divine warrior, beating me in a fair duel and forcibly holding me down and tying me up and throwing me into a bed. Wait, why's she doing this? These weren't the terms we agreed to during the duel! "Lucia!?"

"Hmm?" Lucia sat on the bed and tilted her head to the side.

Don't act stupid! "Untie me, please."

"But you'll run away," Lucia said and blinked.

"Yes! Which is why you shouldn't do this in the first place!" I'm a weapon spirit! I'm meant for combat, not..., not bed stuff!

"Huh? Do what?" Lucia asked with a smile. Her tail twitched a few times as she sat on her ankles and rested her hands on her knees. Her eyes twinkled. "Say? Aren't you hot wearing all those clothes after sparring? I can help you with that."

Desperate times call for desperate measures. Retreat into mini-DalDal!

"Eh!? Durandal!? Where'd you go?" Lucia grabbed at the fallen ropes on the bed, her head swiveling from side to side. She paused and sniffed the air before frowning. She grabbed my weapon body and held it in front of her face. It was almost as if she could see me inside. "That's not fair!"

"Uh, Lucia," Puppers—I mean Gae—said. "Don't you know anything about weapon spirits? Namely, the weapon part of their name? We're meant for fighting."

"But you're just a sock," Lucia said. I still find it quite humorous how Gae was turned into a sock spirit. Back then, in the days of the Godking, Gae and I were always compared as the two strongest weapon spirits out there. But Gae's been reduced to a mere house pet, and I am now weaker than the master I serve. Far, far weaker, but that's a good thing. A spirit can only grow as strong as their owner. Before, I was limited to the peak of spirit warrior due to Roland failing to surpass the wall to divine warrior. But now, I can pass that wall. It's a bit sad when I think about it. Even Roland lost to the passing of time.

"Yes, you reduced me to a mere sock spirit, but what I'm about to tell you, you should engrave into your memory," Pup—Gae said. "Spirits are created from seeds found in nature. We're grown by our owner's qi. But seeds have a double meaning—if Durandal gives you his seed, he'll die."

"If Durandal gives me his seed..., he'll die," Lucia said and furrowed her brow. She gasped. "You can't be serious!"

He's not. It's a complete lie. I never expected my old rival to bail me out of this situation. Is this what it means to be brothers in suffering?

"I'm dead serious," Gae said. "Unless he breaks through to the legendary realm, he'll definitely die if he engages in the activities you want to engage him in. I don't know why he didn't want to tell you it himself; maybe he thought you wouldn't believe him."

"Gae Bulg is right. I have to break through to the realm of legendary warriors before, uh, yeah. And to do that, *you* have to break through the legendary realm first. Only then can I grow stronger. My strength increases with yours." I still have to absorb a lot of her qi to advance to the divine realm and undergo a period of refinement. When Roland first became a warrior, I awakened. When he became a spirit warrior, I unlocked the ability to manipulate my weight. When I become a divine weapon spirit, what will I gain?

"No way," Lucia said and collapsed onto her knees. "My happiness! It was right there!" She ground her teeth together and made strange chattering noises before standing up. She cupped her hands over her mouth and shouted, "Ilya!"

A few seconds later, that spoiled demon walked into the room. She sighed and asked, "More hot chocolate?"

"Yes, please," Lucia said, her face returning to normal. A moment later, she stiffened when Ilya handed her a steaming cup. "Wait! That wasn't what I called you here for. Are there any divine beasts near the Godking's Brawl? I need to consume their cores. For my future offspring, I have to do everything I can to become a legendary warrior."

Now probably wouldn't be a good time to tell her weapon spirits are sterile, huh? And disregarding that, weapon spirits are beings of logic. We have no emotions; our purpose is to defeat the enemy and teach our masters. Strange, why did I recall a time where Lucia was trying to comfort me as I cried? …That didn't happen. I'm a weapon spirit, dammit, and I'm going to be the best one there is.

"For your future offspring?" Ilya asked and furrowed her brow. "I don't get it. Why do you have to be—guah!?"

Gae flying tackled Ilya to the ground. "Not one more word out of you," Gae said with a growl. "I live in Lucia's socks and she never takes them off. If your question causes me to witness something I never want to witness, then there will be a reckoning involving your head on a pike."

"Lucia!" Ilya struggled on the ground. "Why are all your spirits so violent!? What happened to Puppers? He was cute and tame before Durandal came along! I knew he was a bad influence; someone that taught you couldn't have been a good person!"

"Hey. I'm a very good and law-abiding non-citizen of your country," Lucia said and puffed her chest out. "Oh, didn't you say you wanted to learn about my past? Once you hear it, you'll definitely see how good of a person I am." Lucia reached over and tugged on Puppers, lifting him off Ilya with one hand and tossing him aside like a dirty tissue. "Here." She patted the spot beside her on the bed. "I'll tell you all about myself."

I feel like Lucia's been sidetracked. What happened to finding out about divine beasts near the Godking's Brawl? What is the Godking's Brawl anyway? Well, as long as she's not trying to tie me to the bed, I'm not complaining. For now, I'll do my best to breakthrough to a divine spirit.

***

"Mm, where do I start?" Lucia asked and tilted her head.

"Childhood." Everyone's personality stems a little from their childhood. I want to know what happened to create such a whimsical creature like Lucia. She should've been super spoiled as the illegitimate daughter of the beast king, right? "Tell me about your parents."

"My parents, eh?" Lucia hummed and rubbed her chin. "Well, they were pretty poor farmers working the fields in a land that was terrible for growing things on. I had a lot of siblings, and I was the youngest and weakest of the bunch. So when winter came around and there wasn't enough food to feed everyone, they sold me to some slave traders. I was about three or four when that happened?"

"Eh?" Huh? Lucia's not really a liar even though she can fall pretty hard into denial sometimes. But it feels like she's really telling the truth. Wait a minute. "But you have a family name."

"Oh, yeah. I made that up," Lucia said and nodded. "It sounds nice, doesn't it?"

You can't just make up a family name! "So you're not a noble?"

Lucia puffed her chest out. "If you believe, you can be anything you want."

...Surely she must've had a fortuitous encounter after becoming a slave, right? Well, of course, she met Durandal. But something earlier than that. "Then what happened after you were sold, if you don't mind me asking?"

"I was sold to a human noble to accompany his daughter. I learned how to fight there. I was pretty good with the mace if I may say so myself." Lucia nodded.

Mace? Wasn't Durandal a sword? "So he treated you well then, like family. That's—"

"Nah, I was still a slave," Lucia said, cutting off my words. "I had to cook and clean and do laundry and all that. And whenever I messed up, I'd be whipped a few times. That's why I'm so tough today." She gave me a thumbs up and a smile. ...She's a lot more cheerful now that Durandal's back. I guess his presence isn't all negative.

"What family was it?" Somehow, I can't see Lucia as a slave. How could someone enslave such a carefree person? It makes me angry just thinking about it. I'm going to teach that family a lesson if I see them at the Godking's Brawl.

"Eh…, I don't remember," Lucia said and tilted her head. "They fell into poverty and had to sell me to the army when I was about nine. I guess I'm pretty unlucky to own, huh?"

"A beastkin in the human army?" Aren't they seriously mistreated? No human in the army would treat a beastkin as an ally considering they're training to fight demons and fae. "How long were you in there?"

Lucia scratched her head and furrowed her brow. "A little over a decade?" she asked. Then she stiffened. "I mean, a few years! I'm young, dammit!" She cleared her throat. "It wasn't too bad if you disregard the lack of food, sleeping on the floor with a thin blanket, and being treated worse than dirt. Anyways, I signed up for Prince Bryant's excursion to a rumored Godking's treasure trove and found Durandal. Due to a freak accident, the prince and everyone with him, except for me, died."

"You mean, you killed him, right?" Puppers asked.

"Shut up, Puppers, you weren't there. What would you know? Think before you slander me," Lucia said, smacking the wolfkin's snout. She wrinkled her nose. "Go sit in a corner, face the wall, and reflect on your actions."

Puppers sighed, stood up, and followed Lucia's instructions. Good. I didn't like him tackling and threatening me at all. I'm not even sure why he did it! "So before you found Durandal, what were you? A spirit warrior?" If I recall correctly, the news of that human prince's death came out around two years ago along with the bounty for Durandal's owner. Reaching divine warrior in two years would be reasonable.

"No," Lucia said. "I didn't even know spirit warriors existed. I knew about the existence of warriors, but I was still a normal person until Durandal taught me about qi."

I thought I was a genius, almost reaching the sixth circle by the age of fourteen. But Lucia reached the realm of divine warrior in two years! What the heck!?

"Why are you looking at me like that?" Lucia asked. She beamed. "I'm amazing, aren't I? C'mon, say it. You're amazing, Lucia."

"…You're very special." I've lived with my father, eating the best kinds of foods and drinking the best types of potions to boost my magical aptitude. We live in an area of highly concentrated mana which makes developing circles two times easier compared to the outside. I started training at the age of four with proper guidance and insight from many magicians with at least seven circles. If Lucia had the same environment, or even a slightly less poor one, while growing up, would she be as strong as Cain?

"Thanks," Lucia said and patted my head while smiling. "Then after I became Durandal's master, I did some training and eventually met you."

"Wait, you just skipped over some really important things. Like, why was Durandal not around? And why are you so afraid of poison in your food?" Those are the things I'm really curious about.

Lucia exhaled and crossed her arms over her chest. "While I was traveling with Durandal, we met someone named Snow Flopsy." Why does that name sound so familiar? "We traveled together for months, but Snow suddenly betrayed me one day by poisoning my food. Durandal did something to remove the poison, but he fell unconscious."

"Flopsy…, like the Flopsy Gang kind of Flopsy?" The one that's been causing trouble for my father? "Is Snow a beautiful rabbitkin woman? My dad said the leader of the Flopsy Gang took control of some baronies via seduction."

"No! Snow's a cross-dressing male! But the next time I see him, I'll turn him into a female!"

"Well, you might see him a lot sooner than expected," a voice said from behind us. My father appeared in the doorway with a scowl on his face. "I apologize for eavesdropping. I was just passing by when I heard something about Snow. She's going to represent Marquis Strous in the Godking's Brawl. She's even caught the eye of the second prince."

"Snow's a he!" Lucia shouted.

My father shrugged. "I'm just reporting what I've heard from my informants." He stared at Lucia. "You have to defeat him at the Godking's Brawl; the marquis is aiming for my position of duke."

"I'll beat him up easily, don't worry," Lucia said.

"I hope that's the case," my father said with a nod. "But he should know of your existence since the marquis attended Ilya's banquet. He might have some unpleasant surprises prepared for you."

"Schemes will always lose to overwhelming strength!" Lucia said.

My father nodded. "It's not much, but take these." He tossed over three dark orbs. Divine beast cores? "Think of it as an investment. And here, I brought you some hot chocolate as well."

"Yes! I'll do my best," Lucia said and received the steaming mug. Why did she look more excited over the chocolate than the cores?

18

"Hey, Durandal."

"Yes, Lucia?"

"Nothing, I just wanted to hear your voice." Ah, it's so nice having Durandal back. "What are you rolling your eyes for, Ilya? You got a problem? Huh?"

"No, it's nothing," Ilya said and shook her head. She looked at her dad who was sitting beside her. "Do you see what I mean now?"

"A little," her dad said. He leaned back into the plush seats of the carriage and smiled at me. "Did you finish absorbing those cores I gave you?"

"Yup, it took about an hour." He should've given me more. They technically grow on trees, don't they? If I redefine a tree to mean divine beast, that is. What's really surprising is hot chocolate actually does grow on trees! It's amazing. "Durandal's made it to divine warrior, and even Puppers became a divine sock." My feet are constantly in heaven. It's amazing. I need to make some divine underwear spirits. I wonder if I'll find any during the competition.

Durandal turned his head. Hey, don't look away from me! "What took you so long to become a divine spirit, Gae?"

"I spend more time dead than alive when I'm around Lucia," Puppers said and lowered his head. That's right, look away! This is called establishing dominance amongst beastkin. It works on demons and humans too. "I … don't want to talk about it."

The carriage jolted, and I almost spilled my hot chocolate. It continued to jolt, bouncing us up and down. And I really did spill my chocolate. "Why the heck is this road so bumpy!?"

"It's the boundary line separating human and demon territory," Ilya's dad said. "It means we're getting close to our destination."

"That doesn't explain why it's such a crappy road." Now that I spilled my drink, I only have eighty-three gallons left in my interspacial ring. I have to ration it carefully or I'll run out in a week!

"No one wants to maintain it," Ilya's dad said and shrugged. Or at least I think he shrugged. Everyone was bouncing around too much to tell. "The demons think of it as the humans' responsibility, and the humans think of it as ours. Thus, it remains in its war-torn state."

"Why couldn't we have just teleported there?" Then I could've lazed around in bed and relaxed until the day before the competition started. But no, we had to take the month-long carriage ride.

"I already told you," Ilya said with a scowl. "A teleportation on that scale requires two arrays. It's like a tunnel, and the humans would rather die before letting us build an array into their territory."

"Mm. I was hoping the answer would change since the last time I asked." A person can dream, right? "But we're almost there then, yeah?" In the past month, I've been sparring with Durandal and Puppers at the same time because I'm stronger than both of them. Mainly because my weapon's a cheat while they can't do anything with theirs. I considered getting magic tools for them to use, but they both refused them because of their pride or something. They're very belligerent to each other at times, always trying to be better than the other. It's funny because I should be their real goal.

And I'm also improving faster than them too! They'll never catch up to me. Nothing can get in the way of my happiness! Durandal also felt pretty bad for only teaching me Breaking Blade and the Steady Mountain Footwork—and the Flying Qi Blade, but that one doesn't matter anymore—so he gave me a list of other techniques to choose from, saying I should pick the ones that suited my fighting style the best. I'm still peeved that he only picked out completely ungraceful and wholly barbaric techniques. I can be graceful! Ah, I dropped my cup. Oops.

Ahem, as I was saying, I learned some new techniques. The first one is called Breaking Tail. I insert all my qi into my tail and swing it like a whip! The second one is called Breaking Fist. I insert all my qi into my fist and punch as hard as I can! The third one is called Breaking Kick. I insert all my qi into my leg and kick as hard as I can! …Dammit, Durandal! He said they were new! Mm. Well, I really did learn one that's different from all the rest. It's called Armor of Slaughter. I can create a shield around my body that absorbs attacks. I do it by inserting all my qi into my body and…. Okay, this sounds exactly like a Breaking technique. I demand a refund.

"Durandal!"

"Yes, Lucia?"

"Teach me a new technique! A new! New! Technique."

"Didn't I teach you four?" Durandal smiled at me and patted my head. I missed these head pats so much. And I guess I was too harsh on Durandal. He did teach me four techniques after all. …Wait! Don't be tricked that easily, Lucia. He's trying to distract you.

"No! No, you didn't. You gave me four variations of Breaking Blade. I could've came up with them myself!" In fact, I did come up with the Breaking Substitute Blade by myself. That's the one where I grab a person and use them as a sword.

"Breaking Blade is the strongest, most practical amongst strength techniques. I don't have much else to teach you," Durandal said. "All that I have left are graceful, feminine techniques."

"Teach me those!"

"Mm, they don't work really well with the Path of Slaughter," Durandal said and played with my tail. "But you know what they say, it's better to master one technique than to learn dozens and not know how to fully use them."

"But I definitely mastered Breaking Blade!" I've used it millions or billions of times by now! I do a thousand swings a day, but not recently because I've been slacking.

"Really?" Durandal asked with a smile.

"Really." If I haven't, I'll give up drinking hot chocolate!

"Then…, can you control the shockwave's trajectory?"

…It's a good thing Durandal can't read minds.

"And have you considered the other uses for Armor of Slaughter other than defense?" Durandal asked.

No. I haven't. If it could be used for offense, then it wouldn't be called armor, right?

"Like I thought, you haven't." Durandal sighed. "If only I were stronger, then I could force you to learn properly. But I can't beat you or simulate a dangerous environment anymore. You don't have to surpass your limits to fight me now." He rubbed his chin. "I should find a dragon for you to fight."

"No, that's okay. I'll just practice controlling the shockwaves of my Breaking Blades."

"Oh, I have a good idea," Durandal said, his eyes lighting up. Dammit. Something bad is going to happen to me. I just know it. Durandal reached over, grabbed the back of my dress, and … is he going to—!? He tossed me outside! What the hell!?

Durandal's head appeared outside the carriage's window. Were they speeding up!? "Lucia, use your Armor of Slaughter to lift yourself off the ground and chase after us. No part of your body is allowed to touch the ground. Every time you make contact with the ground, I'll throw out a cup of hot chocolate."

I knew Durandal didn't have kind intentions when he asked to hold onto my interspacial ring! But I was tricked by stupid head pats! Armor of Slaughter! My qi surged around my body, and a faint layer of red light appeared on my skin. This should be enough to keep me off the ground, right? But Durandal seriously underestimated me. I could run faster than two horses pulling a carriage with my eyes closed and on one leg while moving backwards. ...Not that I'm going to do that to myself.

"You're not high enough off the ground," Durandal said from up ahead. A splash of brown liquid flew out of the window. No! My chocolate! Dammit, Durandal! I'm not going to take it easy on you during our next spar! I transferred some of the qi armor from my arms to my legs. The red light grew thicker around my feet, and I was even higher up. Was I running faster too?

"Higher."

This isn't enough? Then I'll use all my qi! The Armor of Slaughter crawled down my body, merging with the qi by my feet. I should rename this to Boots of Slaughter. And now I'll just grab onto this part of the carriage here and hitch a ride...? It slipped away! Why's it going so fast!?

"How long will you be able to maintain this speed?" Durandal asked, his voice coming from inside the carriage.

"Until we arrive at our destination," Ilya's dad said. "They're simple eighth-circle, speed-boosting spells."

Gah! Don't mess with me! Faster legs, faster! If this much qi can't keep up with a stupid carriage, then I'll put all my qi into one foot at a time. But constantly switching is tiring.

"If you don't keep up, I'll toss out more chocolate," Durandal said, his head popping out of the window again. I was very tempted to throw mini-DalDal at him, but I had to concentrate on shifting my qi. "Oh, you're getting the hang of it. Good job." That's right, praise me! And let me back onto the carriage while you're at it. "Can you make the carriage go any faster?"

"She's keeping up?" Ilya's dad asked and popped his head out of the window as well. He flinched and slipped back into the carriage when I met his eyes. "Yeah, I can make it go faster."

"Don't you dare!" This is almost my limit! Why did I throw away my haste dress? Right, because Ilya could cast haste. "Ilya! Buff me!"

Ilya's head popped out of the carriage. A second later, she yelped as she was pulled back inside by Durandal. "Sorry, Lucia! I tried!"

A green light covered the carriage, and it sped up even more. Stop doing that! I'm really going to be left behind at this rate. How do I increase my speed? Think, Lucia, think. Aha! Speed is relative. To increase my speed, I just have to decrease theirs! Alright, mini-DalDal, let's do this. "Breaking—"

"Hot chocolate shield!" Durandal shouted and placed three barrels of hot chocolate on the carriage's rear.

…Drat. Then I'll destroy the road! "Breaking Blade!" A beam of red light flew out of my sword, creating a massive fissure that ran diagonally across the carriage's path. The horses neighed and stopped…? Why aren't they stopping!? Steam puffed out of their nostrils as they charged forwards and walked on air, easily passing over the fissure I created. The carriage rolled along as if the road was completely flat. That's not fair! I was the one who complained about the bumpy carriage ride, and now that I'm gone, the carriage isn't bumping anymore? Like I thought, there is no god.

"At the pace we're going, we'll only need a few hours before we arrive," Ilya's dad said from within the carriage. "I believe in you, Lucia."

Wait! I'll really be left behind! And I have no sense of direction; what if I get lost!? Ah, I'm speeding up? "P-Puppers?"

From my socks, Puppers let out a sigh. "Apparently, I'm the only one who thinks it's a stupid idea to antagonize a divine warrior. And you're my master after all; I have to help you."

…Maybe I've treated Puppers too poorly in the past. He's a good person. In my time of need, he's the only one who offered a hand. Well, Ilya tried, but Durandal blocked her. "I've wronged you, Puppers."

"If you really felt that way, you would call me by my actual name, Gae Bulg," Puppers said. "Don't I deserve at least some respect for being a divine warrior?"

"Mm, but Gae Bulg was a spear spirit. It'd be too confusing to call you that." People would definitely look at me strangely if I had the prince's, err, rare special monkey's weapon spirit. "You're a sock spirit now. New spirits should get new names, yeah? How about Mr. Puppers? I'm willing to give you that."

Puppers fell silent. "I think I'll stick with Puppers," he said after a while.

Well, I tried.

***

"Ah, it looks like we're here," my father said as the spells increasing the carriage's speed and the horses' stamina dispersed. "Pretty big place, huh? It didn't look like this thirty years ago. They've done some major construction works."

I followed my father and Durandal out of the carriage. In front of me, towering above, there was a transparent wall with thousands of patterns scrawled upon it. The mana radiating off the structure made my stomach churn. Were the humans trying to show off their empire's might? If a group of seventh-circle magicians operated the spell formations on the walls, they could easily repel a couple of ninth-circle magicians.

A massive crowd of people were gathered around the walls, camping in tents and other shoddy shelters. A few looked homeless, but the majority of them were demons and beastkin. There were one or two clusters of elves and dwarves, but they were by far the minority. Hundreds of stalls were set up along the road leading to the wall where a relatively tiny gate waited.

"I finally caught you bastards!" a voice shouted. Footsteps that sounded like thunder echoed throughout the area as Lucia ran towards us, the ground cracking and fracturing underneath her feet. The next set of travelers were going to have a tough time traversing through those broken roads. I pitied them. Lucia ran up to Durandal and raised her sword over her head. "You! How could you…." She froze as the mob of people turned their heads to stare at her. "The heck is this? Why's it so crowded!? You told me there were 60 competitors!"

"Mm, no," my father said and smiled. "There's 20 guaranteed competitors from each empire, but anyone, as long as they're under 30 years of age, can compete. After all, Cain is hunting for talent. Though rare, there are some talented commoners out there."

Yeah, Lucia was one of them. I didn't tell my father about Lucia's past. I figured it wasn't my place to tell.

"So I have to compete against all these people here? They're all kind of weak, don't you think?" Lucia asked and tilted her head. The glares coming from the surroundings intensified. Lucia snorted and crossed her arms over her chest. "What? Got a problem? Fight me."

"Lucia…, I don't think you should provoke this many people." What happened to Lucia? I thought she got nervous around crowds. "Aren't you nervous?"

Lucia slapped Durandal's back, causing him to stumble forward. "With him here, what do I have to fear?" She stuck her chest out and smiled while staring up at the sky, striking a heroic pose while her tail twitched a few times. So it was Durandal. Again. The instant he came back, Lucia's and Puppers' personalities changed. I don't like him. All I did was make him apologize for his master's misdeeds. He didn't have to, to..., I don't want to talk about it.

"Mm, well, we're not here to mingle with the commoners," my father said and walked forward along the road. It was surprisingly clear given the amount of people nearby. A few discontent beastkin and humans approached us, but my father let his mana out in a massive surge, knocking them off their feet and throwing them back dozens of meters. My father tilted his head up and swept his gaze over the crowd before letting out a snort. Everyone averted their eyes, and even the merchants manning the stalls stopped shouting. How could my father, the duke of the Tristam Empire, allow random rabble to approach him? It wasn't often I got to see my father's domineering side. I know he always dotes on me.

"Whoa, what was that?" Lucia asked, her eyes glistening. She poked Durandal's back with her sword. "Why couldn't you teach me something useful like that? Ah! I'm supposed to still be mad at you for making me run that whole way!"

"Oh, what's that over there?" Durandal asked and pointed behind Lucia. She turned her head around, and Durandal pulled out a steaming cup of hot chocolate.

"I don't see anything strange?" Lucia asked. She turned back around and blinked as the steaming mug was forced into her hands. "Ooh! Thanks! You're the best."

My lord. I knew Durandal wasn't a good person. Watching Lucia fall for something that even a child could see through was painful. It really makes me wonder if there's a god in this world. How can someone like Lucia become a divine warrior while people like the Godking couldn't? Lucia hummed as she followed after Durandal, sipping on her cup with her tail swishing from side to side. I sighed and followed after them.

As one of the nobles with a guaranteed spot, my father was allowed to enter the city with his entourage, us, before the day of the competition. Of course, that also meant everyone else who had a spot could enter it as well. We passed through the gate without any issues. The buildings were to be expected of the humans. Their designs were a bit lacking, trying to emulate the sharp, crisp edges of demon architecture while trying to mimic the gracefulness of the fae at the same time. Unfortunately, it failed at both, becoming some sort of odd mishmash between the two cultures. The Godking really was a good human, or maybe the humans took after the Godking— appropriating other cultures and claiming it as their own invention. It's an open secret amongst nobility that the Godking claimed credit for hundreds of things he didn't do, including inventing the new magic system of circles and creating the world's strongest weapons and enchantments.

The streets were empty, which wasn't a surprise. We came here extra early after all. The trip should've taken a much longer amount of time, but Durandal decided to have that impromptu training session with Lucia. Well, it was almost empty. A human with curly blond hair and green eyes approached us. Behind him, there were three women around Lucia's age and one old man who was wearing a suit. One of his eyes was closed with a jagged scar crossing over it. They were wearing clothes that I recognized as the robes of nobility. It was in one of my father's books on etiquette. The man with the curly hair stopped in front of my father. He jutted his chest out and stared him in the eyes before saying, "Crown Prince Algar greets Duke Pentorn."

My father raised an eyebrow. "You know me?" he asked. "Then I greet the crown prince in return. Do you have some business with me?"

Algar shook his head before staring at Lucia who was blowing on her hot chocolate. She dipped her fingertip into her cup and flinched, bringing her finger back and sucking on it. The prince's eyes changed from narrowed to widened, and he cleared his throat. "I have business with Durandal's owner," he said with hints of hesitation in his voice. "That's her..., right?"

Lucia raised her head and blinked. "Huh? How'd you know?" she asked and tilted her head. She brought her cup to her lips and blew on it again before taking a sip. Halfway through swallowing, she froze. "I mean! No! Wrong person."

Algar pointed behind us. I turned my head. There was a piece of paper on the wall of a nearby building, and I squinted at it. ...It was a full-body portrait of Lucia with large text beneath it. I read it out loud, since I knew Lucia couldn't read, "Lucia Fluffytail. Owner of Durandal. Slayer of princes. Betrayer of the fae. During an expedition with Prince Bryant, she obtained Durandal and slew everyone who accompanied her before crossing the border and entering the Tristam Empire. She now works under Duke Pentorn as a representative to attend the Godking's Brawl. This informational flyer has been brought to you by the Flopsy Gang. This mark, as many magicians will know, is a brand of truth, guaranteeing nothing on this document has been falsified." Next to the text, there was an array that I recognized as a truth brand that pulsated with mana.

"Gah!" Lucia shouted and ran up to the poster. She tore it down, ripped it to shreds, and stuffed the remains into her mouth before swallowing. She coughed a few times before drinking her hot chocolate in one gulp, clearing her inner passageways. "Fucking Snow!"

Algar stared at Lucia as if she were a strange creature with thirty legs and twenty eyes. "There's, uh, thousands of those flyers everywhere, including the capital and some port towns.... You, you're not going to eat them all, are you?"

Lucia sighed and hung her head. She raised it and placed her hands on her hips. "Alright then," she said. "What do you want from me?"

"I'm willing to buy Durandal from you," Algar said. "Gold, property—"

"Impossible!" Lucia said, shaking her head. "Demand something else."

Algar furrowed his brow. While he was hesitating, one of the girls behind him asked, "Excuse me, Miss Fluffytail, do you know anything about my brother Lan? The last time I saw him, he was chasing after Durandal."

"Ah! You're Evelyn the Witch!" Lucia said, pointing at the girl who just spoke. "Are the rumors true? Did you really poison your husband on your wedding night?"

Evelyn's eye twitched. "I did no such thing. Please don't slander me." She bit her lower lip. "About the prince…"

"Nope," Lucia said. "No idea what happened to him. I heard from some mercenaries that he was killed by Snow Flopsy though. But you know what they say about mercenaries and rumors."

"I do," Evelyn said and nodded. "So there's a chance Lan's still alive."

"He's dead, Evelyn." Puppers appeared next to Lucia. "She killed him."

"Puppers!" Lucia shouted. "What are you doing!? I was just beginning to like you!"

Puppers stayed silent as Evelyn stared at him, shock painted on her face. Ah, so Gae Bulg was passed down to a prince … who Lucia killed. Great.

"I've thought of something," Algar said, breaking the silence. "But it's a bit of a sensitive topic." He approached Lucia and whispered into her ear. What was he saying for Lucia to not instantly reject? Maybe it wasn't about Durandal? The prince took a step back and smiled. "So, do you accept?"

"Really?" Lucia asked, her eyes wide. "If you don't keep your end of the bargain, I'll beat you up. I can definitely do that, you know?"

"I swear on my title as crown prince," Algar said with a nod.

"I'll do it!" Lucia said and beamed.

Stop keeping me out of the loop! I want to know! Lucia better not have been tricked by the promises of hot chocolate or sweet foods again. It's upsetting that's something I even have to consider.

***

"Hey, Lucia," Durandal said after Algar left. "What did he want from you and why did you agree?"

"It's a secret!" This is between me and the crown prince. It's highly illegal, which is why I have no intentions of sharing it with Durandal or Ilya! And I won't even say it in my thoughts because Ilya and Durandal are mind readers. Think happy thoughts like steaming hot chocolate! The payoff for the request is going to be great; I can't wait; though, it might take a while.

"Oh my lord," Ilya said and bit her lower lip. What was her problem? "I really feel like she's been bribed with sweets." Hey, I'm not that easily fooled. I'm not a child. Besides, even if I was tempted by sweets, how would that be any of her concern? Jeez. I'm an adult, and I'm completely responsible.

Ah! That reminds me. "Puppers! How could you blatantly lie to Evelyn like that? I didn't kill Lan! I don't even know who Lan is." I killed a rare spirit monkey to obtain Puppers, remember? It was a bit persistent and knew how to use a spear, but it definitely wasn't a person. Puppers should be thanking me for freeing him from that monkey's clutches. How can I punish him for slandering me like that? I could poison him and feed him to a divine beast! …Well, I do that regardless—I need something better. I could force him to spar with me and beat him to death! …I just realized I never treated Puppers that nicely.

Puppers looked at me, shook his head, and disappeared into my socks. Looks like he's going to give me the silent treatment again. Right, I'll punish him by not speaking to him. Think of how devastated he'll be when my lovely voice is always present around him, but never directly addressing him. It'll be torture. Gah! "Don't flick me!"

"You were thinking something weird," Durandal said. "It's fine if you want to keep secrets, I won't keep asking."

"Is it? Is it really?" Ilya asked.

"Mm, probably," Durandal said and shrugged.

Why does it sound like the two of them don't trust me? It's not like the world's going to end just because I made a deal with the crown prince to—ah, I almost spoiled it. Positive thoughts! "So where do we go now?" I want to go shopping! I saw so many neat things outside on that road, but I didn't say anything because Ilya's dad looked like he wanted to keep up his fierce expression. It wouldn't have been nice of me to ruin it by telling him to wait so I could look at the displays. He's a bit like Durandal in that aspect. Why are men so prideful?

"I was going to reserve some lodgings for us," Ilya's dad said. "Why? Is there something you wanted to do? The request the crown prince gave you, perhaps?"

"No, that's not going to happen for a while." It isn't! Really. I promise. They'll probably forget about it by the time I fulfill the deal, or if their memory's anything like mine, they'll forget about it as soon as I'm out of sight. "I want to go shopping. Maybe there'll be spirit seeds that I can plant in my underwear."

"In your underwear...?" Ilya's dad asked. Was that concern on his face? Don't worry, I'll make sure they're female spirits! "Why..., no, never mind. Then I'll be waiting at the Demon's Peak Inn. I trust you'll be able to find your way there after you're done?"

"Nope! Let me take Ilya, and then it'll be fine."

"What? You're a wanted person right now! I don't want to get involved," Ilya said and pursed her lips. "Besides, you have Durandal. He's so ... confident. His sense of direction should be good, right?"

Durandal looked away.

"Nuh-uh. He's even worse than me when it comes to navigation."

Ilya's face fell. "What about Puppers?"

I'm not sure…. The only thing I know about Puppers is his ability to soften my socks and poison the enemy. Is he good at directions? Can he cook?

"I'm an ex-spear spirit, not a map spirit," Puppers said from my socks. "The only navigation I have to do is finding my way to my opponent's vitals."

Easy there, Puppers. You're a sock spirit now, remember? Just do your job and make my socks nice and fluffy. "And there we have it. You've officially volunteered to lead us to the inn after we're done shopping."

"What volunteering? I've been conscripted," Ilya said and glanced at her dad. He smiled at her and nodded. As usual, he's on my side when it comes to bullying Ilya. I'm not quite sure why that is, but I won't question it. Ah, did I say bullying? I meant guiding. Mhm. "This is ridiculous. How come a divine warrior doesn't know how to differentiate north from south? You just look at the sun and know."

"Not everyone can be as smart as a mage, Ilya. It's called tradeoffs. I get super strength, you get super brains."

"There are some smart warriors out there," Ilya said and sighed but led the way despite her complaints.

"Well, those aren't real warriors."

"Technically, they aren't," Ilya said and shrugged. "They're called battlemages, people who've crossed the first wall in martial arts and magic. None of them have been able to cross the second wall though. Their combat prowess is amazing, but their potential caps early on. The path of the magician is the only way to the top…. Unless we're talking about someone like you."

"Why can't they pass the second wall?" That's the one from spirit warrior to divine warrior, right? Just shove some cores down their throats and bam! Evolution.

"Magicians can't do what you did. Cores are painful for us to absorb, remember?" Ilya sighed before waving a badge at the guards. What was that? Her family emblem? How come I don't get one? The gate opened, and the sound of the rabble outside filled the air for a second before it fell silent. Everyone had turned to stare at us again. I should buy a cloak; I'm tired of being stared at. It's squirrel nature! The only things that stare at squirrels are those that want to eat squirrels. Hmm. Would I taste good?

Eh, I probably would considering divine beasts are always trying to eat me instead of chase me out of their territory. But that doesn't mean I plan on tasting myself! ...Puppers did say I'd regrow limbs if I lost them, right? Lucia! Stop thinking strange things. Shopping, remember? It's great that all the stalls form two neat lines all the way along the road. Even without Ilya, there's zero chance of me getting lost this way.

"What did you see that you wanted to buy?" Ilya asked, grabbing my hand. Was she nervous? Probably not, knowing her, she was making sure I didn't run off without her. Which I totally wouldn't have done. Like I've said hundreds of times before, I'm a responsible—ooh, acorn stew! "Don't move so fast!"

Ah, oops, almost ripped Ilya's arm off. Oh wells. "Give me a bowl, mister." The person manning the stall was an old man. Above his head, there were two triangular ears. He had a big bushy tail that hung to the ground. It was gray with black stripes, or was it black with gray stripes? How can you tell? The old man smiled at me; some of his teeth were missing. Compared to all the other stalls, his was a bit rundown with shoddy craftsmanship, but it was the only one selling acorn stew! He pulled a wooden bowl out from under his counter and ladled a generous helping of stew into it from the pot in front of him.

"An extra portion of meat for the beautiful young lady," he said, taking another scoop from the pot.

"Thanks!" I knew I was beautiful! I took a sip and looked at Ilya. "Do you want a bowl?"

"I thought you had to eat like a tiger to become a tiger," Ilya said and rolled her eyes.

"Even tigers drink acorn stew!" Huh? The old man and I looked at each other. We both had said the same thing at the same time. This is fate! I grabbed the old man's hand with my free hand, retrieved five gold coins from my interspacial ring, placed them into his palm without letting anyone else see, and curled his fingers around them.

"Live a good life, mister. You deserve it." No wonder why people of the same race stick together. They think alike! Humans are so emotional and greedy. Demons are so cold and logical. But beastkin, beastkin are generous and kind! Only another beastkin could understand me. ...Disregard the fact my family tried to drown me before selling me to slave traders, and the fact that Durandal and Ilya can read me like an open book. Well, maybe with the gold I gave this man, he won't have to drown a future grandchild.

The old man cautiously lifted one finger before closing his hand even tighter than before. "Thank you, beautiful miss," he said and pocketed the coins in a flash. "Your kindness, I'll remember it forever."

Mm, this stew's delicious. I haven't had it in so long. While training, who has time to pick up enough acorns to make a stew? And no one sold acorns either because humans and demons can't appreciate fine dining! Well, demons had hot chocolate which comes from miniature black acorns that grow on trees, so I guess they're alright.

"What's that?" a voice asked from behind me.

"Acorn stew, a meal fit for pigs and cows," an older voice said. Mm, happy thoughts, Lucia. It's been so long since you had good-tasting stew. Don't let some ignorant men ruin it for you. One sip at a time. Savor the taste. Swirl it a bit with your spoon.

"Then why's the expression she's making saying it's the greatest thing in the world?" the voice asked. Okay, what does this person look like to have the qualifications to sound so arrogant? Oh, he's a lionkin. Beside him, there was a grouchy fellow with black feathers, a beak, and a pair of wings for arms. Behind him, there was a neat formation of guards. The lionkin tilted his head and stared at me before sniffing the air. He slapped the crowkin's shoulder. "Fetch me some."

The grouchy crowkin's—or was he a black birdkin?—face cramped. "Your Highness, this meal isn't suitable for you. If your father finds out—"

"Are you going to tell him?" the lionkin asked, glaring at his companion.

The crowkin flinched. "N-no," he said. "I just—"

"Then do as I say," the lionkin said with a growl.

"Right away, Your Highness," the crowkin said and glared at me before approaching the stall. What was his problem? And why am I meeting so many princes in a single day?

"You," the lionkin said, turning his gaze onto me. "You look familiar. Where have I seen you before?"

Probably on a poster put up by Snow. But I'm not going to tell him that! "Maybe you've fallen in love with me at first sight?" I am a beautiful young lady after all.

The crowkin coughed and nearly dropped the bowl of stew that he had just received. The lionkin furrowed his brow and looked me up and down. Don't tell me he was seriously considering it. "No. That's impossible."

You don't have to be so blunt either!

"Your stew, Your Highness," the crowkin said and handed the lionkin the bowl. Then he turned around and glared at me, drawing a line in front of his neck with his wing.

I ignored him and stared at the lionkin instead. He brought the bowl up to his face and sniffed it. I could sense Ilya and the old stall owner behind me tensing. Wait, why was Ilya tensing? The lionkin frowned before bringing the bowl to his lips. Ilya and the old man sucked in their breaths. The prince took a sip. His brow furrowed as he spat into his bowl. He tossed the bowl onto the ground. "This tastes like shit. Break the stall down and bring me the owner's head."

Wow! What the fuck? Killing someone for such a nonsensical reason!? If I killed people based on the quality of food they made, Ilya, Durandal, and Puppers wouldn't be alive right now. I placed my bowl of stew down and drew my sword, but the old man grabbed my arm. "You, you don't have to be involved in this," he said. "This old man doesn't have many years of life left. There's no reason for you to die with me. No beastkin can disobey the tyrant."

The lionkin's formation of guards stomped towards us. The surroundings fell silent as everyone turned their eyes towards the show, none of them intent on stepping in.

"Is this how beastkin nobility treat their people?" Ilya asked, stepping in front of me. She's so brave! "No wonder why you animals are the weakest amongst the fae." Hey. Rude. No need to make things personal. "Ice, I know I don't use you often, but listen up! Let those who oppose me learn the meaning of cold. Frost Nova!"

A bright white light engulfed the soldiers in the formation. When the light disappeared, they were frozen solid. Or at least their armor was. Chilled breaths and banging sounds came from inside as the soldiers struggled to break free.

The lionkin's eyes narrowed. "A fifth-circle spell cast within a few seconds? You're a sixth-circle magician. Who are you?"

"Ilya Pentorn, daughter of the Duke of Tristam." Ilya snorted and tilted her head up. Compared to her dad's domineering pose, Ilya's looked cute, but at least she was trying.

The lionkin's face fell. He walked up to the armor sets and knocked on them with his hands, breaking the ice. "How long are you buffoons going to keep embarrassing yourselves? Let's go."

Whoa, Ilya scared them away and I didn't even have to lift a finger. ...That probably was her plan, wasn't it? I vaguely recall something Ilya said about not fighting random people at the Godking's Brawl..., but that was such a long time ago—at least a couple of days. It wouldn't be my fault if I forgot.

"Thank you, Your Grace," the old stall owner said and fell to his knees while lowering his head.

"Don't thank me," Ilya said and gestured towards me. "You should thank her. I only did that because there would've been a huge mess if she killed a prince over a bowl of stew."

"A bowl of acorn stew! Acorn! If you say I killed someone over stew, people would think I'm crazy. That's why you have to specify acorn stew, so people know I'm perfectly sane."

Ilya rolled her eyes and ignored me. Wow. "Though I don't think the prince would care too much about you, you should probably pack your stall and lay low. If you need a new place of employment, you can come work for the Pentorn family."

The old man nodded before rotating on his knees towards me. "Thank you," he said and lowered his head.

"No problem!" It's not like I had to do anything. And the conflict was resolved peacefully. There's no way a war would start between the demons and the fae because of some incident over acorn stew, right?

***

"So what happened?" my father asked as I entered the Demon's Peak Inn. Behind me, Lucia was humming to herself while holding a massive barrel filled with acorn stew. She insisted on leaving it out of her interspacial ring because, in her words, acorn stew only gets better with age. It's not going to turn into alcohol, is it? I hope not. A sober Lucia is already a bit too much on my blood pressure. "You look kind of glum."

"I might have offended one of the beastkin's princes." It wasn't my fault! If Lucia hadn't bought that stupid stew, none of it would've happened. I had to interfere when I did to prevent things from really becoming bad. If Lucia killed the prince, the beastkin would take an aggressive stance towards my father once they found out she associated with our family. Then the humans would have a headache since the Godking's Brawl is being held in their territory. There's so many balances of power that have to be maintained, but this ignorant squirrelkin walks all over them like they're the branches of a tree. She's going to cause a war one day. I can feel it.

"Might have?" My father raised an eyebrow. He patted the open seat next to him and waved at the person waiting by the counter. Other than the receptionist, we were the only ones inside the inn. I took a seat next to my father while Lucia sat across from us, placing the barrel beside her. She took a bowl out of her ring and ladled herself a generous helping before passing it to me.

"Heat, please."

I couldn't help but sigh. I touched upon the sixth circle of magic at the age of fourteen. Yet Lucia only sees me as a convenient food warmer. I heated the soup before passing it back to her. "The prince was going to clash with Lucia over a bowl of acorn stew. I didn't want her to cause any major incidences, so I stopped his guards and declared my name."

"Mm, you did well," my father said. Wait, what? He was actually taking my side? Maybe having a bloodthirsty Lucia chase after us while we were riding the carriage made him realize how insane she actually is. Father, you've realized my plight! "It'd be great if you continued following her to prevent incidences like these." ...I should've known. "Other than that barrel of stew..., what did she buy?"

Lucia ignored us while eating with her eyes closed. I thought it only happened in stories, but pink hearts were floating around her and her mouth had turned into a squiggly line with the end of a spoon sticking out of it. Some days, I think it would be nice to experience life as Lucia: something as simple as acorn stew or hot chocolate can make her so happy. But then I remember I don't want to be crazy.

"She bought a ton of spirit seeds. I tried telling her it was a bad idea to have so many spirits around her, but she didn't listen to me."

"It's just some qi, right?" Lucia asked after swallowing. "Puppers and Durandal are barely noticeable. What's two or three or sixty more? Besides, they're not going to be used for combat."

"Servants, then?" my father asked. Some people had weapon spirits just to carry things around for them. Those who can't afford interspacial rings usually load up a spirit with bags and use them as a pack mule. Of course, some people don't want to spend their qi on that and recruit slaves instead. Lucia probably had to carry the human army's supplies since she was a beastkin, huh? Anyways, using weapon spirits for combat has become long outdated since the rise of magicians. Sure, there are some spirits who can cast magic, but they're highly inefficient with mana. At most, they can be bodyguards, but weapon spirits are limited by their owners' qi. How come there aren't any magic spirits that consume mana instead of qi?

"Nope!" Lucia said. "Comfy underwear! Ever since Puppers became my sock spirit, my feet have been in heaven. All my clothes shall feel that way!" Her eyes gleamed as she took a bag out of her ring and placed it on the table. It made clinking noises and a few marbles rolled out. "Show me the best seeds, Ilya."

"Why would I know?" I really don't. I'm not interested in spirit seeds at all. Without any qi to manipulate a spirit, what's the point?

"Because you know everything?" Lucia asked and tilted her head to the side. "I don't mentally call you my encyclopedia for nothing."

"Please don't refer to a sixth-circle magician that way...." I don't know if I should be happy for being mistaken as smart or if I should be ashamed for being looked down on that much by Lucia. My abilities are more than just expositing information about the world like some crappy literary device! Didn't she see how I disabled those guards earlier? I'm not inferior; I'm just younger than her by nearly a decade. You know what? I'm going to compete in the Godking's Brawl as well. Maybe I don't have the guaranteed spot, but I can still compete against all the commoners and work my way up! I'll just have to surrender if I encounter Lucia though.

"Mm, no can do," Lucia said and shook her head. "Even if you become a seventh-circle magician, I'll continue to treat you this way. Only when you're older than me will I acknowledge you as an equal! Just wait a few years, and you'll be older than me in no time."

...Sometimes, I can't tell if Lucia is actually really smart or not. She says the dumbest things, but I don't know if it's on purpose or not. I'll never be older than her! Alright, Ilya, new goal. Forget becoming strong enough to hold the position of duchess. Become strong enough to teach Lucia a lesson! ...Though, it might be easier becoming an empress if she continues improving at her current rate. By the time I pass the wall to the seventh circle, will Lucia be at the peak of divine warriors?

Mm, well, all I have to do is do well in the upcoming competition. Cain is searching for talent to nurture; though, I don't know why, he's willing to invest in the talented. If I show my worth as a fourteen-year-old sixth-circle magician, my path to the tenth circle should be a smooth one if he helps me. My father might've asked Lucia to represent him, but that doesn't mean he wants me to sit on the sidelines and be a cheerleader. I think. Does he? Well, even if he does, I'm almost an adult. I can make decisions for myself! Second place, here I come! …Realistically, I should aim for the top ten. Yeah. Tenth place, here I come!

19

Wow, time sure does fly when your own weapon spirits are trying to stab you repeatedly with spears while you're drinking acorn stew. It's already the day of the competition. You can stop trying to stab me now.

"Your Armor of Slaughter has greatly improved," Durandal said and sighed as he stowed his spear. I think he's been feeling frustrated ever since he lost the ability to abuse me. It's not my fault he's a sadist! "But how do you know where I'm going to stab when you're not even looking at me?"

"Oh, that just happens automatically." The best part about the Armor of Slaughter is its autonomous function. I just have to circulate my qi like I'm using the Path of Slaughter, and the armor will detect incoming attacks and reinforce my body appropriately. It's a complete cheat! I love it. The downside is it takes a lot of qi to maintain. But that's okay because I have these improved bones of strength carved out of divine qi! …I'm not addicted, I swear. I can stop whenever I want. My willpower's increased a lot ever since Durandal returned to my life. I'm fine. Really.

The door to my room swung open. "Are you ready, Lucia?" Ilya asked. She was wearing a set of blue robes. They looked normal, but I could see thousands of strands of mana crawling inside of it. Ilya blinked and lowered her head while lifting her arms a bit. "Like my robe? My father helped me enchant it. Anyways, we should hurry."

"What's the rush? I thought we got to skip the boring stuff since I already have a spot." The preliminary rounds for all the people who weren't nominated were supposed to happen first. There were thousands of people outside, but the people who hosted the competition guaranteed it wouldn't take more than a few hours to sort through all those people. How were they going to do that? A giant free-for-all?

"I'm competing," Ilya said and placed her hands on her hips. "And I'm not going to be disqualified for being late. So hurry up and finish your acorn stew."

Ilya's going to compete? But she's so … tiny. I mean young, that's the word, right? "Will you be okay?" I finished up the rest of my stew while Ilya nodded.

"I'll be fine," Ilya said. "Do you know how hard it is for normal people to cross the first wall before the age of thirty? Out of all the competitors, you and Daniel are probably the only ones who've crossed the second." Who's Daniel again? "Daniel's the crown prince." Nice one, mind reader Ilya.

"Didn't I trounce Daniel at the banquet with Rogath's spells?" I did, didn't I? "I'll just do that again. Doesn't that mean I'll get first place?"

"You probably will get first," Ilya said with a nod. "But there won't be enough mana in the vicinity for you to use your magic tool. And you can't underestimate people, got it? The Godking stood at the top of the world despite never crossing the second wall by reaching the peak of spirit warrior and sixth-circle magician. I've asked around, and Algar's supposedly managed to do the same." Algar? "Algar's the human crown prince. The one you made a deal with, remember?" Okay, stop with the mind reading.

"Mm, whatever." I'm a divine warrior! I'm stronger than the Godking! What do I have to fear in this world? This competition's going to be a complete walk in the park.

"You're not listening to me," Ilya said and shook her head. She walked out the room and I followed her. We headed to the giant coliseum in the center of the city that we weren't allowed to approach before. On the way there, I saw the marquis that Snow was supposed to be representing, but that bastard was nowhere to be seen. I tried looking for him this past week, but I got tired of beating people up who were looking for Durandal. Ilya had to beg me to stay inside the inn before I started another world war.

"This crowd's pretty big...." It was huge. The streets were completely filled. Could the coliseum even fit that many people? It was a two-story building at most, and it wasn't that large.

"The coliseum was personally built by Cain," Ilya said. "The space inside is larger than the space on the outside like an interspacial ring."

Oh, so it was like one of those pocket dimensions Durandal was stored in. I hope it doesn't bring back bad memories for him. Well, it's not like he can see anything since he's currently inside mini-DalDal. ...He can't see anything, right? It wouldn't make sense if he could. Everyone knows the saying swords and fists have no eyes. That's definitely the context the saying was created for.

The coliseum was like a whole new world once we stepped inside. Literally. The skies were no longer cloudy, and the sun shone directly overhead even though it was only morning. There were no walls, and the floor was made of green grass and dirt. It was nothing like a coliseum. "Um, Lucia," Ilya said with a furrowed brow. "Didn't you hear what I said?"

"The space inside is larger than the space outside, right?" What about it?

"No, the part I said after that," Ilya said and bit her lower lip.

"Nope, wasn't listening."

Ilya sighed and hung her head. "I said you were supposed to enter the other doorway to go to the spectator area where my father was waiting. Why'd you enter the competition grounds with me?"

"Oh. Well, that's fine, isn't it? Anyone can compete, right?" This'll be a good warmup! Who wants to fight me? I'll take on anyone! Hear me roar!

Ilya sighed again. "I know what you're thinking, but the preliminary isn't about fighting. It's about talent and ability." She shook her head. "Well, you have both of those, so you should be fine."

***

If Lucia wasn't going to take our guaranteed spot, then it should've been given to me instead…. Why did she enter the competition grounds as well? Everyone already knows what she looks like due to the posters plastered all over the city, so all their eyes are going to be on her. It's a good thing we're in a massive crowd; it should be a little difficult to pick her out at least. Right?

Dozens of lights flashed as circles appeared on the ground. Was this part of the competition? From above, a giant screen displayed tons of spectators, all of them looking down on us. A few of them stood up and leapt towards us. Were they trying to enter the competition grounds? As their bodies hit the screen, the circles on the ground erupted with pillars of light. When the light dispersed, the people who had jumped were in front of us. What the heck!? Why did so many people with guaranteed spots decide to join the preliminary?

"Lucia Fluffytail!" a voice rang out as a beastkin with green scales growing on his arms and face pointed towards us with a spear in hand. "For the grievances against my blood brother, you must be punished."

Wasn't this snakelike person the crown prince of the beastkin kingdom? Don't tell me his brother was the lionkin that Lucia nearly killed over stew. And how are lions and snakes even related at all? Unless, of course, their father was a promiscuous fellow with multiple wives. Ugh, that just leaves a massive headache for all the descendants fighting over the throne later.

"Lucia Fluffytail? That's her?" a few voices murmured. The people stepped away, and the crowd parted as the nobles with guaranteed spots approached us. There were at least four dozen of them. How come they all forsook their spots? What if they failed the preliminary round and disappointed the nobles they were representing?

A few more whispers of Durandal, betrayer, and acorn stew drinker rang through the air. Before the nobles could reach us, a voice boomed throughout the competition grounds. "Silence. Everyone has gathered." Floating above us, a demon with long red hair that flowed down to his lower back crossed his arms over his chest. He looked at us and furrowed his brow. "The fifty of you wish to compete in the preliminary as well? If you fail here, you won't be able to partake in the brawl even with your seeded spot."

Everyone looked up at the demon without saying a word. Sweat dripped to the ground, and a few people had even fallen to their knees. Lucia was frowning at the demon, her tail twitching rapidly. I whispered to her, "Is your tail stiff?"

"A little," Lucia whispered back. "I didn't think it'd ever stiffen again after reaching the divine realm. Mm, it's a good thing Durandal didn't let me slack off."

"Very well then," the demon above said. "Some of you may know me; my name is Cain Thunderfire, the host of this year's Godking's Brawl." Ten circles appeared around his body, each of them golden in color. Hints of lightning and fire flickered around them, crackling like thunder. "There are some simple rules: no killing, stop when I say stop, and no magic tools allowed. Any questions?"

Lucia's hand shot up into the air. "Question!" she shouted. Cain's gaze landed on her. "What if there's this really, really slimy bastard that I want to kill in this competition? Can I kill him anyway even if it breaks the rules?"

"You'll be disqualified and judged by your respective empire's laws," Cain said.

Lucia frowned and furrowed her brow. "Oh! What if he's just too weak and dies in one hit?" she asked, her tail perking up. "I'm super strong; and I'm not good at controlling my strength. Accidents happen all the time, right?"

Cain frowned. A few other people chimed in before he could say anything. Daniel's voice was the clearest. "I agree with Lucia. Accidents happen all the time. How do we show off our abilities if we have to tread on eggshells? If I cast any seventh-circle spell right now, hundreds of these people would die. Am I supposed to limit myself? I'm willing to bet some people here can't even survive a fourth-circle spell. What if I underestimate the opponent and limit myself too much, causing a loss?"

"You're Daniel, the crown prince?" Cain asked. "What you say makes sense, but the competition is structured in such a way that killing another person will be very hard to do. You'll see when it starts. I decided to modify it a bit compared to the previous decades'."

"I understand," Daniel said and nodded.

Lucia tilted her head. "So can I accidently murder him or not?" she asked and scratched her nose.

Cain sighed. "A judgment will happen if it comes to pass," he said. "If you really must kill someone, make it look like an accident as much as you can."

"Nice," Lucia said and gave me a thumbs up. …Wasn't her motto, 'I'm not a murderer'?

"And without further delay, let the competition begin," Cain said and waved his arm. A glass ball fell towards the crowd and landed in a beastkin's hands. "The first test is simple—a measure of talent. Squeeze the glass and insert your mana or qi or both. If the orb lights up, you pass. If it doesn't, you fail."

I wonder how it works. Does it measure the amount of mana or qi you can produce and match it with your age? How would it even tell your age in the first place? Well, everyone has to pass the same test; it should be fair. One orb seems kind of slow though.... Oh, and there's another. An orb fell towards my head, and I caught it before it hit me. Squeeze and insert mana. The orb lit up, and a second later, my surroundings distorted. I was no longer in the meadows but a gray flatland with nothing to be seen as far as the eye could see. A few others were with me—this was probably the next stage for those who passed?

***

Ah! Ilya vanished! Did the orb teleport her somewhere? It stopped glowing and fell to the floor after she disappeared. Hmm, I really don't like teleportation magic after being tricked by that stupid acorn in the forest. But I have to do this to pass the preliminary and find a chance to kill, err, accidently murder Snow. Let's see, what did the man in the sky say I had to do? Squeeze and...

Ping!

"Uh, Mr. Announcer! Host! Mr. Firethunder!"

"You again?" the man in the sky asked. Hey, if you didn't want me asking questions, you shouldn't have asked if anyone had any questions. Jeez. What do you mean, me again?

"The orb broke." I pointed at the shattered fragments on the ground. I didn't even insert my qi!

"It broke?" the man in the sky asked. The other nearby contestants turned their heads and stared at me. It's not my fault! I just followed the instructions! "Let me see." Another orb dropped from the sky and landed in my hands.

"See, squeeze..."—*ping!*—"and it broke again." It's a good thing my hands are so calloused from swinging mini-

DalDal all the time or I might've been injured by all these fragments.

"Interesting," the man in the sky said and rubbed his chin. What are you doing trying to look so profound for? You don't even have a beard! "Let's just say you pass for now."

Ah? But it didn't light up. The man in the sky waved his hand, and my vision spun around like Rogath casted Topsy-Turvy on me. A few seconds later, the world cleared up and I was standing in a land of gray. Just gray. Even the sky was a slightly lighter shade of gray than the ground. Oh, it's Ilya. "This is the next testing ground?"

"Apparently," Ilya said with a nod. She looked around and scratched her head. So far, there were only a few hundred people in the area with us. It was a lot less sweaty and gross compared to the previous place. I swear, some of those catlike beastkin had no idea how to bathe themselves, thinking licking their skin would keep them clean instead. "Cain's really rushing this competition compared to the previous ones. Is he in a hurry?"

"Maybe he has a date." That's possible, right? He's supposed to be the strongest person in the world. If he were single, that would be a little disappointing, no? At the very least, he should have a harem of five people after struggling to reach the top. No doubt, he should've swayed one ice-cold maiden's heart with a lively barbeque, or he saved a fiery beauty in the nick of time when she was being hunted, or perhaps he even took care of someone stronger than him while they were injured. Who knows? As the strongest person in the world, there's no way he lived an uneventful life. …Now that I think about it, my rise to divine warrior was pretty uneventful. If anything, I only met two people: Ilya and Snow. And they're both women! Well, Snow's not, but he looks like one.

"You think of the strangest answers to everything, Lucia," Ilya said and shook her head. Hey, I think they're very reasonable answers; otherwise, I wouldn't say them. "Is Snow here?"

"Nope, I don't see him. I don't think he's the type of person to do preliminaries when he can join the finals directly." He's like a rat, very opportunistic. I checked the other competitors just in case he was in disguise, but I really didn't see him. Everyone else was clumped up, forming cliques of demons, humans, and beastkin. There were also some really short people and some really pale-looking fellows with pointy ears. Were they part vampire bat?

"Those are elves," Ilya said. "And those are dwarves. They're part of the fae. Like you. Shouldn't you know this at least?"

"Nope, never learned it." All I was taught was how to be a slave and how to use a mace.

"It's been a while since I've seen an elf," Durandal's voice said from mini-DalDal. Hey! Maybe fists and blades do have eyes? "The last one was..., right, the elf child that Roland kidnapped. I can't remember her name. Marilyn?"

She should be ancient then, right? There's no way she'd be participating in the brawl for people younger than thirty.

Ilya tugged on my sleeve. "Is that elf approaching us?"

Don't tell me that's Marilyn's descendant seeking revenge! There's no other reason for an elf to approach me. Unless she has business with Ilya?

"Lucia Fluffytail!" the elf girl shouted and drew a massive greatsword out of nowhere. It was at least twice her height and width. Then again, she did look around six years old or so. "In the name of justice, surrender Durandal!"

"...This girl, do elves have problems with their heads?" I looked at Ilya, but she looked just as stunned as me.

"No...," Ilya said and scratched her head. "Elves are generally smart, level-headed people."

"Nearly a century ago, the Godking kidnapped my grandmother and subjected her to unspeakable deeds!" the elf said, pointing the sword at me. It wobbled a bit like she couldn't hold it steadily. "I've come seeking justice, and I'll only be satisfied when one of the culprits, Durandal, is in my hands."

Ah! I was really right! That usually never happens!

"I guess she's just going to be unsatisfied for the rest of her life, huh?" Ilya asked me.

"Yup." Well, even if she is here for revenge, that doesn't change a single thing. I'm never giving up Durandal. Without him, I'm a literal sobbing wreck, and I never want to feel that way again. "I'm not handing over Durandal, so shoo. Go away. I bet no one likes you."

The elf's face turned red as she gritted her teeth. "Evildoers must be punished," she said and raised her greatsword into the air. She nearly toppled backwards due to the weight, so I decided to help her by poking her on the forehead. She yelped as she fell over. Tears sprang to her eyes as she pouted.

"You made a little girl cry, Lucia," Ilya said. "Is this a hobby of yours?"

Have I ever made Ilya cry? Why does she sound so bitter? Oh, right. She did cry after helping me sell those penises. Hmm. Oh, wells. "Shouldn't there be a lower bound for ages like how the upper bound is thirty?"

Ilya shrugged. "Talent is talent. She's passed the first test at least. Maybe she's older than she looks? Elves do age slowly."

"Don't speak as if I'm not here!" the elf girl said as she struggled to lift her sword. I poked it with my finger, and she fell over again. Hey, this is pretty fun. "I curse you, Lucia Fluffytail! In this lifetime, we'll forever be at each other's throats! Neither of us can live while the other's alive!"

Wow, that's some heavy stuff right there. Are all elves like this? I don't think I ever promised anything that drastic when I was still just a child. I know! I'll sacrifice some of my hot chocolate and make friends with her. I bet she's just grouchy because she's hungry. I pulled a cup out of my ring and held it in front of her face.

"What's this?" the elf girl asked. "The ground up and heated remains of a treeman's unborn child!?"

"No, it's hot chocolate. Try some."

"Oh." The girl brought the cup to her lips. "It's good. I can have this?"

"Mhm."

The elf girl bit her lower lip. She glanced at the surface of the chocolate, then looked at me. I smiled at her. She brought the cup to her chest. "Maybe you're not a bad person.... I renounce my curse! For now, we're acquaintances. My name's Mirta."

"Nice to meet you, Ilya Number Two." I placed my hand on Ilya's head. "This is Ilya Number One. Children should get along with one another."

Ilya Number One and Two shouted at the same time, "I'm not a child!"

Mm. They're getting along so well already. Before I could say anything else, a massive crack appeared in the light-gray sky. The man in the sky from before stepped through, and the gaping portal closed behind him.

"Congratulations on passing the first part of the competition. The second portion will begin shortly."

***

Cain's words echoed through the area, causing all the competitors to straighten their backs and stick their chests out. Compared to just a few minutes ago, the number of people have been reduced by way more than half, leaving about three hundred to five hundred people. It's hard to get an accurate count. Mirta, the elf girl who was even smaller than me, bit her lower lip and stared up at Cain. Did she dislike him?

"While the first test was highly efficient, I have no doubt the spectators are cursing me for showing them such a boring round," Cain said with a chuckle. "This one will be more interesting to watch." As he spoke, his hands were moving in circular patterns, and the world was distorting. The ground shifted until everyone was standing in a neat straight line. A massive black pillar fell from the sky, slamming into the gray earth, but oddly enough, it didn't make a sound as it landed. "Behold, a pillar."

No one said a word as Cain hovered in the air. I hope he wasn't waiting for a response to that. A few seconds later, someone called out, "What about it?"

Cain smiled. "I'm glad you asked," he said. Oh lord, my image of Cain is changing by the second. I thought he was a valiant hero, but his need for attention is almost as bad as Lucia's. Are all strong people childish? No, I can't judge Cain by a singular display. I'll believe in my childhood hero. "The goal of this test is simple: to see how well your talent translates into actual ability. Attack the pillar. The further it goes, the higher your rank. Did I mention the ranking process begins now? Remember, only the top hundred people will get prizes."

"Then I'm starting first?" a voice asked from the front of the line. Lucia and I were somewhere near the back, but the man's words were still transmitted clearly. Without a sound, the ground shifted upwards and a staircase was created with every person on their own step, allowing those in the back to see over those ahead.

"Begin," Cain said. "One at a time."

The first man nodded and walked up to the pillar. He was a human without any distinguishing features. If my life were a story, I'd mistaken him for generic fodder character A. Generic fodder character A let out a shout and punched towards the pillar. His fist was set ablaze and increased in speed. A loud cracking noise echoed through the air ...

followed by an ear-piercing scream. Generic fodder character A fell to the ground, clutching his arm while letting out sobbing noises. The pillar hadn't moved.

A few people sucked in their breaths and stared at Cain. He shrugged. "I never said it would be easy. Next!"

A demon stepped down from her position and approached the pillar, eyeing it like a mercenary would eye a beast. She crouched next to the pillar and slammed her hands on the ground. The earth rippled like water, and dirt surged up like a wave. Smart. If you can't move the pillar, move the ground beneath it. It's a shame it didn't work; the pillar remained unmoved as the wave of earth passed around it like water would pass a rock in a river. The demon sighed as she stood up and shook her head.

"The pillar moved by a millimeter," Cain said from above. A scoreboard appeared in the air, two names appearing on its list. Besides the feminine name, there was a number one. Beside the generic sounding name, there was a zero. "Next!"

And thus, generic character after generic character attacked the pillar with all they had. After a hundred people had gone, the new high score was six millimeters, achieved by a person erupting a volcano underneath the pillar with a combination of third and fourth-circle spells. The next person had a familiar face. Wasn't that—"Ah!" Lucia said. "It's the acorn stew hater. Down with the heretic!"

Acorn stew's not a religion!

The lionkin turned his head and glared at us. So it seemed like everyone's voices were transmitted easily throughout this plane. Mirta gasped when she saw the fiery look in the lionkin's eyes. "My mother was right! Beastkin men will target me because I'm adorable and helpless looking!" She gulped and hid behind Lucia, her actions causing the lionkin's face to darken.

The lionkin shook his head and roared, a surge of qi billowing out of his body. Cain's eyes lit up as he rubbed his chin. "A peak spirit warrior. At such a young age too. It's a shame his presence makes little girls cry."

The lionkin, who was in the midst of walking towards the pillar, collapsed upon hearing Cain's words. He shook his fist at the sky. "It's not like that!" he shouted. "Your words hold a lot of weight; please, don't slander me like this!"

Cain shrugged. "Just attack the pillar. I'll still reward you if you end up in the top hundred."

The lionkin hung his head and trudged forwards, his earlier momentum gone. Poor fellow. First he encountered Lucia, then he … encountered Lucia again. Am I the actual poor fellow for sticking by Lucia's side? Another roar shook the plane as the lionkin charged towards the pillar, opening his arms like he was going to hug it. "Path of Desire: Lion's Charge!"

"See, even your path reveals your true colors," Cain said, raising an eyebrow. "But you moved the pillar 15 millimeters, not bad. You've more than doubled the previous high score."

The lionkin snorted as he stopped releasing his qi. He glared at Lucia before stepping off to the side where all the other contestants who had finished were waiting. A few of the lionkin's lackeys let out praise and fawned over him, but Mirta wrinkled her nose and said, "I can do better than 15 millimeters."

More generic cannon fodder went, none of them passing ten millimeters. The next person of note was Daniel. He interposed three seventh-circle spells and unleashed them at once, blasting the pillar back by three whole centimeters. His face fell upon seeing the result, and he muttered, "What is this thing made out of?"

"A legendary beast's bones," Cain said from above, crossing his arms over his chest. "You did well, doubling the previous pervert's record."

After another hour of waiting, it was finally Mirta's turn. Which meant my turn was next, then Lucia's. Mirta gulped and looked at Lucia before walking down the steps, approaching the black pillar. Currently, the top hundred was filled with scores of three and four, with a noticeable gap between the twentieth and twenty-first score which jumped from four and a half to six. "I can do this," Mirta said as her sword appeared in her hand. Due to its weight, she nearly fell off the step, but she managed to catch herself at the last second.

"Do your best, Ilya Number Two!" Lucia shouted. Stop calling her that! Does Lucia really see me the same way as she sees this girl? I'm not as clumsy or naïve as her! Lucia nudged my shoulder. "Hey, you should cheer for your little sister too."

"She's not my sister! Elves and demons aren't even vaguely related." And, honestly, I don't see Mirta doing well at all. Compared to all the other people who went before her, she's super tiny. She might be talented enough to step onto this stage, but there's no way a five or six-year-old child can translate that potential into actual results.

"For my grandmother!" Mirta shouted, her tiny high-pitched voice echoing through the area. She struggled to lift her greatsword into the air above her head and waddled to the pillar. A green light encompassed the blade, and dozens of golden lines burst to the surface of the sword like veins on an arm. The greatsword rumbled, emitting noises like a growling dragon as the faint image of a reptilian head appeared in the air.

"A dwarven-forged weapon of the highest class, enchanted with a divine inscription created by a high elf," Cain said, his eyes lighting up. "I didn't know Marilyn had broken through to the peak of the divine realm."

"Roar with all your might, Y'terasi," Mirta shouted and swung the greatsword down. The edge of her sword touched the pillar, and the world fell silent as the aura encompassing her blade disappeared. Everyone held their breaths, unmoving. ...But nothing happened.

"Was that it?" someone behind me asked. "That—"

An explosion went off, cutting off the rest of his words. Mirta flew backwards while the pillar remained in place, a violent vortex of wind expanding between the two. Faint sounds of a roaring dragon filled the whole plane as a transparent claw extended from the vortex and smacked the pillar, causing it to lurch forwards.

"Two centimeters," Cain said while waving his hand. A bubble of wind caught Mirta before she could crash into the ground. "It's a pity your strength isn't strong enough to bring out the full potential of your sword."

"That was amazing, Ilya Number Two!" Lucia shouted, pumping her fist into the air. "Introduce me to your grandmother later so she can enchant my stuff too!"

Wait. That wasn't supposed to happen. How could Mirta push the pillar back by two whole centimeters!? That's second place! "Mr. Thunderfire, aren't enchanted weapons cheating?" There was a rule about magic tools. Shouldn't this fall under that? There's no difference between the two!

"Do you think its cheating?" Cain asked, raising an eyebrow.

I could tell everyone behind me, except for Lucia, was nodding as well. "A magic tool allows a person to cast a spell that they might not normally be able to. An enchanted weapon allows someone to do the same. If a magic tool isn't allowed, why are enchanted weapons?"

Cain gestured towards Mirta. "If I gave you her weapon"—Mirta's eyes widened and she hugged her sword to her chest, or the hilt at least since it was too big—"would you be able to do the same?"

"Well, no. Enchantments have restrictions. If I were an elf, maybe."

"Then, if this sword were a magic tool, would you be able to do the same?" Cain asked, a faint smile on his lips.

I think I know what he was getting at. "In other words, since the weapon can only be used by Mirta, it's allowed?"

"Correct," Cain said. "And if you don't like that answer, then it's also because I said so."

Is that really how the strongest person in the world should behave? Because he said so? Power comes with responsibility! He's just like Lucia! Give me back my childhood hero. Lucia bumped me from behind. "It's your turn," she said, pointing at the pillar. Right. Focus. Even if Mirta gets special treatment, that doesn't change the fact I'm aiming for tenth place. How far do I have to hit the pillar? One centimeter, I hope I can do it. No! It's not I hope, it's I will! Wait, I should aim for one and a half centimeters since Lucia hasn't gone yet.... In the end, isn't it just doing my best? Distance shouldn't matter, just hit it as hard as I can.

But first, I should make sure of something. "Mr. Thunderfire, are consumable items allowed?"

"Are they magic tools?"

"No."

"Then they're not against the rules."

Great. "Hey, Lucia. Can I get a bone of focus and all the bones of strength you can spare?"

"I demand an equivalent exchange of hot chocolate later," Lucia said. A pile of bones that nearly towered over the pillar appeared in front of me. They exuded a dense qi that could almost be touched, and it felt like I was facing a divine beast. There were a few shouts, but I ignored them as I stowed the bones in my ring, consuming the focus one first.

Magic, though seemingly complex, is actually simple to use. Everyone's body has certain points that influence how mana transforms when it passes through: the heart creates a dense thick mana suitable for earthen spells. The head creates bright mana suitable for light spells. The bladder creates a, well, liquid-like mana perfect for water spells. By circulating mana through these points, spells are created. The number of times you can circulate your mana through a point in one spell depends on the number of circles you have. Five passes through the heart and four passes through the lungs create the fifth-circle spell Sandstorm.

It's possible to circulate your mana through all the manipulation points in your body, giving it every single attribute, but your mana will stretch thin by then. The first-circle spell that combines every point in someone's body is called Chaos Orb. The second-circle spell is Chaos Spike. Chaos Spear is the third. No one's been able to achieve more than three full circulations, or if they have, they didn't write down the results. People generally focus on one or two spell types because it's easier to circulate their mana to them more times. But if I have a near infinite supply of mana thanks to the bones of strength Lucia's provided, wouldn't I be able to circulate my mana through all the points in my body six times? Mana might be consumed at an exponential rate with every circulation, but it's feasible!

Today, I, Ilya Pentorn, will go down in history as the first person to cast a sixth-circle spell of the chaos attribute! ...Or I'll be the idiot that blew herself up after consuming a hundred divine bones of strength—a prime example of things not to do. I really, really hope it'll be the former. I mean, in theory it should work. ...Right?

***

What's Ilya doing? All she's been doing is standing in front of the pillar while consuming bone after bone. I hope she knows how many barrels of hot chocolate those are worth! Because I don't. But she won't scam me, right? "Go, Ilya Number One! You can do it."

Oh, she's doing the same thing as Daniel did. Her mana's hovering behind her like a completed spell. She's trying to stack them on top of each other, but why does she have to use so many bones? Speaking of bones…, didn't the man in the sky say the pillar was made of a legendary beast's bones? Could I … absorb it? Hm. Hmm. Hmmmmm. I'll try it when it's my turn!

Whoa, Ilya's completed another spell. My skin's actually feeling a little tingly from all the mana in the air. This feels a little like Daniel's attack, but how? Daniel was a seventh-circle magician who stacked three spells while Ilya's weaker and only stacked two. Even I can do some simple math and realize something's not right. Mm, well, at least there's this barrier that the man in the sky created to protect the onlookers. Oh, it's a third spell! She's still making more?

Four…, five…, six…, seven…, eight…, what comes after eight again? Oh, right. I only forgot for a brief moment! Nine…, ten…, ten and one…, ten and two…, ten and three…. Is it just me or does Ilya look like she's bloating a little around the waist? And her veins are bulging a lot; I'm pretty sure that's not normal. How many spells is she at now? I lost count.

Crack.

What was that? There's a scratch in the air…. The barrier? Before I could check, Ilya's voice boomed in my ears. "Before the earth, before the sky, before the world…, there existed chaos!"

Ah! Who turned off the sun!? And my Armor of Slaughter is automatically activating, which means I'm being attacked? So the barrier really broke. …Is Ilya going to be okay in there? I'm not sure how I'd survive without someone as convenient as Ilya hanging around. Who else would I get to explain random things for me?

"This feeling is familiar," Durandal muttered from mini-DalDal. "But I'm not sure why. Chaos magic? I'll remember it."

"What do you mean?" Hey, Durandal. You can't just say something cryptic and foreshadowing like that and then disappear without a sound. "Hey. Hey. Durandal. Hey. Are you ignoring me?" Ever since I became stronger than him, Durandal turned super boring. Durandal's just not Durandal if he can't express his sadistic side. Not that I want him to! I'm not a masochist, alright? Ah! That reminds me! I'm supposed to be giving him the cold shoulder for throwing me out of that carriage. Right, that's why we weren't talking to each other much. Mhm. Every relationship has their own problems.

The sun turned back on! Ilya looks completely fine! Everyone else is on the ground groaning and clutching themselves! Oh, that's not something I should be rejoicing over, huh? "Ten centimeters," the man in the sky said, ignoring everyone except for Ilya. "Very, very impressive. Are you alright?"

"I'm ... fine," Ilya said while gasping. "That ... felt great!"

"You're Ilya Pentorn, correct?" the man in the sky rubbed his chin and asked. "I think it's safe to say you'll be in first place for this part of the competition. Though using those mana-regenerating consumable items may have been a bit excessive."

Ilya shook her head. "I'm not going to be first," she said. Eh? Who could beat that score? It's already three times greater than Daniel's! "She is." Ilya pointed at me. Oh, right.

The man in the sky stared at me. What kind of expression was that? I'm not something you should be gawking at. "Her?" the man asked and looked at Ilya. "Are you sure?"

"I'm positive," Ilya said and nodded. "If bones had a nemesis, it would be her."

"Interesting," the man in the sky said and looked at me again. "Then show me what you can do, nemesis of bones."

Don't give me a weird nickname! I'll show you what I can do! "Step aside, Ilya! The main character's here to steal the spotlight!" Ilya rolled her eyes at me. "And don't forget you owe me hot chocolate."

"I won't, thanks," Ilya said and patted my shoulder before standing off to the side next to Ilya Number Two. Did the barrier only break on the side with all the people who've still yet to go? Well, it sucks to be them! ...Disregard the fact that I was on that side too.

Okay, first, let's see if I can carve anything on this bone. Don't fail me now, mini-DalDal. Here we go.... And nope. "Hey, Durandal. Why can't I cut this thing?"

"You forgot to use your qi."

Oh. Right. I shouldn't have given that bone of focus to Ilya. It was my last one. Well, hopefully I can carve one out of this pillar. "Unrelenting Path of Slaughter: Continuous Breaking Blades in a Specific Pattern!" It's working! The engraving's being carved; although it looks a bit crude, but that's okay. A few more slashes and ... it's done! "Finishing hit! Unrelenting Path of Slaughter: Palm Strike That's Not a Disguise to Absorb Things!"

And just like that, the pillar completely dissolved into nothing. The plane fell silent. That's right; I'm awesome! Be amazed!

"What did you do!?" the man in the sky shouted. "Zero! Zero distance!"

"Eh!? No way!" It totally moved while I was slashing it! "It moved! It totally moved!"

"Negative! Negative ten thousand meters!" the man in the sky shouted. "Last place!"

Fight me! "If you didn't want your pillar to be destroyed, you shouldn't have asked everyone to hit it!"

"Wait!" Ilya said. "Don't do anything just yet, Lucia. There's still a chance for first place in the coming rounds. Calm down!"

I'm perfectly fucking calm! Don't tell me what to do!

"Don't fight," Ilya Number Two said. "This is a peaceful place. Grandmother wouldn't want you two to fight here."

The man in the sky, or should I call him the man on the ground, snorted. Another black pillar appeared beside him. It looked about four times bigger than the last one. "Previously, you did a combination of attacks. You were only allowed to do one. By the rules, I should disqualify you. But, being the magnanimous man that I am, I'll give you a second chance. One attack."

"That's the way," Ilya Number Two said and nodded. "My grandmother would like this better."

…One attack? It felt pretty light when I was swinging at it. Maybe I'll just pick it up and throw it? Yeah, I'll throw it at the man on the ground. This discriminatory bastard.

"What are you…, are you trying to…?" That was easy. I looked at the man on the ground. Target acquired! "What the hell…?"

"Catch!"

***

I didn't know how to react when Lucia lifted the pillar and threw it at Cain. Apparently, Cain didn't know either. By the time it was right in front of him, he still hadn't moved. He barely managed to move his head out of the way, but it still clipped his shoulder, creating an awful cracking noise. The pillar continued flying through the air like a beam of light, showing no intentions of falling. Cain tumbled along the ground like he was hit by, well, by a massive pillar that weighed a lot of tons. By the time he stopped rolling on the ground, the pillar had landed as well.

Everyone fell silent for the second time in a very short timeframe. I wonder how much my father is regretting having Lucia represent him for this decade's brawl. Lucia's voice broke the silence. "Hey, why aren't you announcing my distance? You announced everyone else's instantly."

Cain didn't react to her words, his body lying completely still on the ground. Don't tell me he died because of that; though, I wouldn't be surprised if he did. At the very least, his shoulder should be shattered, maybe a few ribs too. Lucia tilted her head before skipping over to Cain. She nudged him with her foot a few times. "Hello? Mr. Man on the Ground? What's my score?"

I should probably stop her. ...But I really want to see what's going to happen if I don't. Does that make me a bad person? Have I become a deviant after meeting Lucia? There's no way that's possible; I'm an honest, down-to-earth, upstanding person. But an upstanding person wouldn't have to reassure themselves about being one, right? Maybe I have become a little twisted. Is it wrong that I don't feel bad about it? I reached the sixth circle and managed to cast an unprecedented spell after meeting Lucia, and all it cost me was a bit of my morality. That's a pretty fair deal in my opinion.

Someone tugged on my sleeve. Lucia? No, it was Mirta. "Hmm?"

"Do you know healing spells, Ms. Ilya?" Mirta asked.

Miss Ilya? Am I that old that I have to be referred to as miss? No, it's just that Mirta's too young, and her elders taught her how to respect people who deserve respect. "Yes, I do. I'm very good at them in fact."

Mirta furrowed her brow and tilted her head. "Then why aren't you healing him?" she asked and pointed at Cain. Lucia was still nudging the poor tenth-circle magician with her foot. I say nudging, but his body was being flipped over every time she made contact with him.

"I kind of wanted to see what would happen."

Mirta blinked. "Huh?"

"I mean, I thought someone else would heal him, you know? I can't be the only one who knows healing spells around here." It'd be weird if I was. Any second-circle magician could cast a simple cure spell, but it seemed like everyone else was a bit too stunned to move. Or they were afraid of approaching Cain when Lucia was kicking him around like that. "Hey, Lucia."

Lucia's legs stopped moving, and she turned her head to look at me. "What? Are you going to tell me to stop? Huh? This magnanimous man told me to do one attack. It's not my fault he got in the way, is it? Huh? Is it? Is it?" With every question, Cain's body flew forward a little as she prodded him with her toes. "This little nemesis of bones is just a harmless little girl who can only smack a pillar a negative distance. There's no way the person in last place knocked out the strongest man in the world, right? Nope, I'm too weak. He's just ignoring me."

I always knew Lucia was a vengeful person, but ... wasn't this a little excessive? It's that weird nickname Cain gave her, isn't it? Ah, this competition has turned into a giant mess. Cain was struck down by Lucia; it wouldn't be a surprise if tensions between demons and beastkin rose. To avoid an international incident—or should I say mitigate—I have to get Lucia to stop kicking Cain around. I think the easiest way to do that is to convince Durandal to stop her. But how would I do that?

Luckily, Cain let out a groaning noise before I had to do anything. Lucia stopped kicking him and took a few steps back, returning to her original position near the area she had thrown the pillar from. Cain sat up and winced before looking at his arm which was hanging limp at his side. His brow furrowed as white light enveloped his body, his bones cracking as they mended and reset themselves. "Did I pass out after being hit by the pillar?" Cain asked Lucia. "How long was I unconscious?"

"You fainted for a couple of seconds," Lucia said, her face looking completely simple and honest. "Sorry, I didn't mean to hit you with the pillar." She scratched her head and tilted it to the side.

Cain frowned and stood up. He winced again and touched a hand to his ribs where Lucia had repeatedly nudged him. "Odd," he said as more white light circled around his body. "I vaguely remember you shouting, 'Catch!' when you threw the pillar at me."

"Nope, I didn't," Lucia said, shaking her head. You totally did! "You can ask anyone."

Cain looked at me, but I looked away. There was no way I was going to sell Lucia out; my safety's the most important thing to me! "She didn't. She actually shouted, 'Look out!' before it hit you."

Mirta stared at me before staring at Lucia. Then she stared at Cain, and turned her gaze back onto me. She opened her mouth to say something, but I channeled a spell and silenced her. Sorry, Mirta, this is how the real world works. It's best if you learn while you're still young.

"The distance...," Cain said, turning his gaze onto the pillar. He shook his head. "Let's just say you're first for now." The pillar rose into the air and landed in front of Lucia again. "Next."

Lucia smiled at Cain before skipping over to me. She patted my head and ruffled my hair before giving me a hug. I struggled, but I couldn't get away, so I gave up. Lucia laughed before she whispered into my ear, "Nice one, partner in crime." Lying to Cain, I guess that could be considered a crime. But no one else said anything to disprove Lucia, so it's not just me!

Speaking of everyone else, my spell had damaged the competitors who had still yet to go. The pillar was also about four times heavier because Cain pulled out a new one after Lucia's absorption stunt. Those two factors made it nearly impossible to move the pillar, causing the next two to three hundred people to obtain zero distance with their attacks. A few people complained, but Cain wasn't exactly in the best of moods after passing out in front of everyone important in the world, so those who complained were directly disqualified. When the last person futilely hit the pillar, causing it to move the grand distance of zero, Cain rose into the air and said, "The second portion of the competition is over. Though some of you did poorly, there will be chances to make up for it. Even if you're in last place, you can still become first if you excel at the remainder of the competition. With that being said, the third part will proceed after a ten-minute break. The first portion tested your talent. The second portion tested your offense. The third portion will test your defense. Do your best to prepare yourselves."

***

"Are you all ready?" the man in the sky asked after ten minutes had passed. "The third portion of the competition is about to begin. He gestured at the scoreboard floating beside him. "Though this thousand point lead that Lucia Fluffytail has may look daunting, it is not insurmountable." The competitors stared at him, then at me. "Okay, I lied. No matter how hard you try, none of you will be as capable as her. But it is still completely possible to wrest away first place during the actual competition."

Isn't this the actual competition? What the heck? Oh, right. Ilya did say this was just a preliminary. I guess the outstanding people get to participate in the actual event? Then what was the reward he was promising us for being in the top hundred? Was that something else?

"And with that being said, let the trials begin." The man in the sky clapped his hands, and the world darkened. But just barely; if it weren't for my awesome senses, I wouldn't even have noticed. But what was super noticeable was the water springing out of the ground! It was already at my ankles and rapidly rising!

"Ilya! Save me!" I can't swim! What is this bullshit exam!? Right before I was about to attach myself to Ilya, we were pushed away from each other by invisible forces in the water. The water level was already up to my hips! I'm going to drown at this rate! And are those fins sticking out from the surface?

"Sharks!" someone shouted.

The heck is a shark? It's probably super tasty, but I don't have time to worry about that right now! If I don't do something quick, I'm really going to die. If, if I can't swim, then I'll kill the person summoning the water! "Unrelenting Path of Slaughter: A Storm of a Thousand Breaking Blades!"

It's working! The water level isn't rising. All I have to do is keep it up, and I'll be safe! Stupid shark, get away from me. I kicked it, but my foot passed through it. Illusion? Or were sharks liquid? I guess it'd make sense if they were since they live in the water.

"Are you trying to kill me!?" the man in the sky shouted from above.

"Yes!" Why is he so damn slippery? Every time I think I have him, he manages to barely avoid it or block it. Then, I have to double the speed of my output! "Durandal, Puppers! You two help hunt him too!" Obviously, Durandal would know how to use Breaking Blade considering he was the one who taught it to me. And Puppers can ... I really don't know what Puppers can do, but I'll summon him anyways! Oh, he can keep my socks dry for me.

"This is a test of defense! Defense!" the man in the sky shouted as blue sword beams accompanied my red ones. Wow, Durandal and I can create a blue and red painting in the sky if we try hard enough. Maybe we could make some bits purple if we hit each other's beam at the right time. Nice! I hit that slippery bastard! But it only scratched his arm? How thick is his skin? "Stop attacking me!"

"The best defense is a great offense! The only way to ensure you won't get hurt is to kill your enemy before they can hurt you." That's what the Path of Slaughter taught me even though I didn't like following it because it was scary at first. But I got used to it.

"That's it!" the man in the sky roared. Ten circles appeared around him, circling in place. Huge black clouds formed in the sky, and purple lightning snaked through them. "Heavenly lightning, tear the skies asunder. Thunder—"

"Wait!" Ilya shouted. "You'll kill us all if you do that!"

"God dammit!" the man in the sky shouted as the lightning dissipated. Nice one, Ilya! Ooh, I hit him again, this time on the leg. My aim's getting better. "Flames of hell, incinerate the world. Fire—"

"That'll kill us too!" Ilya shouted.

Sweet! Four-hit combo! Keep distracting him, Ilya. He'll be dead in no time. I'll save us all from this watery grave.

"Stop! Stop!" the man in the sky shouted. The water levels are receding, keep attacking, Durandal! "The test's over! The third test is over! You goddam chipmunk, I said stop!"

He can't be talking about me, right? I'm part squirrel. Chipmunk tails are thinner, and chipmunk beastkin are totally less cute than squirrel beastkin. Yeah, he must be referring to someone else.

"Lucia! Fluffytail! If you don't cease this instant, I will skin you alive and feed your remains to your sword spirit!"

Oh, so he was talking about me. "I'm part squirrel, you know? Not chipmunk." Mm. The man in the sky looks angry. It's probably because no one else did as well as me during this test. Update the leaderboards! I want to see how many points I got. Another thousand? That'd be nice. …Why isn't it updating? "Hey, Mr. Flying Target, what about the test results?"

"I hate this job," the man in the sky said. "The world should just burn. Let the plant devils overrun everything, I don't care. Next generation? Forget it." He exhaled. "Calm down, Cain. Calm down. It's just a stupid chipmunk"—

"Squirrel."

—"lady. A stupid squirrel lady. You don't have to let her get under your skin like this, yeah? Okay. Great. You're doing great, Cain."

Wait, didn't he say something super ominous just now. Something about plant devils? But that's not even the most pressing issue! "The leaderboar—dgh!?"

Ilya stuffed something in my mouth! "Please, stop talking."

This, this—! Oh, it's a cookie. Is it made with acorn flour? When did Ilya get something like this and how come she hasn't been sharing it with me? It's not bad at all—pretty tasty. I deserve it after all that hard work I did during that last test. I sent out over two thousand Breaking Blades, not counting Durandal's.

"In one minute, the fourth part of the competition will begin," the man in the sky said. "It's a simple test of comprehension. No attacking allowed! Instant disqualification for anyone who breaks the rules, understood!?"

Comprehension? Like learning a new skill? I'm good at that; this should be easy. A tablet fell from the sky and landed by my feet. What's this?

"The technique you'll be comprehending is written down on the tablet in front of you. There must be utter silence; anyone who speaks will be disqualified. You have one hour. Begin."

What's with the impossible exams!? I can't read!

***

This tablet … makes no sense whatsoever. What the heck is this language? Is there even anyone here that can read this? Judging by the looks on people's faces, they can't decipher it either. What's Lucia doing? Is, is she licking it? Did she figure something out? I have reservations about eating food that fell on the ground, but for the sake of this exam…. Who am I kidding? There's no way I'm going to lick this tablet. Absolutely none.

Ah! Daniel's licking the tablet! And now Mirta! Everyone's gone crazy! Sounds of slurping and disgust filled the air. Don't tell me this is how you're actually supposed to comprehend the tablet. There's no way Cain would test us like this, right? And I refuse to believe Lucia figured something out! But … everyone else is licking it. …Just one taste won't hurt. Blech, it tastes like cabbage.

Crunch.

What was that? It sounds like rocks being ground up. Wasn't there supposed to be utter silence? Of course, it's Lucia. She's eating the tablet now!? And Cain's acting like this is perfectly normal! Could comprehension be digestion? Did Lucia actually figure out the exam before anyone else in this room? Let's try reading the words one more time. This character with the squiggly part, I've seen it before, but where? Doesn't it resemble the way mana flows through my heart transformation point if it's the third part of a spell? If each of these characters are pictures of mana flows, then—

Crunch.

Utter silence, people. Utter silence! Why the heck is that lionkin eating the tablet too!? Calm down, Ilya. If each of these characters are pictures of mana flows, then this could represent the fire attribute. This one would be wind. Would this be light? It kind of feels similar to the way mana flows in my head. Now that I think about it, does mana flow the same way for everyone? What about the people who fight with qi? How are they supposed to figure this out? I'm not sure if I'm on the right track anymore. But—

Crunch.

Daniel too!?

Crunch.

Mirta, you'll break your teeth if you eat that! It can't be that I've fallen under an illusion spell, right? Is this the actual test of comprehension, whether or not you can see through an illusion? Maybe I—

"I understand!" someone shouted and stood up. "This is an illusion! There's—"

"Disqualified," Cain said. He flicked his finger and the man who had just shouted disappeared.

...Was that also part of the illusion? To throw me off track? Am I thinking about this too much? It's okay, Ilya. Trust in your senses. Follow the previous train of thought with the images and mana flows. ...But it's very hard to do that with everyone eating their tablet! It's like studying in a room full of people chewing with their mouths open. This is absolutely infuriating. What happened to the utter silence rule? Ugh, whatever. I'll just circulate my mana in accordance to the pictures.

But how is it read? Left to right like human books, top to bottom like the fae's, or right to left like demons'? It's possible that it's not even read in either of those manners; then I'll plot out every one of those paths for my mana to flow and pick the one that makes the most sense. Left to right requires mana to flow from the head directly to the toes which seems highly inefficient. That automatically filters out right to left as well. Top to bottom then? Or bottom to top. There's still fifty minutes left according to the timer in the sky that Cain created. I'll definitely comprehend this tablet!

Crunch.

And people are still eating their tablets. Ignore everyone else, I have to believe in myself! ...But a quick check on what Lucia's doing wouldn't hurt. ...She's sitting on a couch and drinking hot chocolate while Puppers is massaging her feet. Unbelievable. Forget it, maybe this really is an illusion and comprehending the tablet will reveal a spell that dispels it.

Twenty minutes later, I figured out the most efficient route. But there was a slight problem with it. The spell requires someone to have at least six circles since it circulates through the head six times. Is it possible everyone was given a different tablet suitable for their level of cultivation? I'd check someone else's, but everyone ate theirs! Literally every single person except for me ate their tablet; and it looks like they're meditating while trying to hold down vomit. This vaguely reminds me of the time I took a test with my peers and everyone took out measuring tools, but I had no idea what they were using them for. I don't want to talk about the results of that test.

Ah, forget it. With my results in the first part of the competition, I'll definitely be in the top hundred even if I get zero points on this portion. I'll just try to cast the spell. It seems like I'll have to rely on some bones of strength. It's a good thing I didn't use all of them while attacking the pillar. I had wanted to, but I felt like I'd die if I stacked anymore of those spells. Actually, maybe I shouldn't cast it right now. This is just comprehension. Surely Cain will ask us to demonstrate what we comprehended. Then I'll just memorize and simulate the mana flow until time's up.

Thirty minutes later, Cain clapped his hands. Everyone opened their eyes and looked up. "Alright," Cain said, "I'm extremely curious. Why the hell did all of you eat your tablets?"

Everyone turned their heads to stare at Lucia, but she had her eyes closed with a line of drool leaking out of her mouth. …She's asleep.

"You," Cain said and pointed at a random man. "Tell me."

"W-well," the man said and swallowed. "I'm just a commoner, sir. I can't read, so there was no way for me to comprehend anything on the tablet. But that girl, she got first place in the attack and defense portions, so I copied her. And everyone else was doing it, so if I didn't, then wouldn't I fall behind?"

Lucia sat up the instant the man pointed at her. She blinked and looked around before looking at Puppers. It seemed like they were communicating silently.

"And how was it? Did you comprehend anything?" Cain asked. Was it just me, or did he look like he wanted to murder someone?

"N-no, sir," the man said and lowered his head.

Cain snorted and glared at Lucia. "It's you again. Why is it always you?" he asked. "Tell me, why did you eat your tablet? You're the one who started it. If it weren't for your actions, no one else would have the moronic thought to actually eat their tablets!" His head swiveled to meet everyone's gazes. "That's right. Each and every one of you is an idiot." Then he glanced at me. "Except for you."

It's a really, really good thing I didn't fall for the peer pressure.

"So what do you have to say for yourself, Lucia Fluffytail?"

"The thing vaguely smelled like acorn flour, so I licked it, and it actually tasted like acorn flour!" Lucia nodded. "So I ate it."

Cain's eye twitched. "And did you comprehend anything?"

"Yes!" Lucia said, bobbing her head up and down. She actually did!?

Cain waited, but Lucia didn't say anything. "And?" he asked. "What was it?"

Lucia stuck her chest out as if she were proud of her actions. "I realized the acorn flour was actually on my fingers from before and had nothing to do with the tablet!" Oh my lord. I knew she was a simple person, but … this is going a little too far. "But since I ate the tablet, there was nothing I could do to change that. And you already said that there's no way I'd lose first place in the preliminary, so I decided to take a nap."

Cain's expression darkened. He looked at me. "For not being an idiot, you get three thousand points. It doesn't matter if you actually comprehended anything or not; apparently, you're a goddam genius compared to everyone else here."

Lucia's eyes widened as my name appeared on top of hers on the leaderboard. "Ah! You lied! You said I would be first!"

I won by default? "C-can I try casting the spell I comprehended?" I'm ashamed to win this way. I have to prove myself legitimately!

Cain furrowed his brow. "You actually figured out a spell?"

Was I not supposed to? Is this an example of keeping your mouth shut to not seem like a fool? "Y-yes. At least, I think I did."

"Go on then," Cain said. "I'm curious."

Alright, here goes nothing! I've simulated it thirty times and nothing seemed wrong, so it should definitely bring about a result. Two bones of strength should be enough. Follow the flow, keep it steady, consume a bone, reverse this portion of mana, circulate it back towards my head, consume another bone, circulate it down to my hands, then back to the head, then back to my hands, and I'm done! Like I thought, it's a spell that requires the use of my palms related to the light element. "Light, don't fail me now, show me your power!"

Mana surged through my body as I pointed my hands at the sky. Two beams of light shot out of my palms, creating massive white pillars that extended as far as the eye could see. Cain moved forward and approached the beams. He placed a black stick halfway into one of the pillars. When he withdrew the stick, half of it was gone. Well, I expected the spell to be more than just a giant flashlight. Four circles of fire and five circles of lightning were necessary to create this!

"Not bad, not bad at all," Cain said once the pillars disappeared. "This concludes the preliminary rounds. These are the final results." He gestured towards the scoreboard. I'm first place? "Everyone with more than zero points have the right to participate in the Godking's Brawl. The top hundred people..., I promised rewards, didn't I? Your reward is simple: You'll be given seeded positions in the upcoming brawl like the sixty people with guaranteed spots."

"That's it?" Lucia asked. "What the heck?"

"You were expecting more?" Cain asked. "Why did you even participate in the preliminary if you were guaranteed a spot?"

"I wasn't paying attention and came here instead of the spectator's area," Lucia said with a nod.

Cain took in a deep breath through his nose. Then he exhaled a breath of black smoke through his mouth. "Everyone's dismissed. The Godking's Brawl will begin tomorrow at noon."

20

That was a total waste of time! There weren't even any rewards. I feel cheated. And Ilya looks exhausted after today's events. When the man in the sky said the preliminary was over, the plane had dissolved, and we were back inside the city. Ilya got a message from her father telling her to go back to the inn since it would've been too hard to find people in the crowd. A lot of people stared at us, but no one got in our way. Even the lionkin from the acorn stew incident avoided me after I made eye contact with him. Does this count as becoming a legend? Mm, even if it does, that doesn't matter because I have to ascend higher than the divine realm to achieve my dreams. Ah, speaking of dreams, that reminds me of my deal with Albert...? Algar? The human crown prince. It's still a secret though!

"So," Ilya said. I was holding onto her hand because she's super tiny and would probably get lost in the crowd if I let her go. "Why is she with us?"

In my other hand, I was holding Ilya Number Two by the back of her belt—kind of like a shopping bag. Her arms and legs dangled uselessly in the air; she had stopped struggling a while ago. Obviously I have a reason to bring her along. "We're friends!"

"Friends," Ilya said. "Right. I'm pretty sure her grandmother's a high elf. I'm not sure how strong she is though."

"Nine circles," Ilya Number Two said. She raised her head, which was a bit red from all the blood rushing to it, and flailed her arms and legs a bit. "She'll rescue me! You better let me go right now."

A voice shouted above the din of the crowd, "Mirta! Where are you!?"

"Gran—" Before Ilya Number Two could give away our position, I stuffed her face into Ilya's shoulder to prevent her from making a sound. The little elf girl struggled a lot, and Ilya also tried to run away, but I wasn't going to let that happen! I was curious about the enchanting process, and Ilya Number Two told me weapons can be upgraded by a whole grade. I'm not sure what a grade was, but I decided I had to kidnap the elf in front of me right away! If I reached the peak of divine realm, and then had Ilya Number Two's grandmother enchant mini-DalDal, wouldn't Durandal directly step into the legendary realm? That saves me a whole lot of work! That's why I have to bring Ilya Number Two away. If I can't befriend her, then I can always hold her hostage. Hah? Someone will accuse me of kidnapping a child? Well, they'd be wrong! This is called pursuing one's dreams.

"Mirta!?"

The voice is getting further away. Nice! Let's hurry back to the inn before the grandmother can track us down. Ilya frowned. "I really don't think this is a good idea."

"Nonsense! All my ideas are good ideas. When have I ever gotten the short end of the stick for one of my choices?" Other than trusting Snow. That was a bad idea, a really, really bad one. I still haven't seen him around. Is Ilya's dad really sure about his participation? Snow doesn't seem like the person to compete for prizes fairly. He'd probably steal it from the winner.

"Well...." Ilya's brow furrowed. "Does almost dying count?"

"No. Only actual dying." Keyword, almost. And Ilya's only almost died around three or four times since she's met me. That's nothing!

"Then I really can't think of a time you've been punished for making a dumb decision," Ilya said and bit her lower lip.

"Is that true? Why does that feel wrong on so many levels? No, that's impossible. Someone like you should definitely get your just deserts with all the bad karma you've accumulated. Ah! Being punished by my teacher! Falling for his trap was definitely a bad idea on your part."

"But then I met you?" I don't really think of meeting Rogath as a misfortune. If anything, I got a super-powerful magic tool and a handy-dandy encyclopedia to boot.

Ilya's expression darkened. "You're right." She sighed and hung her head. "There is no god."

Don't equate my lack of divine punishment to the lack of a god! I'm sure there's someone out there plotting out our lives as we speak. Oh, we've arrived back to the inn. That was quick. I need to take a nap and relax. I already finished my daily one thousand swings of my sword while attacking the man in the sky. And I get to sleep in since the competition starts at noon. Life is great!

"Um, Ilya," Ilya's dad said when we entered the suite. He pointed at the bundle I dropped on the ground. "Who's that? A guest?"

"This is Mirta," Ilya said. "Lucia kidnapped her."

"Help!" Ilya Number Two shouted. "Hel—" She stopped shouting when I placed a mug of hot chocolate in front of her on the ground. "For me?"

"Yup!" The easiest way to placate someone is with good food. The second easiest way is to cut their head off, but that'd ruin the whole point of me kidnapping Ilya Number Two. You can't ransom off a dead hostage! …Well, you can, but you wouldn't get as much. "We're friends, right?"

Ilya Number Two stared at the cup. Her lips quivered before she lifted her head and stared at me. I did my best to smile at her. So why did she look so scared? I'm not scary! Didn't we already establish our friendship during the competition? Ilya Number Two's stomach growled. She swallowed her saliva as she grabbed the hot chocolate. "Right, we're friends."

"You're just like Roland," Durandal said from mini-DalDal. "I'm starting to wonder if it's an issue with me."

"I'm just like the Godking?" That's right! Aren't I? I'm the strongest warrior in the world, and I own Durandal! If I fought with the Godking in his prime as I am right now, I'd definitely kick his ass. At least I think I'm the strongest warrior in the world. Ilya's never heard of a divine warrior except for me, and she's super well informed.

"I'm pretty sure Durandal was saying that as a criticism," Ilya said and pursed her lips.

"That's right!" Ilya Number Two said. "The Godking kidnapped my grandmother, and now you kidnapped me!" Then she glanced at the hot chocolate in her hands. "But we're friends.... Then is it really kidnapping?"

My face is turning red from all these compliments. I'm an incredible person now; it's unbelievable. Just a few years ago, I was a punching bag for the army. A few years before that, I was a slave. My life's really changed after meeting Durandal. That's why I love him! "You're the best, Durandal!"

"I know I'm the best, but what am I the best for in this particular moment?" Durandal asked, raising an eyebrow as he neatly received my hug. I'm not even angry at him for throwing me out of the carriage anymore. Well, maybe just a little.

"Mirta! I found you!" The door to the suite flew off the hinges before I could say anything to Durandal. An elf lady walked into the room ... followed by the man in the sky? What was he doing here?

***

I knew kidnapping Mirta was a bad idea! Her grandmother tracked us, and Cain followed her as well. But why is Cain here anyway? It can't be that those two are together, right? It'd be bad for a demon to associate so closely to the upper echelons of elven society. We may be at peace, but tensions are still running high. There's tons of unofficial skirmishes happening at our borders in the lawless lands. Then again, anyone will attack anyone in the lawless lands regardless of race.

"Elder Marilyn, Lord Thunderfire," my father said, rising from his couch. "What brings you to this duke's humble residence?"

"Mirta!" Marilyn said, ignoring my father while rushing into the room. "Are you alright!?"

"Oh," Lucia said, stepping behind Mirta and placing her hand on the little girl's head. "You must be Ily—Mirta's mother! Mirta wanted to come along with us, so I brought her here and gave her some hot chocolate. We're close friends." She smiled at Mirta who was shivering. "Right?"

"R-right," Mirta said after swallowing her hot chocolate. "Grandma, this is Lucia. And this is Ilya. They're nice people."

Marilyn furrowed her brow. "I'm Mirta's grandmother," she said to Lucia. "Not her mother. How dare—"

"Not her mother?" Lucia asked, her eyes widening. "But you look so young!"

Oh my lord, Lucia's trying to trick Mirta's grandmother like she tricked my father. There's no way a high elf would fall for such blatant flattery!

Marilyn drew her head back and raised an eyebrow. She smiled at Lucia. "Really? You think so? I do take good care of my skin."

She fell for it! There really is no god!

"Is she a friend you made during the competition, Mirta?" Marilyn said, crouching by Mirta and patting her head. "I saw her perform. All three of you did very nicely. But you shouldn't eat tablets just because everyone else is, alright?"

Cain cleared his throat, and everyone turned to look at him. "Sorry for dropping by uninvited," he said. Was he here because of Lucia? Did she infuriate him that much? He was getting antsy during the competition, especially during that third one with the defense. He almost killed everyone with tenth-circle spells because of Lucia. Wait. Why's he looking at me!? I'm not the culprit! I'm a victim too. "It's been a while since I last saw you, Duke Pentorn. You raised an impressive daughter." He paused and smiled. "And I just happened to be searching for a disciple."

What? Disciple? Me? Father looks confused as well. "Ilya's already Rogath Winemark's disciple," my father said and rubbed his chin.

"A relic from the past," Cain said with a snort. "He's been alive for how many years and still only a magician with eight circles? Ilya's potential must be nurtured carefully; Rogath can't do that. I can."

"A relic from the past?" Marilyn asked and raised an eyebrow. She smiled at Cain and crossed her arms over her chest. "Then what does that make me?"

"An even older relic," Cain said with a smile. "Perhaps an antique? Or prehistoric even."

Wow. It seems like Cain and Mirta's grandmother don't get along well at all. They just coincidentally arrived in our suite together? I suspected it during the competition, but Cain's … crass, nothing like the person I thought he'd be. He has a perfectly valid reason to be arrogant since he's the strongest person in the world, but I expected him to have a more noble character like a hero in a story. With his current personality, isn't he more attuned to the antagonist's role?

Mana fluctuated through the room, and I had to take a step back. Were the two going to fight? Why in our inn of all places? Lucia tugged on Mirta's grandmother's sleeve, and the pressure in the room disappeared. Lucia's actually going to mediate between two people? Isn't she usually the cause of

419

destruction? "Hey, hey," Lucia said. "If you enchant my stuff, I'll help you beat him up."

...I spoke too soon.

"Am I being underestimated?" Cain asked, raising an eyebrow. "This is certainly an unpleasant feeling. I've been wanting to teach you a lesson, chipmunk. Give me a reason to."

"Eh?" Lucia tilted her head. "You want me to be your disciple? No way!"

"Disciple?" Cain asked. "No! That's not what I mean by teaching you a lesson. Ugh, dealing with idiots is so frustrating. And even if you thought I wanted you to be my disciple, how could you refuse instantly like that?"

"Well, there's nothing you can teach me," Lucia said with a nod. I'm pretty sure Cain can teach you a lot, Lucia. Like learning how to read. Or how to distinguish north from south. Lucia raised her hand and pointed her sword at Cain. "And I don't like you. Your face is too thin for your wide body. It's weird to look at."

Mirta's grandmother snorted before laughing. "Did you hear that, Cain? I may be old, but at least my body's proportionate."

Huh, Cain's face is a little narrow now that I can see him more closely. And his torso is a bit wide in an unflattering way. He's not fat, but he's not ... normal-looking either? I don't know if I'll be able to see him the same way again.

"This is a guest of your house?" Cain asked my father, ignoring the sword in front of his face. "Is she free to be as unbridled as she likes?"

My father's expression darkened. What a tough decision he has to make, I'm glad I'm not the duchess yet. Should he take Lucia and Mirta's grandmother's side, or should he take Cain's side? What decision would I make? Just how much stronger is a tenth-circle magician compared to one with nine circles? There's the wall that has to be overcome, but could Cain win if everyone in this room were to turn against him?

Lucia's an idiot, but she's not a bad person ... as long as she doesn't mistake someone for a rare spirit beast. Cain's a genius, but his character's not that great. But the pressure he could put on my father if he's offended would be a lot greater than the pressure Lucia could put on. My father could possibly lose the position of duke if Cain complains to the emperor about my father's behavior. Speaking up for Lucia in this scenario could also be seen as speaking up for Mirta's grandmother, a high elf. If people learned my father favored an elf over a demon, there wouldn't be good opinions about him. The obvious choice is to placate Cain and coax Lucia to calm down with sweets.

"I apologize, Lord Thunderfire, but could you please leave?" my father asked. "Right now, I'd like to relax with friends. I'd be happy to accommodate you back at my home in the future."

...Or I thought about it too much.

***

"This...," the man no longer in the sky said. "I know you may be a bit muddleheaded from her presence, but do you understand the implications of telling me to leave?"

What implications? If Ilya's dad wants you to scram, then scram! I can totally take this person on in a fight; my tail hasn't stiffened in his presence. Can it be that I'm as strong as a tenth-circle magician? Wouldn't that make me the new strongest person in the world? Mm, I really want to try fighting him now. Huh? He's leaving?

The door closed as the man no longer in the sky left the room. Ilya Number Two's grandmother raised an eyebrow and looked at Ilya's dad. I wonder if she's married. Wouldn't it be weird if Ilya Number One and Ilya Number Two actually became sisters? Wait, no. If they got together, then that would make Ilya Number One an aunt-in-law to Ilya Number Two, never mind. Ah, I can't believe the tenth-circle magician wanted me to be his disciple though. I can't even use magic.

"Why'd you turn Cain away, Father?" Ilya asked her dad. "Wouldn't that cause a lot of problems?"

Ilya's dad smiled. "Why? Were you looking forward to being his disciple?"

Wait, what? Wasn't I the chosen one? Mm, it'd make more sense if it was actually Ilya since she can fart out flames. Could it be that I don't know how to read situations properly? No way, that's impossible.

Ilya lowered her head. "I was for a little," she said. "But he was rude and a bit cold. I don't think I would've gotten along well with him. I'm sure if I hadn't met Lucia, I would've appreciated a teacher like that."

It's nice to know I leave such deep impressions on people. After traveling with me, no one else can satisfy Ilya! That's the second-best compliment I've received! The first is being compared to the Godking. Durandal said that all the Godking was good for was manipulating children, but that is impressive in itself! Look at how I've created a relationship with someone who can enchant items by bribing a child with hot chocolate. And look at how I became best friends with nobility by dragging around a duke's daughter. It takes skill to be this conniving! Not that I'm a bad person, I'm practically an angel with a fluffy tail.

"You know how nobles have been trying to undermine my power for a while now, right?" Ilya's dad asked, folding his hands and placing them in his lap. "Sending men to pose as bandits. Belittling my ideas during the imperial court. Cutting off trade routes. Bribing cooks to poison my spices. Those kinds of things?"

Ilya nodded.

"The only reason why I can't stop the problem completely is because it's not within my power," Ilya's dad said, leaning back. "But I'm a duke; who's above me? The emperor. Maybe the crown prince. And powers beyond the empire's control."

"You're saying Cain is trying to bring our family down?" Ilya asked, her face paling.

"I didn't want to believe it," Ilya's dad said and shrugged. "But after seeing how he behaved today...." He shook his head. "You couldn't see it because you were participating in the competition, but the reactions on the lesser nobles' faces upon seeing Cain confirmed it for me. A baron bordering our territory can easily be squashed if I complain to the emperor, but what if the baron has the backing of a tenth-circle magician?"

Ilya bit her lower lip. "Does that mean the emperor is against us as well?"

"He's adopted a wait-and-see approach," Ilya's dad said. "Since it's already come to this point, I might as well bring the background to the foreground and garner some support with the elves while I'm at it." He stared at Ilya Number Two's grandmother.

Jeez, politics is confusing. Life would be a lot easier if you could beat up anyone you didn't like without worrying about the consequences. But it wouldn't be fun to get beaten up by someone just because they didn't like me. That's why I have to become stronger than everyone else in the world, so I can beat everyone without getting beaten myself! All this talk about beating is making me hungry for some eggs. I'll make some food while Ilya and her dad figure things out.

"Ily-Mirta." Oops. Almost called Ilya Number Two by her nickname in front of her grandmother. "What do you want to eat for dinner? I'm a really good cook, you know?"

"Roasted rose petals and ginger roots," Ilya Number Two said. "And bean curd with olive oil."

"Yeah, I don't have that. Pick something else like steak. Steak sounds good, right?" Don't name things I don't want to eat! Why would I keep those things stored in my interspacial ring anyway? My space is very valuable; how else am I supposed to fit all my gallons of hot chocolate?

Ilya Number Two tilted her head. "Um, can I pick something else?"

"No. I gave you a choice, but you didn't pick something practical, so I chose for you."

"But roasted rose petals are practical…."

"Too bad. Welcome to the real world, kid." Looks like steak is the unanimous decision for tonight's dinner! "You're fine with steak too, right, Mrs. Mirta's Mom?"

"Well it seems like I don't have a choice," Ilya Number Two's grandmother said. She nodded at Ilya's dad. "I'll be imposing upon you tonight. I apologize for the trouble."

"It's no trouble at all," Ilya's dad said. "A friend of Ilya will always be welcome in my home."

"I've heard a lot about you, Duke Pentorn," Ilya Number Two's grandmother said. "But I hadn't heard you stepped past the eighth circle. And I certainly didn't know your daughter was this impressive."

"You flatter me," Ilya's dad said. "Everything is thanks to Lucia. Without her enlightenment, I would've been stuck with eight circles for a much longer period of time. She's also the reason for Ilya's meteoric rise. Half a year has passed since they first met, but Ilya jumped from the third circle to the sixth. If Mirta sticks around her, I bet she'd see vast improvements as well."

I never thought receiving compliments could be so embarrassing. I guess that makes me a humble person. Why am I so virtuous and amazing? I deserve a medal.

21

It's been tough since I removed the poison from Lucia's body and accepted it into my own. Before I went to sleep, I might as well have been a god in front of Lucia. After I woke up, I was comparable to an ant. But now, after months of cultivating and training within the space in my weapon body, I'm finally strong again. Though I can't be stronger than Lucia, at the very least, I'll be her equal. Her body might be overwhelmingly more powerful than mine, but I should be on par with her with the thousands of techniques I know! Or at least that's how it should be.

"Eh?" Lucia tilted her head to the side, propping my weapon body up on her shoulder. "You sure you don't want Puppers to help you? You might last a little longer if he does."

Today's after-dinner spar with Lucia has, once again, been a complete loss for me. It's not fair! She's only adept in three techniques: Breaking Blade, the Steady Mountain Footwork, and her Armor of Slaughter. But no matter what I try, I can't win. The weight of her sword let's her win in any direct collisions. Her Armor of Slaughter reacts faster than she can, blocking any sneak attacks. Feints don't work on her for a similar reason. The few times I manage to scratch her, her wounds heal in a few seconds. Though an attack fully infused with qi can pierce her armor, the speed of the strike slows down, and if she grabs my weapon within that time, I immediately lose because nothing can escape from her grip. She's like a towering mountain; how do you fight a mountain? Truly, her body was blessed by the earth. An ordinary person has no hopes of matching up to her, magician or not.

As her weapon spirit, I will never be able to pass her, only able to grow alongside her. That's under normal conditions. Before, I was stronger than her because she wasn't my original owner, but finding a new master that's stronger than Lucia to surpass her is impossible. Which leaves one other method: enchantments. Unfortunately, the only divine enchanter I know just so happens to be this high elf who's spectating on the side. I say it's unfortunate because a long time ago, Roland kidnapped her with my help. Did I mention that every time Roland kidnapped a child, I'd be forced to play the antagonistic role? After the child was thoroughly terrorized by me, Roland would swoop in like a savior, elevating his existence in their eyes.

So it's safe to say Marilyn despises me. Elves have great memories despite their long lifespans. You think they'd forget things that happened over fifty years ago, but they don't. "And history repeats itself," Marilyn said, clapping her hands. "The spirit gets whipped by its master."

"Hey! Don't make fun of Durandal. He's trying his best." Lucia frowned. Don't you understand that your sincere concern hurts a lot more than being insulted by an elf? Yes, I'm trying my best, but my best is not enough. "In the upcoming fights, I'm going to let him fight for me, so he can rebuild his confidence."

"Mm." Marilyn smiled and nodded at Lucia. "I never thought I'd enchant a weapon spirit that once imprisoned me. Now that I've seen how you use a sword and how he fights, would you like to begin?"

"Yes, please!" Lucia nodded. She had wanted to enchant me after I reached the peak of the divine realm for a chance to break into the legendary realm, but Marilyn had crushed that hope. Unless Marilyn broke through to the legendary realm, all her enchantments would only operate within the divine realm. There would be no chance of me breaking through, so Lucia decided to upgrade me right away. This won't be my first time being upgraded, but Marilyn was going to wipe the slate clean before applying better enchantments. Maybe after being enchanted again, I'll uncover a new skill. I thought I'd gain a new ability after breaking through to the divine realm, but I didn't.

"Ah! But can you enchant my socks first?" Lucia asked. "I want to see the process done on Puppers before you do it to Durandal."

Marilyn raised an eyebrow. "Sure," she said. "But you know my enchantments never fail, right? Whether I enchant Puppers first or Durandal, there'll be no difference."

"That's great and all," Lucia said and tilted her head, "but I wasn't worried about failure. I just want to make sure you don't touch them in inappropriate places during the process." She nodded twice and placed her hands on her hips.

Marilyn coughed. "Inappropriate places? Like where?"

"Like their penises," Lucia said with a straight face. Luckily, Ilya had covered Mirta's ears before Lucia had answered. That demon girl really can read Lucia like an open book.

Marilyn coughed again. A strange expression appeared on her face. "A little touch can't hurt."

"No touch!" Lucia snarled and bared her teeth.

Marilyn took a step back. "I was joking," she said and raised her hands into the air. "There will be no inappropriate touching during the process. In fact, I won't even have to make contact with their spirit bodies. There's no reason to get so … prickly."

Lucia's tail deflated. "Oh. Okay." She nodded and handed over a pair of socks with paw prints on them. Why was Ilya inspecting Lucia's feet? Was she counting Lucia's toes?

Marilyn's nose wrinkled, but she accepted them gracefully. "What would you like enchanted on them? Speed? Durability?"

"Can you make them softer?" Lucia asked, her eyes shining like little stars. "And make them fluffier too."

"Softer? Fluffier?" Marilyn asked and raised an eyebrow. She glanced at Pup—Gae Bulg, who seemed to be crying in a corner of the room. "Are you sure?"

"I'm absolutely positive!" Lucia said while bobbing her head up and down.

Marilyn made another strange expression. "Well, here goes."

A series of runes flew into the air and encircled Marilyn's body. I've seen this process thousands of times, performed by myself during my period of isolation. Of course, I've only seen a success happen once. I don't see how Marilyn's actions were any different from mine back then, but apparently they were. A few moments later, there were some flashing runes on the surface of the socks, and Gae Bulg's fur coat seemed to become more voluminous and glossy.

Lucia put her socks back on. "It worked!" she said and closed her eyes while wiggling her toes. "Great! Now do Durandal."

Marilyn chuckled and stared at me. "Do you want him to be softer and fluffier as well?"

Please no.

***

Guess who else has been upgraded to be softer and fluffier and better in every single way!? Not Durandal! Me! Well, the ribbon on my tail was enhanced to be softer and fluffier, not myself, sadly. But Durandal also got an all-around upgrade. Before, his weight limit capped at 35 tons. Now, he can go up to 70 tons; that's a 100% increase! I thought it was a 200% increase, but Ilya corrected me. Not only that, but Durandal claims he's no longer directionally challenged. Can you believe that? I can't, and I won't let him test it because we'll get lost.

"Now don't forget what you said to me," Ilya Number Two's grandmother said. "You said you'd help me beat up Cain if I enhanced your items."

"That's right! I'll definitely forget it though, so you have to remind me when the time comes." I've accepted I have a weak memory, which is why I started a diary recently. Ilya's trying to teach me how to read and write, but it's tough. So I just draw pictures of the events that happen. I'm an excellent artist if I may say so myself.

"Maybe you'll get the chance to today," Ilya Number Two's grandmother said. "I wish you the best of luck during the competition. Be sure to take care of Mirta for me."

"Will do! Let's go, Ilya Number One and Two." Today's the day of the Godking's Brawl. None of that preliminary crap that didn't really count for anything. Well, it let Ilya Number One and Two compete, so I guess it did count for something after all.

Ilya nodded and grabbed Ilya Number Two's hand. "Do you know the format for the competition, Lucia?" Nope! "Of course you don't, why'd I even ask? So the appropriate follow-up questions are, do you want to know and are you going to pay attention if I tell you?"

"I want to know, but no guarantees on paying attention." I can't promise things I'm not sure about. It's unethical.

Ilya sighed. "Well, I'll monologue on the way there, I suppose," she said and shook her head. "The competition is not a normally structured tournament where people face off one against one and half the people drop off after a round. A lucky person can rise higher than someone they're weaker than in that scenario. The brawl is a ranking system, not a luck-based system. Most likely, there's going to be a test to determine everyone's general levels of ability. Then, the climbing portion will begin. The people at the bottom of the ranking list will be allowed to challenge anyone above them and claim their spot, causing everyone else to drop one place. At least, that's the format the brawl's followed for the last five times."

"Then what's the point of seeded positions? Like our reward from the preliminary." Don't tell me it was really, really pointless. But I wouldn't be surprised if that annoying man gave a hundred people a useless reward.

"People in the seeded positions start higher up," Ilya said. "They get a tiny bonus on their evaluation test. The main advantage is they need to fight less to climb higher. After all, everyone partaking in the brawl is a talent. Fighting against someone will drain your energy. The less people you have to fight, the easier it becomes."

"So you're saying my battle plan should be to take last place, then challenge the first place person before the competition ends? When would the competition end?" Well, I'm not going to do that even though that plan makes a lot of sense. I have my promise with Al.... Why do I keep forgetting his name? The crown prince. I have to keep my promise with him for that sweet, sweet reward!

"The competition ends when no one wishes to issue a challenge within thirty minutes of the last fight," Ilya said. "The longest brawl took place forty years ago and went on for three days."

Three days? That must've been super boring to watch. And we've arrived at the coliseum just as Ilya finished explaining things, how convenient. I wonder what the evaluation system's going to be like. Wouldn't I just get first place again if it's anything like the preliminaries? That annoying man wouldn't do things to make my life more difficult, would he? Well, it doesn't matter since I already have a plan!

"That's Lucia Fluffytail, watch out for her."

"I heard she attacked Cain during the preliminaries. Is she crazy?"

"Did you know she's afraid of water?"

"There isn't even a Fluffytail family in the whole beastkin kingdom. I checked."

"If you want to distract her, throw acorns at her or bribe her with hot chocolate."

Why are so many people talking about me!? It's a good feeling though. The first step to becoming a legend is to have plenty of people spread rumors about you. I should hire some bards to sing good things about me all the time.

"That's Ilya Pentorn over there. She's the world's youngest sixth-circle magician. She's only fourteen! I heard all the families are planning on sending suitors to her coming-of-age ceremony."

"So what if she's a sixth-circle magician? She's the first person to ever cast a sixth-circle chaos spell. Even Cain's never done that."

Hey! Focus, rumor spreaders. I'm the legend here, not Ilya. Jeez.

"And that little elf girl over there, she's Mirta, Marilyn's granddaughter. You all know high elf Marilyn, right? She's the only person able to place divine enchantments on items. She dotes on her granddaughter a lot, so whatever you do, you can't hurt Mirta."

Even Ilya Number Two gets rumors spread about her!? I should stuff these traitors into a bag and hide them away from the public. They're side characters; side characters should stop stealing the main character's limelight. And the main character is me, just in case anyone didn't know.

Gah! Ilya poked me. "Are you thinking weird things again, Lucia? Did you hear my question?"

"Nope, wasn't listening."

"I asked if you saw Snow. That's him over there, right?" Ilya pointed at a beautiful bunnykin woman. Man. Cross-dressing bunnykin man! It's Snow! He really showed his face!

"Snow Flopsy! You're dead!" The bunnykin's eyes widened as I charged at him. "Unrelenting Path of Slaughter: Breaking Fist!"

"W-wait!" the bunnykin shouted. Wow, his voice really turned much more feminine. Shouldn't it have gone down in pitch instead of up? Ah? I missed? "You have the wrong person! I'm not Snow! My name is Reena!"

Huh? Did he really think I'd fall for something as stupid as that? "Unrelenting Path of Slaughter: Breaking Tail! Breaking Kick! Breaking Fist! Stop dodging, damn it!"

"Please, stop! I'm really not Snow!" the bunnykin said with tears in his eyes. "This is the seventh time I've been mistaken for him!"

Caught him! "So you're saying you're not Snow and happen to look exactly like him?"

"That's right," the bunnykin said, nodding his head. "Can you please let go of my ears?"

Is this bunnykin really not Snow? Huh, there's no Adam's apple. Did he get rid of that? "Let me check something."

"What are you—!?"

What...? There's really nothing down there. Is he, no, is she really not Snow? "You're really, really not Snow?"

"I, I can't get married anymore," the bunnykin said and hung her head. "I've been tainted."

"Nonsense, I washed my hands before I left the inn. I'm perfectly clean." At least I think I washed my hands. I'm pretty sure I did.... But how does Snow have a female doppelganger!? And she's wearing sandals without socks, so unless Snow abandoned Bouncykins, his Adam's apple, and his penis, then she's really not him.

***

"Hey, Durandal, use your strange sorcery of reading beastkin like open books and figure out if she's really Snow or not."

I'm afraid my powers of reading beastkin only works on Lucia. But just by inspecting this woman's aura, she's nothing like Snow, and there's no signs of Bouncykins coming into contact with her. Weapon spirits are pretty sensitive to each other's auras. In fact, I can sense at least thirteen other weapon spirits in the nearby vicinity, not including Pup—Gae. "She's not Snow, Lucia. You should probably let go of her ears before they break."

"That's right," Lucia said and released the poor bunnykin's ears. "Don't even think about turning into Snow or I'll kill you."

That's an unreasonable request. Is it just me, or has Lucia become a lot more unbridled after becoming a divine warrior? I suspect it has something to do with the strange path she took. Unrelenting Path of Slaughter..., I don't even have to wonder what she did with a name like that. Slaughter implies she won her fights effortlessly. Winning fight after fight after fight must've boosted her confidence to extreme levels bordering on arrogance.

"I, I understand!" the bunnykin said. "I won't even think of changing my gender!"

"Good," Lucia said and nodded twice, sticking her chest out. "Now get out of my face. You're making me feel inferior."

The poor bunnykin scampered away while Ilya and Mirta approached us. "That wasn't Snow?" Ilya asked. "Are you sure he didn't just use a gender transformation spell?"

Lucia stiffened. "Does that exist?" she ran after the poor bunnykin and tackled her to the ground, grabbing her by the ears and dragging her back to us.

"You didn't let me answer," Ilya said and sighed. "There's no such thing as a gender transformation spell." She looked at the crying bunnykin. "And she doesn't have any traces of magic on her. I thought you were sensitive to mana."

"Oh," Lucia said and released her unfortunate prey. "You can go."

"For real this time?" the sniffling bunnykin asked. "Or are you going to tackle me again?"

"If I said you can go, then you can go!" Lucia shook her fist at the woman, causing her ears to stiffen. No matter how I see it, she looks exactly like Cottontail. Could she be related? But before I could ask, she ran away.

"Hey, Lucia. Just because she isn't Snow, that doesn't mean she's not related to him in some way, shape, or form. You should probably—"

Lucia disappeared before I could finish my sentence. An ear-piercing scream filled the air, and the crowd parted as Lucia dragged back the sobbing bunnykin. "This is abuse! Guards! Guards! Somebody help me!"

"Whew, she almost got away." Lucia wiped her brow with the back of her arm and deposited the limp woman by her feet. "It's a good thing I caught her in time."

The bunnykin sniffled. "W-why are you doing this to me?"

"So you might not be Snow, but how are you related to him?" Lucia asked and placed her hands on her hips. "And don't say you're not. Bunnies can have up to a dozen babies per litter! I bet you're related to him in some way, shape, or form."

"At the very least, you're related to Cottontail Flopsy, correct?"

"C-Cottontail's my grandmother," the bunnykin said. "I'm Reena Flopsy."

"Then you're Snow's sister, cousin?" Lucia asked, tilting her head to the side.

"N-no," Reena said, shaking her head. "I might be his half-cousin? I don't know the right term, but my grandfathers are completely different from Snow's."

Well, that's new. Cottontail had more than just Roland as her lover? It's a good thing Roland's dead or there'd be a massive shitstorm. But, wow, I never thought Roland would be cuckolded. That's..., wow. Should I be angry at Cottontail? But she's already dead.... Ah, forget it. The heavens will handle it. But still, wow. Why would she...?

"What!?" Lucia shouted with bulging eyes. It looks like she figured it out. "You—"

"Not so loud, please!" Reena said and covered Lucia's mouth with her hands. She flinched and drew back after realizing what she had done. "I, I didn't mean to do that. I was nervous."

"Then are you working together with Snow?" Lucia asked, tilting her head.

She's not going to tell you even if she was, you know?

Reena shook her head. "I'm not! I swear."

"I can't trust you," Lucia said. "You look too much like Snow."

"The gates are opening!" someone shouted. It seemed like the Godking's Brawl was about to start. Lucia said she'd let me and Puppers fight by ourselves during this competition. I'd like to see how I compare to the talent of this generation. ...This is not the old bullying the young. It's, hmm, teaching? Yes, it's teaching. As a member of the older generation, I have to teach these punching bags—err, star pupils how to fight properly.

"A-are you going to let me go?" Reena asked, tears in her eyes.

"Nope! You're coming with us," Lucia said and looped her arm around Reena's waist. "Keep your friends close and your enemies even closer. You're sticking to me like a third arm. Let's go, Ilya Number One and Two. We have a legendary beast core to claim!"

"There's only one beast core for first place," Ilya said.

"*I* have a legendary beast core to claim!" Lucia said. "You two can, uh, struggle for second and third, I guess."

Ilya sighed and shook her head before entering the coliseum. She might be an annoying brat, but she's sensible. I'm glad Lucia met someone like her while I was asleep. Who knows how much more differently Lucia would've turned out if she hadn't? Lucia told me a little about her experience while I was asleep, but I have a feeling she omitted a lot of details. Puppers told me she was indistinguishable from a wild beast when he first met her. I was afraid Lucia would never be able to trust someone again after Snow's betrayal, but I'm glad my fears didn't come true.

***

"The Godking's Brawl will begin shortly." What's with that annoying man and his need to be in the sky all the time? The coliseum changed a lot from its previous two appearances. Instead of a grassy meadow or ruined flatland, it looked more like a traditional coliseum with a giant elevated circular platform in the center. On the arena platform, there was a little statue of a fat man sitting cross-legged.

"There are three hundred and sixty of you competing today, and if you look along the walls of the coliseum, you'll see a matching number of cushions. Take a seat."

Reena had stopped struggling, so it was easy to carry her along. I dropped her onto the spot next to me which had the number fifty-eight on it. Ilya Number One and Two sat beside us. All the competitors looked like a long line of ants pressed up against a wall. At the number one spot, that lionkin who hated acorn stew was sitting with his head in the air. He saw me staring and sneered at me. Really? I kicked your ass in the preliminary, you heretic. I'll do it again in the real thing.

"Number one, approach the center of the stage," the man in the sky said. He wasn't even going to explain what was going to happen? At least Ilya described the process fairly well. How did it go again? Eh, I forgot. "Place your hand on the statue's head and insert your mana and qi. Those of you who took the preliminary should be familiar with this process. Instead of making the statue light up, it'll spit out an exact number for the leaderboards." A board appeared in the sky next to the floating man. He really has a thing for boards and numbers, huh? I know how to read numbers since Ilya taught me! But names are still a bit too difficult.

The lionkin approached the statue and grabbed its head. He grunted before shouting, causing the statue to light up. "First, my mana!" he said, and a bright, neon-colored thirty appeared on the statue's chest. "Then, my qi!" He roared, and the number jumped from thirty to six hundred and twenty. At least, I'm pretty sure that's six hundred and twenty. No guarantees!

Then, unreadable—to me—characters appeared on the leaderboard followed by 620 and the number one. The lionkin nodded before walking back to the cushion. "Wait," the man in the sky said. "Don't sit just yet. Seat number two, approach the statue."

A scrawny man with a beard hobbled up to the platform. He placed his hand on the statue and inserted his mana, which made the number 540 appear. Then he inserted his qi, and the number jumped up to 1,140! The lionkin glared at the scrawny, bearded man, but the skinny person was unfazed. He's also a bit green. Green? Like he's covered in mana? Is that a disguise!? It's Snow, isn't it!? For now, I'll put this person on my kill-if-encountered list. Huh? I'm not a murderer. This is a justified list! I don't know how to justify it, but it's totally moral because I said so.

I wonder what the numbers mean though. The calculating system should make sense, right? Well, I'm sure my goals will be accomplished regardless. After the scrawny man, no one else broke four digits until Daniel. His mana score was a whopping 1,150, but he didn't even try inserting any qi inside. Maybe he didn't have any.

"I think I figured it out," Ilya said.

What's there to figure out?

"Zero to a hundred represent circles one to three. One hundred to six hundred are circles four to six. And six hundred to twelve hundred should be in between six and seven circles." Ilya nodded to herself and smiled.

How do you figure something like that out? It's because of Daniel, isn't it? Since he's a seventh-circle magician, it makes sense. Maybe she researched the other competitors and figured out their power levels and compared them to the numbers appearing. Damn, I'm smart. That's totally how Ilya did it. This is what happens when a squirrelkin consumes a legendary bone of focus! If we could put our minds to things, we'd rule the world. It's a shame acorns are so darn distracting though.

"But does that mean anything to us?" Reena asked.

"Of course," Ilya said. "Know your enemy and know yourself to increase your chances of victory."

"Seat number fifty-seven, this is the third time I'm calling you," the man in the sky said. "Damnit, Lucia! Get up here."

Oh, fifty-seven was me. I totally knew that. Alright, secret plan, begin! "First, I insert my mana!" Ah? The statue's turning darker? Eh!? 2,400!? But what's this little dash next to the number? My mana's that amazing? Doesn't this ruin my plan!?

"Negative 2,400…," Ilya said. "That means your number is lower than zero, Lucia!"

How!? How do I have less mana than none!? Well, forget it. I'm definitely getting last place with this. Goal one, success! "And now my qi!" But I didn't actually send in any

438

qi, I just pretended to. Eh!? "Negative 4,800!?" But I didn't even send in any qi! "This thing's broken!"

"Oh?" the man in the sky asked. "How unfortunate. It worked for everyone else. I guess the statue just doesn't like people who attack the host of the competition. Stand off to the side, please. Seat number fifty-eight, approach the statue."

So I was rigged to fail regardless! I see how it is, Mr. Man in the Sky. Even though I may have wanted last place, I wanted to achieve that by myself, not by underhanded means! How dare he help me? I'm going to punish him after this competition's over.

After I went, Reena scored a 400 combined total. Ilya scored 600 and 0. Ilya Number Two scored 50 and 300. I didn't keep track of anybody else and directly claimed my last-place cushion. "So, Lucia," Durandal asked. "Why did you want last place again?"

"For the heroic story!" Obviously. What makes a more riveting tale? Lucia Fluffytail claimed first place by an overwhelming amount and kept it? Or Lucia Fluffytail, the girl with zero talent, struggled against all odds from the very bottom to the top, beating talent after talent with her persistence and determination? The bards are going to have a field day with an underdog story! A peerless genius can't attract the hearts of the commoners; even the Godking struggled to the top as a common villager. "And there's that deal with the crown prince I have to keep. Just remember, when you fight the princes, you have to cripple them but not kill them. That's what he requested of me."

"So he's using you as a tool to secure the throne," Durandal said with a nod. "That makes sense. And what did he promise you?"

"A noble title, territory, and a mansion with lots of servants! We're going to live there and have lots of children in the future!" This deal with the crown prince, it's the first step towards my dream!

***

I'm not sure how I feel about Lucia's request to cripple the princes. But I suppose that doesn't matter, does it? A weapon spirit shouldn't feel. We're tools meant to serve. I guess that makes Pup—Gae Bulg and me bad weapon spirits, huh? Well, I'm not sure if Gae even counts anymore since he was converted into a sock spirit. He's become a lot more sensitive and touchy. It's understandable. I'll let Gae deal with the competitors who aren't princes since he used to be royalty and all.

"The princes," Gae Bulg said as he materialized next to me. "Let me fight them."

…Or not. "You know what to do?"

"Lan lived a terrible life in the royal palace," Gae Bulg said. "He had no talent in magic. His mother was a commoner. He was forced to play a fool in order to survive. The years of stress built up, causing him to become paranoid. After a while, he refused to see his own mother because he thought she would kill him. I'm not sure if he even trusted me." Gae Bulg ground his teeth together. "The princes are the ones to blame, especially Algar. Crippling them should make Lan rest easy on the other side."

"Ah, we're not fighting Algar," Lucia said, smacking Gae Bulg's back. "He's the future emperor and the key to my dreams. If you dare ruin my dreams, I'm going to demote you to a single sock spirit."

Didn't Lucia buy a bunch of spirit seeds before the competition started? "Lucia, what happened to the spirit seeds you bought before that you wanted to plant into all of your clothes?"

Lucia wrinkled her nose. "All of them were men! So I threw them away." She hung her head. "That was my favorite set of underwear too. What a waste. Isn't there a way to determine their gender beforehand?"

"No. And female spirits are quite rare compared to males." The only woman spirit who I knew was Vera. And Roland had a lot of weapon spirits. I'm not sure why that is; I never really thought about it before. Ilya would probably know. But that's not my problem; I have to focus on sharpening my technique.

"I'm going to meditate for a bit." It's been a long while since I've fought someone other than Lucia. I've been secretly watching some mages cast spells; I think I can deal with them if I take advantage of the flaws in their defense. A battlemage may prove to be more difficult to defeat if he's able to cast while moving. I'll use this time to simulate a few battles since it seems like it'll be a while before everyone else finishes. "Tell me when the fighting begins."

I don't know how much time passed, but Lucia summoned me out of my weapon body. "Is it starting?"

"Yup!" Lucia said. "The last person just had their numbers checked."

Cain's voice echoed through the coliseum. "Now that the general ranking has concluded, the next portion, the brawl, will begin. The rules are the same as the previous brawls. For those of you who don't know them, ah, I really don't want to explain." He sighed. "But I'll do it anyway. Pick someone and fight them. If you win, you take their position on the leaderboard and they take yours. You can fight as many times as you'd like. To speed things up, up to ten battles can happen at once. Killing is not allowed; feel free to severely injure each other though. The competition ends ten minutes after all the platforms are unoccupied. Fights end when one side is incapable of fighting or surrenders." He yawned and snapped his fingers, causing the circular platform with the statue to split into ten separate pieces. "Remember what you're fighting for. There are rewards—actual ones—for the people in the top ten. I'm also establishing a clan. Anyone in the top hundred can join."

A few people murmured to each other, but Cain ignored them. "With that being said, let the brawl begin." He looked around, but no one moved. "If none of you want to fight, we can end this in a neat ten minutes and have it be the shortest Godking's Brawl in history."

"It's your turns to shine, Puppers and Durandal!" Lucia hopped onto the largest platform. "I, Lucia Fluffytail, challenge the fifth prince of the Ravenwood Empire! I forgot your name, but I'm challenging you! Get your royal ass up here."

A man with a scowling expression stood up. He wore a full suit of armor with chainmail underneath the plate. Attached to his back was a massive greatsword. Was that the weapon spirit, Balmung? So that old fart was still around.

I looked at Gae Bulg. "Can you take both of them?"

Gae Bulg grimaced. "It'll be difficult. The fifth prince is a battlemage; though, he's not as strong as Algar. And Balmung is at the peak of spirit warrior."

"Then I'll fight Balmung. I can use him as a benchmark to see how much I've grown." Should I use a sword? My last duel with Balmung ended in a narrow victory on my part. But I've taken a liking to the spear since I've met Lucia. "Lucia, pass me a spear."

"And me," Gae Bulg said.

"Here you go," Lucia said and tossed two spears towards us. "Luckily for you two, I managed to pick these up on the way here." Where did she get them? These aren't low-class goods that you find for sale in a street stall.

"Ah!" someone from the crowd, a dwarf, shouted. "My family heirlooms! How does she have them!?"

"Lucia...?" Did she...?

"Found them on the floor," Lucia said with a cough. "Do your best! The enemy approaches."

"So you're the one who killed Bryant and Lan," the fifth prince said as he drew the greatsword on his back. "Balmung."

A man with flaming red hair appeared beside the prince. One of his eyes was closed with a diagonal scar running over it. Weapon spirit injuries healed by themselves unless the spirit chose to keep their scars as a sign of pride. It makes no sense to me, but that's just the type of spirit Balmung is. "Durandal," Balmung said. "It's been a while. Is that a spear?"

"No, it's a really flat sword. If you had both your eyes, you'd be able to tell."

"This injury is a reminder to myself. And today, I'll reclaim my honor. Don't make an excuse after you lose." Balmung raised his arms, and a two-handed sword appeared out of nowhere.

"Prepare yourself, murderer," the fifth prince said and pointed his sword at Lucia … who was sitting down and sipping on a cup of hot chocolate.

"Ah," Lucia said and blinked. "Think of me as the final boss. You have to get through my underlings before you can fight me. Don't forget to cripple him, Puppers."

"I won't," Gae Bulg said. His eyes narrowed as he pointed his spear at the fifth prince. I raised my spear and pointed it at Balmung's throat. Balmung steadied his sword in his hands. The fifth prince mirrored Balmung's stance. We stared at each other. …And continued to stare. When does the fight start?

"Ah, that's my job as host, isn't it?" Cain asked. "Let the first fight of the Godking's Brawl begin."

***

Go, Durandal! Go, Puppers! When I was in the army, I always dreamed about having a weapon spirit. Now I have two, and the feeling is just as I suspected. It's amazing! I don't even have to lift a finger; all I have to do is give Durandal and Puppers some qi, and they can do all the fighting for me. Ah, you've really come far, Lucia. Good things really do happen to good people. The world is just.

"Durandal!" The red-haired weapon spirit seemed to know Durandal. Well, it makes sense considering the princes are royalty and royalty tends to have access to the best stuff. But why is he so weak? "This is impossible! Ninety years ago, we were evenly matched. You, how!?"

Durandal didn't answer, stabbing repeatedly with his spear. His movements were so graceful, so refined, every thrust aimed with precision. ...So why the heck couldn't he teach me to fight like that!? I want to be refined and graceful too! Ah, I broke my cup from squeezing it too hard. It's a good thing only the handle shattered or else I would've wasted precious hot chocolate.

Anyway, how's Puppers doing against the fifth prince? Despite Puppers being a side character totally eclipsed by my brilliance, he's actually not that bad of a fighter. He fights almost exactly like Durandal does, but he shouts and grunts a lot more. Occasionally, he also attacks with his tail and teeth—benefits of being a wolfkin spirit. His attacks, even though they follow the same movements, are a lot fiercer too. But there's still some elegance in his savagery. How come I'm the only one who fights like a brute? Mm, well, if Durandal fights like a girl and I fight like a guy, then it works out in the end.

"You, coward!" the fifth prince said while gritting his teeth. "Stop hiding behind your weapon spirits and fight me like a warrior!"

"Why would I do that?" Seriously? What's the point of a weapon spirit if they don't fight for you? I worked hard to be this lazy! "Besides, you have one too. Ah, watch out."

The fifth prince screamed as Puppers' spear entered his shoulder. I tried warning him, but he didn't listen. Oh wells.

Puppers body tensed as he roared. "Path of the…!" But the next instant, his voice lowered and I had to strain my ears to hear him. "…Sock. Explosion!"

The fifth prince screamed again as his arm was blown off of his body, leaving a gaping wound where his shoulder used to be. The prince's weapon spirit shouted, "Zeig!" and disengaged from Durandal. I thought Durandal was going to take advantage of that moment of weakness, but he didn't. Well, that's Durandal for you; he only likes beating people who have all their attention focused on him.

"How dare you, Gae Bulg!" The prince's weapon spirit rushed over to the prince's side. He took one look at the prince's injury before raising his head towards the sky and shouting, "We surrender! Someone, please, heal the prince!"

The prince's weapon spirit glared at me like I had stabbed a helpless puppy. A portal opened in the sky and a human dropped next to the prince. The human cast a spell that stopped the bleeding, but it didn't look like the prince's arm would regrow anytime soon. That should be enough for Algar, right? I almost feel like a bad person now, but I'm just abiding by the rules of the world. For someone to gain something, other people have to lose something. It's harsh, but it's true. Resources like land and food and gold are limited; there's only so much that can go around. To achieve my dream, I'll crush any opposition!

"I challenge the fourth prince! Come, avenge your brother and win back the royal family's honor. Unless you're too scared!" If I don't provoke the princes enough, they're definitely not going to fight me. Which is why I'm acting uncharacteristically arrogant. It's actually really fun to be this free without worrying about any consequences. When I was a slave in the army, even looking at the lowliest soldier the wrong way could get me beaten. If I insulted the princes back then like I'm doing now, I'd be lashed over a thousand times until I died.

The competition ground fell silent as a few of the competitors turned to stare at a man dressed in a white robe. He was sitting on the cushion with the number 200 on it. Was he the prince? And didn't the man in the sky say ten battles could be fought at the same time? Why's everyone just watching? Mm, well, that doesn't matter to me. After Durandal and Puppers beat all the princes, I'll claim first place and take a nap.

"I accept your challenge," the man in white said. It looks like he was the fourth prince, but he doesn't look like Algar or Lan or even Bryant. How can siblings look so different from each other? I mean, look at Snow and Reena. They're practically the same person. And Snow didn't show up to the competition unless he's in a disguise. I suspect he's the scrawny man with the beard that scored 1,140 on the leaderboards since I couldn't see anyone else with a layer of mana covering their body.

"Why are you helping Lan's killer, Gae Bulg?" the fourth prince asked. "Regardless, I will teach you the difference between a warrior and a mage. Pay for the lesson with your life." He held out his hand, and a staff appeared on his palm. He held his other hand out, and a shield covered his whole arm. "Ancile, come on out."

A bulky weapon spirit, holding two tower shields that looked more like a pair of massive doors, materialized in front of the fourth prince. The prince retreated to the edge of the platform and chanted while his weapon spirit glared at Durandal and Puppers. Durandal and Puppers exchanged glances. Could they communicate with each other through their minds? If they could, then they've definitely been gossiping about me behind my back!

Without saying anything, Puppers charged at the shield spirit while Durandal circled around to approach the prince. I did the very important job of lighting a bonfire to warm up some of my chocolate since magic tools weren't allowed. A heating spell would've been nice.

***

It's time to test whether or not Bouncykins' words were true. A warrior can't fight a magician even if the magician is at a lower tier of strength. Lucia's already disproved that claim, but, quite frankly, Lucia's special. She's blessed by the earth with an outrageous ability to recover her qi in the matter of seconds as long as she's on the ground. Her physical strength is enormous, and her ability to regenerate wounds is ridiculous. Sometimes, I wonder if she really knows how strong she is compared to everyone else. Even if Lucia hadn't found me, she'd still be a monster after discovering qi.

Compared to Lucia, I'm weak. The only aspects I'm better than her in are experience, technique, and concentration, but her instincts are comparable to my experience and technique while her lack of focus is fixed by consuming bones. It's fitting, I suppose. A weapon spirit shouldn't be stronger than their master; otherwise, how could they be called master? Now that I'm weaker, I'm really going to miss the days I could bully her. Well, I'll have to make do with humiliating her opponents instead.

"Fire, engulf my enemy. Flare!" The fourth prince summoned a sheet of fire which obscured him from view. Meanwhile, Gae Bulg clashed against Ancile, using his flexibility to fight Ancile's stiffness. Even though Ancile was bigger, Gae Bulg was holding the advantage in strength. Well, that's to be expected when one's a divine warrior spirit while the other's a spirit warrior spirit. As for these meager flames, a simple layer of qi around my body is enough to let me pass safely. I don't have the Armor of Slaughter like Lucia, but the concept is similar.

The fourth prince's smiling face greeted me when I passed through the flames. "Rise!" he said and tapped the butt of his staff against the ground. Pointed spears of earth shot out of the ground towards my legs and chest.

This level of magic isn't enough to stop me. Steps of the Phantom: Illusionary Grace! If Lucia's Steady Mountain Footwork is the embodiment of strength and stability, then the Swift Phantom Footwork is the embodiment of speed and flexibility. It's actually extremely similar to the footwork Snow uses, the same one that doesn't seem to work on Lucia.

The fourth prince's smile widened. He stomped his foot down. "Grease." A layer of light spread out from his foot, coating the arena ground.

"Ah!" Lucia shouted. Was she in danger? "My hot chocolate's slipping away! What the heck is this?" I'm disappointed in myself for even questioning Lucia's safety. But as her weapon spirit, I couldn't help but turn my eyes away from the fourth prince when she had shouted—that little motion cost me. An invisible force crashed into my spear, but I had no way to support myself after the floor became as slick as oil. "Whoa, Durandal was sent flying!"

Please don't state the obvious, Lucia. It was your fault in the first place. While I steadied myself, the fourth prince pointed his staff at me. "Thunder, trap the weasel. Lightning Cage!"

A thunderbolt rained down from the clear sky, striking the ground beside me. An instant later, a crackling cage of white lightning formed around me. I tested its strength by sending out a bit of qi. I could escape, but not without suffering some injuries.

"Fire and earth, combine your strengths. Magma Pillar!"

Heat bubbled out of the ground beneath me, and I jumped through the lightning cage. The lightning clung to me, shrinking while dancing against my skin. It felt like hundreds of snakes biting me, but staying inside would've been a lot worse. The pain isn't an issue—how is he reading every single one of my moves? It feels like I'm fighting while two steps behind. It's upsetting to admit, but a warrior is predictable, a magician is not.

The fourth prince grinned like a savage. "Darkness, roam free. Pain Amplification! Aggravate Wounds! Mana Detonation!"

The lightning circling around my body turned black, and the shocking feeling increased by at least tenfold. Everywhere the lightning touched, blood poured out as my skin was lacerated. Before I could do anything, the lightning exploded, creating craters in my flesh. How unpleasant. So this is the difference between a magician and a warrior? But I'm no longer an ordinary warrior. While the prince laughed and chanted another spell, my injuries were already healing. The wounded flesh wriggled and reconnected like mating worms.

What would Lucia do in my situation? Her attacks seize the flow of the battle, building momentum nonstop, forcing her opponent to defend without giving them a chance to strike back. It's unrefined with no thought behind it, but it works. "Breaking Spear!"

Qi, shaped like a spear, flew out of my weapon as I thrust it forward. Lucia should have enough qi to support me if I let out an onslaught of spear qi. "A hundred Breaking Spears! No, a thousand!"

"Ah! That's clearly plagiarizing my super-secret final technique!" Lucia said, but I ignored her. I lost the initiative when the prince greased the floor; I have to gain it back and force him into a corner. He won't be able to plan as many steps ahead if the pressure's great enough.

"Earth, protect me. Diamond Wall!"

My spear qi crashed and dispersed against the transparent wall that rose out of the ground, but I didn't stop. I refuse to believe Lucia's qi is weaker than a sixth-circle magician's hastily formed wall! Dozens, then hundreds, of qi spears flowed like waves, crashing and disappearing against the diamond shield. Cracks formed along its surface with every strike, and Gae Bulg and Ancile stopped their struggles to stare.

"Earth, protect me. Diamond Wall! Diamond Wall! Diamond Wall!" The fourth prince shouted and slammed his staff against the ground repeatedly. "If one isn't enough, then I'll summon two! If two aren't enough, then I'll summon three! Give up! You'll run out of qi before I run out of mana. Your master's powering two of you."

"Ten thousand Breaking Spears!" I believe in Lucia's nonsensical strength! Even if she's powering both Gae Bulg and me, she'll last longer than the prince.

"R-ridiculous!" The fourth prince took a step back as the first two walls he summoned shattered. "You want to fight a war of attrition!? Bring it on!" He took out a potion and drank it before slamming his staff against the ground. "Earth, protect me. Diamond Wall!"

This might be the most pathetic fight I've ever participated in. But struggle is necessary for growth. My next fight against a magician won't be as shameful as this one; however, right now, I'm fighting for victory, not honor! If ten thousand Breaking Spears aren't enough, then I'll do twenty thousand. A war of attrition may be what Lucia's best at considering how many bones of strength she has lying around. What a foolish prince.

***

What happened to Durandal's graceful fighting style? He's devolved into, into..., well, something like me! He totally stole my super-secret final technique too! Ah, and he's using up a lot of qi. How come his qi spears are weaker than my qi blades? Shouldn't they be on the same strength if he's using my qi? Mm, I'll test a Breaking Blade on the diamond walls and see. "Breaking Blade!"

A red line flew out of my sword towards the fourth prince. It touched the diamond wall, and instead of crashing and dispersing against the surface like Durandal's attacks, my qi continued through it like a hot knife through butter. It went through the second wall, and third, and fourth, and, oh, there were only four walls. I don't understand why that was so difficult for Durandal to do. I know I'm stronger than him and Puppers combined, but the difference shouldn't be that great, right?

"Lucia?" Durandal stopped attacking. "I thought you weren't going to fight?"

I wasn't planning on it, but my curiosity got the better of me. "I was testing something."

"Oh," Durandal said and nodded as he put his spear on his back.

"Arron!" the shield spirit shouted. He pushed Puppers back in exchange for a wound and rushed over to the prince's side. My Breaking Blade didn't just cut through the diamond walls. Well, at least the prince is still alive, right? He's missing part of his arm and leg, but they'll grow back, I'm sure. The crown prince wanted me to injure his brothers enough to prevent them from taking the throne for at least three months. I'm not sure why he wanted three months, but an arm and a leg should take that long to grow back, right? Maybe the emperor's going to die in three months. Mm, well, that's not really my problem. I'm technically a criminal according to the Ravenwood Empire's laws since I ran away from the army. And killed two princes.

"This revenge for Lan," Puppers said as he approached me, "feels a bit too easy. The years of suffering Lan went through by these prince's hands…. He was powerless to fight back. I don't think he would've expected the person who killed him to avenge his injustices."

I'm not beating these princes for Lan's sake, but as long as Puppers is happy, I won't bother correcting him. "Next! I challenge the third prince of the Ravenwood Empire!"

Everyone in the crowd turned to stare at a man with a scraggly beard. He grimaced before standing up, approaching the stage. "Is there a reason you're targeting my brother's and me?" he asked as he climbed up. "Perhaps you're angry at the mistreatment of beastkin in the army. I know about your past. I think everyone here does."

For some reason, something about this prince's face makes me want to punch it. "I'm going to personally fight him. You two can rest for now." Puppers and Durandal nodded before standing behind me. "Let's start."

"Wait." The third prince held up one hand. "Let's talk before we fight. I can pardon all your crimes as long as you surrender right now. Swear loyalty to me, and—"

"Breaking Fist!" It's great how his guard was completely down. He still managed to avoid the punch to the face, but I clipped his shoulder as he retreated. As expected, he flew off the stage with a loud crash. Ah, that was super satisfying. What was he saying about pardoning my crimes? The crown prince already promised me that without any loyalty swearing required. "Next! Second prince of the Ravenwood Empire. I challenge you!"

A sharp-looking man wearing a blue robe with a popped collar appeared on the stage. Was that teleportation? Maybe it was a movement technique; I didn't sense any mana. "Hello, Lady Fluffytail," the second prince said and bowed. "You're challenging us princes because of my brother Algar, aren't you? There's no need to deny it. It's obvious my brother has a hand in this."

Algar didn't say I had to keep the deal a secret, but it was obvious he didn't want anyone else finding out. The second prince smiled at me—his face isn't as punchable as the third prince's. All the princes really do have different mothers, huh?

The second prince glanced at Algar. "Whatever Algar is offering you, I'll offer double."

"Really?"

"Really." The second prince clasped his hands behind his back. "I'm in charge of the empire's finances. Algar's in charge of the military. Who do you think has more wealth to spare?"

Does that mean I'll receive two times the land, two titles, and two mansions? "Deal!"

"Wait!" Algar shouted and ran onto the stage. "I can offer more!"

The second prince didn't even look at his brother. "Whatever he's going to offer now, I'll double it. You just have to cripple him instead of me. I imagine that shouldn't be a problem with your strength."

Will Algar offer even more now? I looked at him, and he gritted his teeth. A barrier went up around the three of us as he waved his hand. "No one can hear our conversation," Algar said. "I'm willing to give you a third of the empire's lands. Everything in it will be yours." He glared at the second prince and crossed his arms over his chest.

"Then that means he'll give me two-thirds?" Whoa. That's a lot more than what I expected, but I'll take it!

The second prince winced. "Two-thirds of the empire is a bit much," he said. "And I don't believe Algar has the ability to gift away a third of the empire. He's no good at politics. He might be capable of leading an army, but he'll make a terrible ruler. As soon as he gives you that land, the nobles will revolt." He smiled at his brother. "I, on the other hand, am more than capable of giving you a third of the land. I assure you there will be no issues with the transfer. Not only that, but I will send the best aides to help your land grow and prosper."

"Half the empire," Algar said. "So what if the nobles revolt? You and I are both capable of shutting them down by force."

"Half the empire is still doable," the second prince said, stepping ahead of Algar. He knelt on one knee and grabbed my hand. Is this how princesses are treated? I'm really liking this prince more than Algar. "And once again, I assure you there will be no issues on your end. Whatever Algar can do for you, I can do it better."

"I concede." Algar sighed and shook his head. "The only method I have now is to appeal to your honor. You and I made a deal. Are you willing to break it?"

"Breaking Fist!" Bye, Algar. I looked at the second prince. "When do I get my land?"

The second prince smiled at me. "As soon as my father dies and I become the emperor. A doctor determined he has three months left to live. It's a pleasure doing business with you; I concede this fight."

***

After Lucia concluded her deal with the second prince, she challenged Daniel, who was in first place, and won without a fight. It seemed like they had already dueled before with Lucia winning an overwhelming victory. The demon prince had directly surrendered and challenged the second place person, claiming his spot at the top of the list next to Lucia. Once that happened, the competition began in earnest, and everyone picked their opponents.

Lucia had pulled out a pillow and blanket, giving Gae Bulg and me the orders to take on any of the challengers for her. I wanted her to watch the following battles, but after I watched them for a bit, I realized they wouldn't help Lucia in the slightest. There weren't any warriors who had crossed over to the divine realm. But I did learn more about magicians and how they fought. I think I should give my throwing knife skills a refresher. They seem like they'd be useful against a magician. Why does a sword spirit know how to use throwing knives? Well, that's what happens when you're trapped in a secluded space for millennia.

But surprisingly—or is it unsurprising?—no one's challenging Lucia. I'm very disappointed. I was looking forward to educating the future leaders of the world.

"Ah!" Lucia sat up as if she had just suffered through a nightmare. "I was supposed to take care of Ilya Number Two! How's she doing?"

"She's around rank 200 right now." I'm surprised she's not last considering her age. Even if her sword is enchanted with a divine inscription, she's still just a child.

Lucia hopped onto the stage. "I challenge Ilya Number Two!"

"You're not allowed to challenge anyone," Cain said from his position in the sky. "You're first place."

Lucia furrowed her brow. "Then, Ilya Number Two challenges me," she said and nodded. "Get up here!"

Mirta rose to her feet and approached the stage. She hesitated before climbing onto the platform. "Um, Lucia?"

"Argh." Lucia fell to her knees and clutched her chest. "I'm defeated. Good job, Ilya Number Two. Go take first place."

"Um." Mirta's mouth fell open before she raised her head and blinked at Cain. "Is, is that okay?"

"Of course it's okay!" Lucia said and appeared behind Mirta. She picked up the poor elf child and tossed her towards me. I caught her and placed her onto the first-place cushion. "If anyone challenges you, just surrender right away. I'll be sure to cripple them and give you the spot back. Now, I challenge the person in third place!"

For the longest time, I thought Lucia was a simple person. I still do. But there are times, times like these, where she does things I would never think of. Blatantly abusing her power to control the outcome of a competition that happens once a decade between the three empires, only she would think of doing something like this. This is a slap in the face to all the top brass. ...I like it. A person whistled past me and crashed into the coliseum wall. Oh, it was the third place person.

"Ilya! Do you want third place?" Lucia dusted off her hands and placed them on her hips.

"I'll climb up by myself," Ilya said from her seat. "But I appreciate the offer."

Lucia shrugged. "Suit yourself."

"What about me?" Reena asked, raising her hand into the air. I don't think Lucia would take good care of you, Reena; you look too much like Snow.

Lucia scratched her head. "Err, I did bully you quite a bit, huh?" Her eyes narrowed. "How about this? Make me an offer I can't refuse."

"Now she's even selling the spots!?" someone shouted. "Lord Thunderfire! Isn't this too much?"

Cain yawned. "If you have the power to sell positions in this competition, then go ahead and sell them. I'm just here to prevent deaths."

Well, it seems like Lucia's going to make a tidy sum today. "Is, isn't this wrong?" Mirta asked and tugged on my pants. "She shouldn't be allowed to do that, right?"

Ah, the innocence of children—untainted by the cruel, cruel world. Time to ruin it for her. "Might makes right. Since Lucia is stronger than everyone else here, no one can stop her from doing what she wants to do. That's how the world works."

"No way...." Mirta's expression darkened. "But, but that's not right!"

"That's life." Was Lucia right? Am I really a sadist? Just because I love seeing people in despair doesn't mean there's something wrong with me, right? Everyone revels in schadenfreude sometimes. "If you don't like it, then you have to get stronger. It's that simple."

"But some people work really hard, and it takes them a really long time," Mirta said, biting her lower lip. "Grandma worked really, really hard, but it took her a long time to be as strong as Lucia. It's not fair."

"Correct. Talented people are blessed." I'm more surprised by how Lucia remained hidden for so long. I wonder if the emperor is kicking himself for not realizing he had a genius within his army that he was treating like shit because of prejudice against beastkin. I bet his expression was glorious when Lucia sent the crown prince flying. I wish I was there to witness it. Maybe I really am a sadist.

"And we have a winner!" Lucia's voice echoed through the coliseum. "Come up and fight me, and I'll surrender." Moments later, a rich-looking demon magician sat on the third-place cushion. And Lucia shouted again, "Fourth-place person, I challenge you!"

Am I destined to never have an honorable master? Perhaps it's because both Roland and Lucia grew up poor that they respect wealth so much. If I had been a noble's weapon spirit, I'm sure my experiences would've been much different. But it's not a bad thing to be raised by Roland and Lucia. Well, not too bad of an experience. There are some times when I wish Lucia wasn't so perverted and more dedicated towards training. After all, the stronger Lucia becomes, the stronger I become. But I suppose after today, I'll have fulfilled my promise to Lucia—making her a legend. Using her strength to manipulate the outcome of the Godking's Brawl while ignoring the nobles' wishes. Negotiating a deal to claim half the human empire. Receiving a divine enchantment. There's no way Lucia's not going to be famous after this with all she's done.

22

Whew, I worked hard. I managed to sell all the spots up to the twentieth place. Around the twenty-first, no one wanted to buy it, so I just reclaimed my spot at the top of the leaderboards while giving second place to Ilya Number Two. And Ilya took advantage of the fact that the third-place person was weak and claimed it for herself. Then she beat up Ilya Number Two and claimed second place. I'm glad everything worked out in the end. As for Reena, she ended up in sixteenth place or so after promising to be my servant for a year. Of course, I didn't accept her offer, but I felt bad for her and gave her the victory out of pity. No one should have to sell their freedom for any reason. Except Puppers, but he was born to follow orders so he doesn't count.

I had to cripple a few people who fought the top twenty, but after the third person, people stopped fighting them. This is what it means by having face! Who dares attack those I want to protect!? It's great. I'm definitely going to be super famous by the end of this competition. I'll have accomplished Durandal's dream. Happy days, many happy days ahead.

But there's just one sore spot. Snow. Where the heck is he? He was definitely supposed to show up as that marquis' representative, but he hasn't appeared. I had Ilya ask around, and it turns out that the marquis showed up to the city but vanished a day later. He probably fell to some dastardly plot of Snow's.

All that's left is to watch these people fight each other, but it's boring. Like seriously, seriously boring. Can I claim my legendary beast core, half the human empire, and leave already? I have to hurry up and become a legendary warrior to truly make Durandal mine! But where am I going to find legendary beasts to hunt? The only way I'm going to be able to reach the legendary realm is to consume a lot of cores like I did to enter the divine realm. Legendary creatures are like dragons, phoenixes, qilin, pixiu, turtle-snakes, five-horned cows, and unicorns. The last time a dragon was sighted was over ninety years ago which the Godking killed. How did the man in the sky get a dragon's core? I'll have to ask him to find new hunting grounds.

Ah, something interesting happen, please! Three, two, one! ...Well, I didn't expect that to work anyway. Maybe if—

"Cain! Help!"

A giant portal opened up in the sky, and the spectators who were watching jumped into the coliseum. There was a roar, and hundreds of people screamed as they fought and shoved to enter the portal. ...I didn't do that, right? That totally didn't happen because of me! I deny everything. I didn't ask for interesting things to occur. Nuh-uh.

"What's going on?" the man in the sky asked while frowning. There was another roar and people were shoved aside as a creature ripped its way through the portal. The people in the way were shredded like paper, and blood rained from the sky. The man in the sky's eyes widened as he stumbled. "It can't be!?" A second later, he fell from the sky and landed with a splat. Is he dead?

"Predator!" someone shouted. "It's a predator!"

Predator..., why does that sound so familiar?

"Lucia!" Ilya grabbed her number two and ran behind me. "You're the only one who can stop it! It's the predator, the thing that prevents people from casting spells. We ran into it while running from Teacher Shinx, remember?"

"Is that why the man in the sky fell from the sky?"

"Is that how you refer to Cain in your head?" Ilya asked. She smacked my forehead. Ow! Why didn't my Armor of

Slaughter activate? "That's not the time for this! We're all helpless magicians and the warriors are too weak!"

More people screamed as limbs and blood were thrown into the air. This predator's obviously quite fierce! It looks like a..., the fuck? "Uh, Ilya? That's the predator?"

"Yes!" Ilya pushed me from behind while trembling. "You have to stop it before it kills anyone else!"

"But..."

"Lucia! Now's not the time for this!"

"It's, it's a giant squirrel! How the hell is that thing the predator!?" It looks like a giant red squirrel with pointy foxlike ears and all! It's too cute to be a vicious beast!

"Lucia! People are dying!"

If they're being killed by a squirrel..., don't they deserve to die? Seriously, the heck? Who dies to a squirrel? Even the man in the sky is running away from it. Does it really stop all mana? Alright, then let's hit it with a Breaking Blade to see how strong its defenses are. "Breaking Blade!" ...Huh? "Ah? Nothing happened."

"You can't use your qi?" Ilya asked.

"Nope." I guess that's why my Armor of Slaughter didn't activate. "Doesn't this mean we're like helpless cows waiting to be slaughtered?"

"Helpless my ass!" Ilya smacked my back. "You can pick up a fifty-ton object with one hand! Go wrestle it!"

"Hah, alright. This will make me super-duper famous, right?" I'll be even more of a legend! The first person to take down a predator, I'll definitely get some recognition for that. ...Wait a moment. Won't I be even more famous if I tame it!? Girl slays predator or girl tames predator and uses it as a badass mount to terrorize all mages.... The latter's definitely more shocking. New goal, acquired! "Future mount, ready yourself for a beating!"

The giant squirrel dropped the bloody person in its claws and raised its head to stare at me. Hah! Its tail is stiffening!

Mine isn't—this'll be a piece of cake. "Breaking Qiless Fist!" Ah? It's running away? "Get back here! Who said you could run!?"

Why is this thing so darn fast? I must be getting out of shape. It's because of all the hot chocolate and acorn stew I've been drinking, isn't it? No! I refuse to believe hot chocolate is holding me back in any way, shape, or form. If I can't run as fast as the squirrel, all I have to do is slow it down. I'll throw something at it! But what do I have to throw in my interspacial ring...? Oh, this is perfect. "Secret Acorn Stew Bowl Throwing Technique! Go!"

Direct hit! The squirrel screeched and stumbled once the bowl hit its leg. It got up to run but stopped for a second. It turned its head and sniffed at the puddle of stew, and in that moment of distraction, I pounced on it. "You're mine!"

***

I'll be honest; I was a little afraid when Lucia charged at the predator. I wasn't sure if she'd win or not, considering the difference between their sizes. If Lucia couldn't use her qi, she was almost like a normal person ... with the bodily strength of a divine beast. I know that's how strong she is, but she's only the size of the predator's head! It doesn't make any sense for her to overpower something that has more mass than her. It's simple applied mechanics. Larger things generate more force, but I forgot Lucia is an existence that isn't logical at all. I think she's the first person to ever kill a predator. ...Kill a predator. ...Kill the predator! "What the heck are you doing, Lucia!?"

"Giving my mount belly rubs!" Lucia said.

I can see that, but why!? Wait. Did she say mount? "M-mount?"

"Uh-huh." Lucia puffed her chest out and patted the predator on the head. "Say hello to Mr. Wuffletush."

"It's a female."

"Mrs. Wuffletush."

"You can't have a predator as a mount!" I'm getting nightmares just thinking about it. A divine beast that disrupts all forms of mana merely by existing. If she ever brought that to the capital, half of our infrastructure would shut down: the streetlights wouldn't work, the refrigerators would break, and the toilets wouldn't flush. It would be a complete disaster.

"Why not?" Lucia tilted her head, and the predator copied her. How the heck are they already that close? The predator's a fierce wild beast that killed a group of ninth-circle magicians. ...Lucia might as well be a wild beast too. I guess, they suit each other? No! Wait. It's definitely because they're both squirrels.

"Everything would break if you kept the predator as a mount."

"That's not true," Lucia said. She patted her hand. "My interspacial ring still works." A bowl of acorn stew appeared in her palm and she fed it to the predator. "See?"

It does work. Why does it work? It shouldn't be working. My interspacial ring works too. Interesting, maybe the capital wouldn't fall into chaos if Lucia paraded it around.... Who am I kidding? The citizens would be terrified. The predator is the bane of mages; there's no way anyone will allow it to live. "You have to kill it, Lucia."

"I'm not killing Mrs. Wuffletush!" Lucia said and hugged the predator. The predator licked her face and wrapped its tail around Lucia's body. "She's too cute to be killed."

"No one's going to allow it to live." Why doesn't she understand? The predator fundamentally breaks society. Everything that people trained for is rendered useless in front of the predator. Years spent dedicated to magic and martial arts, wasted because of a giant squirrel. In the presence of the predator, a commoner might as well be as strong as a noble. Something that threatens the position of a noble can't be allowed to exist. I don't approve of such thinking, but that's how it is. If Lucia keeps the predator as a mount, her life will be in danger.

"Oh really?" Lucia asked and pulled a saddle out of her interspacial ring. When did she buy a saddle and why does it fit Mrs. Wuffletush perfectly? No, Ilya! You can't acknowledge the predator's name! Lucia stood on the predator's back and glared at everyone in the coliseum. "Then I'll kill anyone who wants to hurt Mrs. Wuffletush! In a world without qi and mana, I'm literally the strongest person to ever exist. If you want to fight me, then bring it on!"

Oh my lord, she's right. Only someone who can kill a predator is qualified to fight Lucia. And Lucia's the only person to ever subdue a predator. Is, is she invincible now? Who the heck brought the predator here!? I need to give them a beating for breaking the world's balance. Wait! That's it! The person who brought the predator definitely has a way to beat it.

"Alright," Lucia said and nodded. "It looks like no one wants to fight. Great." She looked at me. "See, Ilya? Everyone's fine with Mrs. Wuffletush's existence."

There's a difference between accepting something because you want to and accepting something because you'd be dead if you didn't. "Then what happens now? I don't think the Godking's Brawl can go on. Besides, you already ruined the whole concept once you sold the top twenty places."

"Lady Pentorn's right," Cain said. "I declare the Godking's Brawl officially over. The top ten should line up in front of me to receive their rewards."

"Wait!" someone shouted. She was covered in blood, and her arm was hanging limply by her side. "That predator…, it's not alone! There are four more outside the coliseum. Someone teleported five predators into the city!"

"Five predators…?" Cain asked, his jaw dropping open. "You're serious."

"Hey! Man in the sky! Give me my legendary beast core and let me out of here," Lucia shouted. Mrs. Wuffletush ran up to Cain and picked him up with her claws. "I don't see Ilya's dad or Ilya Number Two's grandmother here. That means they're still outside."

That's right! Even Father would be helpless against four predators!

"You, you're going to fight them?" Cain asked Lucia.

"Shut up! Give me my core and open the exit!" Lucia shouted. She grabbed Cain and stripped him naked before tossing him off Mrs. Wuffletush. "You were taking too long, so I took a slowness tax!" As Cain hit the ground, a portal opened up in the sky and a few people jumped through. "Go, Mrs. Wuffletush!"

The people who were entering the coliseum screamed as Lucia's predator bounded towards them. A few peed their pants as Mrs. Wuffletush ran past them and leapt outside, the portal closing behind her. And in the end, I started calling the predator Mrs. Wuffletush. If Lucia saves the people outside, they definitely wouldn't bother her about owning a predator. Or five. She's not planning on taming them all, is she? Well, even if she is, please let her save my father in time.

***

Everything's a mess. A huge, ugly mess. There's dead people everywhere. And limbs—there's lots of limbs as well. But no sign of any predators. Who did this? Practically every important person was here for the competition; this is like declaring war on the whole world. It's probably Snow, that crazy bastard. I have no evidence, but my hunches are only wrong 80% of the time! That means there's a 20% chance I'm right. I was already wrong four times this week, so that means this was definitely Snow's plot! And Ilya said I didn't know how numbers worked.

"Can you track the other predators, Mrs. Wuffletush?"

Mrs. Wuffletush nodded and sniffed the ground. A second later, she dashed off at speeds faster than I could run. Faint screams were resounding from the distance, but they were getting closer with every step Mrs. Wuffletush took. How does she run so fast? It's because she has four legs, isn't it? I bet I could run just as fast as her if I had another pair of legs.

"It's another one!" someone shouted. "We're doomed!"

More screams ensued as Mrs. Wuffletush leapt into a barricaded area. There were a dozen or so people hiding in an alley, and a destroyed building blocked off one end. But that didn't do much to stop us from entering. The people dashed away, and I didn't stop them. Why would I? I'm only here for Ilya's dad and Ilya Number Two's grandmother. "Mrs. Wuffletush, can you locate Ilya's dad's scent? Ilya was the short person who was with me. Ah, I have some of her dad's shampoo over here, smell it."

Mrs. Wuffletush stared at me like I was an idiot. Then she shook her head. Well, I guess even giant squirrels aren't like dogs. I was hoping her sense of smell would be enough to track Ilya's dad down. Wait a minute…. "Puppers!"

"This is degrading," Puppers said as he climbed out of my socks and hung his head. "I'm not a dog."

"Shut up, you're already a sock spirit; how can you fall even further? Can you track him or not?"

Puppers sighed and opened the shampoo bottle before sniffing it. He handed the bottle back to me and pointed his nose towards the sky while closing his eyes. His snout twitched, and he sneezed. "That way," he said while rubbing his nose and pointing in the direction we had just come from.

"Why didn't you tell us that before we came here?" I patted Mrs. Wuffletush and urged her back towards the coliseum.

"You didn't ask," Puppers said and sighed. "You're just going to leave those people behind? What about the predator? It should be close."

"I'm not a hero! The dad and grandmother pair are my top priority right now. Everyone else can wait." That's how the world works. If something happened to Ilya's dad while I was saving a bunch of random people, I'd never forgive myself. I don't think Ilya would forgive me either. "Hurry up, Mrs. Wuffletush. I'll be sure to treat you to something even better than acorn stew if we can save them with no issues!"

Mrs. Wuffletush's speed increased even further, and I was almost thrown off of her body. Good thing her ears are right there to hold onto or I really would've fallen off my mount. How embarrassing would that be? "Keep giving directions, Puppers!" ...Why isn't he responding? "Puppers?" Ah! He fell off!

"Keep going straight!" Puppers yelled. "I'll go back to help the—" His words cut off and he disappeared and reappeared beside me. He coughed. "Uh, I forgot I had to stay within a certain range of you or that would happen. We're getting really close to the smell, slow down a bit."

I patted Mrs. Wuffletush and she bounced to a halt. Puppers sniffed the air and squinted. "That way," he said and pointed towards the right. I tugged on my mount's ear, and she whirled around.

"Go! But why aren't there any screams? Maybe they managed to hide from the predators—that must be it. They can't be dead." Ugh, I feel sick. I hate the feeling of dread so much; it reminds me of my time as a slave. But this time, I actually have things to lose. Please be alright, Ilya's dad and Number Two's grandmother!

"One's coming! Now!"

Huh? Doesn't that voice sound like Ilya's dad? Wait! What the heck are those people doing up there!?

"Set it on fire!" That *was* Ilya's dad! But what's he doing standing on the roof with a barrel of something that smells suspiciously like oil? Ah!

"Stop! Stop! Don't set anyone on fire!"

"Huh? Lucia?" Ilya's dad asked from his position on the roof. "Are you riding a predator?"

Before I could respond, someone threw a torch into the alleyway I was in. The walls and ground were set ablaze. "Gah! Mrs. Wuffletush, up, go up!" I think my tail's on fire. I think Mrs. Wuffletush's tail is also on fire. Why is it always the squirrely tails that get set aflame!? How come Puppers' tail is perfectly fine?

Mrs. Wuffletush climbed to the top of the roof, and smacked her tail repeatedly against the tiles. I joined her, and it didn't take long for our tails to stop burning. But they weren't fluffy anymore. I look like a rat. "Who threw that torch!?"

"S-sorry!" a demon shouted and dropped to his knees, banging his head on the roof. "It was instinct!"

"What's going on, Lucia?" Ilya's dad asked, stepping in front of the kowtowing man. "Where's Ilya? Is she alright?"

"Ilya's fine. Mrs. Wuffletush ran into the competition area, and I tamed her. Ilya's still hiding around in the coliseum since it's dangerous out here." I'm glad Ilya's dad is safe. Phew. And Ilya Number Two's grandmother is also here! Two birds with one stone! "Il—Mirta's fine too."

"Thank the lord," Ilya's dad said and exhaled. "When those predators came out of nowhere, I thought I was going to die. If it wasn't for Marilyn's quick thinking, our group would've perished at the start."

"Quick thinking?" How'd they escape from a group of predators?

"I threw a barrel of acorn stew in the opposite direction we were running to," Ilya Number Two's grandmother said. "I was saving it for you after I saw you helping Mirta out during the competition, but I couldn't hold onto it in the end. Sorry."

"Your strange taste indirectly saved our lives," Ilya's dad said.

There's nothing strange about my taste!

"So what's the plan? Have you taken care of the other predators? There were five of them, including the one you're riding." Ilya's dad furrowed his brow. "And I hate to admit it, but I can't help you. Not with a predator present."

"I'll take you two back to the competition area, then I'll beat up those other predators!"

Ilya Number Two's grandmother made a strange expression. "You're actually willing to risk your life to save those being hunted? You … didn't seem like a hero."

"Huh? Saving people? How am I supposed to make an army of predators with only one of them?" Mrs. Wuffletush alone isn't enough to make me a real legend. I have to leave behind a terrifying legacy! "There better be some male predators amongst the four."

***

"So … I just climb on?" Ilya's dad asked with a frown. He glanced at Ilya Number Two's grandmother before raising an eyebrow at me. What? Mrs. Wuffletush is very friendly; ignore the blood on her claws and chin. Those were simple misunderstandings. "Like … like she's a horse?"

"No, like she's a squirrel. Just hop onto the back." I forced Puppers back into my socks because he was taking up space. "You too, Grandma."

"What, what about us?" one of the demons asked. Behind Ilya's dad, there was a group of about eight people. There was no way Mrs. Wuffletush could carry them all without looking super awkward. And my mount has to look fabulous all the time!

"No space, sorry."

"I have money!" the demon said. "Please, take me with you. What if the predator comes back? I'll die."

"Mm. I guess there's some more space now." Looking fabulous means nothing if you're poor! "All of your belongings—that's the price for a ride on a predator. When are you ever going to get another chance like this?"

And with eight new interspacial rings tucked away in a safe place, Mrs. Wuffletush took off with ten more passengers on her back. They didn't slow her down a single bit, and we made it back to the coliseum without an issue. But.... "How do we open the space?"

"You just jump in," Ilya's dad said. We were in the seating area, facing the empty arena. How were the spectators able to spectate us before? Maybe a scrying orb like the one Ilya and I had in that inn back in the desolate mountains? "A portal will automatically open if you jump above the space."

"Let's go, Mrs. Wuffletush." Now that I think about it, how does Mrs. Wuffletush understand our language? I thought people avoided her since she killed things. There weren't even any descriptions of the predator's appearance. Maybe she's a genius who picked up the language during the short time she was in the city? That must be it. And people say squirrels are stupid. Hah.

"There's another predator!" someone shouted the instant we appeared inside the coliseum's space.

Ilya stood up. "No, wait! That's just Lucia."

"I brought your dad back, Ilya." I motioned for Mrs. Wuffletush to shake, and the passengers fell off like fleas. "I'm going to go back out to find the other predators. You stay here to protect them, Mrs. Wuffletush. Also, Ilya, come over here for a second."

"Yes, Lucia?" Ilya asked as she approached me.

I bent down and whispered into her ear, "Use Mrs. Wuffletush and extort everyone here of their interspacial rings.

It's a protection tax! If they disagree, force them outside. Oh, and say it was the man in the sky's idea, so the people don't hate me."

"Lucia…"

"I'm serious! If I come back and you don't have as many interspacial rings as there are people here, then I'm going to tell your dad about those books you keep underneath your bed."

Ilya's eyes widened as her face turned red. "Lucia!"

"That's right! I know about them. Now hurry up and extort them; I won't be gone for long." Leaving Ilya behind, I … don't know how to leave this area. "Uh, how do I get out?"

"Close your eyes, place your hands on your hips, and spin around five times while chanting, 'I'm gullible,' ten times in a single breath."

"I'm gullible, I'm gullible, I'm gullible, I'm gullible, I'm gullible, I'm gullible, I'm gullible, I'm gullible, I'm gullible, I'm gullible." Who made that stupid way of exiting the area? The world's spinning, but at least I'm outside. Now, if I were a predator, which way would I run? Ooh, something smells nice over there. That way it is!

How far does the predator's qi and mana canceling effects extend? I still can't run with my Armor of Slaughter to boost my speed. At least I'm still plenty fast without it. Ah, there's screaming in the distance. Please, lord, let the predator be a male!

"Help! So—"

The shout was cut off by a scream just as I turned a corner. A woman was lying underneath a giant black squirrel—well, half of her was. The other half was impaled on the squirrel's claws. Her head turned to the side, and she stared at me. One arm rose weakly into the air, then fell uselessly to her side as her eyes glazed over. The predator turned its head, dropping the woman at the same time. It snarled at me as its tail stiffened. Male? Female? I can't tell from here.

"Hey, cute little fella." Maybe if I use sweet words, it won't run away from me. "I have some acorn stew. Want some?"

The predator screeched and lunged at me as I took out a barrel. Its front leg went wide as it swiped at me, its claws cutting straight through a wall as if it didn't exist. Great! It didn't run! I stepped forward and caught the squirrel's leg by its wrist, or is it ankle? Well, it doesn't matter because I caught it! "Qiless Breaking Throw!"

The predator screamed as its back crashed into the ground. Darn, no penis. Well, another female wouldn't hurt. I pinned the predator's front legs with one hand and wrangled its hind legs together with my own legs and tail. I should save the taming portion for later; for now, I'll just keep it tied up with…. A regular rope won't work, huh? Not while it's awake, at least. Then I'll knock it out! Ah, but first I should extort the people around it. "Ah, it's so strong! I can't hold on much longer!"

The people around me shivered. There were only ten of them or so who were still alive. The dead ones were already being looted by … Durandal? How come I didn't notice him come out?

"Wait, you can't?" Durandal asked with a strange expression on his face. "I thought predators were easy for you to wrangle."

"Are you robbing the dead?"

"Waste not, want not," Durandal said with a nod. "Roland taught me that along with where and how to search a corpse in an efficient manner."

"Oh. Carry on then." The survivors were looking at me as if I had two heads. I'm not strange! "Ah! My strength, it's running out!" I coughed. "But if I'm given interspacial rings or precious jewelry, I'll be able to hold on long enough for all of you to run away."

"I-isn't this extortion?" one of the survivors asked.

"Ah! One of the predator's legs got free!" Stop scratching me, dammit! These funds will definitely trickle down to you in the future!

"Here!" someone shouted and threw an interspacial ring at me. Durandal caught it and checked it before nodding.

"There's still around nine more of you," Durandal said. "I'm sure nine interspacial rings will definitely give my master the strength to hold on."

"You two are perfect for each other," Puppers said from my socks. "This is unbelievable. I'm ashamed to associate with you two."

"Stop slacking and loot the corpses as well," Durandal said and reached into my socks, pulling Puppers out like he was a piece of laundry in a basket. "There's a lot we have to do and not a lot of time. Hop to it."

***

"Do I, do I really have to?"

"Yes, I'm sorry about this." I lowered my head and accepted the ring the emperor gave me. Lucia could've threatened me with anything like my life or my livelihood, but she had to use such an underhanded method of targeting my secret books! "These were Cain's orders."

"You mean Lucia's, right?" the emperor asked.

I coughed and turned my head. "No, they're Cain's." Lucia's pet predator growled, and I jumped half a foot into the air. "Y-yes, Mrs. Wuffletush! We'll move onto the next person right away!" I know Lucia left behind Mrs. Wuffletush for our protection, but that's like sending a lion to guard a flock of sheep! I've had dozens of near-death experiences while journeying with Lucia, but this, this is unreasonably scary! A predator could kill me in its sleep, and Lucia expects me to wield it as a tool to extort people. At least everyone's cooperating. Even that angry, stew-hating lionkin didn't say anything when he handed over his interspacial ring. And the people that didn't have interspacial rings gave up everything except for their underwear. I feel like a villain. But I'm acting under orders! My dignity is at stake here; I can't be expected to sacrifice myself for the good of everyone else, can I? It's not like I'm enjoying extorting people of their valuables. I'm a victim too!

"Ilya...."

"Sorry, Father, but you too." I'm an unfilial child. "Please, I don't know what Mrs. Wuffletush will do to you if you don't hand something over."

My father sighed. "Very well," he said and handed over his interspacial ring. "I suppose it's a fair price for my life."

Mrs. Wuffletush stuck her chin into the air and snorted twice. Then she looked at the two trembling elves beside my father. "You too, Mrs. Marilyn. And Mirta." Mirta looked at me with wide eyes while hugging her sword. "Lucia will return your sword to you when she gets back." Maybe. Don't quote me on that. Knowing Lucia, she might not. Mirta pouted as she handed me her greatsword. Before I could take it, Mrs. Wuffletush grabbed it and ate it in a single bite.

Mirta cried out, but Mrs. Wuffletush swallowed and tilted her head to the side. The expression on her face said, "What? You got a problem? Fight me."

"...I'm sure Lucia will help you get a new sword." I'm a liar too. An unfilial, lying extortionist, that's what I've become. Lord, where did I go wrong? When was I led astray? Who am I kidding? I already know the answer is when I met Lucia. If only Teacher didn't have those stupid traps set up to capture beasts. He could've waltzed outside his laboratory, went to the desolate mountains, and subdued some beasts there, but no. He insisted on leaving traps in the southern pass instead.

Hah.... Anyway, moving on. It didn't take too long to collect the rest of the interspacial rings and other various protection taxes. When is Lucia going to return? I don't like the way Mrs. Wuffletush is staring at the people around us. If she ate someone, Lucia would probably pretend like it didn't happen, but I'm not going to tell Mrs. Wuffletush that. I'm just afraid she'll figure it out on her own. Why is she so smart? It's bad enough for Lucia to own a predator, but owning a smart one too? Not to mention she just ate a sword.

"I'm back!" A giant portal appeared in the air as dozens of people streamed into the coliseum. Lucia appeared at the very end…, holding onto a rope with four unconscious predators attached to it. "Ilya! Stuff!"

I ran over to Lucia and handed her the spoils I gathered. She looked at Mrs. Wuffletush and asked, "Did she extort everyone?"

Mrs. Wuffletush nodded.

"Nice," Lucia said and patted my shoulder. "You're the best accomplice someone can ask for." I'm not an accomplice; I'm a victim! Don't slander me in front of everyone! "At least that's one good thing that came out of this."

One good thing? Did she not get what she wanted? "Is everything okay?"

"Look at them," Lucia said with a scowl. She pointed at the four unconscious predators. "Do you see anything wrong?"

"I see four creatures that can kill me if their legs twitched the wrong way. That's pretty wrong."

"No, it's not that," Lucia said and grabbed one of the predators. She flipped it over onto its back and spread its legs apart. "Now do you see anything?"

…What. "Um, no?"

"Exactly!" Lucia said. "That's the problem. None of these predators have penises! How am I supposed to have an army of predators without any males to make babies?"

"Ah! Lucia! Help!" thankfully, someone cried out so I didn't have to respond to Lucia's nonsense. It was Reena, the bunnykin that was Snow's relative.

"Snow!?" Lucia shouted and ran over to Reena, pulling out her sword. "I finally found you, you bastard!"

"I'm Reena! Reena!" the poor bunnykin shouted, covering her ears with her hands while lowering her head and crouching. She pointed at the group of stunned men behind her. "But they know Snow! They mistook me for him and tried to give me a report!"

…Are Snow's subordinates idiots? Well, maybe Reena really does resemble Snow that much.

"I know you're looking for him, and they're his underlings," Reena said. "I did well in reporting them to you, right?" Her eyes twinkled as she looked up at Lucia. Her ears were twitching, and her bouncing tail was practically saying, "Praise me." Do all beastkin behave in that manner? I've seen Lucia act that way to Durandal before. Wait, don't tell me Reena subordinated herself to Lucia. That doesn't make any sense.

The men behind Reena exchanged glances with each other. Then they looked at Mrs. Wuffletush. They dropped to their knees and placed their hands over their heads. "Please, don't kill us! We'll tell you everything you want to know!"

23

Though there's some of Snow's subordinates in the coliseum with us, I'm not interrogating them. I'm letting Ilya's dad do that instead. I have something much more important to do: counting my spoils! One interspacial ring..., two interspacial rings..., three inter—no! You have to check inside of them, Lucia! Phew, I almost did something stupid. Alright, let's see what's inside.

Who the heck does this interspacial ring belong to? The only thing inside of here is meat! Rows upon rows upon rows of meat! Oh, wait. It doesn't matter since it's mine now. At least, I won't have to worry about starving even if I disappear into some desert somewhere. But that's not going to happen; I didn't raise a flag! I'm going to happily retire into the countryside—which is half the human empire's lands—and live peacefully with Durandal after I become a legendary warrior. There will be no searching of any deserts.

Now that that's settled, let's continue investigating the spoils! Inside this interspacial ring that looks like a wedding ring..., there's nothing. It's actually a wedding ring. I should return this. Then, let's designate this table as the returned-stuff table. Okay. Mm, moving onto the next ring. There's ... a pile of men's underwear with printed yellow ducks on them. I'm starting to question if this is a good idea. Well, at least I can sell the ring for a decent price; I'll leave the underwear on the table.

Why are there cleaning supplies in this interspacial ring!? I thought interspacial rings were expensive to obtain! Valuable stuff should be kept in them: jewels, money, beast cores, erotica! What is this crap? ...Well, let's keep the cleaning supplies for now. Who knows? There might be a time where I won't be able to use my magic tool to clean things. Ah, who am I kidding? Cleaning supplies are going on the table.

This is like the holiday where people give each other wrapped gifts that I never got to partake in, but the gifts hold crap and the box is more valuable than what is inside. How will I be disappointed this time? This ring has beast cores! Lots and lots of ... regular beast cores. They're not even spirit beast cores. I, I guess I can use them as paper weights. Or sell them for some snack money. I could probably get a barrel of hot chocolate or two for these. Yeah, every little bit counts.

And this interspacial ring has a ton of books. I can't read, so they're totally useless to me. Onto the table they go. Wait, actually, I could probably sell these too. Back into the ring they go. Sorry, person who just stood up to reclaim them. Oh, wait. That person was Ilya's dad. I could return this ring to him. "Catch!"

"Many thanks, Lucia."

"Lucia! Your giant squirrel ate my sword!"

Huh. What the heck is Ilya Number Two saying? Squirrels don't eat swords. "Uh, yeah. Okay." Sometimes children have no idea what they're talking about. Jeez. What's in this ring? Women's underwear? But ... they're all different sizes! Which pervert does this ring belong to? Isn't this mark on the ring the royal family's seal? "Which idiot prince keeps women's underwear inside of their royal seal? If you admit it, I'll give it back to you!"

"That, that's mine!"

Huh? Isn't that Evelyn the Witch? The person who poisoned her ugly arranged husband? That means all the underwear of different sizes are hers? "Oh, here."

"Thank you," Evelyn said with a red face. She checked inside the ring and froze. "Uh, actually, this isn't mine. Do these all belong to different people? No way, this is Algar's ring…? I've definitely seen him wear it before! And these panties are mine! Algar! What the hell!?"

Oh boy. I guess it's a good thing I broke off my deal with Algar when his second brother came along. I almost worked with a pervert. Maybe I'd have become perverted myself. Ugh, I'm shivering just thinking about it—I'm a chaste, upright person! I can't go around associating with people who steal women's underwear.

"I didn't do this," Algar said when Evelyn confronted him. "I swear!"

Mm, not my problem anymore. What's in this earring? Nothing, it's just an earring. Well, I can sell it since it's not as valuable as a wedding ring. Probably. Hopefully there's no sentimental value? Man, now I almost feel like a bad person. Almost. Away this earring goes before I start feeling guilty! And inside this interspacial ring, we have … a legendary beast core! This one is the man in the sky's, isn't it? There's one, two, three, twenty, twenty-five, thirty-seven, forty-two, sixty-seven… Sixty-seven legendary beast cores! Holy crap! Not only that, but all their bones and organs and valuable bits are here! Hey, valuable bits means scales and skin and horns, not penises. Penises fall under organs. But this ring's capacity is huge! What the heck is it made out of?

"Having fun inspecting my ring?" the man in the sky asked.

"Yes!"

His face darkened. "Return my stuff to me and I won't hold you accountable."

"Mrs. Wuffletush! Teach this man his place!"

The man in the sky screamed as Mrs. Wuffletush pounced on him. The flimsy clothes he had borrowed were torn to shreds, and bloody scratch marks appeared all over his skin.

"Mm, that's enough. Good girl!"

Mrs. Wuffletush puffed her chest out and then looked at the ring. Did she know what was inside? Divine beasts would definitely want to consume legendary beast cores to evolve, right? But I have to consume these too to break through to the legendary realm! Mm, I'll consume them one at a time until I break through, then I'll give her the rest. That should work. I'll start right now! My dream is waiting for me to take it! What if I lose the ring in an unexpected accident? This is called being proactive!

"Mrs. Wuffletush. Guard me as I break through. I'll give you the remaining beast cores if you do. It only took me thirty-something divine beast cores to become a divine warrior. It should only take that much to become a legendary warrior. There'll be plenty for you! Understand?"

Mrs. Wuffletush nodded. It's a good thing beasts are so loyal, unlike Snow! Even though I've only known Mrs. Wuffletush for a few hours, I feel completely at ease with her. Maybe it's because we're both squirrels. My instincts tell me she's not going to betray me, and if I can't trust myself, then who can I trust? "Durandal, Puppers. You two help as well."

"What about those four?" Durandal asked, pointing at the unconscious predators. Phew, I almost forgot about them.

"I'll breakthrough outside. They can't talk after all. They won't be able to chant 'I'm gullible' ten times to get out." With that, I grabbed onto Mrs. Wuffletush and completed the nonsensical ceremony to leave the coliseum. Then I took out the legendary beast cores. "I'm starting!"

***

Looking at Lucia stack legendary beast cores into the empty space in her lap when she crosses her legs just seems … wrong. "This isn't right."

"What do you mean?" Gae Bulg asked. "You mean the way to exit the coliseum? It definitely doesn't have anything to do with that chant. Maybe it's the spinning around that does it. Or someone on the inside knows how it works and teleports

Lucia outside when she's done. Either way, I agree, it's not right."

"No, it's not that." I don't care about exiting or entering a space. "I mean the absorbing of beast cores. A martial artist should strive to breakthrough his bottlenecks via his own power: enlightenment, experience, effort. All of those should contribute to advancing to the next level. But Lucia…, Lucia's using drugs loaded with impurities to forcibly enhance her body. It's not right."

Gae Bulg shrugged. "Clearly she did something right," he said. "Look at her; she's a divine warrior. Neither Roland nor Cuchulainn broke through the wall on their own despite their experience and effort. She found a way when her predecessors couldn't. So what if it's using drugs?"

"Think about it. If she advanced to divine warrior by consuming divine beast cores and she's going to advance to legendary warrior by consuming legendary beast cores, what's she going to do when she becomes bottlenecked at the peak of the legendary realm? She will always be behind in the world if she has to consume those higher than her to advance. She can't blaze her own path to the pinnacle of martial arts if she relies on eating stronger beasts to get there."

Gae Bulg shrugged again. "Maybe her path won't bring her to the peak, but if she continues growing at her current rate, she'll get awfully close." He shook his head. "Besides, she's blessed with that body that's loved by qi. She absorbs beast cores at a rate much faster than everyone else. I'm sure Roland would've consumed more beast cores if his body allowed him to."

"Maybe I'm just bitter." Ah, the world's truly unfair. Roland struggled at the peak of spirit warrior for a long time. When he couldn't make any advancements, he dabbled in alchemy, enchantments, magic. He tried everything to break through, but died without being able to. And Lucia just whizzes by all her bottlenecks by cheating. If Roland saw her progress, he'd probably cry. Well, he wouldn't. He'd definitely plot to kidnap Lucia and dissect her to figure out how she does it. ...Am I sympathizing with Roland? After he locked me away for over a millennia? Something's wrong with me. A weapon spirit has no need for empathy.

"One dragon core," Lucia said in a singsong voice. She picked up a core, and it dissolved into her hand. She reached into the pile and pulled out another core. "Two dragon cores." She hummed and picked up another core. "Three dragon cores."

Gae Bulg turned to look at me. "You're right. There's something immoral about this," he said. "I just can't quite figure out what it is."

"Eight dragon cores," Lucia said. Her eyelids were drooping, and her voice was slower than before. She picked up another core. "Err. Ten? No, that's not right. Seven? Ah, that's going backwards. Ten and three? Gah! Forget it, back to the start. One dragon core." The core disappeared into her palm. ...Did she forget how to count? Or did she not know in the first place? "Two dragon cores." Her head bobbed down and up. "Three dragon ... cores." A line of drool appeared by the corner of her mouth. "Four ... dragon ... cores...."

Is twelve cores her limit? That's outrageous. A normal person can only consume one core at a time before needing to rest. And if it's a core of a beast that's stronger than them, then they can only wait for a longer period of time. But all Lucia has to deal with is a little drowsiness.

"She's going to explode," Gae Bulg said with a frown. "I thought she was going to the last time she did something like this, but she didn't. There's no way her luck will hold out a second time."

"I think Lucia knows her limits. She won't do something that'll make herself explode."

"Gah! So tired!" Lucia sat up and pinched her cheeks before shaking her head. She pulled out a mug of hot chocolate and drank it in one gulp. "Phew. That was close. I almost passed out there. Where was I? A second set of eight cores consumed?" She stowed away the mug and grabbed a core. "Seventeen dragon cores."

She learned how to count again after drinking hot chocolate? Wait a minute. That mug had an inscription on it! "Gae, did you see the inscription on her cup?"

"Yes," Gae Bulg said. He gave me a strange look. What was that expression supposed to mean? Only I can look at others as if they're idiots. "She sculpted that cup out of a divine beast's bone and inscribed a focus inscription on it. You didn't know?"

"When did she do that!?"

"I think you were monologuing to yourself inside of your weapon body when she did it," Gae Bulg said. "She did it after the preliminary competition."

I need to pay more attention.

"Twenty-five dragon cores." Lucia's head bobbed up and down again. A droplet of drool fell onto her leg. Her eyes closed for two seconds before opening again. "Gah!" She pulled out her mug with more hot chocolate inside of it. Well, would you look at that? It really is sculpted out of a divine beast's bones. I wasn't aware a bone engraving could work that way. "Ugh, this is a lot more difficult than I thought it'd be." Lucia shook her head and grabbed another core. "Twenty-six dragon cores…. Ah, I give up."

She's done?

"I'll just absorb sixty cores at once and be done with it."

What. "Wait! You'll explode if you do that!"

Lucia blinked at me while the cores in her lap disappeared at a rapid rate. "Well, that's that," she said. Then she fell over backwards and fainted.

***

Like the last time I used cores to break through, this time I also had a bad dream where I was being chased by dozens of dragons instead of divine beasts. Surprisingly, dragons are easy to kill. You just have to rip off their wings to prevent them from flying away, then their legs to prevent them from running, and finally their face to prevent them from biting you. I haven't figured out how to stop their fire-breathing yet, but they usually die a few minutes after ripping off their faces. Though, I'm not quite at the level of the Godking where he could kill one in a single strike. But I'll get there soon! Maybe after I break through to the legendary realm, which should happen after I wake up. Like now! ...Any second now. All the dragons are dead. Hello? Don't tell me I really exploded.

"Ah, Lucia, you're awake."

It's Durandal! And I'm lying on his lap while staring up at his face. Mm, everything is right in the world: the sky is smoky, the trees are on fire, screams are filling the air. ...The fuck happened while I was asleep? And why's the ground wet? "Uh..."

"Did you turn stupid?" Durandal tilted his head. He scratched my ears, causing shivers to run down my spine. "Better? Are you alright?"

I didn't want to leave the comfort of his lap, but I sat up anyway. What the heck was going on? Why's Mrs. Wuffletush injured? And where's Puppers? And Durandal's missing half a leg!? His face is super pale too! "Durandal! What happened!? Why are we in a forest and not the city? How long was I out for?"

Durandal exhaled. "It seems like you broke through to the legendary realm safely. That's a lot of qi in your body. It feels endless—like I could get lost in it." He smiled at me, staying seated because his leg was half-missing! Why is his leg half gone!? "While you were breaking through, Snow somehow managed to teleport a dragon into the city. Mrs. Wuffletush, Gae Bulg, and I barely got you out of there. Gae Bulg poisoned himself and jumped into the dragon's mouth, saying that's what Lucia would've done. What the heck was that about?" Durandal exhaled and closed his eyes. "Anyway, I'm going back into my weapon body to recover. I'm not going to tell you something unreasonable like fight the dragon. I'm already proud of you for reaching the legendary realm. But quite a few of your friends are still in the city with the dragon. If you don't want to lose them…"

Durandal smiled as his body disappeared and entered mini-DalDal. Mrs. Wuffletush looked at me and pawed at the ground. "Right, the left over cores." Where did I put them? Here they are. "Will you evolve right away if you eat them?"

Mrs. Wuffletush shook her head.

"Then I'll give them to you later. Right now, I have to save Ilya. Since you're injured, you can wait here." Did Mrs. Wuffletush fight the dragon directly? Her fur's mostly burnt off and bloody, and she has gashes everywhere. She must be seriously injured if she hasn't recovered yet. "Just hide for a bit; I'll be right back."

Snow teleported a dragon into the city after bringing in five predators? I don't know what his final plans are, but I'll do everything in my power to disrupt him! Oh, and I have to save Ilya and Ilya Number Two. Yeah, that's definitely the number one reason why I'm going to slay the dragon. But Durandal didn't tell me how long I was passed out for. Maybe everything's already over? I hope not. I finally found friends of my own; I don't want to lose them so soon. No one's allowed to take them away from me!

"Let's"—the ground shattered underneath my feet as I took a step forward—"go…?" I took another step, and the ground cracked even further. Why's the ground so soft? No way! Don't tell me I became fat after consuming all those cores! …Phew, I still look like me. Mm, this vaguely reminds me of a conversation I had with Durandal once. I think I asked him if someone could be as strong as a dragon if they consumed enough cores. Then Durandal said something along the lines of it's impossible to get enough cores. How many did he say was required? Thirty? And I had … sixty. That means I wasted thirty cores! Oh, it also means I have the constitution of a dragon now.

Wash your neck and wait for me, Snow's dragon! I'll recreate the Godking's achievement today with a Breaking Blade! But, I just realized there was something I was forgetting. "Mrs. Wuffletush."

Mrs. Wuffletush's head appeared from behind some bushes. She tilted it and blinked.

"Which way's the city?"

Mrs. Wuffletush pointed behind her, the opposite way of where I was originally going to go. It's a good thing she's not directionally challenged like me. Why is that though? We're both squirrels! Life really isn't fair; why can't it ever be unfair in my favor? Well, that's just how life works; I should stop complaining and save Ilya! Ugh, but there should be a way to lessen my volume when I run. Maybe I'll jump? Dragons can fly, right? And since I have the constitution of a dragon, I should be able to as well!

I put all my strength into my legs and leapt into the air. It's working! Ah, not really. I can't change directions. Or increase or decrease my speed. Or stop myself from crashing into the tree! Who put this tree here!? Well, at least my skin's thick enough that it didn't hurt. And some acorns fell off the tree, sweet. Stop! Lucia. Ilya, remember? Right, forget the acorns! I have important things to be doing. Maybe I can fly to the city? If I jump a little harder than last time, I might be able to.

After crashing into another tree, I figured out that my focus bones' effects ran out. And the ones in my interspacial ring aren't working anymore. Don't tell me I've grown immune to the effects after becoming a legendary warrior. I demand a refund! Mm, but becoming a legendary warrior's not all bad. Maybe I can breathe fire like that dragon in the sky too. ...Nope. Well, it was worth a shot. Wait. Dragon in the sky? I'm here! Wait for me, Ilya; I'll save you!

***

After Lucia's sudden departure from the space inside the coliseum, everyone else decided to leave as well once someone noticed she left four unconscious, but alive, predators behind. Why did she keep them alive...? I thought it'd be safe outside, but that's when the trouble started. A massive dragon descended from the sky, and there was nothing we could do to stop it since Mrs. Wuffletush was still in the area. She fled after sustaining heavy damages, and Cain was getting ready to fight the dragon, but one of the predators from inside the coliseum woke up and came out. I'm not sure how it figured out the exiting method was to spin around five times, but it did.

The only reason why I'm alive right now is because of the man riding on top of the dragon, Snow. At least, I'm pretty sure that's Snow given Lucia's description of him. He looks like Reena, but he has a flower clipped to the base of his ear, making him more feminine. Well, I thought it was clipped on, but my father pointed out the roots growing from Snow's head. Evelyn, one of the princesses of the human empire, paled and fainted at the sight. I'm not sure why. She did mutter something about Bryant though. Currently, we're at a standstill. There's four predators surrounding us from the back and the sides, and there's a dragon facing us from the front. By us, I mean every single person from the coliseum. I really dislike predators. They make me feel so helpless. Why the hell did Lucia not take them with her!?

"So," Snow said from atop the dragon's head. His eyes were bloodshot, and veins bulged on every surface of his exposed skin. "These are the people in charge of the sky and earth plane? Quite a pitiful lot, aren't you?" He jumped off the dragon and landed on a predator's back. He patted the dragon's leg. "Burn the rest of the city down. Smoke out the survivors and kill them."

The dragon roared and flew into the air, flapping its massive black wings. It had yellow eyes, four legs that were as thick as tree trunks, and a tail that was as long as the rest of its body. I've seen pictures of dragons before, but I never thought I'd see one in real life. I thought they went extinct.

"You're Snow Flopsy," one of the human survivors said. "Was all of this planned by you? The predators? The crazy squirrel girl? The dragon? How are you controlling them? What do you want from us?"

"Snow Flopsy, yes," Snow said and tilted his head. His mouth didn't seem to be moving in time with his words—like they were delayed while coming out of his lips. "But not quite. You can call me Snow Larkspur. I've joined the Larkspur family, and you'd do well to follow me. In fact, that's why I've come here. I want to invite"—his head swiveled around like a broken puppet's—"all of you"—blood leaked from the flower on his ear—"to my family."

There's something seriously wrong with him. I'm getting shivers just by looking at him. He doesn't seem like a person anymore. It's jarring. The way he moves, the way he talks, the sound of his voice, and the dead look in his eyes, all of it makes me think he's already dead and controlled by someone.

"Has anyone heard of the Larkspur family?" a human asked. "Are they from the fae? There's no such family among the humans and demons."

The lionkin that despised acorn stew shook his head. "There's no Larkspur in our lands either."

Where the heck did Lucia go? What is she doing? Whatever she's doing, I hope she hurries it up! I hate this feeling of powerlessness. I hate it. I can't cast spells because the predators emit some kind of energy that disrupts my mana.

But how? If I can figure out how it's being interrupted, couldn't I take measures to prevent the predators' effects?

Snow clapped his hands once. Then twice. Then he lowered his arms and blinked hard. "The Larkspur family is not from your plane. We're from the wind and thunder plane."

Cain's face paled, and he hid behind me, even crouching behind my back. What the hell? Why was Cain hiding behind a fourteen-year-old girl!? "Lord Thunderfire!" I whispered in my fiercest voice. "Have you no shame?"

"Sshh!" Cain shushed me and peeked through my arm and my side to see if Snow was watching. "I don't get along well with the people of the wind and thunder plane."

"Have you been to the place he's talking about?" I asked while Snow was distracted by other people's questions. "By plane … does he mean another world?"

Cain glanced at Snow. The rabbitkin seemed intent on doing a question and answer session. "You could say that. Once you reach the legendary realm, you'll understand. Just think of the Larkspur family as a family from another country where dragons are as common as scavenger crows. Compared to them, all the royal families might as well be country bumpkins."

"You're serious?" I've never heard about this. Not even in any books. Well, there were some vague creation myths and legends that might fit with this scenario, but those are myths and legends!

"You saw the dragon, didn't you? After discovering their plane, I … fell into despair for a while. I finally reached the peak, but I realized I was just a big fish in a little pond. That's why I hoped for you to be my disciple, so I could raise the next generation to be strong enough to protect our plane. I'm not the first one to discover their existence," Cain whispered. His eyes narrowed. "The Godking did as well. He used Durandal and Vera as seals to prevent our plane from being found once he realized the disparity between our planes' strengths. But that idiot squirrel girl undid one seal. These plant demons have been invading our lands ever since Durandal chose her as an owner. It was only a matter of time for a major family in the wind and thunder plane to figure out what was going on."

"You said you didn't get along well with them? So you can't negotiate for us?" I wonder if this is how wild beasts feel like when we encroach on their territory and cut down their trees and homes. It's not a pleasant feeling at all.

"I, uh, stole some dragon cores from their family," Cain said, his face cramping. "And may or may not have killed one of them to do it."

"So what will it be, ladies? Gentlemen?" Snow asked, his voice echoing through the whole city. Even the crackling of the flames and the roars of the dragon were drowned out. I shivered and met Snow's gaze, stepping in front of Cain. "Now that you know the circumstances, will you swear loyalty on your souls to my family, or will you choose destruction?"

"What do you think, Ilya?" my father asked. "Become puppets for some plant people or death?"

Snow pointed at the acorn stew-hating lionkin. "You, make your choice."

The lionkin stared at the ground. He clenched his fists. "I want to live!"

Snow nodded and pulled a seed out of his bag. "Very well," he said, offering the seed to the lionkin. "Put this up your nose."

The lionkin hesitated before grabbing the seed. He grimaced and took in a deep breath as he positioned the seed on his finger. Then he jammed it up his nose. A second later, his eyes widened and bestial screams rang out of his mouth. A green tendril snaked out of his ear and grew into a bud. Then it blossomed into a purple flower. A line of drool fell from the lionkin's mouth as his eyes glazed over.

Snow smiled at the sight and pointed at the human standing next to the lionkin. "Make your choice."

"I, I'd rather die than become food for a plant!" the man shouted and charged at Snow, brandishing his sword. The predator underneath Snow blurred, and the man was bisected by a single swipe.

"Foolish," Snow said and shrugged. His gaze locked onto a woman who tried to run away. The dragon dashed over from its position in the sky and breathed a breath of flames on her before she could get very far. Even her bones had turned to ash.

Is this how I'm going to die? By having a plant shoved up my nose which will eat my face? That's a depressing way to go. Maybe I should just let the predator kill me. It seems less painful.

"Breaking…"

Was that Lucia's voice? How far away was she?

"Blade!"

The world turned red. It was as if blood had been smeared on everything: the sky, the ground, the people. The phenomenon lasted for a few seconds. When the world regained its color, the dragon in the sky became a headless dragon in the sky. Its head, which was falling towards the ground, blinked and shifted its gaze around while opening and closing its mouth. Its wings continued to flap as if its body hadn't realized it was already dead. Then it froze, and the massive dragon plummeted towards the ground with a crash.

Lucia's laugh echoed through the city, and the predators all stiffened before rolling onto their backs while playing dead. Then a flying squirrelkin girl … slammed into a nearby streetlamp. Maybe it wasn't appropriate to say she flew. I'll try again. Then a falling squirrelkin girl slammed into a nearby streetlamp.

***

490

I did it! I killed a dragon with a single sword strike! It's unfortunate I crashed into a lamppost afterwards, but at least I made it to Ilya. She didn't get eaten or burned. It looks like I didn't take too long to break through the divine realm. Ilya Number Two is scared but safe. Her grandmother's fine too. And Ilya's dad looks unhurt as well. All the important people are accounted for. And there's Snow!

"Snow, you bastard! It's time for you to meet your maker!" I charged at the bunnykin and raised mini-DalDal into the air. I couldn't use my qi since there were predators around, but there was no way Snow was going to escape my strike! My speed was an uncountable number of times faster than it was before. And I can see every minute movement of his.

The bunnykin screeched and raised his hands in front of his face. "I'm Reena! Reena!"

Oh. It's a good thing my strength increased too, or I might not have been able to stop my sword in time. Phew.

"Snow's over there, Lucia," Ilya said and pointed at one of the predators. Underneath the predator, a pale figure was struggling to get free. Its legs and stomach were pinned by the predator's weight. On top of the figure's head, there was a pair of bunny ears. It's Snow! "There's something wrong with him though. I think he's already dead."

A flower was growing out of Snow's ear. It was purple and a bit creepy, but it did make him look more feminine. It made me a little jealous. Bluish-green veins were decorating the surface of his skin, and his eyes were bloodshot but glazed over at the same time. "That's really Snow?"

What happened to him? I walked over and crouched in front of him, but he didn't seem to notice me. He was still trying to crawl out from underneath the predator. They weren't even that heavy. Mrs. Wuffletush only weighed about three tons, and this predator's even smaller than her. I know Snow poisoned me and all, but it feels a little wrong to kill him when he's not paying attention to me. So I poked his head with the tip of my sword. "Hey."

Snow stopped moving and looked up. His eyes widened before narrowing. He sighed as his arms' movements ceased, and he rested his chin on the ground. "There was another legend in hiding? And you seem to be unaffected by the giant squirrels. How inconvenient. Mm, well, the family should understand if I fail."

Snow's voice didn't sound like the one I heard way back when. Maybe he went through puberty? It doesn't seem like he recognizes me. "Hey, Bouncykins. Are you there?" I lifted the predator off Snow's body to check his feet. He tried to move, so I brought my sword down and cut off one of his arms. And he didn't even scream. Am I disappointed? I'm not a sadist! There's no way I'd be disappointed about someone not screaming when I cut them. But Bouncykins isn't there. Snow's not even wearing socks.

"What happened to you, Snow?"

"You knew me?" Snow asked and raised his head. Blood continued to pour out of his shoulder, and the veins on his body were shrinking back underneath the surface of his skin. "Interesting. I don't have any memories about someone as strong as you."

"Who are you?"

"Snow Larkspur."

I looked at Ilya. "Did I get the wrong person? Is he another one of Snow's cousins like Reena?"

"That's definitely Snow Flopsy, Mrs. Fluffytail." One of the henchmen who reported to Reena earlier stood up and bowed towards me. "He created the Flopsy Gang again after it was destroyed the first time. I was one of the new gang's founding members. While adventuring, he thought he found a space with treasures, but when he came out, he had that flower on his head. Then he started changing."

"And you still followed him?" Ilya asked.

The henchman shivered. "I didn't want to die. He still treated us well as long as we did what he asked."

Then ... doesn't that mean Snow's already dead? I was cheated! How dare he die before I killed him!? "You bastard, give Snow back to me!" I grabbed the flower on Snow's head and pulled at it. Snow screeched like a dying pig as a bloody root came out of his ear, attached to the flower. It was nearly three-feet-long and there were bits of brain-like matter attached to it. Ew.

Snow's body shivered and convulsed. He thrashed around on the ground like a fish out of water, and his eyes were rolled upwards so that only their whites showed. Blood gushed out of his ear and shoulder, and I wasn't sure if I should've cut his head off to put him out of his misery or not. Luckily, he stopped moving a few seconds later, and his eyes rolled back down. They were clear but a bit dull. "L-Lucia...?"

"You're Snow Flopsy?"

A weak laugh escaped from Snow's lips. "I won't apologize for what I did. You deserved to be poisoned after treating me like you did during our travels." His eyes dimmed even further as his eyelids drooped. "Just kill me. Please."

...This isn't the revenge I had in mind. Where's the despair? Where's the begging and pleading? He should be on his knees, praying for someone to save him. He should have a strong will to live! This, this is pathetic. I was poisoned by someone like this? "Where's Bouncykins?"

Snow exhaled, and his chest and stomach deflated. "Dead."

Dead? "Beg for your life, dammit!" Ah, why are my eyes hot? I'm not crying!

"I refuse..., dummy."

"Snow Flopsy! You're not allowed to refuse!"

"Idiot...." Snow's eyes closed.

"You can't die like this!"

The corners of Snow's lips turned upwards. "Stu...pid."

Ah.

Snow's dead.

Am I crying? Who's cutting onions? Fucking flower, what are you looking at? I stabbed the flower with the long, bloody root and tore it to shreds. It screamed, but it didn't make me feel better. Wasn't I supposed to feel better after getting revenge? Why don't I feel better? The hatred's gone…, but nothing replaced it. I was promised happiness; where's my happiness? Snow, you bastard. You were the shittiest first beastkin friend a person could've made. And you didn't even let me say goodbye. I hate you.

24

The world is great. After the Godking's Brawl, I got my promised reward of land and a living space from the second prince right away. The emperor that was supposed to die of an illness in three months had been trampled to death by a predator, so the second prince ascended the throne. Algar tried to contest it, but since he turned out to be a pervert who stole even his second sister's underwear, no one supported him. I only found out after the second prince was crowned that Ilya had stuffed all the miscellaneous items into one ring, which happened to be Algar's. Talk about a stroke of bad luck, but that's not my problem!

I was given the half of the empire that was closer to the demons and fae, but I don't really mind even though Ilya says I'm being used as a buffer. The closer I am to the demons and fae, the closer I'll be to Ilya and Ilya Number Two. Also, my portion of the empire is the more wooded one. The predators love it. After Snow died, I rounded up all the predators and tamed them with my fists and acorn stew. Thinking back, I should've left that dragon alive instead of killing it. I could be riding a dragon right now if I hadn't, but I was too preoccupied with killing one in a single strike. At least that action made everyone see me in a new light.

To the common people, I am a savior! To the nobles, I am a savior! To the ruling class, I am a disaster! Everyone in the world knows Lucia Fluffytail scored first place in the Godking's Brawl, robbed the man in the sky of his treasures, tamed a group of predators when others could only tremble, and slew a dragon in a single strike! Compared to the Godking who tamed a phoenix, isn't taming a group of predators much more incredible? After all, the Godking just tamed a red baby bird. I tamed a savage beast with a history shrouded in blood. Before I took action, no one even knew what the predator's fearsome appearance looked like since all who saw one died.

I'm still a bit peeved that there were no males amongst the batch though. I went for a short romp through the desolate mountains, but I couldn't find any there either. According to Ilya, predators might not be native to our lands, whatever that means. All I know is my dream of having an army of predators probably won't come true anytime soon. A shame, really. As for my other dream, Durandal and Puppers are working hard to cross over to the legendary realm. I can't wait for the day Durandal crosses over. Speaking of the legendary realm, after I got used to controlling my strength, it doesn't feel like a lot has changed. The only noticeable difference is the density of my bloody qi when I use it. I made Reena piss herself by circulating my qi. It was hilarious.

Ah, Reena. She's living in my territory now—along with half the population of the human empire. I tried kicking them out, but the second prince said they came with the land, so I should keep them. So now I tax them cocoa beans and acorns. It's really nice having someone manage your own lands for you. There's no way I'd be willing to spend that much time and effort growing things on my own. And Reena takes care of Mrs. Wuffletush and company. It's funny. I used to be a slave, now I'm practically an empress. Aren't I an empress? I think I am. The three factions are treating me like I'm another faction of my own. Ilya's reputation amongst the demons increased a lot because of that. Everyone knew she was my encyclopedia! Err, friend. So the demons treat her extra well in fear of provoking me. This is what it means to have face! The day has finally come!

And since I accomplished Durandal's goal, he's been getting depressed a lot less recently. He doesn't sigh as much as before, and there's always ice cream around to cheer him up when he's feeling down. There's lots of cookies and cuddles too, but he doesn't ask for cuddles very often—at all—so I have to drag him to bed using force. Even though he makes an upset face when I interrupt his training, he enjoys our time together. I know I do!

Durandal had promised to make me into a legend, but thinking back on my journey to legendhood—is that a word?—didn't I accomplish almost everything by myself? Durandal still tries to claim credit for my achievements because, according to him, he set up my foundation. I can't help but roll my eyes at that. All he did was torture me into compliance while teaching me a few techniques. But I guess I wouldn't have gotten as far as I did without his initial guidance. He also feels like I'm not a real legendary warrior because I used beast cores to advance. And I think there are some merits to his words. There were a few more people who came by with plants growing out of their heads, and none of them have referred to me as a warrior. They call me a fierce body practitioner instead. It's hard to understand what they're saying about different worlds and whatnot, and the plants growing out of their heads remind me of Snow, so I kick those people out of my territory and into the demons'. Ilya says Rogath likes studying them, so it's totally okay.

So now, here I am, at the top of the world. I have my own mansion, my own workers, my own hot chocolate and acorn stew factories. I have two good friends: Ilya and Ilya Number Two. Wealth is meaningless to me now; the days of saving and scrimping for a month just to buy a rusty old firestarter are over. I still have that little metal bird. I don't need to start any fires, but I like having it around. I don't have to work as a punching bag or a luggage porter in an army anymore. I don't have to go to sleep hungry and cold. There's no more crying myself to sleep and struggling to wake up. And most importantly, I have Durandal! And he's the only thing, err, person I need in this world!

"Durandal!"

"Yes, Lucia?"

"Head pats!"

Ah, that feels good.

Afterword

Thanks to Sharda Hartly for supporting me on Patreon!

Feel free to check out my website at www.virlyce.com.

A sequel is planned for the future.

If you enjoyed the story, please leave a review. It helps me out a lot. Thank you for reading!

Other books by me available on Amazon:
The Blue Mage Raised by Dragons

Printed in Great Britain
by Amazon

45881988R00298